NO LONGER PROPERTY
SEATTLE PUBLIC LIBRARY
NOV - - 2017
BY:_____

NAIVO

BEYOND THE
RICE FIELDS

Translated from the French
by Allison M. Charette

D0187790

RESTLESS BOOKS
BROOKLYN, NEW YORK

Copyright © 2017 Naivoharisoa Patrick Ramamonjisoa
Translation copyright © 2017 Allison M. Charette

First published as *Au-delà des rizières*
by Éditions Sépia, Paris, 2016

Excerpts of this text appeared, in slightly altered form, in *Two Lines*
as "The Call of Tangena" and "How to Become a Slave."

All rights reserved.
No part of this book may be reproduced or transmitted without the
prior written permission of the publisher.

This translation was made possible by a grant
from the PEN/Heim Translation Fund.

First Restless Books paperback edition October 2017

Paperback ISBN: 9781632061317
Library of Congress Control Number: 2016940787

Cover design by John Gall
Text designed and set in Garibaldi by Tetragon, London
Printed in Canada

1 3 5 7 9 10 8 6 4 2

Restless Books, Inc. 232 3rd Street, Suite A111
Brooklyn, NY 11215

www.restlessbooks.com
publisher@restlessbooks.com

*In memory of my mother, my first source of inspiration,
and my father, constant support and irreplaceable
adviser.*

*To Lovasoa, Soafy, and Ibonia, for their patience, and
for giving me more love than I deserve.*

*To Mitondrasoa, who may one day discover a new face
on a familiar presence.*

*To Jean-Claude and Patricia, old companions on the
journey and accomplices from the very first step.*

NAIVO

To my boys.

AMC

CONTENTS

BEYOND THE
RICE FIELDS

BOOK 1

Kotrokorana
Ny voalohany ihany
No mahamanina
Fa ny aoriana
Tselatra sy varatra be ihany

Rumbling storm
The first sound of thunder
Is a bittersweet pang
The ones that follow
Are but flashes of lightning

MALAGASY HAINTENY

1   *Tsito*

EVERY TIME I WATCH THE *FAMPITAHA*, my heart aches, and I can again see Sahasoa, where I spent the first years of my life with the People Under the Sky. I can again see Fara, who was crowned queen of the competition. Back then, we still rolled the gate stones across the entrances to our villages, every night, before dusk fell. The rice fields were bounded only by the swampland, teeming with life, and by the limits of human labor. That was the age of childhood fancies and the first schools, of bullfighting, nighttime stories, and chameleon battles. What remains of that now? That world is slowly fading from my memory, its edges frayed by the passing years, washed away by the tide of time like the old sun-bleached bamboo stalks from our fishing rafts. It erodes under the here and now, like our red walls under the monsoon rains.

No, nothing stirs my soul as much as a procession of girls coming around a clay wall, richly dressed for the fampitaha dance competition. Their eyes sparkle with a child's desire to please; at least that has survived the test of time. Their ribbons and flowers are a feast for the eyes and spirit. When they dance in our dust-covered streets, curving their wrists and bending gracefully at the waist, the finest fruits of the great wide past burst forth, reborn. The old tree is granted new life in its tiny seeds.

Despite the passage of years, I remember my arrival in Sahasoa in great detail. I still remember that sun-drenched morning during the Alakarabo moon when Rado brought me to the village. As we walked through it, children flocked to us, raising a cloud of dust. Even the dogs came up to sniff me. I felt very fragile. Lost, filled with fear.

"*Haody*, Nenibe!" said Rado, walking into the hut. "Is anyone here?"

Fara and Bao were at the market. Bebe was alone, burning incense in the northeast corner. I'd followed Rado but stopped at the door, dazed.

Everything was new to me. I was assaulted by smells, sounds, and lights from every corner of the house. The placement of objects was unpredictable, threatening. The bed looked fit for a funeral. The *sinibe* was a weird color. The *sahafa* looked like the wrong size.

"*Mandrosoa tompoko! Tonga soa!* What have you brought us?"

Even the central-midlands drawl—which I've now adopted—made me instinctively afraid. It reminded me of the slave market, of the soldiers. The welcoming words opened my wounds again.

In my far-off childhood, my father had often spoken of this tribe, the long-eared Merinas, whom he called "*amboalambos*"—pig-dogs. The elders described them as underhanded beings, merciless and cruel. The forest people, my people, had always valiantly resisted their attempts to invade, hiding at the slightest warning in the impenetrable, age-old forest. But one day, my village was taken by surprise and destroyed. Soldiers descended on my community in the early dawn, like a cloud of evil red crickets, sowing death and desolation. Amboalambos were the enemy.

That first day, seeing Bebe with her drooping ears in the shadowed hut, I recoiled, horrified.

Yet the elder woman's home became mine over the years. Mine, like the foreign shore where the waves spit you out after a shipwreck. Like those makeshift underground shelters to run to before a whirlwind, where you unexpectedly find new faces. And a new destiny.

2

How to Become a
Devoted Slave

I'VE KEPT A HABIT from my early years among the amboalambos, of massaging my wrists and ankles. I do it for hours on end, whether sitting, squatting, or lying down, whenever I can, to circulate my blood. I never could shed the compulsion. Sometimes in the morning when I wake, I look at the Creator's rising sun and contemplate my own hands and feet in amazement. I still wonder if I'm truly free.

Rado bought me at a slave market. When he brought me to Sahasoa, Fara was seven. I was two years older than her, but I looked a year younger, and I still spoke with a lilting forest accent. My home village had been razed to the ground when Radama's troops attacked. All the men were killed, and the soldiers looted all our possessions. Having captured the women and children, the king's troops kept a handful as trophies and sold the rest at the slave market. They killed my father and my grandfather, my two older brothers, my two paternal uncles, and my maternal uncle. My childhood memories are haunted by bodies littering the ground.

At the time, children were going for thirty to sixty piasters on the slave market. Young girls were popular for their domestic use. Older girls were more expensive, and beautiful captives could bring in eighty piasters. Little boys were sold for an average of thirty piasters, but any with a particular skill were worth more.

I was sold for forty piasters. It was a good price.

Sometimes I laugh, because I've realized that even the memory of the dealer—a foul man with formal speech, so typical of that time—has become a weirdly precious treasure. My owner was a smooth-talking hawker. A career man, he was good at his job, not like those soldiers who captured and sold indiscriminately around the countryside. His is a permanent mark in my memory; time will not alter it.

This occurred during the last crescent of the Alakarabo moon, in the fifteenth year of the Sovereign King's reign.

This is essentially how the dealer sounded: "What would you say to a little slave to distract you, my good sir? This one right here will enchant your evenings with the melodious sound of his *valiha*; the ancestors will bestow their favor upon you! His music is fresh as the dawning dew-covered day, more poignant than the setting sun on the hillside! This slave is as small as a louse and as black as the inside of a cooking pot, but his fingers have been blessed with inspiration by the most benevolent of our forest spirits!"

I never knew the dealer's name. I must have had occasion to hear it, but I never retained it. Perhaps because I didn't want to.

Rado didn't intend on buying a slave. But he came over anyway. I was squatting among stacks of baskets and sacks of grain. My ankles were chained together, and I looked aggressively, silently, at this strange man walking toward me. What did he want? Nothing good. Probably to hit me, hurt me, like so many others had done since my capture. Seeing Rado's interest, the dealer whose name I've forgotten held a stringed valiha zither out and ordered me to play. The customer was waiting. I acquiesced with a grimacing smile; showing too much malevolence would have led to punishments later.

Rado seemed interested.

"How much?" he asked.

"You won't regret this choice, good sir! You have a rare opportunity. The ancestors have surely brought you here. It was just this very morning that a noble lord offered me a pair of sheep for him, but I refused; I wanted to keep him for myself, you understand. My wives just love the valiha. The second in particular, the youngest, she goes into raptures whenever she hears its wistful chords."

As he spoke, the merchant gestured invitingly with a knowing smile, which Rado returned coldly.

"So why are you selling him now? Is he sick?"

"Oh no, not at all! He's in perfect health! He also never begs to be allowed to play, which is a welcome quality. You know the proverb, 'A slave skilled at the valiha: when you ask him to play, he refuses, but as soon as you speak of work, he goes mad for music!' You won't worry about that with this one—"

"You still haven't told me why you want to sell him."

Without answering, the dealer turned to me and barked, "Get over here, you!" I shuffled forward, the chains fettering my feet.

The dealer clamped his hand onto the top of my head and turned me around, showing off my limbs and thin torso.

"He's called Tsito. He's a little skinny, but he comes from good stock. He'll work hard and won't bother you. I broke him in very well."

Rado examined me carefully for marks of abuse. I lowered my eyes. It wasn't allowed, looking at a master. I've also kept that habit, lowering my eyes when I talk to people. It's very hard for me to hold someone else's gaze.

Slave traffickers procure their merchandise in several ways. The simplest is to buy them from soldiers when they return from the countryside, as happened with me. They can also do the village circuit, traveling around to the many families enslaved because of debts or poverty. Sometimes, dealers will send their henchmen to capture ordinary people who get lost on the roads or venture out alone a little too far from home. The most common technique to break them in is the trial of water, which consists of binding the captive's hands and feet and plunging their head into a tub of water until they start to suffocate. The procedure is repeated over several hours and only stops once the victim declares, convincingly, "I confess that I am your slave and that my ancestors are your ancestors' slaves."

I'd been broken in well, as the dealer said. Very well.

Slaves who don't show marks of violence aren't necessarily better treated. But Rado couldn't know that. The only visible marks on me were dark furrows that the ropes had left on my wrists and ankles. In some ways, these marks recorded the least violent aspect of enslavement: being bound. In a twist of irony, the body does not preserve any outward sign of the most brutal part: suffocation, temples threatening to burst, slipping unutterably toward death.

Well, actually, mine did. I was two years older than Fara, but I looked one younger; until well beyond my captivity my body refused to grow, which was the only way my bones and muscles revolted. As an adolescent, I sometimes wondered if my ancestors were punishing me for enslaving them to the ancestors of the amboalambos. And of the nameless dealer.

The slave trafficker shoved me toward Rado and heaved a deep sigh.

"I've decided to part with him, good sir, because I have a large family to provide for. You must understand, I am a poor man. I don't have the means to feed one more mouth—"

Rado interrupted his little speech: "You still haven't told me the price. And where is this child's mother?"

"She died, my good sir! Along with the rest of his family. That is, alas, the harsh law of war. You'll be taking in a little orphan here. You know what our ancestors said: 'A crying orphan, only pitied by the back of his own hand.' Through your purchase, you will save him!"

My owner pulled a mournful face, ever the true professional.

In that moment, I was wracked with despair, and tears sprang to my eyes. The dealer was lying again. All of my other family members had been sold. Those who trade in men find it wiser to get rid of the adults first, for if parents see their offspring leave before them, they become uncontrollable. Some even attempt suicide. In any case, the merchandise is spoiled and is harder to sell.

This seller was definitely a career man. Night made me a confidante, tied to the foot of his bed: he sighed and reminisced sadly about the time when the business of lost men still flourished. Ever since the Sovereign King ceded to British pressure and prohibited the export of slaves, the trade had languished.

I never saw any of my family members again.

But I found Fara.

3

The Story of Fara, Daughter of the Fampitaha

RADO, FARA'S FATHER, was a coarse man, weathered, with powerful calves and shoulders as sculpted as the red granite of Mount Ankaratra. He was a *mpandranto* trader from the belle époque under Nampoina's reign. He drove cattle herds to the ports in the East and North to exchange them for rare goods, which he then unloaded in the highland markets. He had a sturdy enough constitution to survive weeks traveling over makeshift, swampy trails, and negotiation skills honed sharp enough to manage networks of local allies, working constantly to evade attacks from the *fahavalo*, the cattle thieves.

Bao, Fara's mother, was a sentimental woman, as our vast hills are so adept at producing. She shone the brightest of all the girls in Sahasoa in her time. Her merry eyes, her high voice, and the alluring way she walked attracted attention from lords and free men. Her neck was graceful and fine, and her wrist supple as a reed. She was the precious girl, coveted by a thousand men to be their companion. Sometimes, many years later, when Rado and I were traveling the road together so he could teach me the ways of the nomad's life, he spoke about that part of his youth with a longing smile. That was an era when a peaceful spirit still reigned among the highland peoples.

Before meeting Rado, Bao had been chosen twice by the community to represent the village at the royal fampitaha competition. The first time, she'd earned comparisons to the very best dancers, though she wasn't even ten years old. I can't say even this without seeing Fara's silhouette stretching skyward, already, shining at the same competition as she entered adolescence. Images surge forth, slipping out of the darkest corners of my mind: impassioned crowds, flower petals raining down, the ringing shock of the drum and the dizzying trills of the flute . . .

Rado, the road-bound adventurer, was star-struck at Bao's second appearance, when she was already a full-grown woman. He fell under her charm, like a wild cricket halted in flight by a field of tender grain.

That occurred during the Alahasaty moon, in the seventh year of King Radama's reign.

Rado was one of his district's most promising young negotiators. By that time, he'd already been allocated over one hundred head of zebus and stocked away over one hundred measures of rice. Young women blushed before his strong will. Parents dreamed of having him for a son-in-law. But Rado, like the chaotic mob rushing up alongside him to the Palace doors, was struck petrified and speechless when Bao began to dance.

The trader found out what he could about her and turned up in Sahasoa the next week. He slept neither day nor night, never stopping until he made her his.

But he was not alone in this quest: after Bao's second performance before the Sovereign, she suddenly became one of the most courted women in the region. The strongest men in the land wanted to hold the pearl of the dance, to win the sky child. During the following moons, her jewelry box was never depleted, and her granary was always filled with rice, to the great joy of her mother, Bebe. Her house was even blessed with the richness of a calf, whom she baptized Ifotsy because of the white spot around its right eye.

Bao was young and hungry for life. She loved the men who loved her, and made herself beautiful for them. Garments of raffia and fiber disappeared from her wardrobe to make way for imported fabrics. She had a set of pearls strung permanently around her neck and set flowers in her hair.

Rado had to tear her from the arms of an officer, push aside a wealthy landowner, and oust the son of the local magistrate. He pampered her, showered her with gifts, drowned her in *barandro* so she'd forget her other lovers. He stayed with her for six months and got her pregnant.

But one day, just as Bao was thanking the ancestors for giving her a descendant, Rado disappeared without a word. He didn't reappear until two years later, breezing through like the wind.

In the meantime, Fara was born.

Rado became enamored with the little girl, but showed less and less interest in her mother.

Bao changed. She ground banana paste for herself to grow fat. Her teeth lost their whiteness, and her hair started to fray. All of her former lovers deserted her hut. The officer turned his head, the landowner found himself a different wife, and the magistrate's son set his sights on a young cousin instead.The only ones left were harsh, miserly laborers and emancipated slaves.

Rado came back from time to time to visit his daughter.

I remember the regret in his eyes when he spoke to Bao years later. Bao didn't know why, which made her sad.

4   *Fara*

I WANT TO BELIEVE that my name is a bearer of good luck.

Even though it's not a name I should bear. Fara is normally a name for the youngest daughter in a family with many children. I'm certainly the last-born of my family, but besides Tsito the slave boy, I'm the only child. To my knowledge, my mother had no other children, either before or after me.

The ancestors say, "Do not cook meat without knowing its name." The unnamed is not cooked or eaten. As my grandmother, Bebe, explained, that's why you must give a proper name to each thing and each being. My friend Vero had a brother, or maybe a sister, who was trampled by zebus just after birth. I wonder what name they would have given it if it had survived. Iamboafetsy, the cunning dog? Ivoalavotsilaitra, the stubborn rat?

My name is a sign for the future: Rafaramanorosoa, the-last-born-daughter-who-shows-the-path-of-righteousness.

There's just one thing that makes me kind of sad.

Most of the other families in Sahasoa, my village, have at least four children. Like Vero: she's the fifth in a family of eight children, three of which died young of illness—not counting the one that was crushed by cattle. It must be fun to belong to a large family. During the Bathing Feast, families like that buzz with joy, their houses burst with shouts and laughter. There are only four of us in this house: my grandmother Bebe, my mother Bao, Tsito the slave boy, and me. My father, Rado, doesn't come back for festivals, not even for the Bathing Feast. He's a strange thing: his head's in the mountains, and he smells like bulls moving to summer pastures.

But I know why I'm an only child, and I know why my name is Fara. I also know why my mother didn't take another husband when my father left. It's not very common: all abandoned women take new husbands.

These things are all for the same reason. Lots of questions have the same answer.

"It's because of Ranaka," Bebe told me yesterday.

She uttered the name and spat out her sugarcane. My grandmother needs more time to extract all the nectar from the sugary reed, because of her missing teeth. The liquid sometimes leaks out of her harelip and dribbles down her chin. How can she play the flute with her harelip? That's always been a mystery to me.

Sitting on the doorstep, she traced pictures in the dust with her big toe and wiped her mouth off with the back of her hand.

"Bebe, who is Ranaka?" I asked.

She looked at me thoughtfully. "Do you know how seers peer into the future of a newborn or a child-to-be? First, they chart the progression of the moon at the end of the pregnancy, then the course of the sun at the hour of birth. That's the first thing they have to do. Ranaka didn't do any of that. He scoffed at the moon and sun."

A boy goes by the hut with his two goats. It's Tovo, Vero's little brother. He's nibbling a stalk of grass, driving his animals with a long bamboo rod.

I get a little bit emotional whenever it's time to clean the hearth.

I like this moment in the late afternoon when the solar eye has partially descended and starts pouring golden light through the backsides of the tree leaves. The fleeing star seems to breathe life back into things, bringing back the light of dawn. The cool evening returns the scent of the earth to the air, after the high noon burned it away. It makes you want to fly back over the paths to the fields.

Sahasoa and the surrounding land are bathed in bronze light that transforms the canals along the rice fields' highest terraces into fiery furrows. The hollow valley is shadowed, but you can still make out the jumble of rocks and brush lining the spring. I glimpse the outlines of children on the path. They're leaving early for the evening water run.

Bebe had mentioned the story of Ranaka earlier, during a conversation with my mother.

I hadn't been paying attention at first, I only listened in when they started talking about me. The conversation was short. Afterward, Bao, my mother, took her loom and sat at the foot of the great fig tree. I hadn't quite caught what they'd been discussing. It was something about a talisman, or a remedy against some sort of evil.

Well. The sun continues to set.

My mother, weaving at the foot of the great tree, like she does every evening, looks at the sky, then at me. I should go clean the hearth. I'm already late. Bebe is sitting at the entrance to the hut, munching on her sugarcane.

Bebe has already told me the story twice since yesterday. Her tale takes on a different color every time, like a chameleon when children hiss at it.

"I want to hear the story again, Nenibe! Who was this Ranaka, really?"

Bebe slowly gnaws her sugarcane, staring off into the distance.

"Do you know the proverb, 'The seer who wants to make the impossible believable is not afraid to make dying men dance'? That was Ranaka. So deep was his knowledge that it could have swallowed up an entire village, cattle and chickens and all."

"But why did he want bad things to happen to people?"

"He didn't wish ill on people. He predicted things."

A white egret cries and flies across the sky in a long, silent curve, before landing on the riverbank with a great beating of white wings. I think it's the same bird I saw fly over the house yesterday, at the same time. How could this man Ranaka's predictions prevent me from having brothers and sisters? My grandmother purses her lips to point at Bao, who is listening to our conversation from afar, weaving all the while.

"I told you: one day, he read her fate in the seeds. Your mother was still sweet and tender as a young shoot. He wanted to make her wither and dry out like a bush in winter."

"Why didn't he want her to have children?"

17

"May my hands be cut off if I have any idea," laughs Bebe. "You shouldn't listen too closely to seers, o piece of my soul. All that knowledge can make their brains turn inside out in their skull. He just said that she had an evil womb."

Bebe spits the moist fibers out into the palm of her hand, examines them, and throws them onto a small pile of garbage by the entrance to the house.

"Yes, he forbade her from having children. He said this, to my own daughter: 'You will die without bearing a child.' In other words, you'll die a death deeper than death itself! If she did not follow his command, he said, she'd be putting the entire community in mortal danger. And misfortune would come crashing down upon the family."

So, I am a forbidden child, like the ones that are born during the Alakaosy moon. It doesn't do anything in particular to me, just weighs down the back of my neck. I'm not sure I know exactly what it means. Bebe is humming a song. I like this one a lot.

> We'll go to the City of Thousands
> To eat the laying hen
> To eat the fatty zebu hump

I wonder why the hearth is always so dirty. I clean it three times a day, but it gets filthy all by itself, even if we're not using it. There's stuff in there that shouldn't be. Wet leaves, stones. It must be Tsito. So I have to empty the basket of ashes and garbage underneath the bushes, to the west of the hut. It's so boring.

Outside, the great red wheel of the sun is already half-hidden behind a hill. Coming back from the garbage pit, I stop to pick out logs from a stack by the entrance. I place one on the block. What does this seer want with me, anyway? Ranaka. Funny name. I find the ax where it belongs, for once, leaning neatly against the wall near the northwest pillar. Tsito usually leaves it lying around wherever. To use it properly, you have to snap it sharply into the wood, without bending your wrist.

I'm happy: I split the first log on the first try.

I wish Tsito were here. I glance over toward the old tree. My mother has finished her work and is folding up the loom. I won't get to play with Tsito before the evening rice meal.

We meet under the old tree in the evening a lot to play and talk. It's a knotty fig tree that hangs out over the path from the slope above it. Its dense leaves cast a thick protective shadow over that side of the yard. Roots snake out of the ground by the path. The tree has a circular hole at its base that makes a natural tunnel, just big enough for a kid to slip through.

After chopping the logs, I sit on the step at the entrance, next to Bebe.

"Tell me again how I got to come into the world, Nenibe. You went to consult other seers, right?"

Bebe clears her throat. She seems more relaxed now that the evening has truly begun. Her voice changes, too, falls into the same inflections as at night, when she tells us stories and legends of *Ntaolo*, the time of the Ancient Ones.

"That's right. But it wasn't easy. This man, this Ranaka, had influence over most of the seers around. People were afraid of him. We had to sneak away, climb unfamiliar hills and valleys. Cross terrifying streams of rushing water, sleep on the edge of a knife. But finally, we found out how to ward off that evil fate."

"Where?"

"There was still an old seer living in a village by the mountains. He was unique, as fragile as a tree on the edge of a ravine. Ramasy was his name. He'd learned how to walk across the days from an *ombiasy* seer from the South, powerful enough to make predictions without consulting physical objects. He said to your mother, 'You will be able to have a child, but only one. The child must carry the name of a last-born.' And that is why, at your birth, we named you Fara."

Bebe scratches her right earlobe a little every time she tells a story. It had been pierced and stretched when she was young to hold the heavy ornamental earrings of olden days. But over the course of the years, the flesh tore completely in half, and now it hangs in two separate pieces, like the cured fillets of zebu that get hung from kitchen ceilings. Bebe often jokes that if a famine hits, she'll cut them off and fry them up to make the manioc and taro taste better.

Bebe is the best storyteller in the village. People say that she's one of the most gifted in the whole region. In the evenings, she brings her stool outside, leans against the old tree, and starts her tales. The gentle hiss of her words is like a beacon; kids come running and quickly make a tight circle around the fig tree.

Ranaka. Ramasy. Do seers have special names?

My mother interrupts our thoughts. "Could you come help me light the fire?"

I look up at her. I still find her beautiful. Her forehead has a roundness to it, her large brown eyes give off a kind of sweetness, and her chest is firm and plump. But her nostrils flare when she's worried.

Bao walks into the hut without waiting for me. She carries the heavy loom without any apparent effort. I've always been impressed by her physical strength. She got it by tackling men's jobs herself: without a husband, she turned the mud clods in the rice fields, for forever. She got it from the fampitaha, too.

Now the village is quiet. The workers haven't come back from the fields yet. There's just two zebus, padding heavily between the thatched-roof huts, followed by a young driver. From the east, there's the dull sound of a pestle being pounded rhythmically against the rice mortar.

I pick up a bunch of logs and sticks and carry them in near the hearth, and I start setting up the wood below the stone tripod.

Will she talk to me about Rado again?

My mother is humming an old fampitaha tune, like she always does when she's tired of working. She puts the loom away in a corner and sits on the bed to watch me make the evening's rice. Tsito won't be long. He went to draw water from the little spring. Bao asked him to make a detour by the river to net some fish. There are always more fish when the sun sets,

20

as if they know that people should want to flee the dark, and so the danger should retreat with them. The fishermen always have the best catches once the water's surface has gotten dark and the rocks in the river have melted into the dark night.

"I hope Tsito catches an eel," I say.

"I'd be surprised if he did," says Bao. "Eels are much too clever to be caught in a net. But I bet we'll have some little fish to eat tonight. Did Bebe talk to you about your father?"

I'm getting a little tired of thinking about my birth. I already knew I was an illegitimate child. I just found out that I'm a forbidden child. But what could that mean?

A log starts to burn. I have to add dry twigs and blow on the new fire for it to catch. As the flames grow, I have to fan air into the hearth to give them more life. I untie a corner of my wrap.

"No, Neny, she didn't. Why? Do you think he'll be back soon?"

"Rado is currently in the North, I've been told. Barely a week ago, he was still somewhere in the West. Your father crosses hills like Darafify the Giant! I hope that he'll come visit us after his trip."

"Where do you hear that, Neny?"

"Rabevala saw them in a village as he came back from Fort B . . . He told me that your father is very busy, but happy with his progress. He and his companions are driving a herd of three hundred head and their journey is coming to an end. They'll head back down the southern road soon."

Bao sighs and her eyes shine with delight.

"Do you remember the last time he came to visit us, when he gave me this silver pendant? I'd never seen such a pretty thing in my life! And he and his companions brought foreign fabrics, too, and salt, pearls by the basketful—so many wares that this country had never seen! Are you listening to me?"

I realize that my parents would have separated with or without the seer's help. At the same time, I see how attached my mother still is to my father, through and despite everything. I can see things that I'd only been confused about before. It's like that dull physical pain from a fall that you can only feel long afterward. My father's indifference, the stubborn hope that drives my mother.

"Why didn't you find another husband when my father left, Neny?"

My mother sighs deeply and drops onto the bed. She stretches out on her back and stares at the stripes of soot clinging to the ceiling, without answering.

"You're still too young to worry about such things."

Not that young—I know the answer. She tried, but didn't find one. Bao had been promised a future of happiness and ease. Then, one day, it all fell apart, for no apparent reason. I was born into doubt and fear. What can I hope from my destiny?

Tsito is late coming home. I miss him.

5 Tsito

The Home of a Hundred
Cattle and a Hundred Slaves

BEBE OFTEN SAID that I had "an old soul."

By that, she meant that I too often showed more maturity than suited a child. It was a rare ability, to act with the gravity and dignity of an adult, but it was just one of the many oddities that destiny had rewarded me with. I also knew how to scratch between my shoulder blades with my thumbnail, peel most fruits with my teeth, and scatter an army of invading rats with my heels—very useful things when your hands are tied.

In Bebe's opinion, the aftereffects of my captivity were summed up in an old proverb: "When the whole household gets a lecture, the orphan learns the most from it, the most quickly." I'll admit that I could never rid myself of the habit of listening in every situation, of never leaving anything to chance.

When my whole family had been sold and I was the only one left with the slave dealer, he built a cage to keep me in. That cage was my world, my universe. I spent my unusable days, and sometimes my nights, in the company of chicken and wild geese, even young goats. Who knows, maybe it was because I lived with animals that I became a man too quickly.

During that period, whether to pass the time or forget my sorrows—or maybe to not lose my mind—I also developed the habit of fashioning tools, molding and shaping everything that passed through my hands. I made wooden spoons, stakes, little scales, spinning tops, bird traps, and various other useful things. Everything that, as I think about it, kept me connected to the family of human beings.

These skills—developed in adversity, as an old soul would be—made it easier for Sahasoa to accept me.

It would be improper for me to lament my destiny too much, for it has been mild with me. I started from the very bottom—I could only go up from there. Rado and Bebe proved themselves the most considerate masters that anyone could hope for. In my very first year in Sahasoa, after the dark eclipse of my family's massacre, the sun shone for me again in a clear blue sky. Rado did take off the same evening we'd arrived, which left me in a state of confusion but free to move around. He simply gave me the valiha that he'd bought from the trader.

"Here," he said. "Use this to brighten your new home. You'll see how pointless it is to try to run away—you'd get lost, and even if you managed to escape the wild dogs, you'd just end up in the hands of slave dealers again. Why even try? Be like the baby bird and wait for your wings to grow."

My wings grew very quickly. And besides, before bringing me to Bebe, Rado had broken me in, too. In his own way.

But it had very little in common with the slave dealer's methods. Rado never used force with me, that wasn't his style. He taught things the hard way, though, toughening me up against life's difficulties by taking me on his journeys down the kingdom's harshest roads: day after day, he taught me about difficult passes and dangerous paths, what signs to look out for, hidden trails. We often moved at a forced quick march and slept out in the open. On those treacherous paths of life, you must react quickly and aggressively to dangerous situations. It was the most efficient education that I could ever have hoped for.

Later, after I was already living in Sahasoa, Rado sometimes still took me with him—to negotiate some business in the North, perhaps just for the company. He was a strict and tortured soul, and gruff, like so many of the Perfumed Lord's great workers. He could walk by your side for a week without saying a word. And he could also confess his entire life to you in one evening at the fire.

Rado had never had a slave before, and didn't want one. He'd bought me for a very specific reason.

My new master had a sensitive heart. The decision to leave Fara's mother hadn't been one he'd made offhandedly. When he'd known Bao, she was young, beautiful, talented, and crazy. The fampitaha queen's eccentricities had left a huge impact on him. But Bao the village girl greatly desired to marry someone, and that—along with her unbridled wish for wealth—wore him out quickly. The early energy soon died off, and the day came when he had to return to more stable relationships.

Rado already had a wife at the time: Vololona. She managed his lands selflessly during his long absences: all his rice fields were well cared for, and his livestock multiplied. Shortly before succumbing to Bao's charms, he'd also promised marriage to a nice young woman named Raivo, a Northerner.

"She had a good head on her shoulders," he confessed to me. "A combination of strength and sensitivity, like all Northern women. She didn't dream of having an extravagant wedding celebration. She just wanted a house and kids."

People said that you couldn't escape a Northern woman. Rado broke things off with Bao and married Raivo. Still, his choice tormented him: he'd become enamored with his now-illegitimate daughter. He didn't think that Fara deserved her situation. He wanted forgiveness for abandoning her, for not giving her a real home. He wanted to give her a present. And that present was me.

"This will be my way of keeping an eye on her and her destiny," he said. "I see gifts in you that will be revealed by the winds of time. Our meeting was not by chance—it was willed by the ancestors."

I believed it.

But what did Fara think?

It would be difficult, even with the corroding winds of time, to erode the memory of the peculiar welcome that my new home had in store for me. It was on a nice, sunny day in Alakarabo.

Bebe and Bao were ecstatic about my arrival, for reasons I couldn't fully understand. The two women were singing, and laughed at everything. Rado was smiling. It was like some sort of celebration.

Then, at some signal I didn't see, Bao took me by the hand and led me into the middle of the yard. Everyone else followed. I saw other village women come running from every direction, holding the hem of their wraps in one hand, peals of laughter ringing out. Bebe clapped her hands and smiled a wide, toothless grin. Children were whistling and imitating the *babakoto* lemur's call. I looked at Rado, worried, but he just kept smiling.

"Look at him!" someone shouted. "Isn't he handsome? Did you see his teeth? His legs? His little penis? I can't believe it!"

Bao pointed at one of the boys there. "Quick, bring her here! Go find her, I want to see them together! Praise be to Zanahary the Creator!"

They brought over Ifotsy the cow and stood us side by side. The animal got a little excited by all the commotion. She let out a string of short moos and kept swinging her head back and forth. She was still a young cow at the time, always eager to be petted. As if encouraged by the shouts from the crowd, she licked my face with her long, rough tongue and joyfully let loose a pile of smelly green dung. Everyone laughed.

Fara had been suspicious of me up to that point, but she also laughed. For the first time, she really looked at me, intensely, with that curiosity-infused stare that belonged so specifically to her.

Then, the women started singing.

> *The village is rich with children*
> *Grandmother is lucky indeed*
> *Her home has a hundred slaves*
> *Her home holds a hundred cattle*

6 *Fara*

WHEN I WAS LITTLE, I had a wooden doll dressed in rags that I named Andriamanorosoa, the Lord Who Shows the True Way. Bebe made him for me. She'd sewed a little pocket filled with burial dirt into the doll's folds. She said that Andriamanorosoa would be my personal talisman.

I was three or four, but I remember that I was already driving Ifotsy the cow to pasture back then, all by myself. Bebe was always amazed that such a big animal would obey such a minuscule person. When Ifotsy deviated from the path to treat herself to wild plants, I'd run as fast as I could to the front, smack her across the muzzle with a branch, and yell, "Aie! Aieeee! *Ho aiza ity adala be ity?* Where are you going, you big dummy?"

"We never thought such piercing cries could have come from such a tiny body," said Bebe. "You have a unique voice. You must study singing someday!"

Ifotsy would jump to the side, surprised by the branch, rolling her furious big eyes. I don't think I even came up to her chest. I wasn't afraid to pull her tail or even block her way—she'd always go back to the path with a regretful moo.

I asked questions of my talisman, Andriamanorosoa, every single day. I begged him for answers about everything that children care about: Who would win the next singing contest? When would we eat zebu meat again? Would I marry a prince from the highlands, a landowner with ten silos of rice? Would I become the wife of a gold-toothed ogre? Would I have porcelain plates, a full henhouse, and a real cow-fattening trough?

Once, I asked him to make a rival girl stumble at the children's fampitaha tournament, and it worked. But one day, the talisman couldn't fend off a punishment from my mother for touching her jewelry, and in a rage

I threw him into the pond and left him there all night long, to punish him back. Heavy with questions and besieged by an avalanche of increasingly crazy demands, Andriamanorosoa eventually surrendered. One morning, I commanded him to dance, like all talismans worthy of such a name should be able to do. I'd vowed not to give him any chance of wriggling out of it, and he couldn't move one thread in his rag loincloth. His time was up. I burned him alive in the hearth.

I watched the Lord Who Shows the True Way get consumed in the rice pot, producing a thick, gray column of smoke. I was already thinking of other ways to win my fortune and princes of light.

The day is breaking.

It's the hour of letting Ifotsy and her calf out. But Tsito took care of that. I can hear them going east, to the pasture. Now I can take care of the morning's rice.

I remember that my mother was horrible to me when I was very little. She pinched me, hit me. She pushed me away in horror if I came too close. I have hazy memories of this, but it affected me. Now I know why. She and Bebe fought a lot because of it. Every time Bao was plagued by some sort of unhappiness, she lashed out at me.

"This child is cursed! She'll turn her horns toward us one day and we'll all perish!"

"Woman, your brain has turned inside out!" Bebe would yell. "You're a fool! Just listen to the tales you're making up about a blameless child! Get out of my sight!"

Bebe is tiny, but she has a terrifying presence when she's mad. Bao would scream and hurl her spindle across the room, then grab a couple of things and storm out, and be gone for several days. I'd cry.

Bao has changed. She's not like that anymore; she probably realized that Ranaka's predictions haven't come true. Finally. That fear and humiliation is just a bad memory. In the evenings, Bao likes to laugh about the latest village gossip. Bebe listens and laughs, too. When Bao really wants a confidante, she'll even tell me about her men. Her lovers. It's funny.

My mother is a little crazy, but she's a gifted woman; that's what attracted my father. She doesn't dance anymore, but when she's feeling especially extravagant, she lets her expressive abilities loose to create a world of marvels, like the fables and legends of Ntaolo, the time of the Ancient Ones that Bebe describes. It happens more often now that Tsito is with us: the slave boy brought a new wave of joy and optimism.

My grandmother likes to tell us about the adventures of Ibonia, the great monster killer and conqueror of the Stone Man, and the tales of Imaitsoanala, the bird-child who became queen, as well as the cruel tricks of the thieves Kotofetsy and Maka, and the ingeniousness of Isilakolona and Imbahitrila, the children who were part human, part tree.

Sometimes, when we're tired of all those old stories, my mother describes the joy of the Blue Forest and the great horn-topped houses of the City of Thousands. Bao could talk forever about the City, where she was the queen for a day during the famous royal fampitaha competition.

"Picture this: a swath of all white, a veritable sea of humanity, stretching halfway up the hills! An infinite number of people, listening to the Sovereign's proclamation in absolute silence. When he pauses, you can hear birds calling and beating their wings in the swamps on the outskirts of the city. Above your head rises the Palace, where thirty concubines await his pleasure. The cannon thunders when he appears, and all the people bow to his will. Did you know that he smiled at me? Me! Oh, that I could have kissed the edge of his shadow! I would have thrown myself off the top of the cliff if he had just said the word!"

Listening to my mother talk like that, I imagine myself roaming the streets of the City of Thousands, mingling with other women in the great markets, climbing the sacred hills. Getting lost in the endless alleys, dancing in the royal dances, visiting Rasahala Lake and the imperial rice fields.

And at night, just when sleep overtakes my mind, I can see the King, fit into his snug, gold-embroidered uniform that makes his serene face and youthful hair glow, fingering his silver-pommeled saber, smiling at me.

The rice is done.

Bebe is praying in the ancestral corner, in the northeast. Tsito will be back from the spring soon. I made herb rice this time, for a change. But I couldn't find the red chilies, the best spice for it. Little green chilies with herb rice—it's deceptive. You bite into them accidentally and it makes you suck air through your teeth and hiss like an angry chameleon. I should wake Bao up.

Bebe knows how to read the future in black sand.

It's a strange art; I don't know if I should believe it. Bao doesn't, anyway. It was always about my birth. After Ranaka's forbidding orders, my grandmother tried to read my mother's paths through life in black sand. She also tried *fano* seeds. But Bao thinks that, in order to understand how destiny is flowing, your mind must be dominated by ancestors in the night. All of it seems like a witch's tricks to me.

They finally agreed to consult the other seer, old Ramasy. Otherwise, no children. And I hadn't even been conceived yet! It was right after the fampitaha. My mother had just met my father and was entertaining notions of marriage.

I was born during the Adalo moon. That's the moon of tears and sorrow, but I'm not sad by nature. I like to sing and laugh. At any rate, Adalo is better than Alakaosy, the moon of terrible fates. None of that prevented Ranaka from wanting to pull me out of my mother's womb and run me through with a long assegai spear. Crazy man.

Time passes quickly. The sun's rays are already lapping the chicken pen. Tonight, I'll do slices of smoked eel to go with the rice. I got some at the market.

I've learned that it's a bad idea to hang smoked meat above the rice silo in the southeast. It draws more rats: rice already attracts them, but the scent of cured meat drives them wild.

And to think that Tsito sleeps there at night, on the north of the silo. I wonder how he manages with the rats.

I have a strange destiny. Bebe and Bao had come back from seeing old Ramasy to try and foil Ranaka a second time. This time, though, it didn't work.

"I can see this child's early years, but her path to the market of no return is jumbled chaos that goes beyond my reach," he told my mother. "Pour out the blood of a red rooster on a tall rock at the north of your home. Wait for the moon's first crescent. Take these herbs, steep them, and bathe in that water two times each day until your pregnancy reaches its term."

He also had her make an offering to the elements of three red pearls and a pair of coral pieces, a request for mercy. As if that could stop an assegai spear!

It terrified Bao how aggressively Ranaka tried to destroy her fertility. He brought the same cruelty to the task as the community did in driving out barren women.

The sky's eye has turned red.

Outside, I hear the slow plod of the zebus coming back.

Bebe has set up her stool in front of the door and is warming her back in the sun's final rays. She's watching me cut the smoked fish.

"Tell me how you thwarted Ranaka's plans, Nenibe."

"You have to cut smoked eel longwise, into thin strips. Not across, like you're doing."

"Why?"

"It saves the meat, and it releases more flavor."

"Alright, I didn't know. So what did you do with Ranaka?"

"Plus, that will help you hang the leftover eel more easily. I don't see how you could hang little diced pieces of eel from the end of a string."

"Bebe, why do you always have to find something wrong with whatever I'm doing? Why don't you ever answer the questions anyone asks you?"

"Because we must respect the order of things."

"There's no order to how you cut an eel!"

"Yes, there is. There is order everywhere. Each object in this house respects an order and an orientation: the bed at the northeast, the hearth in the center, the sinibe at the east of the hearth, the rice pestle in the south-west. That's the foundation of their sacred virtues. The eel is no exception."

"Fine. Next time, I'll buy shrimp."

"Oh, you cook very well for your age. You'll make a wonderful mother."

"Thank you, Nenibe."

"'The desires of the mind fade with ease, but the passions of the womb resist even the butcher's meat hook.' Do you know that proverb?"

"No. What does it mean?"

"Ranaka had become very powerful. He was no mere seer: his family served as guardians of talismans passed down from father to son. His ancestral defender was called Mandatsivoho, because it had the power to cut down those who believed they'd vanquished it."

"Why passions of the womb?"

"Imamo princes had called upon his services to conquer their rivals. It was said that the Sovereign King planned to name the Mandatsivoho a royal talisman. There were many who believed in it."

"Is that why you called the lord of the province for help?"

"Yes. At the time, the old lord of the land, Andriamaro, was still alive. He was dying, yes, but still alive. His bones had rotted so much that he had to crawl around his hut. He couldn't even be carried on his slave's back. He drank three pitchers of barandro rum every day, and even refused to have lice picked off of him. And his wrath had grown greater than ever: he was known as Andriamaro the Furious."

"And he took pity on us?"

"Despite his bad health, Andriamaro was still absolute ruler over the four towns and villages in his province. We'd gotten along very well since we were young. I could even say that we were linked together by old passions of the womb."

"What?"

Bebe laughs her reedy laugh. An uncommon flame dances in her eyes. It's like Bebe is young again. She continues, secretively, "And that leaves its traces, even into old age. I wasn't always dry as an old mortar without a pestle, you know, o light of my life. There was a time when even lords

32

knew my bed, and Andriamaro was among them. I wasn't as beautiful as your mother, but my teeth were white and my voice pleasing."

"But how could anyone love a woman with a harelip?"

I regret it as soon as I say it. Bebe's not offended; she gets up, comes over, and takes my hand. She has me feel the edges of the gaping crack.

"Do you feel a twisted nerve or any shrinkage of the flesh?"

"No, why?"

"That tells you that it's not a birth defect."

"You mean your harelip appeared when you were already an adult?"

"I mean that I've never had a harelip. The thing you feel is the scar from a wound."

"But how did that even happen?"

Bebe laughs bitterly. "Jealous women, plotting shrews. The ancestors say, 'A banana threatened with a knife will eventually be pierced.'"

She waves her hand like it's not important. I realize that youth once lived in her, too. It makes her an entirely different person to me. Her hair wasn't always white and her face wasn't always scarred.

Bebe sits down. "Andriamaro was still a judge. Ranaka would never have dared confront him."

Bebe laughs again, a small laugh, bright with the memory of Andriamaro the Furious, the quick-tempered old lord of Ambohimanelo. Passions of the womb: that's how Bebe won the first round against Ranaka.

7   *Tsito*
Rasoaray's Pond

I CAN'T COUNT the number of times I was cast in the role of a prince or king in our childhood games. And every time Fara called on me for the task—so incompatible with a slave's—my soul leapt, unfailingly. In the space of a brief but intense moment, it was as if such a metamorphosis could happen in real life. As if the Creator would suddenly change His tune and sweep away the sorrows that had stricken my young life in one fresh puff of air, like a great cyclone.

"You're the Prince of Light and I'm the Cloud Lord's third-eldest daughter," Fara would say. "Don't forget, you have to transform into an ant so that you can startle me when I bathe in the lake!"

She said that with such a severe but endearing tone, the kind that children take when they're giving instructions to someone smaller.

I think my inextinguishable desire for emancipation may have been born during those moments, sprung from emotions rooted deep in old tales and given ingenious new life in a child's mind. My path to being a free man began on the banks of that enchanted lake—which, when it comes down to it, was nothing but a pond just to the south of Sahasoa.

Rasoaray's Pond.

We usually went there on Thursday mornings, because that was market day in Anativolo and adults had other things to do besides look after children.

The group of friends was made up of Fara and myself, Vero and her little brother, Tovo, as well as a few other interchangeable children from the neighborhood.

We'd leave early for the pond. We waited for Bao and Bebe to set off for the market, which they'd do soon after the morning rice meal, because the best bartering or buying opportunities at Anativolo would only last the first few hours. The two women usually wouldn't come back until nightfall. As they left, they told us to clean the house, and we'd rush to scour the pots, put everything away, and sweep the hut. When all that was done, we had to go fetch water. That was the moment we waited for. As soon as the first call came from the neighbor kids—"*Ndao ô!*"—we raced for the forest and freedom, as fast as our legs could carry us. Most times, we dropped a few pitchers and gourds behind a rock, so that we could carry more important things under our arms.

With the distance of decades, that explosion of tightly contained joy still hits me with all its dizzying force. That is what freedom tastes like—and I've never tired of it since.

For my princely roles, I carved a curved scepter out of hardwood, like the ones the highland lords had. Fara put flowers and leaves in her hair and stuffed a myriad of accessories into a sack, which she'd put on as soon as the village was out of sight. But before crossing the village moats, Fara and I always took a detour past Vero and Tovo's house. Tovo had the heart of a hunter, and he'd bring slingshots and a bunch of sharp and pointed implements in a satchel. Vero wanted to be a soothsayer, so she was partial to sacred and mystical objects.

To get to the pond, we followed a trail along the rice fields. The dense dew would still be hanging on the grass, making our bare feet damp. The misty air would smell fresh, perfumed, unlike any other time of day. The big, beaming sun would slowly appear over the hills to the east, revealing Sahasoa from the light morning fog.

Once we arrived, we'd face off in the realm of imagination to let off our pent-up energy. We'd be so impatient at the beginning that we'd all talk at once; it made for a chaotic din.

"Let's play *diamanga*! No, *atsipilavaka*! With real coins! Nobody's gonna be able to beat me if we use coins!"

"Nuh-uh! We want to play *raosi-jamba* or fampitaha!"

"A chameleon race! A beetle battle!"

We'd spend the day like that, frenzied and enthusiastic, our energy never dropping for a second. Happiness gathered us up into its great big warm arms. We didn't stop until we got hungry, which we'd slake with grilled crickets and wild berries.

But the best times, the ones that still glow in me today with their restorative light, were when we played *tantara tantara*.

Fara and I always gave our performance last, when everyone else was finally tired from running, fighting, and screaming at the top of their lungs. Silence would settle, with only the spring marring it with crystal tinkling from the east. Our voices echoed off of the pond's silvery surface.

"Do you not fear my father, the lord and master of the heavens?" Fara would cry, clattering her stone charms. "Do you not know that tornadoes stand guard over his dwelling place, and that the rushing waters bend to his will? O, take care: you are only a man of the earth!"

"I fear nothing," I'd reply. "I've made a secret pact with the powers of the forest. I will survive all calamities! For you, my princess, I will explore the deepest rivers and hunt down the dwarf hippopotamus. For you, I will fell the great forest and fertilize the endless plains!"

Our friends, paying little attention at first after having played so hard, slowly let themselves be lulled into the fantastic stories that escaped effortlessly from our intertwined words.

And in the evenings, when a storm brewed in the east, we'd end our games and head home with regret. In the wet season, the fat drops of the first downpour would usually catch us on the path, and we'd get back to the village with our faces soaked, as bolts of lightning split the thick, dark clouds hanging over the valley.

The storms, the lightning, it was the anger of the Cloud Lord, whose breath was the wind and whose voice was the rolling thunder. As we watched the rain continue to fall, squatting inside our huts, we'd think of the pond and its playful fantasy setting.

Yes. Rasoaray's Pond.

There was a story, which was part of our lives. And our destinies.

The elders told the tale of two dead boys who had been fished out by farmers one morning. Their mother's name was Rasoaray. The drowning story, along with the unusual path to reach the pond, made all the kids curious. I remember that Fara paid special attention to it, after the unexpected connection was made between that event and her own troubles with destiny.

There were contradicting rumors about the circumstances surrounding the death of Rasoaray's sons. Some said that they'd dived in to try to get the gold coins that someone had tossed in. Others claimed that they'd thrown themselves into the water to escape from a pack of wild dogs, after they'd been caught outside the village trenches at night. Where did the truth end, where did the story begin?

Whatever the case, Rasoaray had lost her mind when her two sons disappeared. Several years later, she still wandered the streets, lamenting her fate to the dogs and birds. Every child around knew her and her story. She'd shaved her head and let her fingernails and toenails grow out in permanent mourning. Her clothes were nothing more than foul rags, with a scrap dragging behind her on the ground like an animal's tail. She'd been a normal woman once, with a husband and two sons, but all three had been lost, and Rasoaray had ended up alone.

Rasoaray's Pond was our fairytale kingdom. I can still see it perfectly, that precious place of my Sahasoa childhood. A small creek sprung from the overhanging rocks and ran down into a natural well, where the villagers would come to fill their pitchers. Near the center, the well took on a dark-blue tint, showing where the water got deeper. From far away, it shone like an evil eye, set back from the pond's waterlilies.

The pond itself, another level below, was really just a little basin hollowed out of the streambed, where water flowed so slowly as to seem stagnant. On the banks, the rain and rising water levels had weathered the red laterite rock, leaving only a fine layer of white and yellow sand. The arid sand struck a contrast with the fertile life of the pond, where the surface was striped with thin arabesques of aquatic insects. Dragonflies peered with bulging eyes at the iridescent waters from their perch on the petals of great white waterlilies.

We played fierce games there; we had to keep our defenses up. The little body of water was far from paths and houses, so no adult would bother us. We could chase each other through the woods, mount stone-hurling battles with one another, climb the tallest trees, and eat all the things we weren't supposed to. All excesses were allowed, all rules abolished.

That was where, like a young *fosa* against a tree's bark, I earned my claws. Where I learned to defend myself, to better understand my peers. This was also where my soul intertwined with Fara's, slowly, with the patience of a climbing vine meeting the steadfast fig tree.

8   *Fara*

THIS MORNING, AT THE POND, Big Faly was telling the drowning story to get our attention. He'd puffed out his chest like a rooster.

"I know how Rasoaray's children died!"

"They drowned. The whole village has known that forever."

"Yeah, but no one knows they were killed, on purpose. Except me."

"How d'you know that?"

"Because I was there. I watched them die."

Faly is the oldest of the gaggle of kids that usually meets along the river. He's by far the biggest and strongest of the boys, and he likes being the leader. Tsito is the smallest and quietest.

Faly likes playing mean jokes. But it backfired this time, and Tsito almost sent Faly to join his ancestors.

At the height of the brawl, in the screaming and splashing, Tsito had grabbed Big Faly by his legs and dragged him to the bottom of the well. The little slave's arms locked around him with the strength of a crocodile's jaws. Afterward, Faly told us that he sunk to the bottom of the well like a stone. He said his blood pounded in his head just like a drum, and his heart beat in his chest like a caged animal, and his lungs were just about to burst. He tried to grab the sharp rock wall, but he just cut his palms. His blood streamed out in long red ribbons in the blueish well water. The silvery surface dropped away, and he realized that he would die.

Right as he was losing consciousness, he saw a spade coming toward him through the water.

There had been several of us at the pond this morning: Tsito and I, Vero and Tovo, Faly and a few others.

Faly had acted out to us how a man had submerged Rasoaray's children in the water until they stopped breathing. Their hands and feet had been tied so they couldn't fight back. The water came up to the man's belt, and he kept a firm hold on them until they no longer moved. Faly saw bubbles breaking the surface as they suffocated. Their mother, Rasoaray, was on the bank, screaming so awfully that all the lemurs and dogs within earshot had run away. Two other men held her as her little ones were killed.

"Who was it?" asked Vero.

"A seer. He prayed and cried as he was doing it."

"Why haven't you told anyone this story before?"

"Because I was scared that those men would kill me, too! My parents forbade me from telling anyone what I'd seen, as long as the seer was working around here. I pushed it out of my mind, but it came back to me this morning when I saw the bushes where I hid, right over there."

He pointed at tall ferns that spread their leafy tresses a little to the west. As we followed his finger, I saw a quail appear from underneath the green thorns. The bird peered at us with its scornful red eyes and disappeared behind a bush. I took that to be a bad sign.

"Your parents?" screeched Tovo. "Who are you talking about?"

Tovo clapped his hand over his mouth right after he said it. Everybody knows that Faly's an orphan who was adopted by Ranjato, the village chief. Faly bared his teeth.

"I had parents! We lived in another village. You got a problem with that?"

The proverb says that a lie likes to dress itself up as a story. But Faly looked like he was telling the truth. His details were too precise to have been made up. And he's old enough to have seen what would have happened several years ago.

My body shook while he talked. I was overwhelmed with a mix of dread and disgust. And I stifled a scream when Faly revealed the seer's name: Ranaka. My history pursued me like a predator.

I stared at Faly without seeing him, imagining Ranaka drowning Rasoaray's children, and I felt like I was suffocating, like I was the one being drowned.

The villagers had found Rasoaray the next morning, slumped up against a large rock. She was humming an old lament, clinging her balled-up clothes to her chest. *"Handeha ho aiza itsy ravorona? Ivorona inona? Vorona asiasy. Asiasy inona? Asiasy vazaha . . ."* Her sanity had flown away when her children's lives were extinguished.

But I found out that I wasn't the only one who was so afraid. And in Tsito's case, it could even become rage.

This morning, right before the fight, we'd been playing mass trial.

Faly and Tovo were both high judges and earth husbands. Their task was to purify the People Under the Sky, to wash them clean of their turpitude and evil intent. As loyal subjects of the Sovereign, they had consented to first submit themselves to an ordeal, and they had chosen the trial of gold.

Trembling with excitement, Vero found a small terracotta pitcher that had been lying around and filled it with water from the spring. She held the vessel out to Faly. Her wide eyes sparkled with curiosity. She wondered whether Faly would die right away, before our very eyes, or if it would happen later. She told me she'd never seen anyone die of poison. I hadn't either.

Vero has a small, slender face. Her bulging eyes take over the whole thing. I'm shier than her; she has an adventurous spirit.

"Wait, we need gold!" someone said.

"And where exactly do you think we'll find gold?" snapped Faly.

"I've got some gold!"

All eyes turned toward Tsito. The slave boy untucked the side of his loincloth and unrolled it warily. A flat, blackish little thing appeared in his hand. Faly grabbed his wrist hard, forcing him to open his hand.

"If that thing's gold, you can chop my head off!" shrieked Tovo.

Tsito pulled his wrist free without a word and walked to the edge of the pond. He thrust the object underwater and scrubbed it against his palms. Then he wiped it off on his loincloth and held it up to the sun. The metallic yellow color didn't leave any room for doubt. It was a gold coin.

"Where you'd steal that from?" shouted Faly.

"I didn't steal it. I took it back from the man who sold my family," Tsito said evenly, holding out the coin. "One day I'll use it to buy back my freedom."

"You're lying. You stole it! Don't think you're gonna get away with it that easy!"

Faly snatched the coin out of the slave's hand with an evil glint in his eyes. I knew instantly that he'd gotten some wicked idea into his head.

"Come on, Faly. Leave him alone, drink your water of gold."

Faly took the small pitcher out of Vero's hands and dropped the gold coin into the bottom. Then he raised the vessel over his head.

"I will now drink this water of gold," he said, his voice ringing out clearly. "If there are lies within me, if a witch is hiding inside me, let this water become poison and let my entrails rot away! Let me be devoured by crocodiles when I cross the river! Let wild animals feast on my body when I walk through the forest! And let my death be as insignificant as a grasshopper's!"

Then Tovo did the same, and the two judges began purifying the people.

For me, they chose the trial of stone. The accused has to reach into a pot of boiling water and take out a stone at the bottom. If the skin on her hands blisters, she is guilty. Lacking a pot and boiling water, they made me use my bare hands to catch a large crab poking around in the pebbles on the shore. I avoided getting pinched and was declared innocent.

Vero got the trial of rice, which consists of swallowing an entire pot of rice broth, then regurgitating the whole thing to prove your innocence. A bunch of bananas filled in for the rice. The amount of bananas that small, delicate Vero can swallow is staggering. Next, Vero gulped down water and stuck a finger in her mouth to make herself vomit. The mush of bananas came back up, and Vero screamed in triumph, her eyes shot through with blood. Tovo felt ill, too, and threw up to general laughter and jeering.

Finally, it was Tsito's turn.

"And you, we're going to purify you by water," proclaimed Faly with a nasty grin.

The slave raised an inquisitive eyebrow at the oldest boy in our pack, who pointed toward the well. Then Tsito understood what he meant. And what he would do.

"No. I don't want to."

"Too bad."

"No."

"I'm the high judge. You cannot defy me!"

"No."

"You're a liar and a thief, and you must be tried. Get him!"

They surrounded him and tackled him into the dirt. Two boys found a piece of vine and tied his hands behind his back. Over protests from the rest of us, they took him to the edge of the well and forced him to his knees. Faly grabbed him by the neck and bowed his head over the well, making up an incantation.

"O spirit of the water, we now submit this insurgent being to trial. If he is guilty of sorcery, if he's plotting against the kingdom, then let his life end here and his body be food for crabs and fish!"

Then Faly nodded to his friends, and together they plunged the boy's head into the water.

They did it again, then a third time. Tsito was suffocating; the sounds issuing from his mouth weren't words anymore.

"So, will you confess to your crimes, you little traitor? You stole the coin! Admit it!"

"Stop it," I yelled after a moment of waiting. "This isn't funny anymore!"

But Faly and his acolytes were stubborn. They liked their game. And they couldn't see the tragedy that stalked them. The globes of Tsito's eyes darted about, a terrible moan came from his mouth. It wasn't just fear. He had ceased to exist in a normal state.

"Say goodbye to your gold coin," said Faly with a sneer. "Since when do slaves have gold? It's cursed gold, sorcery! And I know just what to do with it!"

He pretended to throw the coin into the pond. It landed in the sand, just beyond the water's edge.

"Okay, come on," said Tovo. "We can stop now. It's not fun anymore." But it was too late.

Tsito wrenched himself free with a roar that froze us all where we stood. His face was unrecognizable. Faly and his friends stood there gaping, wide-eyed. With a single shove he had knocked over the three boys who'd been holding him, three solid young men who were all a head taller than him. This thing couldn't be Tsito. He glared at them with unspeakable hatred, stomping his feet like a *morainqy* wrestler.

Then, before Faly realized what was happening, he found himself launched backward with incredible force. The slave had charged straight at him like a horned ram. Faly got headbutted right in the stomach, and they tumbled together toward the well.

But it was not yet their destiny to perish.

"What's all this? Are you both completely mad?" a man yelled, as he ran toward our screams.

He thrust his long spade into the water. His reflexes saved their lives.

He was a farmer who did not normally take the detour past the pond to get to his rice field. He was only there because the ancestors willed it.

9   *Tsito*

Ibandro and the Undivided Piaster

BEING A MALE SLAVE in a home of women had many advantages.

I had a lighter load of chores, and discipline was minimal. Here, too, it would be wrong of me to complain. On the rare times that Bao or Bebe went to market, the basket I carried wasn't too big. And the only somewhat demanding work that fell to me was the water run to the spring and working in the fields. And the water runs, I carried out with no small amount of pleasure, as excursions to the spring afforded me immense freedom. As for working the family rice field, it was collective work performed in high spirits.

I was entirely spared a slave's weightier obligations, like carrying the master's baggage on my back, or even the master himself, anytime he left the house.

It was in such a stance, with an adult man astride his back, that my friend Ibandro first appeared to me one day. And every time that I think about Ibandro today, the preeminent servant, that is the dominant image: of a man-carrying man.

Ibandro was the head slave of Andriantsitoha, the provincial lord. Whenever he appeared in public places in his domain, he preferred to go on Ibandro's back rather than in a litter. Lord Andriantsitoha was still a young man back then. He had a strong presence, but his youthful features were contorted by his permanent worried expression and frantic eyes.

Eyes that never stopped moving, desperate to explore heaven and earth in search of friends or enemies. His bearing was a sharp contrast from the calm of his head slave.

That day, I was accompanying Bao to market. The pairing of the lord and his mount made for a unique spectacle. Villagers jumped out of their way and greeted Andriantsitoha with deep bows.

The first thing that you noticed about Ibandro was the size of his neck. A wondrous apparatus, thick as a bull's, it gleamed with sweat even when he wasn't carrying anything. At its base, it expanded into a vast spread of dorsal muscles, the most imposing set I've ever seen. Ibandro was a creature of colossal strength. In the *tolonomby*, wrestling barehanded against zebus, I've seen him seize the stockiest males by their horns and fell them in a single, powerful twist.

"Mistress, who is that?" I whispered to Bao.

"That's the lord of the province, Andriantsitoha."

"And who's the man carrying him?"

"That's his slave Ibandro. He's the strongest man in the province."

"Is that the only thing he does, carry the lord around?"

"It's an honor to carry the lord. He has a lot of power as head slave. Everyone is afraid of him. He's envied by many free men."

While we were talking, Ibandro set Andriantsitoha down at the entrance to a rich man's house. When the lord disappeared inside, the slave sat on the steps and cast a shadowed look over the villagers, who went about their business. People kept a respectful distance from the giant, and many excused themselves as they passed.

"*Manao azafady ô!*"

"*Ndao re tompoko!*"

I wondered what sort of authority Ibandro had. I couldn't take my eyes off of him. Not the smartest thing I've ever done. Curiosity ate at me, and it must have showed on my face. He stared right back at me and furrowed his brow. I watched apprehensively as he stood and approached us with his thudding steps. Bao seemed even more awestruck by his stature than I was. He was so tall and broad that he blocked out the sun.

"*Azafady tompokovavy!* Excuse me, mistress," he said. "Who is this boy? I've never seen him around here."

My fear became suffused with admiration: this man had a seductive confidence and freedom in his tone of voice. It was no ordinary thing to see a slave coming up to a free woman like that and questioning her so baldly.

"This is my new slave," Bao answered. "His name is Tsito. My husband bought him for me a few moons back."

My mistress smiled uncertainly. Her slightly fazed eyes showed quite some regard for this man. She didn't try to hide it, but instead attempted to make conversation. "Please, Ibandro, do you know if your master will soon consider the dispute between those two families over their rice fields?"

Ibandro ignored her question. "Where is he from?" he asked, towering over me.

"From the southern forests, I believe."

"Has he been broken in well? He looks insolent. I can take charge of his education if you'd like. Send him to see me in Ambohimanelo on Wednesday."

I was terrified. That giant could crush me with one swipe of his enormous hand and pluck off my limbs like a cricket's. As he spoke, he furrowed his brow, and his disconcerting black eyes kept shooting in my direction. His invitation to Bao sounded more like an order.

To my distress, she responded immediately. "But of course, I'd be very happy to. I'll bring him to you myself!"

As we walked away, Bao explained that Ibandro knew most of the children in the province by name and appreciated their company. It wasn't entirely reassuring.

Ibandro had his own personal hut on the south side of Andriantsitoha's estate, which sat on the highest hill in the province, in Ambohimanelo's main town. I'm always emotional when I think of that place.

The view from the hilltop swept over the province and its clustered towns. To the north sat Tendroarivo, like a sentinel, an old colony with

familiar red walls, founded by the Zafimanelos, Andriantsitoha's ancestors. Anativolo, the exchange market, was to the east of that region. In the
west, the border of the province ran along a dense, marshy forest, where
we used to hunt moorhens. And to the south, as the river valley stretched
out, was Sahasoa, Fara's village, with a cluster of huts overlooking a ring
of terraced rice fields.

Ibandro owned a cow and a rice field, which he had other slaves cultivate
while he accompanied his master. He was richer than most free men, but
had no wife or children. All of that merely fed the rumors.

"Are you hungry?" he asked as soon as Bao had left.

When my answer was no, he looked at me suspiciously.

"Slaves are always hungry. You must eat something every time the
opportunity arises. It is extremely important to eat. I never decline food."

He picked up a container full of slices of cooked taro and held it out
to me. I helped myself, and he did the same. My fear melted away, and I
ate with relish.

He looked me over sternly as he chewed. "Why are you so small and
skinny? Tell me how you got here."

Ibandro had me tell the story of my capture in detail, followed by my
life in captivity and how I met Rado. He only stopped eating every so often
to listen and glance toward his master's hut.

"Do you know what the servant's undivided piaster is?" he asked, once
I'd finished my story.

My answer was no.

He pointed to Andriantsitoha's house. "It comes from a proverb: 'The
servant's undivided piaster is the master's esteem.' Do you understand
what that means?"

"No."

"It's your master's respect that will allow you to regain your freedom
one day."

"Why an undivided piaster?"

"That's the price that all slaves must pay to the Sovereign or his lord
to buy back his freedom. From now on, this maxim must be your code

of conduct. You must please your master at all times, make sure that he always reaches the highest satisfaction."

That code was basically the only one that my friend and mentor taught me. At the time, I was unable to comprehend the full impact of those words. And even today, they are still just as rich in teachings and as parsimonious in meaning as life itself. Only Ibandro, I believe, that broad-shouldered giant, could fully understand.

Ibandro was born a slave. His father had been bought as a child by Andriantsitoha's father, from soldiers coming back from the countryside. The old provincial lord, named Andriamaro, had educated him and paired him off with a slave woman who died in childbirth. Ibandro's father had told him, his only descendant, that his homeland was in Bara country, far to the south. He'd been tortured all his life by the desire to return to his country and find his relatives, but had died without fulfilling his dream. Ever since, most likely in his memory, Ibandro had been taking slave children under his wing, the ones that somehow ended up adrift in the province.

It had only happened twice before me, since the region was set back fairly far from the major commercial routes. The first child, Ikoto, had been brought by a herdsman from the North. He'd been nothing but skin and bones, after his successive masters had undernourished and mistreated him. He died of fever and a bad cough two moons after he arrived. The second, Inaivo, an Anosy boy, was luckier. Bought by the daughter of an important local figure, he followed his mistress to Île Sainte-Marie, where she married a *vazaha* who emancipated the little slave and gave him a job on his plantation. Ibandro took great pride in him.

Ibandro had me come to Ambohimanelo every Wednesday. First thing we'd do was to sit in front of his hut and eat. He said that a scrawny slave was a dead slave. He believed that the soul starts to wander when the stomach is empty. He hated slender people; slimness made him anxious.

Ibandro had a reputation for being a respectful, obedient slave, with irreproachable behavior. It would be difficult to find a single incident in the province's recent past that he could be blamed for. But young Ikoto's death had affected him deeply. Changed him quietly. One day, a villager told me about how the herdsman who had mistreated the young slave had eventually fled to another district, for fear of being killed: upon meeting the herdsman in the market one evening, Ibandro had sworn that he'd take out his heart and spleen and eat them. This had caused quite the stir among the Council of Elders, and other slave owners had started to panic, convinced that the brutish giant would come to slit their throats. Andriamaro had been forced to intervene. He'd reprimanded his favored slave in the presence of the Elders and sent twenty piasters to the community to make amends. They had accepted the gesture, and the incident had been declared closed.

I became aware very early how greatly injustice, cowardice, and betrayal appalled Ibandro, and how dangerous that could be when combined with his big heart.

For that reason, I could never tell him about my confrontation with Big Faly, even once Faly and I became sworn enemies; he might have nabbed and snapped him like a wisp of straw. Without once thinking that he'd be signing his own death sentence by killing a child. I much preferred to learn from my friend and to grow up peacefully like the baby bird in its nest, sheltered from larger confrontations under his protection.

In Ambohimanelo, Ibandro had me carry big rocks and swing a heavy ax, even wrestle calves barehanded, to make me stockier. He also wanted me to hone my craftsmanship, so he introduced me to the province's master carpenter, an individual named Ratefy. He was a taciturn man whose wife, Ravao, had family in the City of Thousands. The couple owned an astonishing orchard, where a vast number of fruits from beyond the seas grew beside vegetables that had been completely unknown to the central highlands two generations earlier.

I went to their house whenever I had a free moment. Ratefy wasn't very talkative, and our conversations were generally limited to exchanges like, "Pass me the bevel. Don't forget to prop it up, okay? And make a pilot hole so you don't blunt the drill bit." Still, he taught me the greater part of carpentry techniques. I could thus dedicate some of the free time afforded me by the kingdom's laws to this art. The dexterity that I'd gained in captivity accelerated my progress.

Ibandro often brought back little trinkets from traveling with his master to far-off lands, like glass beads, wooden utensils, and scraps of fabric, all of which he distributed among the children in the area. In exchange, they picked fruits and roots for him from the woods, which he ate voraciously. For me, Ibandro brought back carpentry tools, so I could start to do odd jobs here and there for my own gain. In addition, my friend sometimes acted as intermediary himself. When, walking through the provincial towns, he spotted, for example, a beam in rough shape or a broken chicken coop, he'd call to the owner with his habitual brusqueness: "It looks like you need this repaired. I know a highly skilled young carpenter who could help you. It won't cost you very much."

And that was how, little by little, I started to save up some money, with the hope of one day possessing an undivided piaster. A real one. And to put it to good use when the circumstances allowed.

10

Bebe, or the Manioc of Saving Grace

ONE OF THE STRANGE THINGS about destiny is its ability to produce equally passionate veins of unexpected closeness and wrenching separations. I believe that Fara's life had been, since its very beginning, one of the best illustrations of that swinging pendulum.

Bebe had many anecdotes to tell us about Fara. I think she did it as much to keep us entertained—slyly dressing real life up in the garb of a story, as she liked to do—as to ward off evil.

She recounted Fara's early moments for us, moments of anguish if there ever were any, during a period when I was slowly rebuilding my own experience of a lost feeling: happiness. This occurred during the spring, in my first year in Sahasoa. Ibandro had cast his wide, protective shadow over me. Soldiers and slave dealers were slowly fading into the past.

Back then, Fara and I were put in charge of protecting the seedlings. This early-season task was traditionally entrusted to children, and we had to get to the rice fields early to do it: at first light, whole clouds of birds liked to set upon the stalks. Any delay could cost us dearly. Some years, especially when migratory crickets struck, too, whole harvests had been ruined before even being transplanted.

I don't think we were ever late for the seedlings, but it wasn't out of a desire to do the right thing . . .

We got up at the same hour as the farmers and hastily threw a few things together, including little baskets of rice that had been cooked the night before. Then, Fara lit the fire for Bebe and Bao while I let the chickens out, a little earlier than at other times of the year. At the third cock crow, we were on our way. We'd hear other children slipping between the huts in the still-dark village.

The rice fields weren't far. We quickly reached the bottom of a valley, where leafy covers were spread all along the edge of the crops; they would shelter us later, once the sun had climbed high in the sky. Until then, we had to drive away the birds and other enemies. To do so, we'd brought along a wide variety of noisy instruments—reed pipes, valihas, flutes, sticks, old pots—or we'd hollow drums out of wheatgrass, or make valiha *veros* from stalks of grass.

That was the fun part of seedling-surveillance duty: before first light, the rice field sprang alive with a clattering din.

Shouts, songs, whistles, drumbeats, a whole battery of cacophonous sounds rose over the morning fog, piercing the still-sleeping fields. The discord made birds take wing, and all the rats in the area clear off, as well as the owls, porcupines, and goats. We farmers waved to each other in that pandemonium, calling out challenges like moraingy wrestlers from one end of the green land to the other.

Ey e, lehiroa o!
Ey e, raha matanjaka e!
Ey e, mba midina o!
Ey e, am-belively o!
Ey e, am-belisangodina o!
Ey e, antongotongo e!

Perhaps it wasn't the best way of chasing away the harvest-eating spirits, but we stuck to it; we called it the *rodobe*, the great rumpus of Sahasoa.

Sometimes, Bebe came with us. She liked to come along on the first days, to give advice and pass on oral history. She told the tale of Andrianjaka, the architect of the great plain, painting the ocean of rice fields with a hundred shades of yellow and green, where villages looked like islands, where the silvery furrows of canals and water beds glittered in the distance, all the way to the mountains' base.

So it was, then, that one day, while overseeing the seedlings, resting from the shouting and uproar, Bebe told us for the first time about the school and the man who saved Fara.

Fara was asking her questions about how the seer Ranaka plotted after her birth. "So did he give up his awful schemes, Nenibe?"

"Sadly, no, o apple of my eye. And Andriamaro the Furious had the bad sense to die shortly after your birth."

"Didn't you have some other old lover who could help you?"

Bebe laughed and pinched Fara's arm, which made her yelp. I wondered what kind of lovers a woman with a harelip and ripped ears could possibly have had.

"Andriamaro was truly a lord of the era of conquests, a man the likes of whom you won't find anymore. When his bones were not aching, he never wavered. Just before his death, he'd woken up in very high spirits, almost healed. He'd even been able to take a few steps in the courtyard, supported by his eldest son, Andriantsitoha, and his favored slave, Ibandro. Beside himself with joy, he had a bull sacrificed and asked for the hump and rump to be brought to him. After feasting on grilled meat, fried crickets, and barandro, he lay down for a quick nap, and fell asleep for all of eternity."

"So did young Lord Andriantsitoha take over from his father and protect us?"

"No, Andriantsitoha was just an adolescent. He didn't have support from the powerful men. Ranaka's hands were no longer tied. We were once again exposed, like the worm under the bird's watchful eye."

Bebe had quickly realized that they had to take action. Ranaka had not remained idle. He'd sacrificed Rasoaray's children and was working hard to have families purified. He said that he'd been having terrible premonitions, that the ancestors were rousing him every night. That the community was in danger.

"That lunatic, he knew how to drum up support from anywhere," the grandmother said. "And it was a favorable era for him: talismans were very popular in wartime."

The seer wasn't afraid to shake Mandatsivoho underneath powerful men's noses as he pronounced curses. Even Andriamaro the Furious had refrained from quashing him, despite his insolence. If it was true that the Sovereign King wanted to use Mandatsivoho, such an action could have been extremely dangerous: the young monarch was a relentless warrior and a fastidious conqueror. "Will you let our ancestors' words be ignored?" Ranaka cried to the villagers. "Will you let evil forces flourish on the great woven mat of the People Under the Sky? The elders speak through Mandatsivoho. They tell us that the kingdom is going through uncertain times and that enemies must be crushed!"

"All you'd have to do would be poison him, right?"

Bebe shot forward and gave Fara a firm slap, making her yelp again. The older woman's hand still hung ready in the air. I backed away slowly.

"That's the last time I ever want to hear such words of sorcery! Who taught you that? Where did you come up with such thoughts?"

"Forgive me, Nenibe."

"What is it that you two do, exactly, with the other ruffians while we're at the market on Thursday mornings?"

"Nothing, Nenibe, we just play tantara by the pond!"

She turned toward me, eyes narrow. "Is that the truth, Tsito?"

"Yes, mistress."

Bebe stared long at us, her wrinkled face etched with sternness and distrust. Finally, she sighed. "For Ranaka, I followed the ancestors' advice. They say, 'Well might you possess the most powerful charms in the world; when you are hungry, you'll trade them for manioc.'"

The day was rising.

That morning, Bebe watched the birds, deep in thought, and smiled to herself.

I picked up a rock and chucked it toward the rice field. A cloud of multicolored birds rose and swirled up to the sky, lingered above the path for a few instants, and landed with a great flurry of wings in the thick branches of a tree ten paces away.

The rice seedlings had grown in nurseries for a moon. The plants were starting to emerge from the water and were easy targets for grain-eaters. In three moons, with the ancestors' blessing, we'd move on to transplanting the paddy. The rice field had already been weeded and the earth turned. The only things left to do before transplanting were flood it and have the cattle tamp it down.

The earth likes to be trodden by zebus; it becomes generous under the hooves of that fundamental animal. But in Ranaka's time, cattle were also sometimes used for trampling other things.

"When you were born, Ranaka wanted to put you in the path of a herd of zebu," Bebe told Fara. "We called on a vazaha to save you. This vazaha was a missionary. His name was Blake."

How many people living today have fallen among the zebus' hooves? Toward the middle of the Sovereign King's reign, the kingdom still practiced the trial of the pen to purify children born during the wicked Alakaosy moon. The evil-bearing child was simply placed before a cattle pen, and someone would open the gate. If it survived, it was considered washed clean of the malevolent astral curse. If not, it merely met the evil destiny that had been born in it.

Fara's grandmother paused, then burst out laughing. "O apple of my eye!" she exclaimed to Fara. "You weren't far off from the truth. As a matter of fact, the vazahas were a kind of poison for Ranaka. And for talisman guardians, too, generally speaking . . . "

"Why, Nenibe?"

"The Ancient Ones say that when manioc and yams were introduced to this land, taro and other roots slowly lost favor in the people's eyes and started to shrivel and dry. Did you know that vazahas are the color of manioc when it's peeled and cooked?"

·   ·   ·

56

Back when Fara was born, Bebe hadn't yet seen a White—except for the Wandering White Man, of course. But she'd heard about them, so she went to the very edges of the district to find one.

Blake had just arrived from England. He was part of the first group of missionaries to whom the Sovereign King had opened the kingdom's door. The vazahas wanted to establish *sekolys*—schools—where, like the Ancient Ones said, children would be taught sacred symbols. Blake's counterparts had made an initial venture in the East, but they'd been massacred by the coastal people, who were much less patient with foreigners than people from here.

Drawing lessons from that failure, Blake had decided to focus his efforts on Imerina, the highland kingdom. It was clearly the ancestors who willed it to be so.

Blake was the manioc Bebe was looking for, sent from heaven.

This occurred in the eighth year of the Sovereign King's reign.

It was a strange meeting, of the manioc and taro.

Ranaka's face expanded with alarm as he saw an unknown, red-faced man surging forward, gesticulating wildly. The villagers who were watching the trial, Bebe aside, thought for a moment that it was an albino, driven mad by the sun, but Blake wore European clothes. Back then, that kind of getup confused people.

"A vazaha!"

Frenzied whispers shot through the crowd. Yes, it was definitely one of those pale-skinned men who came from across the seas. Great beads of sweat sparkled on his forehead and rolled down into his eyes. Several women ran away squealing. Terrified by the Englishman's yellow hair and eyes set with their brilliant-green irises. And his voice.

"*Stepy baky! Stepy baky! I saly naoty alao io tu prosidy!*" he barked.

What manner of tongue was that? What was this man saying?

Ranaka hesitated. The other man kept coming.

Nonetheless, once the moment of shock had passed, the seer tried to show proper consideration toward the vazaha, and he forced a smile.

Bebe, gently lobbing pebbles at the birds in the rice field, guffawed again as she described the face of the talisman guardian. "Ranaka was not brazen enough to go against the ancestors' principles: 'You must not judge the stranger with his yellowish face, but think of his family on the other side of the earth.' Remember that, children: every person from far away carries in him the sacred virtues of his own kind, and thus deserves respect."

If you ask me, Ranaka couldn't ignore that the Sovereign had welcomed the missionaries with open arms either.

"You are most welcome in our lands!" the seer boomed. "And may the Perfumed Lord and the ancestors bless you!"

In a strong yet slightly strained voice, he declared himself the vazaha's loyal servant, offering to lend him his belongings and even his wives and children to make use of as he pleased. He proposed, according to the customary phrasing, carrying him on his back and on the top of his head.

But as for Blake, he didn't understand the language of the ancestors and didn't seem inclined to any such arrangement.

"Two bulls had already been released in the pen," recalled Bebe. "Ranaka couldn't give in without losing face. A confrontation would have to happen."

The story had a lively ending, as might be expected.

Ranaka tried to seize Fara and put her in front of the cattle pen. Blake got in the way, violently. The time for civilities had passed. After a few blows, Ranaka went and got a *kibay*—a bludgeon. He rounded on the vazaha with an evil glint in his eyes. Everyone stepped back, believing that the white man's hour had come.

But the foreigner, plunging his hand hastily into his pockets, grabbed a vial of ink from somewhere inside his clothes and threw the contents in the *mpitaiza sampy*'s face. It made a huge black spot on the talisman guardian.

Ranaka stopped dead, blinded, dumbstruck, the mayhem and raging curses cut short. What did the gesture mean? What was that sorcery? Finally, the elders intervened. The village chief himself stepped in between them. Other important men were alerted, even the young provincial lord.

The trial of the pen could not happen that day as planned. A stinging blow for Ranaka.

And that wasn't all. The authorities decided to suspend the ancestral sentence indefinitely. The Council of Elders was troubled by the fact that a vazaha had intervened in a traditional process. They interpreted it as a sign from the ancestors. They decided to wait for a clearer vision to come and refused to make any rash decisions. More repudiation and humiliation for the seer.

And in reality, Ranaka could never win. One moon after those events, saving grace came from the Palace. The Sovereign King, master of destiny's flowing current, long pressured by his English friends, abolished the trial of the zebu throughout the kingdom.

Fara was saved.

11 *Fara*

RADO HAS AGREED to bring me to the City of Thousands.

My father goes to the big city regularly for his business. He's never wanted to take me before now, because of the danger. Bebe looks worried, but I think Rado's made his decision.

"I want her to see the City. I have to go there to learn about silkworms and the zebu markets in the Great South; I'm not too familiar with them. Might as well take advantage of the opportunity for her to discover the City."

"But she's never left the province, she has no experience traveling! She hasn't even been to Tendroarivo yet!"

"You don't have anything to worry about. I'm not bringing any merchandise along this time. No herds. We will attract much less attention and be more mobile. Plus, we'll only walk in daylight, even if it doubles the length of the trip. We'll sleep in friendly villages along the way."

Rado explains the reasons for this journey to us, but Bebe is only half-listening, watching me, her brow furrowed. She knows she won't make my father change his mind. I think she's even a little annoyed with me for not helping her.

"I want to clear up some rumors that have been circulating ever since the Sovereign forbade exporting slaves," says Rado. "I see big changes on the horizon for the kingdom's commerce, and I know that they'll all come from the capital. In my line of work, you have to know how to anticipate things if you don't want to be left out of the game."

Bebe sighs. "Shouldn't Tsito come with you?"

My father is an experienced traveler, he can pick out both dangerous passes and the quickest routes. I wasn't afraid of anything.

On the very first day, we pushed deep into thick forests with crystal-clear rivers cutting through them that it seemed like no human being had ever crossed. There were ferns as tall as a man and ivy climbing toward the treetops like knots in a sky-bound net. Orchids wafted a delicate scent into the air. Clouds of insects flitted about in glowing streaks of light. Lemurs with black and white coats clung to branches and watched us with great big surprised eyes. It was strange and exciting.

Then we crossed a swampy plain where birds thrived. I spotted egrets, moorhens, partridges, wild ducks, many other species I didn't know, of all sizes. Tsito managed to slingshot a teal duck with shimmering plumage. We roasted it that very night.

We carefully avoided some crocodile-infested waters. The only actually difficult parts were the cattle trails, where the mud was so deep that it could have swallowed up a child. Rado carried me on his shoulders to get through. Tsito jumped from rock to rock and hung onto bushes.

We were received like lords in every village we spent the night in. People aren't stingy with their hospitality: they're very happy to share the family rice and mattress, and they'll throw a feast for you. As incredible as this seems, they all seemed to know my father. Tsito and I, we slept through their long conversations around the fire.

"Soon, you'll only be able to trade zebus for powder and guns. But that merchandise is reserved for soldiers and higher court dignitaries, which means that ordinary folk like us are going to be excluded!"

"I hear the Sovereign is sick. All the alcohol the Whites are giving him might be sapping his health, and the fevers and injuries that he incurred during his military expeditions have left their marks, too."

"They're saying he's getting more and more unpredictable and cruel—"

"Careful, keep your voice down."

"—and much less inclined to consult the elders."

Walking only became harder near the end; the slopes got steeper and steeper, and I started to feel the effects of the altitude.

Approaching the capital, the hills cleared. It didn't feel as lush as the great forest, but it was calmer and nobler. The views were magnificent:

they made you feel like you were looking out over the whole world. More than once, we thought we spotted the City of Thousands in the distance, but Rado set us straight: they were only large towns around it. When, on the evening of the seventh day, he finally told us that it was in sight, we could only see faint lights, because it was already so dark. It was forbidden to enter the City at night, and we had to sleep at the gates. Fortunately, an old woman who lived not far from there gave us a place to stay.

The next day, I didn't open my eyes until light hit the undersides of the leaves. Rado and Tsito had gotten up earlier, at the hour of laborers, but hadn't woken me. I emerged from the hut, my heart thumping.

At first, I only saw a forest. What I was looking at could only be the royal hill, though, with the Sovereign's house materializing on its peak. Where was the City? The steep hill was covered with a thick, dark forest that looked more like blue. That's when I remembered its old name: Analamanga, the Blue Forest. I didn't see the buildings until my eyes adjusted: they were the same color as the forest. The thick bamboo houses stretched along an invisible spiral line that rose all the way up to the top, where the Sovereign's residence sat enthroned. And then I finally heard the City, and felt it breathing, like some enormous creature.

We're here. First, we make a wide circle to the south. There are some construction projects the Sovereign recently launched, and Rado wants to see how they've been coming along. Soon, we're crossing a vast site being leveled by thousands of laborers. Almost entirely naked, red with dust from head to toe, men and women, and even children, are all working here, as far as the eye can see.

The prisoners pass us without seeing us, without paying any attention to us. Some have crazed eyes beneath masks of mud; all waver as they walk. Tsito watches them without a word. The next site is less sad, fortunately: it's the construction site for a new satellite palace for the Sovereign. The silhouette taking shape already makes you think of parties, tournaments, a luxurious life. Rado says that most of this work is being done by vazahas; they have already left their mark on the city.

We come back up the west side, because Rado wants to call on an acquaintance who lives in a place called Andavamamba, the Crocodile's Cave. We walk through tall grass for an hour. I can hardly tear my eyes from the royal hill, rising in the distance to our right. The person Rado's looking for can't be found. People tell him that he went to the market.

We keep going north for a bit, then we turn east to go around a large pond that they call Anosy.

We get out of the way a lot to let sedan chairs go by. Some of the litters are long and richly decorated, sometimes even followed by a long train of slaves; it's a stunning sight. The porters, hardy men, have enormous calluses on their shoulders. The richly dressed people they carry look annoyed as they peer down on the commoners. One of them is wearing a bizarre hat, and his skin is as pale as an albino's: it's a vazaha. Other important men, not as rich or stingier, travel on a slave's back.

We climb a steep slope, and a little further on we pass the Friday market on our left. It's just north of the Champ d'Or, where Mister Hastie's estate is—he's the King's chief adviser. The market is filled with grave mounds, and some people set their merchandise right on the tombs themselves. Are denizens of the City so money hungry that they no longer respect their ancestors' resting places?

Rado stops for a moment and scans the merchants' stalls, then seems to change his mind. "Let's go see the Palace first," he says.

We keep climbing southeast, on a path that becomes more twisting as the slope gets steeper. After a while, we get to a little ledge where nothing blocks the view.

I'm speechless.

The royal citadel towers on top of the hill, its shining presence competing with the sun itself. The Sovereign's residence is recognizable by its red, white, and yellow bands, and the thousands of glittering silver nails around the entrances. On the highest knoll next to the King's residence are the two residences for the royal wives and concubines. The citadel is built from interlacing wood and topped with a row of lances, for both defense and decoration. From where we stand, we can also see the sacred houses

63

where the remains of our founding ancestors lay and, a little further off, the royal stables, armory, and school. It's even more beautiful than my mother described.

This city is my destiny. I was born to live here someday.

Soon, we're back at the edge of the market. Rado is leaving us alone for an hour or two to take care of a few things. He gives Tsito a few parting instructions. "I trust you now—you're an intelligent, experienced boy. Do not leave the market for any reason, it's safer that way. I'll come back to get you near that big tree over there, when the sun is at the rooftops."

"Why can't we come with you?"

Rado seems annoyed by my question. "Some of my contacts are dangerous men, who can change into starved wild beasts in the blink of an eye. They'd be willing to eat their own father and mother. Some of them have been involved in the slave market. I came without my friends this time. It's best to be more careful."

I'm slowly getting used to the motley market crowd. Tsito doesn't seem impressed at all. He must have gotten that confidence from traveling with my father. His presence is making me more confident, too. Soon, my curiosity returns, and I start dragging him all over the place. We start at the fabric sellers, dawdling there for a long time. Tsito is getting irritated, but I just want to have two sets of eyes.

"Come here! Look at that! Look!"

"Don't shout. People are staring."

The buyers fascinate me even more than the vendors. My eyes feast on the City girls: their most commonplace gesture has a heavenly mystique about it compared to our provincial mannerisms. Even the sound of their laughter, revealing teeth whitened by liana and *tambolo*, sparkles like the song of a sacred spring to my ears.

I shiver with envy at the colorful cotton fabric from Mojanga that they wear, their noses in the air. I'm finally seeing it—the imported fabric that people talk so much about, sewed into shirts. My neck is cramping from all the turning, to see bracelets, necklaces, and earrings crafted from such new and strange wood and mirrored metal. I recognize the favorite hairstyles of the young Thousands ladies, with their elaborate structures.

"I'd love to be dressed and styled like these women!" I say.

"No one would be caught dead wearing clothes like that in Sahasoa."

"But I'm not going to stay in Sahasoa. I'm coming here. I'll have a rich and powerful lover!"

After seeing the silkworm sellers, we start heading over to the iron-mongers, and the crowd surges.

"Move! Up there! Out of the way!"

Tsito sees the danger immediately. With lightning-fast reflexes, he throws himself on top of me and rolls us to the side, and I shriek. Tsito jumps back up and drags me three steps backward. Other people get trampled underfoot. I hear cracking bones among the screams.

One part of the peaceful market crowd has transformed into a fero-cious beast. It's led by a handful of muscular men who thundered across the square like bulls in the Bathing Feast. Their eyes have a sinister look that testify to a long practice of hunting men. At first, it's impossible for us to see who their prey is; the crowd presses in around the place where he's finally been captured, and the dust billows over the action in yellow clouds.

But the pursuing crowd soon starts moving again, more slowly, like a snake. At the head of the column, men shout and wave, opening the way for a compact group holding the fugitive. Behind them, women, children, even self-respecting fathers follow closely.

"To the dais!" the crowd shouts.

"Come on!" says Tsito, pulling me along.

"No! What's that? I don't want to go!"

"We have to! I have to know who was being chased," he shouts, drag-ging me through the crowd.

I don't even have a chance to get angry. This is another Tsito, different from the meek slave that goes to the rice fields with me every day. This one has the same hardened look as my father.

"What are you going to try to do? Will you know the person they caught? I don't get it, I'm scared!"

"It's nothing, I just have to check. Stay with me, Mistress Fara, and you'll have nothing to fear!"

The crowd gets denser as we get closer to the earthen platform. We use our elbows to sidle up just behind the front. Then it gets much harder to keep moving forward. Everybody is tense, tempers flare, they don't seem to have any desire to let us past.

"Who is it? What did he do?" Tsito asks a man.

"A traitor. He took what belongs to the King and was involved in plots against him. He was sentenced by the Sovereign almost a moon ago, but he managed to escape. People recognized him when he tried to blend into the crowd at the market. He'll get exactly what he deserves."

Tsito stands on tiptoes. "What does he look like? A young man? I can't see."

As Tsito tries desperately to catch a glimpse above the forest of backs and shoulders, I find a gap.

"Come on, through here!"

A bunch of kids manages to get out in front. I follow as they go. Tsito comes with and quickly scans the scene.

"Okay, good. Let's go. Nothing else for us to do here . . . Fara?"

But I'm not listening anymore. I'm looking at the man on his knees, held firmly by three others. A fourth saunters behind the prisoner, grabs his hair, and yanks his head backward. Holding the man facing the crowd, he takes the knife hanging at his side and slits the straining throat. The captive shudders violently and lets out a howl that fizzles into a bloody gurgle.

"Come on! Don't look at that!" says Tsito, pulling my arm.

But I can't tear my eyes away from the criminal's bulging ones. His executioner, slicing vertebrae and tendons with one hand, severs the head completely and hoists it overhead to show the crowd, while the body spasms and slumps over. My entire body begins to shake.

"He got just what he deserved!" I hear from the crowd.

"That'll make his friends think twice!"

I don't see what happens next. I think I temporarily fainted. A few instants later, I'm running, but I slam into a human wall. I fall, get up, and run again. I fight against an angry wave. Finally, I get to the edge and dive into the trees, far away from the crowd. I hear someone fuzzily calling my name, far far away.

I run as fast as I can, turning up the first path that led away from the marketplace. The howl follows me. The decapitated body runs behind me and tries to grab me. I'm too scared to turn around. "Hnnnngh! Hnnnngh!" I run faster and faster, never stopping, never looking behind me.

I don't regain my senses until I reach some sort of clearing, an eternity later. I can't hear the crowd's screams anymore. My legs don't want to carry me anymore.

At first, I don't notice what the weird long rods are, stuck into the ground all around me. I'm more preoccupied with whatever was behind me.

Shaking all over, I slowly turn around.

It's a dog. Huge, fat, with reddish hair, glowing eyes. Its chops are bared, showing long, pointy canine teeth. My eyes hunt desperately for a way to escape, a tree to climb up.

Then I see the heads. They're stuck on long bamboo pikes. Some of them are already skulls, without skin or flesh, their eye sockets gaping; others still have some of their faces. Bones are scattered below, left behind by the dogs, rats, and birds.

On the right, another mongrel appears, then a third on the left.

They're both just as fat as the first, bloated with human flesh. I open my mouth to scream, but no sound comes out.

Tsito has just enough time to grab a large branch to brandish against the dogs. He followed me. He didn't abandon me. I am petrified, defenseless. We're still ten paces apart. We won't do much good against the ravenous pack. Tsito takes a step forward, wielding his improvised weapon, trying to intimidate the beasts.

"We have to at least get back to back. Walk backward toward me, slowly. Don't take your eyes off them."

We're surprised even to reach one another. The dogs growl and stare up at us with their bloodshot eyes, but don't yet attack. Tsito even makes one of them back off with a good whack of his club.

Soon we're standing back to back. We wait for the assault, but it doesn't come. Tsito looks carefully at the dogs.

"They're scared," he says.

They're not scared of us—that's impossible—but something else. They smell something coming, and hesitate.

"What are you doing here?"

The gravelly voice, the muscular body, the inhuman eyes: we both recognize him at the same time. He's the one with the criminal's head, which he'd tied to a stick to carry over his shoulder like a bindle. He's not alone: two of his buddies are a few steps behind, dragging the rest of the body on a rope tied around the feet. That's who the dogs had smelled coming. What they were waiting for: food.

"What are you doing here?" he repeats.

"We got lost."

One of the men launches himself onto the biggest dog, slicing through the air with a machete. The animal yelps and cowers, its hide cut by the sharpened steel. The three men guffaw. The other dogs whine and growl with hate. These creatures who feed them their own brothers' bodies are also their worst enemies.

Dogs on the outskirts of the city are so accustomed to human meat that they'll attack people and devour them if they walk around alone or too late at night.

The men throw the decapitated body at the bottom of the bamboo pikes. Their boss sticks the head on one of the free pikes. Then they step far back. The dogs launch themselves onto the body.

The executioner and his friends watch the show, morbidly fascinated. I feel sick again. The sounds of chewing and tearing flesh, punctured by wild growls—it's unbearable.

"Come on, let's go," says Tsito, pulling me by the hand.

"Who said you could leave?" says the boss, his eyes never leaving the dogs.

Tsito stays silent. The man spits on the ground and slowly wipes his hands on a corner of his wrapper. After watching the dogs a little longer, he wanders nonchalantly up to me and seizes my hair.

"I like this one. Where're you from?"

Tsito doesn't move.

"Come on, where's your voice? Don't you know how to talk?"

I look helplessly at Tsito. The other men snicker.

"Hey, Ramy, since when were you interested in little girls?" says a voice.

I would have recognized that voice in ten thousand. The two henchmen jump, but the one named Ramy doesn't flinch. He stares coldly at Rado as he approaches. Tsito grabs me so I don't run straight to my father. That's smart—it's better not to trigger anything.

Rado puts on his friendliest airs and steps confidently forward.

He is armed only with his walking stick. Only curiosity and no small astonishment must be keeping the other men from falling on him. My heart beats wildly.

"My apologies, my lord, but I don't seem to know your face," says the boss, in sickly honeyed tones.

"So, you don't recognize your own brothers anymore? Do you so easily forget the ones who have shared food with you? Do you scorn the shoulder that supported you and the eye that showed you the path?" says Rado in a patronizing tone. He plants himself right in front of Ramy, a broad smile plastered across his face.

The other man hesitates. Rado's tone echoes like an insult. Ramy probably wants to make sure he's not making a mistake.

"Please know, good sir, that it brings me great pride and honor to be counted among your friends, even if your name, my lord, has not yet come to me. Please forgive me for my tiny memory. Although, as the proverb goes, 'Better a small soul respected by his friends than a great soul who perishes in vain,'" says Ramy ironically. He waits patiently for an explanation. He has all the time in the world.

Rado smiles wider. "The number of men who have worked in my service far surpasses a thousand, two thousand souls, although not all have worked directly with me. But I know each one of them as well as an animal in my pasture; each one is as dear to me as a member of my own family. Your father's firstborn, Njato—he was in my party barely two moons ago, driving a herd of a hundred head toward the eastern banks. How's he doing now? Has his tendon healed? I'll be honest with you, without my brothers' helping hands, his bones would be decorating the plain as it burns today!"

Ramy's expression changes. "Who are you?"

"Come on, Ramy! You're gonna make me upset! Did you not take up a rod and thrice strike the water of your birthplace and swear an oath of loyalty two years ago at the Bathing Feast? My interests align with those of my blood brother, Ndriana. Last year, you helped acquire cattle in the land of Bezanozano rebels, which showed your courage and valor."

"Ndriana is your blood brother? But then—"

"Him, a few others . . . Do I really need to list them all? In our fraternity, as you know perfectly well, we prefer work done right, with the ancestors' blessing, to a useless reputation that'll eventually be taken advantage of by villains and rogues! The proverb says, 'The tree that grows too high will be thrashed by strong winds.'"

The one called Ndriana and his men, whom my father has sometimes mentioned to me, are not hired hands like Ramy and his friends. They are true warriors, sometimes called to serve the Sovereign himself. To my relief, Ramy and his two friends instantly turn into the most agreeable company.

"Ha ha! That was a devilish plan, that operation with the Bezanozanos, eh my lord? Do you have any ones like that coming up? You can always call on us!"

"Yeah, maybe we don't have Ndriana's cunning skill in the art of war, but we have sturdy arms and we're not afraid of anything!" adds one of the goons.

"I've noticed that. Looks like the dogs are finding that out at their own expense," says Rado, with a note of sarcasm.

Ramy takes my father collegially by the arm. "Quite right, my lord. You still haven't told me how I might be of service to you. You appeared so suddenly that we took you for a fahavalo thief!"

"I was looking for my two slaves here," Rado says, gesturing to us.

"Oh, they're yours? We were wondering what they were doing here. This is the convicts' yard, it's one of the most dangerous places they could be. We were going to leave them in the authorities' capable hands."

Rado, too, acts like he forgot how the other man was leering at me. "Thank you."

"You know what? We can accompany you for some of the way, if it's not inconvenient. The fringes of the City are dangerous—"

"No point. I left ten of my stoutest companions on the outskirts of the market while I followed you into this forest. And I know you're anxious to get your hands on your hard-earned money from the earth husbands. In fact, we should all get out of here quick: if my friends are left waiting, they might come and butcher all your dogs, and you wouldn't have your cleaning crew anymore."

"Ha ha ha!"

As soon as we're out of earshot, Rado roars at Tsito. "Why did you disobey me? I told you not to leave the market!"

"When that horde of people took off after that traitor, I was afraid it might be my master."

"Why?" my father asks, surprised. "Do I seem like a traitor to you?"

"No. But times are changing, and more and more people are becoming prey."

Rado stops walking, looking confused. But loud footsteps marching behind us interrupt their conversation.

I shout out loud, "Iada, look! Their hair is short!"

A military patrol is passing by. The soldiers wear scarlet tunics, the ones that people often confuse with the clothes reserved for nobles. Tall feathered hats make them look even more European. Some people don't like short hair, because it's a sign of mourning. It doesn't bother me. I am overcome with admiration.

We suddenly realize that Tsito has disappeared.

"What is it now?" my father yells.

We find him behind a house on the side of the road. His eyes blaze with hatred, and he's shaking.

"What's wrong with you? Are you insane?" I say.

Rado makes me be quiet and takes the slave by the shoulder to calm him down. He turns to me and murmurs, "Most of his family and all the men in his village were massacred by those soldiers in red. He was hunted and captured by them, like prey."

BOOK 2

Mpanelanelana ny sarotra
Toa tamotamo

To mediate the difficult
As saffron does

MALAGASY HAINTENY

12 *Tsito*
Blake and the Vazimbas

PERHAPS IT'S A NECESSITY that every morsel of life be a mixture of good and bad. Few stretches of time brought me closer to Fara than our shared years of schooling, few moments were closer to my heart. Yet those same times also saw the birth of the deep-seated animosities that would eventually tear our community apart.

Bebe decided to send Fara to learn from Blake shortly after telling us about the white man's first meeting with Ranaka the seer. The English missionaries encouraged parents to send their younger slaves with their children, which is why I am able to tell this story, which is why I am the man I am today.

But what kind of man have I become? What parts of my personality do I owe to Blake and the Europeans? In what corners of my soul do rice fields and the ancestral colors still hold fast?

Back when we started attending school at the mission, very few people in the highlands knew how to read and write. Writing as the Europeans conceived of it was a very new thing—for us, only the ombiasy who advised the sovereigns, as well as a tiny number of insiders, knew how to decipher the sacred *sorabe* writing passed down from the ancestors.

In school, our way of seeing the world was radically altered. I'm sure that I'll remember my first day of class until age blots out my memory and empties my skull. We'd departed for the mission on a cool morning in the Adizaoza moon. The rice fields were still silent, awash in the silvery grayness of a new day. Roosters were nodding off after the flurry of waking up, perched on low red walls, and sleepy snorts came from the animal pens. Our friend Vero had joined us, escorted by her parents. Even Bebe, despite the stiffness in her legs, was intent on making the trip. Bao alone had refused to come. She believed that seeing Blake again would bring her bad luck.

Farmers on the path greeted us with curiosity, spades over their shoulders.

"*Fa andeha ho aiza izato izy?* Where are you going?"

"*Any an-tsekoly!* We're taking the children to school!"

"*Hay! Masoava ary Tompoko!* Oh! May you find happiness!"

The school was located outside of the Ambohimanelo domain. It was a large hut built on a shaded little plot, with a thatch roof and white-slat walls with an adjoining hut; it looked very nice. There were about twenty students in all, including a handful of adults. The children, of various ages, came from all the surrounding villages. New students arrived every month, and others left at the same rate, never to return.

Blake received us in his office, a converted room in the attached hut. He was a tall man with red hair and green eyes. He had a strong voice and hewn features, like those of our mountain men. He recognized Bebe and congratulated all the parents on their decision.

"*Tonga soa ato amin'ny tranon'Andriamanitra!*" he said, in his exaggerated accent. "Welcome to the house of God!"

Since the school was a rather significant distance from Sahasoa, it was decided that we would come two or three times per week, preferably on Mondays, Tuesdays, or Fridays. Some of the other students in this seed of a school only came one day a week, when their chores allowed. Others only had class every other week, or just showed up whenever it suited them. The missionaries were perfectly accommodating.

We started that day.

A few moments after the meeting, Bebe left and we found ourselves—Fara, Vero, and I—sitting on the mat in the large room, watching the other students tracing letters on a blackboard, with a kind of envious fear. Rose, Blake's assistant, introduced the pupils by name as they wrote: Rasendra, Imbitika, Andrianary . . . Some of them, feeling us watching them, wrote with a flourish. We'd never seen a blackboard before. Once they'd written down all the symbols, Rose pointed at the chaos with a stick and had them spell out loud. The whole class read in unison, at the top of their lungs: F, A, B, D . . . To our commoner's ears, it sounded like a song of praise, or a magic prayer.

Then, Rose picked up a piece of chalk and wrote five words in a row, under the letters, that the students rushed to be the first to read.

"*T-o-n-g-a s-o-a . . . Tonga soa! T-S-I-T-O . . . Tsito . . . Fara . . . Vero! Tonga soa Tsito sy Fara ary Vero!* Welcome Tsito, Fara, and Vero!"

The sentence of welcome was repeated seven times, in a clamor of childlike voices. Everyone looked at us and clapped their hands. I was speechless. It was hard to believe that I—the lost child, the slave—could also acquire such extraordinary knowledge. I looked at Fara and Vero: they'd been knocked completely off course. Something was happening. A new link had just bound us together.

We made rapid progress. It took Fara and me relatively little time to learn the alphabet; the missionaries' flexibility in teaching, established in response to a fluctuating head count, also allowed the ones who wanted to, who could, to go faster. Rose always put in the time needed to instruct us individually or in small groups. She and Blake were always willing to go in a different direction and explore new interests.

This method was generally beneficial to all of us, but it had a miraculous effect on Vero. School proved to be quite an exceptional experience for our friend, a real transformation. We got the impression that she knew words before letters, full sentences before words.

The moons passed quickly.

"Today, Vero is going to read the Epistle to the Ephesians, chapters one and two," Rose announced one day, her face beaming.

She'd found out that the little girl had figured out whole chunks of the text without any help, guided only by her insatiable curiosity. We barely knew how to read, but she was already navigating verses and chapters of the Bible with ease. We deciphered selected passages, snippets of stories, while for her, the Books themselves were her tools—the whole things. She didn't read. She devoured.

Vero dedicated herself entirely to the Christian religion barely one year after starting with Blake.

Our friend's spiritual climb was certainly escalated by her inordinate intelligence, which we'd already seen before we started school. Among the group at the pond, Vero had always been the one motivated to undertake the most radical exploits and the most extravagant stunts. She loved crazy dares and was completely unrestrained in brandishing the obscene challenge phrase: "By my father's incest, I'll do it!"

Although frail, shorter than average, and with a pair of bulging eyes, Vero was a ball of energy who brought overflowing passion into everything she did. One day, she told us in one sitting every adventure of Kotofetsy and Maka, and even Ibonia—her favorite story characters. Another time, she stole three soldiers' uniforms from under their noses while they were washing on a riverbank near an encampment. The soldiers had to return to their camp naked, but they found their clothes the next morning, folded neatly in front of their tent.

Vero's conversion to Christianity fueled passionate opinions, because of how quick and spectacular it was. Some of the provincial children, including Faly, showed increased hostility toward us. They accused us of becoming pretentious and haughty, of trying to command their respect with ill-gained knowledge. We were just "slaves to the Whites," they said. One day, the vazahas would force us into the basest menial labor, and we'd have it coming. In return, we treated them like jealous imbeciles.

Faly's aggressiveness was focused on me in particular. He had quite a talent for slanderous proverbs.

"Hey, what are you, even?" he jeered. "At best, 'a slave wrongfully set north of the hearth, who has trouble digging himself out.' But don't look too far: 'Slave you are, leader will never be.'"

Some adults eyed us with almost as much suspicion. I admit, the sight of Vero on the path with her heavy book, with her unique attitude and speech, it inspired gossip. Ever since she'd been baptized, Vero never separated herself from her Bible. She was one with the book, consulting it endlessly, never flagging.

Her unusually strong connection to the Word gave even more credence to the wildest rumors that gullible folks exchanged about the vazahas: they said that the vazahas transformed children into raving lunatics, destined for some later sacrifice, and that, at night, men in black tried to lure innocent people to isolated places to devour their hearts. And outside of that, it was still a delicate situation, as many people feared that school was a way to take a census of the population, which would lead to new taxes and duties.

But the new religion—spreading rapidly across the land, its missionaries like generals waging a war—took the main part of the blame.

In the beginning, the villagers in the area had been very welcoming to the vazahas' activities. Blake and Rose had trained their best students, including Vero, to fill their roles. The deputies worked with a zeal, and an increasing number of farmers learned their *latinu* letters. Villagers flocked to outdoor reading sessions and listened devotedly to the young masters, who took advantage of their attention to extol the virtues of the *Baiboly* and the strength of *Jehova*. Rose also healed the sick with European remedies, and preached that *Jesosy Kristy* could even bring the dead back to life. She bandaged scabies wounds and made dressings to soothe aches from cold drafts.

But a talisman guardian grew furious as he watched his clients leave him to rush over to the vazaha healer. One day, he burst into the school to spew threats.

"This land is sacred! All those who do not respect the law of the land will be crushed! *Kapao fa manimba ny tany!*"

Blake was away that day. It took everything Rose had to make the man leave.

After that incident, the relations between the missionaries and the community elders started to deteriorate.

This occurred during the moon of Adimizana.

·   ·   ·

79

After the sampy guardian's interruption, Blake spiraled into more aggressive and chaotic behavior. He laid into Rose and his deputies, berating them for being unable to defend the values of the Baiboly, and started heading expeditions to the villages, usually bursting with anger. His green eyes glowed with a strange light. The farmers were shocked, being more accustomed to Rose's gentle nature and the young masters' passionate eloquence. People started to fear him.

During an outing with his students one evening, the vazaha spotted a group of people gathered around a little mound. He asked what it was.

"That's a *vazimba* tomb, sir. The vazimbas are the former masters of this land. People bring offerings to them and make requests. Lots of people come here to pray," explained a student.

"I see. Always the same pagan beliefs. By now, I reckon that you've been in touch with the Divine Truth for long enough to renounce all of that. It's time for you to learn the most dramatic way to do that. I want you to know that Kristy is more powerful than all the vazimbas in the world!"

Having said that, Blake made a beeline for the group of people and told them that they shouldn't pray to the vazimbas, for there was only one living God, the God of Christians. The villagers were stupefied into silence, so he climbed on top of the vazimba tomb and tried to stir up the crowd, entreating them to abandon their idolizing and turn toward the true God.

"If the vazimbas are really so strong, why aren't they able to strike me down as I trample on their tombs?" Blake shouted.

Some of the farmers—and even two or three of the students—fled, terrified by such desecration. Blake leapt off of his improvised platform and walked among the crowd, the people still uneasy but buzzing with whispers and questions.

"Look, touch me! Here! Am I dead? Have I turned leprous? They can't do anything to me, they can do nothing in the face of Kristy! Here is my challenge: come see me tomorrow, the day after, whenever you like, and see for yourselves whether or not I've fallen ill, whether I'm on the brink of death or not! Kristy is stronger than vazimbas!"

He looked like he'd gone mad. We waited, petrified with fear, for the sky to rend in two above our heads, or for the farmers to take out their knives and slice into the vazaha's blaspheming flesh. But nothing happened. Then, no longer in his right mind, Blake went over to a tree growing next to the tomb, where more offerings had been piled up.

"What is this?" he asked, turning to us.

"It's a sacred tree of the vazimbas," a student answered. You shouldn't touch it. They say that any who are unlucky enough to touch it die within three days."

His eyes blazing with eerie joy, Blake ran to the tree, grabbed a branch, and broke it off with a snap. A shiver ran through the gathered crowd. "Come see me in three days!" he shouted. "Come and see!"

The next day, one of the school boys fell deathly ill. He had pains all over his body and fell into violent convulsions; his eyes turned white and blackish spittle frothed from his mouth. Rose and Blake flew to his aid and gave him *ody vazahas*, their own remedies, but they had no effect. But then, right at the hour of the rice mortar, the episode stopped. The student went back home and showed up the next morning as fresh as a young bull. But when the day started to dim, the episode came back, only to stop, like the day before, when the sun hit the rice mortar.

The sickness came back every day at the same time. The boy sometimes spouted incomprehensible monologues in a grownup's voice, but once the crisis passed, he didn't remember what he'd said, or what had happened. The third day, another student got sick in the same way, at the same time. And the next day, two others had the same symptoms.

Blake must have felt he was going insane.

The students were convinced it was the vazimba curse. "You shouldn't have desecrated the sacred tree!" they cried. "We're all going to die!"

But on the fourth day, in desperation, the missionary threw a whole pitcher of cold water into the face of one of the possessed children, who instantly came back to his senses. Encouraged by this, Rose did the same with the other three and got the same result. The students were awestruck, and the feat increased Blake's renown throughout the region. The vazaha had felled the curse of the land's former masters, the holy water of Kristy had conquered the vazimbas! New zealots hurried to the mission's doors over the next few moons, hungry to know everything about this new power. But the seers scoffed and objected, saying it was illusion and luck—they practiced that kind of ritual three times a week.

"Actually, that's already saved my skin once, when I had to defend myself against a talisman guardian who wanted to kill me," Blake explained, when I asked.

"You drove him back with holy water?" I asked.

He laughed, which, for him, was a sign of dismay. "No, we didn't have any holy water. I didn't have anything besides my ink well to defend myself—I'd always kept one in my pocket so I could write anytime I wanted. I threw the ink in his face, and that stopped him."

The year of rising tensions was clinched by an event that would change our lives forever: King Radama's death.

Blake was reading a Scripture passage on the Apostle *Paoly*'s imprisonment, when farmers from the neighboring town burst into the school.

"Return to your homes! The Sovereign has turned his back! Everyone must observe the mourning period!"

Blake frowned, but he didn't dare defy that order. Classes were suspended until further notice, which Fara and I weren't too upset about: the missionary's crazes had created a confrontational atmosphere toward the guardians of the ancestral ways, and Rose had redoubled her efforts to get the children and their parents to convert to the religion of Kristy, which was producing further friction.

There was a great turmoil among the people. Messengers went from village to village to spread the sad news.

"Heaven and earth have been rent apart, the Sovereign has turned his back!"

Villagers came running from every direction. "Where, when did this happen?" they asked.

"No one knows. It has most likely been some days now since he went to slumber. They hadn't told the people. We've just found out. The City is restless. The Guard is on alert around the Palace."

The latest news kept coming from the City. Mavo had been proclaimed queen. She took the throne under the name Ranavalona.

"May Ranavalona be blessed!" new messengers shouted in the streets. "May her reign last for a thousand years!"

When Fara and I got back to Sahasoa, we saw distraught people screaming and running around. Families shouted to each other across the village. All homes were busily preparing to go into mourning.

Bao and Bebe, standing before the familial hut, their faces worn, waved their arms to us. "Come quickly! The Sovereign has turned his back!"

The day that the Sovereign's death was announced, Bebe asked Bao to cut all the family members' hair. The rules of royal bereavement had to be scrupulously observed, under pain of death. All the People Under the Sky had to cut their hair three times during the year of mourning.

In that funereal moon of Asorotany, as soon as the news hit Sahasoa that the great Radama had joined the community of ancestors, Bao left to gather the rumors flying across the district. Back at the familial house, she cut Bebe's few hairs and spoke excitedly of what she'd learned.

In the battle for succession, the army's generals had led Mavo's faction and emerged victorious. They had instantly begun to enforce their will upon all the land and everyone in it, whether they be mere subjects, provincial lords, or princes. Many were in danger of being knocked down by this wave of violence, and some would vanish entirely, body and belongings.

"Andriantiana, the governor of Foulpointe, was strangled with a silk wrapper. Ramanetaka just narrowly escaped. He set off in a boat for the island of Anjouan. People are also saying that Radama died from drinking, and that Mavo had his entire reserve, hundreds of casks, thrown off of the Ampamarinana cliff. She also ordered all the pigs chased out of the gates, so that the City could recover its sacred virtue."

"I heard that she was angry with the converts," Bebe said. The old woman was staring pensively at the strands of hair that were strewn about her on the ground. Bao finished cutting the last of her bangs. Black hair mixed with strands whitened by time.

The elder woman picked up a clump of hair and held it up to the daylight to examine it.

Bebe's frail figure, with an almost bald head balancing on top and lit by a ray of sunlight, cut a stark shadow on the wall.

"Life," she said, "is a mixture of sweet honey and bitter aloe."

13

Andriantsitoha and the Wandering White Man

LATER, I WOULD UNDERSTAND how Ranaka's passion resulted from the changes affecting our communities, most notably the intrusion of vazahas into our family life. Blake had saved Fara, but it was actions of that same Blake and those like him that had imperiled her in the first place.

Few people today have retained a memory of that fierce war—yes, it was most certainly a war—that changed the face of the kingdom. A conflict fought on multiple fronts, where destinies could shift in an instant.

When I told Ibandro about Blake's proselytizing excursions, he explained that vast conflict, in which Sahasoa was only a small field of operations. Ibandro, like many People Under the Sky, was fascinated by white men's knowledge, and he'd encouraged me to acquire as much education as possible. But Blake's provocations shocked him. They sowed disorder, and it took all our efforts to clean up afterward.

He remembered Ranaka very well and told me that it was Andriantsitoha, his own master, who had brought the seer's career to a conclusive end.

"The defeat by the vazaha missionary intensified Ranaka's madness. He started seeing all kinds of catastrophes on the horizon. The ancestors came to flog him with thorny branches; they weren't letting him sleep! He yelled at whoever cared to listen that Mandatsivoho was crying every night, and that every morning he needed to mop up the river of tears that had streamed from the little perfumed lord."

"Was it a powerful talisman?"

"Yes. Everything happening seemed to prove the seer right, and more villagers came to pray to Mandatsivoho every day."

"What was happening?"

"All sorts of odd things. No surprise there—we really were on the verge of catastrophe. Thirty-six young women in Tendroarivo, for example, all fell ill at the same time from *ambalavelona*. At the same time! It was a distressing sight: possession, mass hysteria, gruesome faces, convulsions. Nobody in the village could handle it. The girls had become as strong as bulls released on Bathing Day!"

"Could Ranaka have put them under a spell himself?"

"Who knows. In any case, no one could fix the problem, and the public pressure was too strong. We had to have him summoned, Ranaka himself, to heal the girls."

Wasn't bringing Ranaka in just like the foolish chicken who sat on a crocodile egg?

Ibandro explained to me that Andriantsitoha, a great lover of strategic *fanorona*, had decided first to play defense. It was imperative to ease the public's mind and help the Tendroarivo girls regain sanity. This occurred in the ninth year of the Sovereign King's reign.

Ranaka arrived screaming: "This is the precipice! This is the fissure! This is the ravine that is trying to swallow the honor of the twelve sovereigns and the twelve sacred hills! Prepare ye, prepare ye!"

The seer had a black bull sacrificed on a *vatolahy* and mixed its blood with burial dirt and holy water. He added herbs of his own concoction and had the possessed girls drink it. It was an incredible remedy, and helped secure his and Mandatsivoho's reputation.

In return for Ranaka's feat of healing, the villagers had to give in to his demands. The seer's remedial sciences defined endless restrictions and obligations for the community.

"The farmers hardly dared breathe without asking his permission," Ibandro laughed. "But really, he drove several families into despair."

86

"How?"

"Oh, he only wanted to destroy all of their descendants, that's all. Or most of them. For he judged them all to have been swayed by the forces of evil since their conception. Rasoaray, that poor woman, was the first victim."

Andriantsitoha made the decision to eliminate the talisman guardian shortly after the death of Rasoaray's children. The whole business had sown fear throughout the province. The water in the rice fields was spilling over.

Here, again, he had to play smart. Andriantsitoha's father, Andriamaro the Furious, had been reluctant in his years to throw Ranaka where he could no longer do harm, for fear of attracting the ire of certain Palace players.

"We knew that some of the influential men in Ambohimanelo were secretly supporting the seer's projects," Ibandro said, "in the hopes of undermining the aging Andriamaro."

Ibandro was sharpening his knife on a rock as he spoke. He blew on the blade and held it up to the sunlight to inspect.

"But they were playing the losing side," he said.

"How?"

"Because the Sovereign King was losing faith in the power of the talismans. Anyone who couldn't catch the new way the wind was blowing didn't stand a chance."

My friend picked up a sugarcane stalk and hit it with the knife. The bamboo was cut clean through. The section of cut reed rolled in the dust.

Ibandro explained that over time the power structures in the kingdom had evolved out of the talisman guardians' favor. Ever since the new King had reorganized his army—with help from the English—he'd had innumerable conquests and lain his fiercest adversaries low with ease. Where his father had won glory with a sharp sense of alliances and games of dissuasion, Radama plowed forward with cannons and bayonets. He treated traditional methods more offhandedly, and his vazaha advisers took every opportunity to mock the virtues of the talismans, even though the same talismans had ushered in the kingdom's earlier expansion.

"The English missionaries were getting more and more influence over Radama," Ibandro said. "They weren't afraid of anything; they went so far as to teach devotion to another people's ancestors and beliefs."

"Even back then? Wasn't it still a capital offense?"

"Not for the missionaries. You know the proverb: 'The Sovereign's word is law; it enters our homes not on tiptoes, but stomping its feet.'"

All of that caused resistance, of course. One day, when the new King decided to cut his hair so he looked like the soldier-kings of Europe, four thousand women from the North marched on the City of Thousands to protest the sacrilege and demand that the missionaries be put to death. The King had the leaders of the protest seized and executed at the city gates, and the movement dispersed, proving that he was, and intended to remain, the master of traditions.

Andriantsitoha had succeeded his father in the meantime, and he now saw that the time had come for action.

Andriantsitoha was just as prudent as Andriamaro the Furious, and considerably shrewder.

He'd inherited the province of Ambohimanelo while he was still an adolescent. The elders had looked after the province in his place for a while, exercising the actual power while consulting him only for show. Some of them had taken a liking to that, and it took Andriantsitoha a few years to reassert control over his ancestral inheritance. Aided by his father's loyal slaves, he'd had to resort to some rather radical measures.

Eliminating Ranaka the seer was one of those measures. It helped secure his authority over the provincial elders. It impressed them, made them think twice.

"What a master stroke!" Ibandro remembered.

To put an end to Ranaka's career, Andriantsitoha exploited the same method as Bebe. There weren't many ways to corner the seer, but he'd already been defeated once by a vazaha, a missionary. Whites seemed to be bad luck for him.

There happened to be one in the area.

The Wandering White Man.

He was a recluse who'd been living on the outskirts of Anativolo for almost a generation. I remember having come across him once or twice when I was a child.

Who didn't know of the Wandering White Man back then? He was often seen hanging in a tree consulting a book or a notebook, muttering into his beard. He made children curious, and the mean ones would throw rotten fruit at him and run away screaming that he'd lost his mind: "*Vazaha very saina! Vazaha very saina!*"

Nobody knew exactly where he'd come from, but he was definitely a white man, not an albino. He was dressed in rags that people said had once been beautiful European clothes, and he had a grim face. Whenever anyone approached, he'd whip out an old pair of binoculars with broken glass, furrow his bushy brow, and stretch out his long, scrawny red neck, like a rooster's.

People said he'd been there since King Nampoina's reign. Back then, foreigners weren't allowed near the City of Thousands—that Sovereign had been just as concerned with preserving the City's sacred nature as with keeping dangerous forces at a distance. The Wandering White Man had been denied authorization to enter the city, but he'd persisted, for reasons still unknown. That added to the mystery surrounding his presence. Some said he was in love with a princess, or maybe even one of the Sovereign's wives. Others claimed that he'd been sentenced to be beheaded in his own country and couldn't go back home.

Nevertheless, the years passed, and the white man kept waiting. His slaves had slowly deserted the house, taking most of his belongings with them. He'd been reduced to poverty and had to work his own land to feed himself. When he had a meager harvest—which he often did, because of his lack of experience—he begged for rations. As for other vazahas, they eventually forgot his very existence. The white man lost his soul while he was still alive.

When we were children, the story of the Wandering Vazaha had attracted us for a specific reason: legend had it that he'd hidden treasure in anticipation of his return to the City of Thousands. There wasn't a single kid in our village who hadn't one day tried to find this treasure. I'm sure a few of the adults believed in it, too. They said that brigands had once snatched the vazaha and brought him into the forest to make him tell them where he was hiding his loot. No luck. They didn't dare kill him, because people said that killing a white man gave you leprosy. They didn't beat him up too badly either, because the village belief was that vazaha blood was a slow poison that made anyone who spilled it go deaf. They tried to sell him at a slave market, but no one wanted to buy him. Not really knowing what to do with him after five days, they let him go.

Andriantsitoha, though, had figured out how to use him to his own advantage.

It was the height of Ranaka's glory, but the seer was far from getting over Blake's affront, and he held a grudge against vazahas.

In the game of power, in fanorona, the young lord of Ambohimanelo had learned how best to choose his angles and strike decisive blows. He suggested that Ranaka keep an eye on the Wandering White Man's movements.

And then, one day, the vazaha was caught performing strange ablutions in the Sahasoa well. This occurred during the Alakaosy moon, a little while after the crisis of the thirty-six Tendroarivo girls with ambalavelona. In the middle of the night, the madman had lit torches all around the pond and was washing himself in the well water, singing at the top of his lungs. The seer fell into the trap. He arrived the next day leading a procession and wearing a triumphant expression; in front, he pushed the Wandering White Man, who screamed like a man possessed.

Andriantsitoha, of course, claimed to be unfit to judge the matter, and sent it before a higher jurisdiction. As expected, the regional high judge stood down as well and sent the case to the Palace. The Sovereign, the great purifying stream, listened politely to the accuser's grievances. The story had caused a sensation, and the whole city clamored to hear the verdict. The Palace judges received an order to investigate the matter carefully and question the white man, while a lavish meal was offered to Ranaka and his friends.

But Andriantsitoha's calculation was a simple one: it was unthinkable that the Sovereign would have a white man executed, or even submitted to an ordeal, what with the current state of the kingdom's relationships with foreigners. Especially putting a half-crazy European to death, a man who didn't even know why he was there! The Wandering White Man's acquittal was inevitable, and was duly pronounced. Consequently, his accusers found themselves guilty of malevolence and attempting to manipulate royal justice, and their heads were cut off, as the law required.

Thus ended the life and career of Ranaka the seer.

Destiny would give me the opportunity to personally know Andriantsitoha, the man who saved many imperiled innocents, like Fara, through his actions. The man, too, whose strange visions led, I believe, to the downfall of many others.

On the Thursday that followed the Sovereign's death, Ibandro asked me to come with him to the City of Thousands. He'd heard of school being suspended until further notice and had immediately thought of me; he wanted to include me in the core group that would accompany the lord to the funereal ceremonies.

After the debacle we'd had in the capital, and because of my aversion to being away from Fara and Sahasoa for too long, my first instinct was to decline the offer. Yet I couldn't refuse; I owed the head slave a considerable debt. He'd done everything he could to make it easy for the community to accept me and to alleviate my life of servitude. Basically, I wouldn't have gained any of the advantages or privileges that I benefited from every day without Ibandro, the most significant ones being my carpentry work and the peace I enjoyed under the "ogre's" protection.

By bringing me to the city of the sovereigns, Ibandro intended to do even more, showing me more fields where I might find my path. And thus, he presented me to Andriantsitoha, someone who, up to that point, I'd only glimpsed from afar.

My meeting with the provincial lord happened that very day.

Approaching a powerful man is always done with some degree of fear. Andriantsitoha, despite his young age, had a thousand men and women at his disposal. But more than that, he was the only person, among all that I'd met, who stirred true fear within Ibandro. That alone gave him supernatural stature in my eyes.

However, I discovered that Andriantsitoha was a tortured soul. Ibandro had confided to me that the province had been subject to predatory actions for a while. The atmosphere toward the end of Radama's rule had encouraged the appetites of all sorts of corrupt officials across the island. Those who'd been left out of the profits from the export markets had come back to prey upon the population. For the first time, people started targeting our province's resources. People with protection on high were helping themselves to the community's lands, livestock, and harvests. Entire families were seized and enslaved.

"The people committing these acts are untouchable," Ibandro explained to me. "We're going to the City to try to solve the problem at its source."

When we entered Andriantsitoha's residence, he was deep in thought on his bed, looking worried.

"My lord, here is the young slave of whom I spoke."

"Very good. What can he do?"

"He's an excellent craftsman; I have overseen his progress personally. He can craft weapons and tools from wood and iron. He also has wide-ranging experience with travel, thanks to his master, a trader. He can hunt quail and moorhen, gather honey, and fish for eel in swift waters."

When Andriantsitoha looked me over, I lowered my eyes. Ibandro was very strict about the rules of respect. It reminded me a little of the time when the slave dealer had exhibited me for Rado—I felt the same mix of fear and confused hope. But Andriantsitoha quickly turned his attention back to Ibandro.

"Make provisions ready for us for four to five days on the road. I need porters, but only a few. I want sturdy, discreet men. And go tell my brother that I need him. I want to give an address before my departure.

Have Manantsindry the seer come also, so that he can read the auspicious days for us."

"If those are your wishes, my lord, I will do as you request. May you grow old alongside your grandchildren."

"One last thing: inform the elders that we must observe the most meticulous respect for the traditions of royal mourning. And tell Vola to come cut my hair."

"*Eny tompoko!* It will be done, my lord!"

Ibandro beckoned to me and we made to leave, when the lord stopped us. "He can stay. I'd like him to help Vola make some preparations."

I understood by the joyful glow that rose in my friend's face that Andriantsitoha was looking favorably on me. But I wasn't about to rejoice in it: "He who changes lords changes status," the proverb says. At Bebe's house, I was more like a child of the family than a slave. That suited me marvelously. I promised myself that my stay with the provincial lord would be very temporary.

"You called for me, my lord?" a feminine voice asked.

Vola, the lord's second wife, was a very young woman with light skin and a delicate figure that her first pregnancies had not filled out. She knew me from having seen me in Ibandro's company and did not seem surprised to see me with her husband.

"Yes, o apple of my eye. Please take the knife and come cut my hair. I must set the example in mourning for our Sovereign King. In addition, I must give an address before my departure. And you're aware that you should also cut all our children's hair?"

"It is done, my lord." Her eyes filled with tears as she looked at him. "Is your departure truly necessary? You know that without you, we are nothing but helpless chicks."

"Yes, it is necessary. This boy will come with us, he'll help you make preparations. Please show him what there is to do."

Andriantsitoha grabbed a vial of perfume and went to kneel in the northeast corner of his house while we took care of things. It seemed, under Vola's worried watch, that he was praying with particular intensity.

．　　　　　．　　　　　．

Andriantsitoha was our lord, and an enigma. A man whose emotions were, at first, very difficult to grasp.

The ancestors of Ibandro's master had supported the highland princes in their unification efforts, and many of them had lost their lives on the battlefield. As compensation, King Nampoina had allowed them to keep their fiefdoms and granted them use of these bountiful lands, which their families had been working for generations. They had even earned the status of kin to the kings. Neither their honor and rank nor the integrity of their communities had been threatened since. But now, all of that was starting to change.

Andriantsitoha answered Vola's worried questions. "You must not let the community get frightened. Andriamady will replace me while I'm away."

"Him?" the young woman fretted. "But he has a child's mind!"

"He will shoulder all of our family's duties if anything should ever happen to me, and also become your husband."

Vola cried out and threw herself at his feet, her face awash from tears.

"You're leaving for so long! Why are you doing this? Won't you take pity on your children?"

"I have no time to listen to a woman's words. Take the knife and get to work," Andriantsitoha said, although he seemed to regret his harsh tone.

Vola wiped away her tears, stood, and picked up the knife. She took her place behind the lord, who was sitting cross-legged in the entrance to his home. The young woman held the first lock of her husband's hair and cut it with a sigh. Andriantsitoha's eyes were already lost in the forests spreading out to the west.

"No, we will not stay in the City for too long. I just have to take care of a few things. I also need to find Rasoa and see what's become of her."

Rasoa was the youngest of Andriamaro the Furious' three children. She'd left to live in the City of Thousands and adopted the Christian religion.

"Tsito, open my trunk. At the bottom, underneath my garments, you'll find a gray and gold book. Bring it here. You know how to read and write, too, is that right? Ibandro told me that you were going to classes with the missionaries. I know you're an intelligent boy."

He took the book that I held out to him, brushed off the thin layer of dust covering it, and smiled to himself. The title was still legible, despite the fading gold letters: "*The Pilgrim's Progress*, by John Bunyan."

"I was given this by the Reverend Jones. I was among the English missionaries' very first students, but not too many people around here know that."

He stopped Vola's hand that held the knife, turned toward me, and fixed me with his intense eyes. Three-quarters of his hair had disappeared. I realized just how young he was.

"Most of my classmates went into a career in administration, others converted to Christianity and became preachers. Some were slaves . . . I elected to return to my dying father's side and shoulder all the duties of the province."

He returned to his initial position, set the book on his lap, and leafed wistfully through it.

"I read and write Latin letters fluently, and I know the language of England very well. These are extremely useful skills in the City of Thousands; the kingdom needs educated subjects. I want trustworthy people at my side. Ibandro never learned to read and write. That's why I'm bringing you with me."

14

Dreams of Kalanoro

WE STAYED IN THE CITY OF THOUSANDS for seven long weeks. But before we left I almost changed my mind and let my friend Ibandro down for the first time. My whole existence had just taken an unexpected turn. The center of the universe had just shifted, and it had a name: Fara.

I can still, today, pinpoint the exact place and time of the upheaval.

When Fara, Vero, and I were on our way home from school, in the early years, we sometimes took a detour through the woods along the river, one hour's walk upstream. The vegetation was abundant there, set away from the slashing and burning of farmers and herdsmen. There, we picked red and black berries, plump and juicy below leafy branches. With a little searching, you could also find bananas as big as your thumb, in bunches that looked like children's hands, with flesh sweeter than honey. Not far from the water grew melons so engorged with liquid that they were as heavy as rocks.

We'd discovered that valley by accident when we'd gone on a hunt for a *kalanoro*, a little long-haired creature with great powers that could make itself invisible. People said the ones that haunted the swamps to the north had one tuft of hair on top of their head and would grant all your wishes if you managed to see them without them spotting you.

We'd covered a lot of ground with Vero and hadn't found a kalanoro, but we'd stumbled on this forest, which was no less enchanted. The place was devoid of people, and the nearest villages were either far downstream or beyond the hills to the west. The valley slowly became our secret place to get away, our faraway fairytale land where no other children could set foot. We frequently found refuge there, ever since the arguments over school had more or less disbanded the pond group.

Fara and I went back there, just before I left with Andriantsitoha.

That escapade fixed the course of my life.

That day, we'd filled a basket with fruit and sat on the rocks at the foot of the little waterfall nestled in the crux of the small valley. We watched black kite birds sweeping across the sky among the scattered clouds drifting lazily away. Our faces smeared with sugary juice, our feet in the lapping ripples, we watched the powerful birds diving into the underbrush whenever they honed in on crouching prey.

"Do you think that you'll leave someday, for good?" asked Fara.

The memory of our time in the City was still burning in our minds, despite the unpleasantness. We'd started talking more often of journeys and faraway countries.

"I like this village a lot, this river, these woods—"

"Yeah, so are you afraid of leaving?"

"Why?"

"I can't wait to leave. I want to live in the City of Thousands. One day I'll get out of Sahasoa."

"What about Bebe? And your mother? Won't they miss you?"

"Oh, stop it! I don't want to die here. It feels like I'm a slave. I want to be free!"

Fara had been obsessed with the idea of leaving for a while. I didn't share it.

"But what happiness would we find in the City?" I asked. By which I meant: "That we couldn't find here."

She didn't answer, maybe because she found the question too naïve. She kept eating her berries, staring off into space.

Ever since she'd seen the City, Fara seemed to be afraid of living a monotonous and empty existence, somehow kept away from real life. Me, though, I got frightened when I saw how attracted people were to the big city. It was both an extraordinary and inevitable phenomenon. I'd gotten to see the waves of humanity pouring into the City from every horizon.

Caught up in that force, villages like Sahasoa would one day be nothing more than stretches of land strewn with tombs and old ruins, deserted by their people.

But I looked at Fara and saw the hope shining on her face. An iridescent dragonfly landed in front of us on a long piece of downy white grass. Something happened, everything changed, and my skepticism disappeared. The feelings that had given me life beside the pond surged in me again, but with new power. A window opened onto an improbable, indescribable joy, onto a new world.

I looked at Fara, my cloud princess. Something in me wanted more: a meeting, a presence, a promise.

All of a sudden, I became the prince of light, for real. The words of the fable flashed onto my lips, with a new, exhilarating taste. What is more delightful—and at the same time more absurd—than adolescent stirring? I took her hand.

"No, in truth I fear nothing. For you, my princess, I will explore the deepest rivers and hunt down the dwarf hippopotamus. For you, I will fell the great forest and fertilize the endless plains!"

She was surprised for a moment, very briefly. We were still children, but in the space of a word ceased to be so. Our eyes met, then fell. That was all. She was my mistress again, I was the slave. She threw my hand down angrily and hurled pieces of fruit at my head, thinking I was making fun of her.

"Slimy little slave! Don't you provoke me!"

I threw both arms over my head to protect myself like a shield, like in a game. I put a servant's servile smile back onto my face.

And yet, that fraction of an instant had shaken me.

A hopeful wind had pounded against the stone gates of my thoughts, a hole had been made in a wall of rigid laws and strict principles, of established practices and deep-seated opinions. The story encroached on reality. It was frightening, and hopeless.

I'm not sure why, but my mind turned first toward our ancestors. I'd never really prayed much up to that point. My elders lay somewhere far in the south, in places I didn't even remember the names of. The Scriptures that Blake and Rose introduced to us had never rung true for me.

But there, in the valley of the kalanoro, the land was as bountiful as it had been in early times, in the time of Ntaolo. Wild game frolicked. Herds of animals swelled in the bosom of the forest, still protected from the advance of man.

Perhaps, unconsciously, I was finding my own origins there? My own source?

Among the dense timber and variegated ferns, we were enveloped by the forest's unique breath, a rustling of leaves combined with a buzzing of insects. There was life—present, everywhere, perched on branches, crouched beneath every root, lying in wait behind the smallest clump of brambles. Nearby, a liquid murmur betrayed a stream flowing between the century-old trees, cut here and there by jumping fish and amphibians. Above, creaking branches were accompanied by bird calls and lemur cries.

At the time, I was making traps out of glue, string, and fiber, and we'd set them in the undergrowth. Several times, we and Vero had brought back to Sahasoa guinea fowl, which Bebe would roast over the wood fire or cook in a stew with roots and spices. When we showed up early in the afternoon, we'd hear packs of wild boars rooting through the tall grass. I remember one day trapping a young male that we had to let go because he was too strong and not too inclined to let himself get captured.

The day I came back with Fara, we found an azure-flecked *soimanga* ensnared in a little net. Together, we carefully unwound the bird, a bringer of luck, and restored its freedom.

Yes, the kalanoro valley reconciled me with the ancestors. After my escapade with Fara, I went back to that place several times, wandering alone. Each time, I stopped at a large rock covered with moss sitting at the edge of the forest, to pray to the masters of the land. In the quivering leaves and shining light of day, I saw the spirits of the first people, the ones who lived here in the time of the first rice fields. Traces of the vazimbas were still visible: four field-lengths away, on top of the closest hills, old tombs stood, bristled with so much grass that they blended in with the landscape.

They had left the coasts behind and ventured into the age-old forest, confronting illness and bad weather. They'd built towns and cities where there had been only rocks and brush, crafted walls and trenches from clay and rock, dug troughs to fatten their animals, raised huts of wood and bamboo, gutted trees to sculpt their pirogues, constructed palaces and great tombs with the labor of a thousand and ten thousand men, and planted pillars in the ground to honor their sovereigns and the Perfumed Lord.

Why couldn't they help me make my impossible dreams come true?

15

The Gospel According to Dadarabe

I BELIEVE IN SIGNS that chart mankind's existence. They may not predict the future, but they'll reveal the hidden face of the immediate or imminent present, and uncover new ways that lives are stirred together and worlds are combined.

En route to the City of Thousands, we passed through a village whose chief, Rabenanahary, had converted to Christianity after a time in the capital. He'd been a talisman guardian before converting. Now, he was fueled by contagious faith, and his status as an elder had helped him convince a large number of people in the community to follow his example. But Dadarabe, as he was called, was illiterate, and the missionaries had only been able to give him a very basic education before sending him back to his far-off village. They'd promised to send a preacher to help him as soon as possible, but no one had ever shown up, due either to forgetfulness or to lack of funds.

When we arrived at Dadarabe's village one Sunday morning, our interest was piqued by the huge Christian cross crowned with bull's horns that welcomed visitors at the entrance.

The chief had summoned all the villagers to the center of town. They were all singing Christian hymns and clapping their hands, while Dadarabe, a Baiboly in hand, recited the verses he'd learned by heart. Three women were shaking in the middle of the crowd, every limb beset by tremors, yelping fragments of phrases in an incomprehensible language. They'd fallen prey to *tromba*, possession by ancestral spirits.

At Andriantsitoha's questions, the master of ceremonies replied that the holy spirits of Kristy, Paoly, and Radama, the deceased sovereign, had entered the village women to lead the community to *Paradisa*, the land of boundless plenty. He assured the lord that the language they were speaking was Hebrew, the language of *Palestina*.

I was blown away.

Upon arriving in the City of Thousands, I discovered a facet of this land's people that I hadn't known before. The City was the place of any and all passions. People there appeared to be both consumed by the desire to do good and strangled by games of power and fortune. Nothing demonstrated this more than the feverish excitement in the neighborhoods of the big city in the year when the great Radama turned his back.

The streets were flooded with crowds. People said the city's population had tripled. Many thousands of people had come from all over the kingdom. The city squares teemed with provincial dignitaries and district lords in rich mourning garb. Everyone clamored to get ahead of everyone else to share their tears and pledge their allegiance to the new Sovereign.

"You'd think we were at Anativolo on market day," I whispered to Ibandro.

For once, my friend was not carrying his master, who waited in the long line like everyone else, with members of his clan. Ibandro and I, along with the other slaves, had been charged with transporting and guarding the gifts brought by the Zafimanelo clan. The line wasn't going anywhere, and we had plenty of opportunity to ponder the mob.

"I'm worried that the gunfire will make everyone panic," he replied.

The royal cannons were shooting off honor salutes, which were only making the crowd more nervous. In addition to baskets and bundles laden with presents, the visitors had brought dozens of zebus, driven by slaves and servants. These animals were added to the ones that the city folk had offered as sacrifices to their prince, and the scene was one of chaos. Two men had already been killed, gored through by bulls driven mad by the wait and the noise.

And yet the guilty animals had been butchered on the spot, and the distribution of meat that followed drew shouts of joy from the neighborhood children and relaxed the atmosphere a little. Throughout the City, the ground was red with blood, from sacrifices. Every night, on the grounds of the Palace alone, eight castrated cattle were being slaughtered.

I thought to myself that Fara would have been entranced by all these scenes.

But Andriantsitoha's face grew more and more weary.

Whenever a group was allowed admission into the Palace compound, they stayed inside forever. It made the wait even more trying for everyone languishing behind them in the blazing sun.

We were in the company of a dozen members of the Zafimanelo clan, who reigned over provinces in the district, and conversation flowed freely. We saw several vazahas pass by with members of the royal family and army generals. I inquired as to their identity from someone sitting next to me, but there was no time to hear the answer.

"Out of the way! Out of the way!"

Our group leapt briskly to the side, suspecting another bull rush. The rest of the crowd followed suit. A provincial prince got shoved and fell into a ditch, exploding into curses.

This time, it was soldiers. Three thousand men running up to the Palace and rushing inside, cutting in front of everyone. Soon, a chorus of masculine cries and lamentations echoed all the way to the riverbanks.

The slave I'd asked—whose mistress, it seemed, had connections to the Palace—finally explained: "The vazahas you saw with the royal princes are former advisers to the Sovereign King and representatives of the European nations."

"And the soldiers?"

"Men who had been the closest to the King during his campaigns."

The shouting crowd was deafening.

I saw Andriantsitoha sigh bitterly, irritated by the wait. The number of groups let in before everyone else was only rising, and we were still stuck far back in the long line.

But we didn't really have anything to complain about: another line to the Palace, next to ours, stretched back endlessly. The poorly clothed people in this line weren't allowed within the *Rova* palace. They shared their tears outside, overseen by the guards.

After the soldiers and vazahas, we also had to let the Palace artisans ahead of us. That group, on the other hand, fascinated me, and I lapped up the city folks' conversations about them. They talked about how the smiths had forged the pirogue of silver that would carry the Sovereign toward the market of no return. Two thousand pieces of silver had been used to execute the work. But the pirogue had ended up being too short, so several thousand additional pieces had been collected to lengthen it. They'd also crafted two gold assegai spears for the Sovereign, as well as ten guns and a silver saber. The carpenters had built the sacred house on top of the Monarch's tomb, as well as the bier of precious wood. The seamstresses had fashioned the tranovorona, the tapestries of mourning, and the purple shroud.

Seeing my interest, Ibandro tapped me on the shoulder with his enormous hand and didn't hide his pleasure. "You'll work in the Palace one day, too, little one. I'm sure of it."

Our group was received into the royal compound after the sun had already set behind the hills. The raised area where the new Sovereign Queen sat was shadowed, and none of us could see her face. We could only make out dark figures. No one was honestly able to say if the Sovereign was present or not. Andriantsitoha appeared greatly frustrated.

Once the Zafimanelos had handed over their presents and shared their tears, Andriantsitoha and the men with him were invited to drink *vokaka*. A pirogue had been filled with the sacred liquid, which was the subjects' pledge of submission to the new queen, heir to the Bull with Large Eyes. All visitors had to recite an oath, dip their goblet into the vokaka, and drink.

I felt crushed by the solemn weight of ritual.

"So what will happen now?" I asked Ibandro.

"There's Andriambelo, the clan chief," he said.

A venerable old man came down toward us from the darkened place where the kingdom's dignitaries stood. He was the oldest of the Zafimanelos, and as such, one of the rare people who had the privilege of remaining at the Sovereign's side throughout the ceremony.

"Our Sovereign Mistress would have me say that our cries and gifts ease her mourning," he said to his friends.

"May she grow old alongside her grandchildren."

Andriambelo seemed pleased.

"I will have the honor of speaking the words of mass purification just after the Sovereign is enshrouded," said the old man. "It will be, as always, an important occasion for our group—I'm counting on you to ensure that the honor of the Zafimanelos will be exalted by this funeral."

Andriantsitoha seemed to be literally drinking in his words. I realized that this was the kind of meeting that the provincial lord had been seeking here.

One of his companions brought him to the patriarch, calling him by his nickname. "This is Tsifa, Dadabe. You may not remember him, for he was naught but a green pumpkin the last time you saw him. He's Andriamaro the Furious's firstborn . . . "

But I was only half paying attention to their conversation: royal servants had just brought out the bulls that would be sacrificed that night. Enormous animals, of the *volavita* variety, like nothing I'd ever seen before in Sahasoa. They were brought to the northeast of the Rova, where a little space had been made. The first was swiftly pushed to the ground and tied with a *mahazaka* rope. Long knife blades glinted in the moonlight. The sight should have brought me joy, but instead weighed on my chest.

" . . . it's true! And how are things going in Ambohimanelo? I simply must come and visit you one day. Did you know my sister is buried in your family vault? She married a descendant of your paternal grandfather's cousin. I'd love to come wrap her in a new shroud someday."

"You must come, my lord. I will have a fatted calf cooked under the glowing embers for you."

The first bull cried long in agony. We reached the main gate as the servants made swift work of him, to a chorus of people clicking their tongues in appreciation.

When our group had finally, to my immense relief, gotten some distance from the Palace crowds, Andriantsitoha confessed the problems his province was up against, and the clan elder's face betrayed concern. "You are not the first to bring this type of incident before me, and unfortunately, there is not a great deal we can do."

"But these people are coming to steal from us and laugh in our faces! They have connections. We can't just let ourselves get pushed around!"

Andriambelo glanced around nervously. He took the arm of Ibandro's young master and lowered his voice. "There are grave things happening around here. People are being executed by guards, or by militiamen, simply because of rumors that they belong to the opposition. It's not that easy to build a position of strength. As long as no one's coming to take your wives and children, count yourself among the fortunate."

Andriantsitoha looked dismayed. "But what should I do?"

"Serve. The better you serve the Sovereign, the less people will dare attack you or yours."

The secret meetings of the Zafimanelo lords were a little obscure to me, and I longed terribly for Fara. However, Andriantsitoha was determined to bring me everywhere he went, for reasons that were unclear to me at the time. I was both flattered and frightened by such unusual consideration.

The day after his visit to the Palace, we went to the house of a woman named Mary. She was a soldier's wife, actively involved in the Christian movement. Mary had taken Rasoa, Andriantsitoha's sister, under her protection.

As we entered the house, he explained, "We'll be able to get more information here."

He seemed to be feeling some emotion returning to the City. The day before, while I'd served him rum and royal zebu meat late in the evening, in a hut lent to him by one of his friends, he told me that he'd only gone back to the capital once since he'd finished school, to see Rasoa. The City had changed, and he thought that the community had lost something. Ambitions were growing, like the pretentious-looking constructions that were surging up in various locales out of competitive anarchy, slowly replacing the houses with blue bamboo walls.

"It's produced an ironic proverb," said Andriantsitoha. "'The City's great houses: the first built are soonest dissatisfied.'"

The forest was retreating in many places. But the trees weren't the only things affected: we'd also noticed people living in a kind of permanent anxiety, where everything was a pretext to take to the streets. People shouted and thronged into crowds for nothing.

The mayhem reminded me of the awful adventure that I'd had here with Fara, with the thief lynched in the market square, and the beheaders. It seemed to me that the populace could transform into a bloodthirsty predator at any moment. How could you find pleasure living in such an environment? Sahasoa was a haven of tranquility and joy by comparison.

"This is the center of the kingdom, the top of the tree, the part that's the most exposed to thrashing winds," said Andriantsitoha.

And in truth, the City of Thousands was buzzing with a thousand rumors that would invariably pop up in the briefest of conversations. The new Sovereign had ascended to the throne through violence, and that spirit of confrontation was spreading through the city. The elimination of Rakotobe, the other claimant to the throne, and all his supporters had proved how willing the new masters of the kingdom were to crush any and all opposing forces. The vazahas didn't quite know if they were welcome or not, which only intensified the intrigue, and there was a haze of disquiet about the composition of the group who had brought the Sovereign Queen to power. That was probably what Andriambelo the patriarch was talking about. Names of high-ranking officers and nobles flew about.

"What's happening at the Palace?" Andriantsitoha asked Mary. "People tell me that different factions are still fighting?"

"There's a good chance that this is just the beginning," she sighed.

Andriantsitoha asked for news of some of the people he knew in the City. "Whatever happened to A . . . ? The last time I heard about him, it was some years ago, during the addresses at the Bathing Feast."

"I'm afraid he was killed."

"That's horrible! What about his family?"

"They were all executed. Only one of his daughters survived, who was in Toamasina. People say that Christians managed to shield her from the men on her trail."

Andriantsitoha nodded in approval of the Christians' charitable act, but he himself wasn't very predisposed toward converts—Ibandro had informed me of that. He didn't trust their fanatical personalities and said that in the long term they were riding a wind that was at least as violent as the one that was starting to rise against them.

The conversation was interrupted by the entrance of Andriantsitoha's younger sister, Rasoa.

"Tsifa! I was sure it was you," she said. "I knew it even before coming in. I would have recognized your voice among thousands!"

Andriantsitoha was yanked out of his thoughts when he heard his nickname. He leapt to his feet to welcome the young woman.

"Look at you, I almost didn't recognize you. What have you done to your hair? And do you really have to dress like that? You know this isn't a good time to draw attention to yourself."

"You're criticizing me as a greeting—you must've gotten old!"

Brother and sister looked at each other for a few moments and embraced. Andriantsitoha was struck with sudden emotion and couldn't stop the tears that sprung to his eyes. Rasoa was also overcome with feeling and cried freely against his chest.

They sat on a new mat that Mary had just unrolled.

"So, you left Ambohimanelo almost a week ago, and you're just now coming to see me?" Rasoa said, smiling and wiping her cheeks dry.

"Yes, well, I went to the Palace to share my tears and get some advice from friends. I couldn't show up unprepared." He smiled at the women. "I'm only a 'peasant,' you know!"

"Oh, my lord, you're too modest," replied Mary.

Andriantsitoha smiled, and I saw a teasing glimmer in his eyes: the distinction between city folk and "peasants" was getting more pronounced as the kingdom was modernized. Fewer and fewer people in the City knew how to hold a spade.

The lord of Ambohimanelo sometimes spoke playfully of the downward spiral. "The great king Nampoina, whose last few years of rule I knew, was still a 'peasant,'" he recalled. "He still worked in his rice field every day!"

I had also noticed the changes that were occurring before our very eyes among the People Under the Sky. In the City in particular, people who lived lives of ease wore fashionable yet sometimes dumbfounding garb. Officers loved to get all decked out in uniforms of European regalia, often paired with long cavalry boots. And on top of that, we'd also pass civilians who had unabashedly embellished the *salaka*, the ancestral wrapper, with a frock coat and top hat.

It wasn't just the clothes or working the land. Coming into the house of Mary the Christian, Andriantsitoha was shocked to see that almost none of the ancestral placements had been respected. A Baiboly had been set open on a shelf in the north with a cross over it. The sinibe sat near the door in the southwest, and the hearth wasn't even there. Worst of all, a broom sat idly in the northeast corner, forgotten by a servant.

"What evil and unhappiness will a home like this make?" he'd whispered.

Even in the Palace, there were more and more signs of European influence, sometimes odd ones. Thus it was that after the ceremonies of mourning the day before, people out late at night had been stupefied to hear European dance music coming from the grand Silver House. The next day, the Sovereign sent early-morning messengers throughout the whole city to inform the inhabitants that the music had been funereal songs and that mourning was still "hard, very hard."

"Now, tell me," Andriantsitoha said to his sister. "What's become of you? You know that the other reason I came here was for you?"

Rasoa didn't answer right away. She ran her fingertips over a little woven wicker basket from him, which Ibandro had just handed to her. The young woman was dressed in the long white dress of the *mpivavaka*, those who pray, and her hair was tied behind her head in a simple braid.

A glimmer of nostalgia flickered across her face as she examined the coral and silvery jewelry in the basket.

"The Sovereign Queen has promised to change nothing of what Radama instituted. We're confident. The number of people asking to be baptized is rising every day!"

"How wonderful. But that's not what I asked," Andriantsitoha said patiently. "I'd love to know what you have been doing."

"I teach classes for young children, and I take care of the mission's paperwork, like I told you in my letters."

"Is it a respectable life?"

"I'm serving Kristy, the Lord our God. He chose the place I must hold in the congregation. He will choose the place that I must hold in his great design for mankind."

Andriantsitoha stood, under the pretext of an aching muscle. He looked annoyed. He rooted himself in front of the open Baiboly and read out loud: "Ezekiel twenty-three, thirty-five. *'Therefore thus saith the Lord God; Because thou hast forgotten me, and cast me behind thy back, therefore bear thou also thy lewdness and thy whoredoms.'"*

The words appeared to make him thoughtful. He sat back down near the two women, calmer, and continued to ask questions. Every time Rasoa spoke, her brother's eyes seemed to tighten a bit more with worry.

Everything about Rasoa's story, which Ibandro told me, reminded me of Vero's. But I couldn't yet grasp what that similarity of paths could truly mean.

Like Andriantsitoha, his younger sister had been one of the first students of the London Missionary Society. Tsifa, three years her elder, had actually insisted to their father that she come to the City of Thousands. He'd always known that the girl's bright mind would find better material to feed and thrive on in the capital than in Ambohimanelo. In those times, enthusiasm for schooling in the City was much weaker, and few people were likely to send their children to the Whites. But their father had agreed to the unusual initiative out of affection for his only daughter.

Enticed by Rasoa's intelligence, the missionaries immediately agreed to take her in. Rasoa quickly found her place in the first group of students who were almost exclusively boys, which made her brother extremely proud.

Andriantsitoha, who at the time was already the designated heir to the Ambohimanelo province, had lots of ambition for his father's domain, and saw his younger sister playing a significant role in it. He'd already decided that he wouldn't stay in the capital.

"He wanted to come back and make his ancestral land a model of expansion and abundance, the envy of the other lords in the district," said Ibandro.

"And Rasoa, what did he want to do with her?" I asked.

"From very early on, she'd wanted to become a schoolteacher. Her brother understood the importance of the new knowledge that the vazahas were bringing. He'd developed a project to open schools in Ambohimanelo. In that plan, Rasoa was the iron and spade that would fertilize the field."

"How old was she?"

"Sixteen. The proverb says, 'Hope cannot vanquish destiny.' She'd absorbed what the missionaries were teaching her, almost too well. I don't know. One day, she just announced that she wanted to stay in the City of Thousands. She'd decided to become a Christian and dedicate her life to the vazahas."

The same thing had happened to Vero. White men's beliefs were reshaping our lives and communities, down to the deepest bedrock.

"That must have been such a disappointment for Andriantsitoha," I said.

"Less awful than for his father, believe me. He was outraged, he wanted to bring her back to Ambohimanelo by force. For a little while, he even considered having the missionaries' throats slit—we almost couldn't dissuade him, it took all our efforts."

"Slit their throats?"

"Oh yes. You didn't know him. Andriamaro the Furious was an old lord with a terribly short temper; there aren't many left like him. But his daughter had seen that coming. She brought a grievance before the Palace, where the missionaries had connections, and the Palace issued a warning. The clan elder had to promise to refrain from any violent interventions." And that was that. Andriantsitoha had to cut his own studies short to assuage the old lord's anger. And everything that was even remotely related to the missionaries was banned from the lord's province. After the death of his father, Andriantsitoha continued to keep the Whites at a distance.

The day they saw each other again, when I was there, Andriantsitoha was again caught unawares by what seemed to me to be the particularly Christian faculty for self-sacrifice. He tried to find out more about his sister's activities.

"When you say that you manage the mission's paperwork, what exactly does that mean?"

"I handle some of the congregation's accounts, and I also translate some of the articles sent from London for us to publish."

"What kind of articles?"

"Articles on faith, and spreading the Christian light around the world."

"And you believe in that?"

Rasoa threw him a disarming look. "I don't know too much, you know, I'm just the translator. The articles are written by very wise and knowledgeable people."

We spent the rest of our time there trying to infiltrate the City of Thousands' spheres of influence. It was not an easy task.

When old Andriambelo said that it was hard to build a position of strength, he was undoubtedly speaking from experience. Several strata of courtiers and dignitaries of dubious rank seemed to have the mission of making it impossible for anyone outside their clan to gain access to the Palace. Everyone in the City defended the tiny privileges they'd gained, and they all seemed committed to keeping newcomers away.

"This City is a crocodile-infested rice field!" Ibandro liked to say.

Andriantsitoha had asked Andriambelo to gain him access to circles where his skills could make a useful contribution; at one point, I realized that he was planning on making me his secretary. I think that the lord of Ambohimanelo still thought that the same thing would happen as did during his studies, when some of his classmates had been recruited to work at the Palace at barely twelve years old. But that era was over: such positions were now subject to fierce competition, with factions and even whole clans clashing relentlessly over them.

Andriambelo introduced him to a dignitary named Andriantsoly. It was difficult to pinpoint exactly what this man's status was in the circles of middlemen orbiting the Palace. He sported an officer's dress and displayed an even-tempered face for his visitors. A portrait hanging on the wall showed him in ceremonial uniform, with the caption: "Andriantsoly, ten-times-honored general of the Royal Army." He exuded the self-importance of those whose power and worth came from deciding others' fates, instead of their own abilities.

"I have the highest respect for Andriambelo," Andriantsoly told him. "He is an elder worthy of being carried on the top of the head. I know that our Sovereign Mistress, may she grow old alongside her grandchildren, has great affection for him. He's a remarkable man. You know it's such a delicate matter these days to know who you can rely on. Our enemies are many, and they know all the criminals' tricks!"

"My desire and haste to serve our Mistress are such that peace has left my soul, my lord," Andriantsitoha replied. "The ancestors compelled me in my dreams to leave without delay, to leave my wives and children behind, to sleep neither day nor night until I'd shared my tears and expressed my eternal devotion to the Queen. She can be secure in the knowledge that she has in me her most loyal and eager slave."

"I thank you for your devotion to our Mistress."

"May the ancestors keep watch over her. May she not know illness, and may she grow old in the affection of the People Under the Sky."

A little of Andriantsoly's frigidity seemed to thaw. He got up from his stool and took a little plate from the shelf, heaped with brown things. He offered the plate to his guest, then took a piece himself, which he chewed with relish.

"How do you find this food?" Andriantsoly asked.

"I've never eaten anything so delicious."

Andriantsitoha later confessed to me that he'd had to struggle not to expel the viscous thing. The taste seemed abominable to him, the smell pestilent.

"What is it, then?" he inquired with feigned nonchalance.

"It's a precious commodity, very much in style among the vazahas. Apparently it has many hidden virtues."

"What is it called?"

"*Chocolat*. But let's turn to what has brought you here today. I'll tell you, I considered the matter a little before your arrival."

Andriantsoly offered him a post in customs administration. The offer seemed respectable and interesting. Everyone knew that, since the slave trade had ended, the largest profits had been made in that sector. In addition, the most important people in the kingdom had stakes in trade businesses, chiefly the Prime Minister and members of the royal family. It could be the ideal opportunity to strengthen those relationships.

"You'll be an official," said Andriantsoly, "in charge of the written registry of transactions, and responsible for carrying out orders from your superiors."

"Superiors?"

"These procedures report to several very important people, including a general and a prince. But you won't be in direct contact with them; you'll have immediate superiors on-site who will tell you what needs to be done."

"Oh?"

"You'll of course be entirely responsible for your own keep. But you'll have the right to have an assistant."

"And how much will this post cost me?"

"One thousand five hundred piasters."

"Huh?"

Andriantsitoha was taken aback. Andriantsoly seemed annoyed and looked away.

"It's a very important posting, I don't understand your reaction at all. Dozens of young men your age, from better upbringings, dream of securing such an advantageous position. Just this morning, I placed a boy from one of another clan's best families in Mojanga."

"In Mojanga?"

"Correct."

"Where would I work?"

"In Toamasina."

"But I want to stay in the City of Thousands!"

Hearing that, Andriantsoly gave him the kind of smile reserved for children who spout whatever comes into their head. Humiliated, Andriantsitoha promised Andriantsoly to consider his proposal, and we took our leave. The dignitary barely accorded us a nod of his head as he continued to eat his chocolats.

Once the late sovereign had been placed in the silver pirogue that would bring him to the ancestral kingdom and his remains had been enshrouded from sight of the People Under the Sky, the Palace gave the order for the sun mourning, the ceremony of final separation from the King.

The entire royal family—with the exception of the new sovereign, who hadn't yet been presented to the people—went to the edge of Tsimbazaza Pond to witness the sacrifice of the black bull with bent horns. The City folk, heads anointed with oil, came to bring the "five grains of rice" offering of separation owed by every household. Then, the people went to the water's edge for the mass purification.

Andriambelo recited his words, a fervent prayer asking that all unhappiness and evil destinies be swept away by the waves and flung into the furthest ravine.

The city's cannons thundered. The funereal ceremonies were complete.

"How did your meeting with Andriantsoly go?" the patriarch asked the young lord of Ambohimanelo.

"It went marvelously. Thank you a thousand times for your help."

"Did you accept his offer?"

"It was very generous, but I still must consider it carefully. I could never commit to something without being worthy of the honor bestowed upon me. I want to be absolutely certain that I can handle the responsibilities."

Andriambelo nodded approvingly.

"You've done well, very well. I won't lie to you, sometimes young people these days frustrate me; they're so pretentious and full of themselves! They're greedy for honor and privilege, and they don't even know how to hold a spade! I'm pleased to see that Andriamaro passed his wisdom onto you, even if the saying goes, 'Only simpletons want to be like their fathers.'"

Andriantsitoha failed in all his attempts to get a strong position in the City. He returned to Ambohimanelo more bitter than when he left.

All this occurred in the first year of the Sovereign Queen's reign.

16

The Elemental Law
of the Fampitaha

WHAT MAKES US MEN who are truly worthy of this land? What specific moments give the People Under the Sky their flavor, their colors? How does our destiny shape itself in secret beneath the watchful eye of time? I believe the fampitaha was, of all the old ways, the one that best conveyed the ancestral spirit. The one in the second year of the Sovereign's reign was one of those rare moments that leaves an indelible mark upon the soul.

The fampitaha was the event: awaited by everyone, the subject of every family's discussions far in advance. No other games could compete with the brilliance of the queen's competition: not the diamanga duels, which attracted the ones who loved fighting; not the *karajia* sparring, which enthralled lovers of the spoken word; not bullfighting tournaments, which could entertain entire villages. Yes, the fampitaha was the one competition that fanned flames highest in the hearts of the People Under the Sky.

That year, our district took part in the trial, the only one whose final event took place in the courtyard of the Palace itself, in the presence of the sovereigns.

But since that time the fampitaha has always been muddled with one image for me, one name: Fara.

One day, Bao left the village very early. The dawn departure surprised us: when she wasn't working the fields or going to market—and especially after some nocturnal escapade—Bao rarely rose before the Creator's great sun. She returned later with a large sack under her arm, making us even more intrigued. She called Fara.

The girl approached apprehensively: her mother held a thin rod in her other hand. But Bao led her into the middle of the yard.

"Dance! Yes, dance, lift your arms! Curve your wrists! One hand on your hip! Faster! Bend at the waist—no, not like that. Watch me! Now, spin!"

A moment later, Fara was dancing under the sun. Her mother guided her with the end of her baton while grabbing fistfuls of flower petals from the sack and tossing them into the air.

Bebe came over clapping and started singing an old tune in the same rhythm. I set down the spear I'd been carving, grabbed my valiha, and joined in. The music, the game, the communal *lalao*—they all scooped us up in their bountiful hands. We simply let ourselves be carried away.

I knew that Fara had secretly been longing for this moment. The joy that lit up her face when she danced proved it. It was a way to reach the City, and she knew it. Why hadn't she taken the initiative earlier herself? When I thought about it, it was simple. It was in her nature to take the time to consider things first. That was the way she was: sometimes full of drive, sometimes too timid, always ambitious but often not confident in her abilities, her own destiny.

Practicing for the contest quickly filled up most of our free time.

Within two days, we'd established a ritual: Bao taught Fara the main steps in the morning, attentive to the smaller details, like how to blink or the way to accompany and prolong her movement with a look or her breathing. Then, Bebe had her sing tunes out of a repertoire that contained moments of joy and deep longing. Near midday, Bao would be back from the market with a supply of strong ointments and ornaments to try on her daughter. Finally, when I returned from the rice fields, I'd take Fara onto my shoulders and we'd practice some steps under the strict eye of our elders.

Now, Fara wanted to win. Her eyes shone, and she opened up more.

We trained in utmost secrecy, usually in the small yard to the south of the hut, so that the fig tree and the shared garden wall could hide us from prying eyes; that way, the best effect was saved for the contest itself, and it prevented us from getting copied by cheats. Bao led the practices, baton in hand: she'd regained her old vitality, shouting and jumping around, her hair shaking loose. As for Bebe, she paced back and forth, grumbling and bent over double in thought, trying to find the best melody and *hainteny* couplets.

The competition was fierce. To win, you had to be excellent. Any girl could participate, but only the most beautiful and talented dared step up to the challenge; the public was cruel and demanding, and took glee in devastating any less talented participants. Fara had at least two rivals at her level: Tiana, a girl from Tendroarivo who embodied the best of grace and charm, and Sahondra, who lived in Ambohimanelo and was the most formidable opponent. Being taller and more svelte than the average adolescent made her imposing enough, but she was also sprightly of spirit and very at ease in her body. She had already taken part in the contest twice, and the jury had awarded her a distinction the last time around. She was the favorite, by far. Sahondra hadn't been eliminated until she'd been pitted against the most brilliant young girls of the whole kingdom.

In comparison, we seemed a little like backward peasants.

But Fara had a secret talisman: Bao.

Bao, whose hands never tired and excitement never waned, brought a queen into being before our awestruck eyes. Bao, who was then, for Fara, the most loving mother in existence. Bao, who knew exactly how to win.

"You must not dance for the men of this earth but for those in the cloud kingdom, for princes and sovereigns, o light of my life," she whispered lovingly as she combed her daughter's long hair.

"I don't know how to do that!"

"Yes, you do. Forget the commoners, their sight is stained with lust and want, with jealousy and meanness. Don't try to please the most seductive man; his desire will be your downfall. Don't try to enchant the richest; he will reduce you to begging."

"So tell me what I should do!"

Bao smiled, stopped painting Fara's eyelids, and took her face in her hands. "Like I've told you: sing for your highest dreams, dance for your most starstruck plans. Then you cannot lose."

Fara grew more confident as the weeks went along, perhaps under the spell of these words.

The trial included ensemble dances that we practiced in a neighboring prairie with the other province children. The public who attended these rehearsals noticed Fara. People found their attention drawn by an allure in the way she turned, the way she moved her shoulders and curved her arms. Her moves were as light as leaves on the wind, fluid as a stream running between walls in the rice fields; her sky-bound steps drew burning lines in the red soil. Under her charm, people clapped their hands to the rhythm.

At night, as I slept, I dreamed of Fara dancing and twirling in the red dust, her *lamba* shawl over her arms and shoulders. I still dream of it today. Where have those precious days gone?

After two weeks, Fara was nearly as lauded as Sahondra, which was already validation in and of itself.

We were fully convinced of her chances when one night, as an exhausting rehearsal drew to a close, her rival approached her, hands on her hips.

"I have to tell you: you dance pretty well and you could distinguish yourself in a village competition. But be careful that ambition doesn't ruin your life. The royal fampitaha is another thing entirely. I shouldn't hide this from you: your legs are too bowed and your bottom's a little saggy. And as for your breasts, maybe you should massage them with something to make them grow; they look sickly, it's a little shameful. At least give me the illusion of defeating you honorably! But hey, do whatever you want—this is just friendly advice."

Life likely never metes out its sweetness too easily, and fate always comes up with clever ways to complicate things. For me, that year was also a period of agony, of being pulled in all different directions.

First of all, Fara and I abandoned the missionaries' school because of everything else we were doing. The two weekly classes were usually reduced to one, or none at all. We weren't the only ones to desert: in the final weeks before the Bathing Feast celebration, Blake decided to close his doors for a while, for a lack of filled seats. He gave new assignments to his assistants and faithful followers, including Vero, sending them on evangelical missions in the wide countryside.

Then, one morning, Ibandro came to our home, which had never happened before. He came for me. We heard him approaching long before seeing him appear at the end of the street; his entrance to the village had riled up the area kids, who followed him and swarmed around like a loud pack of courtesans. Ibandro had a huge smile: Andriantsitoha wanted to see me, to give me an important job.

My soul fell lifeless. I had to abandon Fara and the whole family in the middle of rehearsing for the fampitaha in order to follow him.

"Tsito!" the lord said upon seeing me. "Come, you will help me; it's been too long since I focused on words and books. I want to refresh my memory, but I need someone to guide me. It will be faster and more enjoyable that way."

I was furious, yes, but also flattered and enticed. Learning, reading, exercising the mind—I missed it all. School had showed me that I could learn just as well as other people and that "everyone is in himself a nobleman," as the old saying goes. But how could I concentrate on reading now? The whole province was preparing for a party. Plus, with Fara participating in the fampitaha, we in Bebe's house now had the chance to achieve one of the greatest honors that a family could dream of.

It was torture, but a short-lived dilemma; yet again, I couldn't refuse Andriantsitoha's offer.

He'd salvaged an old trunk with books and notebooks that he and his sister, Rasoa, had used during their classes with Reverend Jones. It hadn't been touched in ten years and was covered in dust. Time, moths, and aphids had destroyed the linings in many of the volumes, and someone had had the ill-advised idea to put a small earthenware urn of alcohol in a corner of the trunk. The urn had cracked, spilling its contents and ruining an entire stack. The cleanup took me hours.

Who was Andriantsitoha? What kind of character was he, really?

Emptying the trunk, I was surprised to find works more varied and diverse than the ones in Blake's library, including collections that the missionary would never have authorized, under any circumstances. I was instantly struck by those books; I'd never seen anything like them before. Perhaps the first missionaries had had a grander vision of their task than their successors did—although I suspected that Tsifa and his co-disciples had probably procured some of these works behind their instructor's back.

I had to go to Andriantsitoha's house every day. But it was, I'll admit, not without a certain pleasure. He would often give me a notebook or pamphlet to take home and read, and we'd spend an hour or two the next day discussing it, watched admiringly by Ibandro. He also had me read texts out loud, interrupting to correct me or share an anecdote.

"Oh, I remember this little tale!" he would say. "The protagonist is shipwrecked on a forgotten island and teaches a savage proper manners. My classmates and I thought that Jones was very much like this Robinson Crusoe, in the feverish energy he brought to everything he did. You absolutely must read the entire book."

So my time was thus divided between the fampitaha and the sessions with the provincial lord. Yes, it was a time of both intense mental activity and awful emotional distress: I grew to realize more each day just how beautiful Fara was, just how precious she was to me. Far from abating, the secret feelings that had gripped me in the kalanoro valley only grew.

And everything that I did, I did for her. I was prepared to become a different man, if that's what it would take for the impossible to become real.

In Andriantsitoha's presence, I took to dreaming that knowledge and reading would one day let me overcome all the obstacles and marry my young mistress.

This outrageous ambition was nurtured by the forbidden books inside the trunk. I couldn't figure most of them out, not yet—just two or three, trying to guess what the sentences meant without understanding half of the words inside. But that was enough to thrill me. *Paul and Virginia* was my favorite one; it described the island of Maurice that was so similar to our own. Tsifa had scrounged up a copy in bad shape—the last pages were missing—but inside was written, "Translated from the French, Paris, Francart, 1801." I didn't know what that meant at the time, but the story transported me with huge waves of emotion, for I found similar traits between Virginia and Fara. In my naivety—and with no illustrations—I imagined the heroine wearing a white lamba, with a tananivoho hairstyle.

I took quite a liking to Paul, who, like me, revealed his feelings for his beloved spontaneously one day. How could I not identify with him? His modest birth raised walls in his path that made my soul ache, reminding me of my own heartbreak and poverty. Fortunately, other stories came to my rescue when I was broken down, other heroes carried me on their broad shoulders when I felt too much like a slave. Nothing was impossible: Othello was a Moor, and hadn't he captured the heart of Desdemona, the daughter of a rich and powerful Venetian lord?

Even Andriantsitoha encouraged me to pursue the risky venture. For yes, my current status is due in part to the lord of Ambohimanelo: my love of writing and diverse ways of thinking stems from that time when we discussed everything freely, outside, him on his stool, surveying his domain, and me squatting on his left, leafing through a book with yellowed pages. But Ibandro's master also impressed certain values on me—which, with the distance of time, have proven more ambiguous than at first encounter. Our meetings continued, stirring up all sorts of opinions that solidified his ambitions and sharpened his grudges. It was there, too, in front of that hut, that I first learned the basics of power struggles.

"I wonder what will become of the kingdom," he fretted, "if men like Andriantsoly—you remember him, the ten-times-honored general of chocolate—take control. Men like him exist only to divide the riches of this land up among themselves; they have no vision for the future. Or if they do, it's hidden away in the stinking folds of their embroidered pants."

"There is much to fear in that, my lord."

"Indeed. I recently traveled to Toamasina and returned very troubled. High-flying riffraff has descended upon the city. Nobles, officers, and vazahas were arguing over commercial profits like rabid dogs. It seems that worthy descendants have been found for the slave traders!"

"Are the families there unhappy, my lord?"

"Yes. And the same thing is happening in all eight corners of the island. Did you know that the governor of Mojanga built up a huge fortune in dollars and almost ten thousand head of livestock and then fled like a rat? Whereas I passed through villages on my way back from Toamasina that had been ravaged by famine and plague . . .

"I miss the reign of King Nampoina, you know," he continued, "even if I only knew it briefly. Back then, most of the high judges were men of great integrity. They were carefully chosen based on their commitment to community values, and their decisions were founded in wisdom. But now, over the past few years, what have you seen? Those who rule over the people are transforming into wild animals. They snatch up the People Under the Sky who fall within the reach of their jaws and rip them apart with their putrid fangs. They live on the currency of iniquity and seize their victims' possessions, swallowing all their shame, defying the infallible eye of the Perfumed Lord himself."

"I hope that the kingdom regains its lost greatness one day, master!"

"You are only a slave, and yet I see clarity and virtue in you, Tsito. Woe is us that we cannot say the same for those monkey brains who govern us. The only thing they know is how to be a vassal for vazahas. To be sure, though, I have absolute adoration for our Sovereign Queen, and she has my unfailing respect forever. She is not of whom I speak.

"This is a sacred land, but it is adrift, at the mercy of outside interests, foreign dealings that go far beyond us. This land is rich, but we're leaving it fit for pigs and stray dogs. What will military officers do, those birdbrained, plotting buffoons? Or princes, with their imbecilic minds as stubborn as a broomstick? Or judges, those fops who whore themselves out to anyone who asks? I don't want to imagine it."

"What about the missionaries, my lord? Don't they have our well-being, our happiness in mind?"

"Oh, don't be so naïve, Tsito. Missionaries make me think of those broad-backed slaves, always willing to help and serve, to carry any burden. But, as the proverb says, 'He who shows his back hides what is in his soul.' Personally, for anything that has to do with the vazahas, I'll stick to the other saying from our Ancient Ones: 'He who has a white soul is like a bird of ill fate.'"

Andriantsitoha was convinced that we had to find our own path, but he admired the kings of Europe all the same, especially Bonaparte. He hated the Whites, but swore by knowledge and artistic progress. He wanted to extract juice from the sugarcane without chewing the fibers. He wanted to seize tools for the future like chewing tobacco: to suck out all the flavor and spit out the rest.

All of which made me a little confused.

I was rather relieved when Andriantsitoha, swamped with other obligations as the Bathing Feast approached, had to suspend our meetings.

Finally, the crucial day of the fampitaha arrived.

The chosen few, who alone among a thousand and ten thousand would go present themselves one day before the Sovereign Queen, were traditionally selected on the last day of the year, the Day of Bathing.

The People Under the Sky had spent several weeks making feverish preparations for the celebration of the new year. The main markets were flooded with streams of humanity that poured in from all four horizons. Fat cattle of enormous height pushed through the crowd, occasionally trampling careless people underfoot. Busy young folks crisscrossed every village square, carrying offerings for the elders.

The Queen's wishes were that the joyful celebrations of her first Bathing Feast would leave wonderful, lasting memories in the minds of the people. Extravagant preparations were being made in the City of Thousands. It was a time of great excitement throughout the realm, and people greeted each other gaily in the street.

The lord of Ambohimanelo had had space set up south of Tendroarivo, where three hills surrounded a basin. Bamboo pikes surrounded the arena's perimeter, hung with all sorts of different colored lambas and topped with flowers and palm branches. The fampitaha was the most popular of all the festivities in the Bathing Feast. A full hour before the trial, the surrounding hills were already packed with spectators, undulating as the locals waved branches and bouquets of wild flowers joyfully. The most beautiful girls of the province were gathered in a prairie east of Sahasoa, where they'd start their parade over to the competition site. We counted long minutes waiting for the signal with Fara.

Sahondra, the favorite, had been placed at the head of the procession. Noticing us a few steps away, she waved to Fara, smiling a killer smile. "Little sister! Why didn't you heed my advice? This is not a game for children; it's a serious trial for grown-up women. Remember what I told you? Why are you seeking humiliation?"

"You've got nothing to worry about," Fara retorted. "I won't dance to make you lose the competition; I'm not concerned about that at all. Your stupidity will do that for you all on its own. I hope to see the Sovereign Queen—that'll be much more thrilling than squashing a little dragonfly like you."

Her taunt was met with laughter and cheers from the people around us. Sahondra's smile twisted into a sneer, and she spat on the ground.

Finally, the signal was given, and we set off.

Our arrival was welcomed by an infinite crowd. The contestants' finery was so rich that it left everyone breathless. The impatient audience was chanting:

> *Come forth! Let them appear*
> *And the most beautiful will triumph*
> *They will be judged*
> *And the ugliest will disappear!*

Old women hollered, children ran in every direction, and dogs howled like the demons of hell. I couldn't control my beating heart.

Fara, in untold beauty, marched in the second row. Her hair was braided with white silk flowers and piled on top of her head in a tiara of leaves and thorns set with silver coins. Her neck was adorned with a silver chain, and her ears graced with red pearls set in copper. She was dressed in linen dripping with thin veils, with her shoulders and legs left bare. The whole ensemble was so ethereal, a perfect image. Bao had worked a miracle.

That was her, Fara, my sky princess. The story had unfurled its shimmering wings under the real sun of mankind, and legend had been made flesh.

Fara was transformed. Her shyness had disappeared. The night before, she had murmured to me, with the same voice and the same light in her eyes as in the kalanoro valley, "I want to go to the City of Thousands. It is my destiny."

People from Sahasoa were there with some of our friends from the pond, including Tovo, and they all shouted out gaily to us as we passed.

"Fara! You are the most beautiful one here! You'll outshine them all!"

"Yes, yes! Show them how well you can dance! None of these other girls come higher than the soles of your feet!"

Then, someone threw a zebu rope around my neck and yanked me backward, choking me and nearly making me fall to the ground. Big Faly—for of course it was him—wearing his nasty smile, laughed as he dragged me along for a few steps like an animal. My breath cut short, I tried to hit him, but he dodged my blows. He was a skilled herdsman

"Hey you, slave, work well or else I'll sell you!" he cackled. "Maybe I'll even have you whipped first!"

Faly only let go and ran off into the crowd when a furious Bao started hurling rocks at him. Still, the ugly joke elicited a few snickers and chuckles from the people around us.

"Slaves have to have fun, too!" someone shouted. "Show us how well you can dance, slave!"

I spat upon the ground, beside myself with anger. The parade had continued, and Bao and I had to run to catch up. Fara hadn't seen any part of it, and was stamping with annoyance.

"Where did you go? I was so worried! Don't ever do that again."

Bao was breathing hard and I was shaking all over. Bebe had quite a job calming everyone down. Faly. Of course he had to do that here, in the middle of the crowd, at the moment of highest stress. What did our ancestors have in store for us?

That day, the full meaning of an ancient proverb was revealed to me: "If the waterfall rumbles, it is because of the rocks; if kings rule, it is because of the *vahoaka*."

Yes, the vahoaka, the people. They were the real Sovereign, and all would bow to their will.

The collective part of the competition happened without any upsets. Warmed up by the bullfights and rounds of rum, the good-natured public took up the competitors' songs quickly. The province's girls pirouetted across the dust in a graceful, multicolored dance, to admiring whoops and whistles. They sang praises to Queen Ranavalona:

> *Tahaky ny voahangy roa tsara venty!*
> *Amidy, lafo be!*
> *Avela, endriky ny trano!*
> *Fihaingoa-mahafa-kenatra!*
>
> *Sady taviny no volony!*
> *Rabodo no anaran'ny zaza!*
> *Rabodonandrianampoina!*
> *Zafin'Andriambelomasina!*

As the individual trials began, the commotion died down and the audience paid closer attention. The tension increased with the competitors' courage.

Twelve girls, the twelve best of the lot, stepped out from their rows to face the merciless sound of the drum, flute, and valiha.

The first dance was an ensemble one, to eliminate half of the group.

Unsurprisingly, Fara passed. Then, the six remaining candidates were submitted to a rapidly alternating set of sung oratories and choreographed movement. They were run through their paces without a moment's pause. When Fara's turn came to sing, her voice soared above all the others, but Sahondra's performance, immediately afterward, was full of expressive and overly humorous gestures that garnered shouts and warm cheers from the audience. After a brief uncertain moment for Fara, they were both let through to the next stage, along with Tiana, the girl from Tendroarivo.

I took a deep breath. We'd reached the most anticipated part of the competition: the free individual presentations.

The song choices and movements were left up to the competitors' discretion, but each dancer had to perform the last part of the dance on a man's shoulders, as befit every fampitaha queen. I would come onstage for that last part.

Tiana performed first, but fell as she was climbing onto her partner's shoulders. She was met with sarcastic jeers as she ran off of the esplanade in tears.

"Oh, too bad! Go train harder to mount a man!"

Sahondra appeared next.

She was extremely beautiful, enveloped in blue. Her hair was braided into two thin plaits on her chest and decorated with blue flowers. Strips of silver hung from her dress, and a bright oval shone in the middle of her forehead. A large blue agate encircled with silver hung from each ear. I doubt many royal princesses could have measured up to her. Half of the men in Ambohimanelo fell in love with her that day. At least.

Sahondra had a very high voice that pierced you to your very soul, and her long, gracefully swaying body bewitched the mind. The public was entranced the entire time she danced and sang. Women babbled in admiration, patriarchs shouted themselves hoarse, children cheered and hollered. When she had finished, lovesick young men whooped and ran over to hoist her up and carry her out of the arena, to wild applause.

But it was our turn. Bao sat at the drum, and I picked up my valiha. Fara took her place in the middle of the dance square.

We'd created a short drama about a sky princess playing in the sand beside a lake. It started slowly, playfully, then unfurled over a long emotional passage, before finishing ruled by the drumbeat's breathless speed. The climax, when the flute came in, was the appearance of the midlands prince: me.

The audience didn't like the first part.

They'd gotten too much of a taste for the other girls' seductive dances. Some of the crowd started to boo.

I looked at Fara. She was losing her composure. I shivered; she was becoming swept with doubt again. She looked at Bebe and me questioningly. But the next part would be the key: Bebe had meticulously arranged lyrics from the most eloquent hainteny verses, and I'd dug deep into the very fiber of my being to compose the accompanying valiha voice. Fara had to outdo herself. But no sound came out of her mouth. She stared wide-eyed at the crowd. Mute. All was lost.

I heard Bao whispering next to me. "Sing, now, for your highest dreams. Sing!"

Fara sang.

She closed her eyes, and suddenly her voice rang out, a clear tone, inexpressible, lifted on the clarion vibrations of the valiha, that long piece of magical bamboo. At the first refrain, all conversation stopped and only a low murmur was left, punctuated by a few drunken shouts, which people shushed. At the second refrain, utter silence fell; the crowd was captivated. Fara's voice rose and soared over the carpet of humanity, caressing the hillsides like a soft spring breeze, swelling and breathing a glimmer of longing into every heart and mind.

> *Tell me how I can keep your love:*
> *If I knot it into a corner of my gown*
> *The thread might break and I could lose it.*
> *If I place it in the palm of my hand*
> *I'm afraid it might dissolve into dampness . . .*
> *Instead, I'll put it in my heart:*

Although it will make me perish
Will that not make me love you all the more?

We had our chance.

We couldn't falter now; we had to keep the intensity rising to the end. At the drum, Bao, sweating, disheveled, was equal to the challenge; she accompanied Fara's every move with unremitting precision, guiding her step by step like the inspired finger of the Creator, until my friend was perched squarely on my shoulders. It was the climax. Bebe let fly a long trill on the flute. I breathed in deeply and set my muscles in motion.

We performed the last three steps with unhurried calculation, so often repeated and refined, holding our breath—and we felt that the audience was doing the same.

Three simple steps, each one with a flourish on the flute and a double drumbeat, like a cresting wave. One, *ba-bum*, two, *ba-bum*, three, *ba-bum*. It was done.

There was silence, waiting, then a thunder of applause and an indescribable, unending roar.

The jury was split and deliberated three times. But the verdict was soon delivered: we had the public on our side. We had won.

The first Bathing Feast of the Sovereign Queen was a time of harmonious communion with the vahoaka, the people, thanks to our victory in the fampitaha. For Fara and me, that feast marked the end of our childhood and the dawn of a new era filled with hope.

My memories of those festivities are vivid, both as sweet as honey and as blazing as the jacaranda in springtime. Our happiness was complete and serene, unspoiled.

Andriantsitoha summoned us to Ambohimanelo to congratulate us on the day of the competition. Bebe was emotional, and Bao was all smiles. Fara and I didn't yet fully understand what had happened. We were intimidated by the enthusiastic shouting and the flower petals being tossed along our path. We were kings for a day.

131

"You gave a magnificent performance, my child," Andriantsitoha said to Fara as he received us. "I will personally accompany you to the City of Thousands, where you will soon appear before the Sovereign."

"My lord, you are too good," replied Bebe. "May you grow old alongside your grandchildren."

When the provincial chief bade farewell to the family, he asked me to stay for a short while to take care of a few things. It was disappointing not to be able to go with Fara; the new year feast had already begun, in the village and throughout the whole province. But Andriantsitoha had been moved by the spirit of lalao, the community games, and was overflowing with ideas. He wouldn't be convinced to drop the issue.

"I have grand plans for this domain, Tsito!" he exclaimed. "I want to make this the most prosperous province in the district. You can help me."

That day, I wrote several letters for him that he sent to his peers scattered across the island. They were about money, support, and loyalty. He didn't release me until the hour of herding the cattle back to their pens. I raced toward Sahasoa.

Fortunately, it was the night of lanterns, and the festivities continued.

When I arrived, the village was just setting off. Bebe, Bao, and Fara were ready and waiting for me. I had just enough time to go get the lanterns that I'd stashed carefully below the rafters.

The hillsides of the province were already burning with a thousand lights. The valleys filled with children singing. Everywhere you looked, luminous processions snaked through the dark, like the paths of stars in the sky, reflecting children parading joyfully in the festival of lights.

"Bebe, why do we celebrate lanterns?" Fara asked as we passed the great rolling gate stone at the village entrance.

We admired the huge variety of the lamps around us. Some, from the poor families, were just a wick protected from the wind by a bunch of leaves stuck crudely together. Others were real oil lamps with a little handle and chimney for the smoke.

Fara and I carried two lanterns whose tinted paper walls danced and flashed red, green, and white. Fara's was in the shape of a house, and mine was a glowing little pirogue. I'd called on all of my skills to fabricate the lanterns' frames. I'd poured all my love into the work. I had the feeling that this would be the last time we took part in the festival of lights, the celebration of childhood.

"We celebrate the light in honor of the life that has been granted to us," explained Bebe. "Each lantern is a sign of gratitude from those who have reached the new year, who have stayed alive until the Bathing Feast. Even the Sovereign lit her candles last night, and the Palace was decorated with a thousand lights."

We didn't get home until a little before midnight, exhausted from walking and sheer pleasure. When the hour of the Bath finally arrived, we gathered around our elder. It was time for the first prayer. Each one of us cupped a small amount of gleaming holy water into the palm of their hands and poured it over their head. Bebe, the first, uttered the prayer of life, and we repeated it in turn.

"Bestow your goodness upon us, O Perfumed Lord, our Creator! Grant that we may reach a thousand times a thousand years! Let illness stay away! Let us never be separated!"

When the night began the second half of its course, we shared poultry and *sosoa* rice. As the oldest, Bebe was entitled to the rump, and Fara and I received the thighs. The elderly woman had cooked the dishes with love for many hours. We ate with delight, like we had the seven elemental royal dishes. Then, a rare treat: Bao rose to dance. We watched her dance by candlelight; we sang and clapped our hands, reveling in our shared happiness.

The new moon could be seen very clearly over the hilltops. Orion's Belt and all the other stars in the sky seemed to be exalting her. It was Alahamady.

At the hour of the sun overhead, the community distributed the meat from sacrificed zebus and every family shared their first real meal of the year. Ikitromalaza the bull, the only one born to the old cow Ifotsy, was thus slaughtered, and Bebe set a part of his flesh aside to cure in fat. We built a fire of his bones to make the red-water medicine, which we'd sell at market later.

This was the Bathing Feast in the second year of the Sovereign Queen's reign. Forty thousand bulls were sacrificed that year, and the meat was distributed to the people.

BOOK 3

Adin'ombalahin'ny mpianakay
Ny mahery tsy hobina
Ny resy tsy akoraina

Bulls fighting within the herd
The victor is not cheered
The vanquished is not booed

MALAGASY HAINTENY

17 *Fara*

YESTERDAY EVENING, Bebe told us the legend of the volcano called Tritriva.

"A young man and woman from a village at the foot of Tritriva fell madly in love with each other one day. They loved each other so much that they decided to get married. But their parents would not condone their union. The lovers begged for compassion, but their elders were unyielding. In despair, the two lovers decided to throw themselves into the volcanic lake.

"On that day, they hugged each other tightly and knotted their wrappers around their bodies. Then they let themselves roll all the way down the slope into the crater and disappeared into the lake's sparkling green water.

"A year later, a tree grew in the middle of the water. Its trunk stood in the very center of the lake. It was swathed in thick, intertwining liana. The villagers believed that the two lovers had transformed themselves into a tree. When their parents heard, they were very sad and tore their hair in regret. The elders made an ironic observation: 'Now at least you know that regret does not come before recklessness.'"

I like the legends that Bebe tells about lovers, but I think something's missing, and sometimes they sound hollow, like a convenient fabrication. Maybe it's because Bebe is too old to really breathe life into those stories. Plus, they're usually a pretext for all kinds of pithy, moralizing sayings: "Regret comes after, not before," "'So-and-so' was so love-crazed that he forgot to notice the setting sun," "Overly passionate love will denounce even brothers and sisters," and others.

I think that Bebe's real-life memories of love have shriveled with time. Evaporated in the sun of old age. Bebe herself, with her wrinkled face, half-bald head, and ruined body, is an arid wasteland, like a dried-up old riverbed. The season of heavy rains has given way to cracks and withered plants dotting dead surfaces that have all been stripped bare.

This morning, as I prepared the morning fire and Tsito stacked the firewood, I asked him a question: "Do you think I'll ever meet a man who'd be willing to risk his life for me? Or a man who I'd be willing to sacrifice myself for, like in the story of the Tritriva lovers?"

He didn't answer. He picked up a whole armful of split wood and sticks and started packing and tying them together. Eventually, he set the pile on top of a stack against the southern wall. Then he looked at me, blinking against the burgeoning glow. The dew had already evaporated and the chickens were starting to stir inside their little pen.

"It's a nice story," he started, "but I really wonder how—"

"What do you think of Faly?"

"Why?"

"Do you think he could be my steadfast tree, my prince of light?"

Every single bundle of wood in the pile fell over. Tsito tripped, I don't know what happened to him. He grabbed the wood as he fell and the whole pile tumbled onto him. Almost an hour of work wasted. That slave is getting clumsier and clumsier.

"Wait, have you gone out with a girl yet?" I asked him.

"I . . . I have to finish picking up this wood, otherwise Bebe won't be happy."

I'm really not happy, I have to say. My grandmother doesn't listen to my questions about love anymore, and Tsito is completely ignorant in that area. Bebe especially can be really annoying. Regret and reckless-ness—what could be more boring than that? Now I understand what that saying actually means: "Dry as an old woman's vagina." No point trying to get any useful advice there.

The only person who knows anything is Bao, my mother. But that's another story. Her love land is a battlefield. She gets just as many bruises and broken ribs as outlines of lingering kisses on her neck. Jealous women, condemning wives. That's no turn-on. And besides, Bao just broke things off with Rainivonjy. She says she doesn't love him anymore, says he's too old, says he can't last. She's going out with other men now. When I ask her what new things she's gotten from her new lovers, besides lasting, she only gives me vague answers before leaving with a nervous chuckle. I really think she's a little crazy.

The day continues. It's the hour of tying the calf to his post. I'm all alone with my loom, near the fig tree. Bao's chasing after her lovers, Bebe is sleeping, and Tsito went somewhere.

At the end of the path, the rice fields are reflecting their last silvery glimmers, slowly starting to meld into the marshes in the distance. The thatched roofs around me in town are being swathed in a thin cloak of smoke. The dull thuds of the rice pestles in the neighborhood dwindle with the daylight, replaced by crackling firewood. The village is already getting drowsy.

I wish Faly were here with me.

Below the old tree the other day, Tovo, Vero's brother, very quietly told us about the latest big thing: two of his friends had discovered a secret affair between Haga and a mystery woman. It was afternoon, just before the Bathing Feast, and Tsito wasn't there—he was still held up with Ibandro, the provincial lord's slave. I sometimes wonder what those slaves do together over there.

Funny story with Haga and the mysterious woman. Haga is a diamanga champion. He lost his left ear in a brawl, sliced clean off by a machete. Even so, a handsome guy. Every boy in Sahasoa wants to be like him, they try to copy the nonchalant way he wraps his arm around his spade when he carries it on his shoulder, they strut around with their legs arched to make their butt stand out like his does. Really silly.

Haga and the woman were spotted together behind the walls in Tendroarivo at an hour of being unable to see zebus' coats anymore. They recognized Haga in the darkness from his bulk, but not the woman. Speculation ran rampant the other day; some people threw out names of rich men's wives. Tovo had his own idea.

"I know it's Saholy!"

"No way!"

"She sticks out so badly! Have you seen how they ignore each other in public? They don't say hi to each other, they don't talk to each other. If they walk past each other, they both act like the other one's just a puff of air or a cloud of dust. Such a tall, handsome guy, and a pretty girl like her? Think about that!"

"Wait, why?" I asked. "What are they doing together?"

There was a very brief silence, exchanged glances. Then everyone burst out laughing, followed by whoops and wheezing. I wanted to bury myself in the ground. I stood out to them, all those simpering pretty boys who boasted of knowing "things." I was on the verge of tears.

"It's not funny!" I shouted.

Finally, they calmed down.

"They're sleeping together," Tovo said.

"Why're they doing that?"

"Because they need some loving. Because it's fun."

Tovo peered at me with a strange expression, then suddenly smacked his forehead. "Oh, of course! I forgot, your father doesn't live with you, does he?"

"No. But my grandmother does."

"What about the other men that go out with your mom, do they ever sleep at your house?"

"Why would they sleep at our house?"

"Okay, I get why you don't know. I promise to show you soon!"

"Show me what?"

More laughter. Teasing grunts. Tongues clicking.

Somebody recited a poem:

> *Swollen gourd*
> *Soft raffia,*
> *The gourmand's eyes*
> *Are fixed on the bottom of the pot*

The libertine's eyes
Are fixed on me.

It still makes me so mad.

Of course I didn't know. So what? Looking back, those pimply kids' meanness stands out clearly to me. Faly's right to hate them. Good thing I got my revenge in the fampitaha; they were speechless. I could have had any adult man at my feet if I wanted. It was a huge blow to their pride.

Faly, though, he's always respected me.

But what surprised me the most in the story about Haga was when we found out that it really was Saholy.

Saholy is engaged to Doda, Ramaro's oldest son. Their family tree has many branches, and they're very respected in Sahasoa: rich, diligent in community service, hard workers, always willing to lend a hand. The father had thirteen children in three different beds. Doda has everything that pleases girls: money, dedication to his work, a strong body.

Only look at that: he's not even married yet and his wife is already cheating on him. Damn Saholy. A girl who's so perfect that flies don't dare land on her. Full of energy, overflowing with joy. A model woman, the aura of a lovable wife, a future daughter-in-law with the ability to win over the most stubborn parents-in-law. Her easygoing nature is complemented by how thoughtful she is to everybody. And on top of everything, she has one of the prettiest faces in the whole district. What could have possibly been going through her head?

It was a shock when Tovo and his friends came to pick me up that night to give me a clear view of what love "looks like."

"Come quick! It's happening!"

I'd been sewing part of my dress for the fampitaha. I barely had time to put my loom away.

We crept silently through the undergrowth. Soon, we heard voices—they were trying to be discreet. A man and a woman. We could see them clearly in the light of the setting sun. They were hurried, quick and eager as crop robbers. I stared at the intimate struggle, fascinated. I saw their intertwined bodies perfectly clearly, in an almost grotesque position. I heard their heavy breathing and the little moans that escaped. I understood things that I hadn't known before.

I had a dream that night.

People dressed in white welcomed me to a house with silver fabric hung on the walls. A zebu head with long silver horns was sitting on a school table in the middle of a large room. A scarlet curtain was visible in the back, concealing a secret door, behind which I heard voices. The people in white drew back and Blake burst out from behind the curtain. He was naked from the waist up, his ear was cut off, and he was brandishing a machete. I woke up screaming.

Faly was the one who opened my eyes to love. I know that now. It happened after the fampitaha, during the Bathing Feast. The last day of Alohotsy, the day that never ends.

We'd gone home without Tsito because he'd stayed with Andriantsitoha. We had to get ready for the new year's eve. For the first time, I thought a little about the other events of the day. Just think, I'd won the fampitaha without knowing what some of the festivities meant! Everyone else knew and probably thought that I knew, too. Ever since Vero, my best friend, converted to the vazaha religion, I haven't been spending much time with the other girls. They're afraid of the pond group and our boisterous games.

Still, I had the idea to ask Bebe. We were getting the chicken ready for the Bathing Feast.

"The day that never ends? That's when everyone goes out to plant the great field."

"The great field?"

"We'll sacrifice Ikitromalaza for Bathing Day. He's not getting much fatter. I'm afraid he won't survive until the next dry season. Go get him from the pen and tie him up out back."

"What's the great field, Bebe?"

"Now now, it's forbidden to talk about. Right now, I'd like you to go get some gleaming holy water for Bathing Day. Ranjato's wife will give you some."

As soon as I left for the village chief's house, I asked a couple village women who I passed on the way. The same awkward, dodging answers. It was like trying to milk a heifer. Only the most roundabout paths for a tradition as old as dirt!

As I walked, I was surprised by how quiet the town was. I passed two men in the street who looked at me with a strange expression, and I hurried away.

The chief's first wife, a woman who's already old, filled a pitcher with gleaming holy water for me. I half hoped to run into Faly—he's their adopted son—but he wasn't there. As I left, I slipped in a couple of questions about the day that never ends, acting nonchalant, but she narrowed her eyes and kicked me out without answering. "It's forbidden to talk about. It's not a subject for children. Now go home, and don't wander off the path!"

Why is everyone insisting on treating me like a child?

I'd ended up with an idea of what I was looking for. It had all become clear. Letting instinct lead me, I headed for the pond. The path had suddenly become a very busy place. It was like every adult from every village was meeting outside the trenches. Everyone in the whole region, almost, was in the woods and fields, leading a hidden life that no one talked about. I moved through the bushes to keep from attracting attention and to spy more easily on adults on the prowl.

I couldn't take ten steps without stumbling on a couple in the thicket. It was like the thing with Haga and Saholy, but on a larger scale: wrappers hung everywhere, thrown hastily over branches; monkeys and wild dogs watched the mayhem of mating people, stunned like me. Among the many strangers and a few acquaintances, I saw Saholy the pretty girl. But this time, she wasn't with her fiancé or Haga, the man with the sliced ear. And three field-lengths away, I found Doda, Saholy's fiancé, talking gaily with another woman on the edge of a rice field.

There weren't just young people, either: retracing my steps, I saw Ranjato, the village chief, stealing away to an isolated cove in the valley, following a slave woman. He looked left and right as the woman pulled him along by the hand.

"During the day that never ends, all the laws that forbid the intermingling of clans are abolished," Bebe finally explained to me later, with a sigh. "Anyone interested in one another can go out together, under the sole condition that they hide. That's how the great field is sown."

"What about married people?"

"They're also free to go out with whoever they please. And it's forbidden to talk about—no one may complain about it."

"Why?"

"The Bathing Feast is a celebration of life, o apple of my eye."

I was baffled. I noticed that Bao had disappeared—she'd gone to sow the great field, too. And this time, there was no risk self-righteous ire from everyone else. So why did the community ordinarily act so severely toward its more "frivolous" members, like my mother?

"That's the law. The Sovereign is the only one above the law and the seasons. The Sovereign alone can ignore clans, prohibitions, and the harvest seasons. The Sovereign's field is fertile all year long."

A little later in the day, I was at the pond with the other children to get ready for the *tsikonona*, the ancestral supper, and the festival of light. It was probably the last time in my life that I'd take part in such childlike games. Big Faly hadn't hung out with that group for a long time—he hated them, called them "empty-headed pumpkins."

That day, though, for some reason, Faly and his friends were hanging around the pond. They sat across the way to watch us. Some of them lounged on the rocks on the side of the pond, lazily chewing betel leaf or the stub ends of sticks. Faly had swung his leg over a tree trunk that had fallen in the last cyclone.

If Tsito had been there, I bet there would have been another fight. Tsito's turned a little pretentious lately, ever since he started spending time with that brute, Ibandro. I think Faly's attractive; there's something mysterious about him, some inner pain that he hides under his cynical exterior. He was adopted by Ranjato when he was seven. I don't know how his parents died.

I got lost in my thoughts and cut myself grabbing the sharp end of a little meat knife that we were using for the tsikonona. I got blood on my clothes.

I looked at the wound—it was superficial, not dangerous. I just had to rinse it with clean water, which I did quickly in a water gourd. As I did, I could feel someone coming.

"Let me see."

Faly had gotten up when I screamed from the cut. He took my hand and looked at the cut.

"It's not properly washed. I'll show you how to do it."

Then, he did something that rooted me to the spot: he bent over and sucked on the wound.

I was flustered.

"You didn't know that saliva is the best thing you can find for cleaning?" he said with a wide smile.

He looked me straight in the eye. I acted cool.

"Thanks," I said. "I'll try to remember that."

He kept looking at me emphatically, up and down, with that smile, and said, "You aren't coming to the great field?"

"Uh, no . . . "

"You should. You have everything you need to have a good harvest. You showed that perfectly well at the fampitaha. I have to say, I was enthralled. And I wasn't the only one."

For an instant, I didn't know what to say. I felt panic rising in me. The only thing I thought of to say was this: "I know. But I get to choose when to sow. And which spade to use."

Faly burst out laughing and walked away, his laughter echoing throughout the valley. He winked at the other kids as he left.

We've seen each other twice since the Bathing Feast.

Now I know it's time to sow.

And I know where to find the spade.

18　*Tsito*

Mount Andrigiba's Lament

IT WAS TIME for me to leave.

As the saying goes, gold without coral and coral without gold cannot make a necklace. Fara and I weren't pearls on the same strand anymore—what good would it do to intermingle any longer? I'd sown a hopeful seed, but didn't know how to harvest what had grown. I'd striven for victory but someone else had stolen the trophy. Big Faly had made a brazen move and won a game that I hadn't understood the full scope of. His are the amorous desires, mine are the insipid consolations:

> *The trees of sweet-smelling wood*
> *Counting two, there finding three*
> *There on the tall mountain*
> *On Mount Andrigiba*
> *They wanted to sleep*
> *Pressed against each other*
> *At least rejoice, oh my soul,*
> *That you do not possess*
> *The one you do not love*

One world was falling to pieces. Yet I refused to abandon my life because of it. After all, wasn't I a slave? I didn't possess anything, I said to myself, thus I had nothing to lose.

Coincidentally, Blake called me to his office around that same time. I had a bitter taste in my mouth as I walked into the little room that the

146

missionary had set up as a place of thinking. Classes had started back up shortly after the Bathing Feast, but I'd become the only one whose path still led to the mission. Fara had stopped attending school to hang out with Faly and his gang. She also dropped the pond group; it had started to die after Vero defected, and now it had completely disintegrated.

Blake's office was a familiar place. I'd read the better part of the books adorning the modest library of white wood shelves. The worktable Blake wrote on had also been crafted in the mission's woodshop. I liked that rustic table; I'd designed some parts of it myself. I took pride and pleasure in looking at those pieces of furniture when I came to talk to Blake after class.

"You asked for me, sir?"

The vazaha was scribbling something in a notebook. His face was wrinkled, and his hair had seemed to be leaning more toward white for several months. He raised his head and looked at me sharply. I'd learned to not be afraid of that coldly fuming look, which always seemed to be peering directly into your soul in search of the slightest trace of weakness or sin.

"When are you going to get baptized?" he asked, surly. "Why are you always delaying the hour when you will follow Kristy's path? Would you rather let evil control your life?"

The missionary looked tired. He usually didn't adopt such a sermonizing tone unless his energy was starting to flag. I sat down silently in a chair across from him and let the storm pass.

"Look at all these people running straight into *Satana*'s arms! The armies of darkness are gathering. Your Bathing Feast is a celebration of sin, no better than Roman saturnalia! *Sodoma* and *Gomoro* were razed for less than that! Look at what's happening these days—I've never seen so many people rallying around *doany* and other demonic altars!"

This was the Blake who had crusaded against the vazimba. He leapt to his feet, as if he'd just realized something. He looked out the window, as if trying to calm his anger. Blake, I guessed, was thinking about everything that had happened since the new sovereign had risen to power. A menacing wind was rising against Christians. Did that matter to me?

He turned toward me, his face now beaming with pride. "We're going to baptize twenty new converts soon! You can be with them! The Good News is spreading through this country, shining like a new dawn. You can't ignore it. Many are those who will soon follow in our Lord's footsteps."

"I promise to think about it."

"Why do you always sidestep the question?" He was irritated. "Do you want to remain a slave? Our only salvation rests in Jesosy Kristy. You know that, you're an intelligent boy. You also know what will happen to those who have heard the Word and ignored it. It's time for you to figure out what you want."

I looked at the ground humbly, smiling faintly. I thought about Fara. But I also thought about Bao and Bebe. I had lots of respect for them. The thing I wanted, which I did not tell Blake, was something impossible: to take a world that had just shattered and piece it back together. I'd made my decision. I would miss them.

Blake sighed heavily and came to put a hand on my shoulder; it was an unusually tender gesture. "You can't come to school anymore. It could be dangerous for you and the other students. The Queen just forbade all slaves from learning to read and write."

Why would the Sovereign Queen do such a thing? I didn't know, and it didn't matter much to me either. I just thought it had to be that way. It conformed to how things evolved. My exclusion was a relief: from then on, I thought, there was nothing that bound me to the past. Going to the missionary's place had become torture. It was time to turn the page.

As I walked along the path home for the last time, I felt a small amount of deliverance as I pondered the bright blue sky. Only the faraway mountains were fading to dull gray as the day started to ebb. I saw herdsmen working their way slowly over the neighboring hills. The zebus' heavy footsteps pounded on the red clay. I took my braided straw schoolbag, walked to the side of the road, and threw it as hard as I could off into the rice fields.

The next day, I asked Ibandro to get me entered into the provincial lord's service. We'd already discussed it. That was also in the order of things. Andriantsitoha had the transfer price brought to Bebe, even though he was under no obligation; as the lord of the province, he also had his subjects' slaves at his disposal. But then again, he was a man of odd principles. Bebe notified Rado, who gave his consent and, Ibandro told me, left the full amount to the family.

I left Sahasoa for Ambohimanelo on a Friday morning at the hour of the rising day. I gave Bebe a small basket of fresh fruit as a sign of gratitude. The elder woman took water in her hand and blew it onto my face as a blessing. Bao was not there, so I left her a vial of perfumed oil as an honor. As for Fara, who was also not there, I left her a letter written in my own hand, which I put in a jewelry box carved from dark *zafimaniry* wood.

The sun would soon reach the rooftops. I took in the sight of my second childhood one last time, especially the bamboo-walled house that had been my shelter. I looked a little sadly at the valley and the river curving away toward the spring and child's pond, and I left.

When I appeared at Andriantsitoha's residence, he was pacing back and forth in front of his door, gesticulating wildly. He'd been angry since morning; soldiers had burst into the town of Tendroarivo, five men under the influence of *rongony* and alcohol. They'd stolen a bull and dragged two girls from their homes as loot. The village chief had tried to stand up to them, but he'd been beaten and left bleeding out in the town square. As the intruders left, they'd killed a slave of the Zafimanelo clan who'd refused to give them his goats.

I arrived to see Vola, the provincial lord's second wife, holding a bowl of steaming herbal tea in her hands. She looked worried—she'd been trying to make her husband drink the calming brew, but he pushed the bowl away every time.

"Tsito!" he said, seeing me. "That does it! I have to do something about this, I must!"

"What might I do for your pleasure, my lord?"

"You're going to help me. I'm going to write to the Palace this time, I'll find the evil and root it out. I'll talk to the Queen herself if I have to. I won't let them walk all over me."

I got straight to work. I took the papers and pen from Bathing Day back out from my new master's trunk. The bottle of ink was still half full.

"Rumor has it that the army will soon conscript thousands of men," Vola murmured to me as her husband finally drank the soothing remedy.

The idea of conscripting troops was devastating. Radama's campaigns still haunted people's memories: forced to provide their own sustenance, thousands of draftees had died of starvation and illness far from home, if they had not already been felled by enemy bullets and spears. Some, seduced by profit and acclimatized to violence, had transformed into ferocious beasts.

First, Andriantsitoha had me write a long letter to the Prime Minister, Commander in Chief. But after reading it back, he tore it up and threw it into the fire.

"No, no, that's awful. It could give the impression that I fancy myself one to teach him lessons. This is a delicate matter. He's an ill-tempered man. He'd crush us."

He sighed, his eyes bitter. "And as it stands, he doesn't even know me."

Then he had me draft, in succession, messages for the Queen's First Secretary, the Minister of Commerce, and Prince Ramonja, but they met the same fate as the first.

"It occurs to me that all of this could have the sole effect of attracting attention to us," he said, defeated. "I cannot ignore reality. It's a crocodile pit; they'll think that we have some treasure to hide."

"Couldn't we contact the officer in charge of the soldiers who committed the crime, my lord?"

Andriantsitoha sat on a stool and surveyed his domain. His answer was terse. "If I do that, I only have two choices: fall on them with five hundred armed men, or go beg them like a lowly slave to return my goods to me. I'd be loath to abase myself before creatures with no more virtue than a herd of swine. They'd feel invincible, they'd take sick pleasure in humiliating us more. As for attacking the royal army, we'd see ten thousand men marching on this province before the next moon to reduce it to ash."

I didn't know what to make of that. Was this the world of free men that I so longed for?

Andriantsitoha decided to call the community elders together to determine what action should be taken. I knew he hated that; some of the ones he'd had to face down to restore his authority after his father's death were still alive. Old grudges had not been erased, and war still simmered just below the surface, but he'd been backed into a corner: there'd been plundering, and the perpetrators were going unpunished. All his hard-won authority was compromised.

Ranjato was among the elders who came to Ambohimanelo that very night. The old landowner brought Faly. So I could not evade my destiny. Less than a day after leaving Fara, I already found myself facing my rival.

Andriantsitoha asked me to observe the elders' reactions and listen to their conversations. He wanted a detailed report. I was supposed to melt into the small group of people that had come with these powerful men, letting my ear wander without being noticed. But Faly spotted me before a single word had been exchanged. He shoved me into a corner and hissed in my face.

"So you up and changed masters just like that? What a shame—Fara and I would have rather you stayed to sweep our house."

I clenched my fists, and tears sprang to my eyes. Faly's sardonic smile widened; he knew I couldn't do anything. He grabbed my arm and clenched it in an iron grip.

"I hear you're making 'big strides, like a slave who dreams of becoming a lord.' Where do you think you're going?"

"Why are you hounding me? You won, and I left. What else do you want?" I spat.

I immediately bit my tongue. Faly cackled.

"Won? Am I dreaming?! Tell me, what were you hoping for, you adorable little dancing fampitaha servant? Oh, Creator! Is it possible . . . No! That's hilarious! Hahaha!"

The people around us called our attention: Andriantsitoha was about to receive the families of the two kidnapped girls. The discussion had begun.

Faly let go of my arm, and I slipped away into the gathered crowd, a new taste of defeat in my mouth.

I was not the only one to surrender that day.

Under pressure from the elders, Andriantsitoha agreed to negotiate with the officer, but would not go there himself. The three village chiefs who were still fit to travel made the trip in his name, escorted by Ibandro and me. My friend's immense presence reassured me: the soldiers would think twice before trying to capture us too.

Faly didn't come with Ranjato this time, but I found his absence more disquieting. Destiny put my enemy on my path too frequently for it to be mere coincidence.

Farmers informed us that the soldiers had set up camp in a hamlet of five or six huts at the edge of the neighboring province. When we got to their makeshift camp, we felt confused and afraid. Several roofs had been burned or pocked with holes, and everyone seemed to have fled. Dogs fought over a zebu carcass in the yard. A pair of ripped boots lay near a smoking hearth, and a threadbare uniform hung from a tree. We carefully made our way toward the houses that were still intact. There was no one there.

"They left," Ranjato said. "They took the girls with them. If we'd come sooner, we could have saved them."

Maybe the soldiers had run away fearing retaliation. More likely, though, they'd left to go hunting somewhere else. It was pointless to try to catch them now. The two young girls were going to end up in a slave market, after the troops had gotten enough pleasure.

At Ranjato's urging, the Council of Elders blamed Andriantsitoha for this calamity. After two days of heated debates, the shaken lord announced that he was going to go to the City of Thousands personally, to, as he said, cut the wave of aggressions that were being committed against his province off at its source. Still, a group of men was sent on the soldiers' trail; they had to at least try to identify what corps they belonged to, try to find out what they'd done with their captives. But there wasn't much hope.

Leave. Go far away. That's all that I wanted.

We spent the next three moons preparing for our departure to the City of Thousands. This time, Andriantsitoha was determined to stay there as long as necessary, which required making some arrangements. He left nothing to chance: he had me draw up a list of people he knew in the City and sent messengers to scope out opportunities. I was also charged, with Ibandro, with raising funds to cover the costs of the journey. The provincial lord was bringing wives, children, and servants; it was almost fifty people in all to lodge and feed, and we would also need gifts and bribes for once we were there. My friend and I traveled the length and breadth of the province, urging the people to contribute; we collected twenty-seven zebus, twelve goats, three dozen hens, and a little over a thousand piasters. We sold all the cattle in a neighboring province except for three, which we kept for the trip; the collected money and the balance of regular taxes made up the initial purse. The amount boggled my mind, and once Andriantsitoha added the amounts that he'd borrowed from his family and clan, I was sure, in my naivety, that we were in a position to buy the Commander in Chief himself.

My new obligations as a provincial lord's slave took up all of my time and energy. I wasn't displeased with my fate, but Sahasoa still plagued my thoughts. The wound was still so raw that I was torn between the desire to see the village again and the fear of reliving my defeat by merely setting foot there. That's why, when it was time to collect money for Andriantsitoha in Sahasoa, I left the task to Ibandro and other servants. Upon returning, my friend told me that Bebe and Bao had asked after me. I was pierced with sadness when I heard that and had to turn my head to hide my misty eyes. I realized just how much I missed the affection of the two women, my second family.

Fara left that year for the City of Thousands, three weeks before us: the Sovereign Queen wanted to have the fampitaha winners dance for her son,

Prince Rakoto, who was taking his first steps in life. Fara had waited for this moment for so long, and it had finally come. Faly and Ranjato organized the trip, because Andriantsitoha was too preoccupied with other things and no longer had an interest in it. Neither Bao nor Bebe were involved in the preparations, which I'm sure made them extremely frustrated; Faly had claimed our victory, even though we'd undergone a great struggle, alone, to rip it from fate's onerous clutches.

When I arrived in the big city with the lord of Ambohimanelo and his retinue, the festivities organized by the Palace had already ended. Fara and Faly did not come to greet Andriantsitoha, even though the rules of respect demanded it at a bare minimum. It wasn't a good sign. Ranjato was there, but I could hardly ask him directly. The village chief's slaves quickly informed me that Fara had been eliminated in the first round of performances, a fight had broken out between her and Faly, and, beside herself with disappointment, she'd fled the group of villagers who'd come to support her. Faly had gone after her to try to calm her down.

They left for Sahasoa the day after, and we never saw them. I felt sad for my former mistress and childhood friend. Her failure was also mine, and I felt her pain. Did her dream have to end in such misery?

Like all visitors, we could not enter the City of Thousands except with the Sovereign's express authorization. When Andriantsitoha was invited to present his offerings and assurances of allegiance at the Palace, he had a crazy moment of hope that he could address the Queen directly, but the formality was overseen much too closely for such ambitions. He stayed in the courtyard twenty paces away, standing under the blazing sun in a rigid pose of humility for the entire time that words were exchanged through vicarious elders. Queen Ranavalona was on her balcony, recognizable from the red umbrella that a lady in waiting held over her. Visibly annoyed, dying to get it over with, Mavo cast only a distracted glance over the two royal zebus led by Ibandro and the baskets of gifts that I and other slaves had carried to her representative's feet.

Andriantsitoha heaved a doubtful sigh as we went out the gate. "I'll come back and be heard," he muttered, bucking himself up. "I'll wait however long it takes."

First, we stayed with a rich member of the Zafimanelo clan, who my master compensated too much, I thought, for the miserly and self-seeking services rendered. The man, whose name was Andrianomena, rented us two huts of dubious quality for an exorbitant price. Andriantsitoha, Vola, and their two children took the larger one, and I shared the smaller with Ibandro. All the other members of the group were sent to Ambohimanarina, a town located an hour's walk away, where Andrianomena had a plot of land. My master asked me to accompany them, and I discovered upon arrival that the plot was a swamp. There was only one half-dilapidated mud house on a tiny mound of earth surrounded by water; you wouldn't even use it to shelter goats. I had to pay area farmers to agree to lodge our people. The same type of misfortune returned the beginning of our time there; far from helping matters, all the letters Andriantsitoha had sent served instead to attract all sorts of parasites, eager to strip the naïve provincial people bare.

Three moons after we arrived, however, my master seemed to figure out the situation and changed tactics. On his sister Rasoa's advice, he asked for and received authorization to buy a piece of land from a member of his clan, in a domain that King Nampoina had allocated to the Zafimanelos. We built three houses there, where all the wives and their children could live. We planted rice and grain fields in the plot's swampy part. Ibandro built a small enclosure, not far from the houses, and filled it with livestock.

Some time later, Rasoa introduced Andriantsitoha to one of the surviving wives of the former sovereign, King Nampoina, who took him into her service.

In all, we stayed in the City of Thousands for over ten years.

19

The Breath of the Bull
with Large Eyes

THE HARDEST THING was not being separated from Fara, but resisting
the temptation to return to her. My first years in the City were years of
waiting, of moments filled with confused and sometimes senseless hope
that I'd be hard-pressed to explain.

We still had strong channels back to Sahasoa. Andriantsitoha had taken
measures to retain control of his domain, despite the distance. Before
leaving Ambohimanelo, he'd put his brother Andriamady at the head of
the province.

"Andriamady will be my eyes in Ambohimanelo, but eyes do not see
the enemy until he is there, whereas ears can hear what is not there, hear
what memory has written in the words of mankind. I will also need the
people to be my ears."

A small number of loyal subjects, herdsmen or laborers, and a few of the
master's relatives were chosen to listen and report on rumors. My master had
created an elaborate system of ways to send his brother instructions, to keep
himself informed of the situation in the province, and, above all, to funnel
money and supplies to the capital—all well before our departure. Contrary
to what I'd initially thought, the journey was not a hastily made decision but
a project that had been planned since long before the Tendroarivo attack.

Furthermore, Andriantsitoha had assembled trustworthy people to help
with collection and shuttle back and forth between Ambohimanelo and the
City. He didn't want to give us that duty; Ibandro's and my presence in the

156

City was too precious, he said, to allow for such long absences. Moreover, the trips could be dangerous, and he didn't want to risk losing us. I suggested Tovo to him—the only member of the gang from the pond with whom I'd stayed on good terms.

Tovo, Vero's younger brother, was both a former playmate and a close friend of Bebe's family. He'd never shown any contempt or hostility toward me. Plus, he hated Faly, which I appreciated. Secretly, I hoped to hear a bit of news of Fara from him, even if I'd forbidden myself from going to Sahasoa out of pride and caution. Andriantsitoha agreed to take Tovo into his service, and I welcomed my friend with a mixture of joy and sadness each time he arrived.

"Vero left Sahasoa and the family home to follow the missionaries," he informed me one day.

I wasn't surprised, knowing Vero's disposition. Times had changed since our school years: the Sovereign had prohibited vazahas from all teaching and preaching activities, and the missionaries were leaving.

"How is she following them, if they're going across the oceans?"

"You think so? If you ask me, they haven't gone. They're hiding in the mountains and forests, waiting for the right moment to pop back up. They haven't exactly concealed their intentions."

Tovo told me that Blake had gathered his students one final time before closing the school. He'd set a challenge before them: "See, I am leaving you this Bible. If it contains not the word of God but that of vazaha ancestors, as your Sovereign claims, then it will be reduced to nothingness and you will one day forget its very existence. But if that is not the case, if the word of the true God is written inside, then nothing in this world will be able to stand against it!"

Listening to Tovo talk, my lips burned with a name that I didn't dream of pronouncing; it would have betrayed my internal agitation. To my overwhelming impatience, my friend only got to what I was most interested in after he'd exhausted every other piece of news from the seven moons that had gone by.

Fara broke up with Faly shortly after they returned to Sahasoa. Tovo didn't know why; the failure at the fampitaha final probably had something to do with it. Fara had had a few affairs after that, but none had lasted. She'd gone back to her loom, Tovo said.

"I often see her sitting under the old tree, you know, the fig tree where Bebe used to tell us stories? She looks a little lost to me sometimes."

"What about Bebe? And Bao? How are they?" I asked, to hide my emotion and change the subject as quickly as possible.

"The grandmother, she's a tree on the edge of a cliff, old boy. We only rarely see her telling the children stories, and that's a bad sign. I think Bao's troubles are weighing on her as well."

"What troubles?"

"You know what Fara's mother is like: men make her live and breathe. The amazing thing is that she still gets so brokenhearted when they reject her. People think she's a little unhinged."

"What happened to Faly?"

"He comes and goes. I don't know what he's plotting. Ranjato uses him for all sorts of things. And speaking of Ranjato," Tovo lowered his voice, "did you know that Andriamady is facing more and more criticism back home? The elders have deemed him weak, and aren't showing him any respect. I feel sorry for him sometimes. Ranjato is the most aggressive. Your prolonged absence is setting tongues wagging. And we're constantly on alert since you left."

"Have there been more assaults? In Sahasoa?"

"No, not in Sahasoa. But there have been more thefts of cattle and crops in the province. Fahavalos even came to the Anativolo market once, in broad daylight, when it was crowded."

"They were brazen enough to attack the market then?"

"No, they just walked around, as if they owned the place. They were there to show their force. Two hundred armed men. Some in military uniforms. Ever since, Ranjato has been pressuring the elders to negotiate with the groups that are issuing the threats, to placate them. They're bringing them goats and sacks of rice, sometimes money, so that they'll spare the village. But that didn't stop them from attacking a farmer and his family two weeks ago; they killed the oldest son, wounded the father, and carried off one of the daughters. The livestock vanished."

I was deep in thought when Tovo left, torn between having to keep pursuing my path and wanting to run back to Sahasoa. My dreams from the kalanoro valley came back to the surface. But at the same time, I was in the City—the place, they said, of all possible dreams. When you have one foot in the pirogue, as the saying goes, it's not an opportune time to try and go back where you came from.

Destiny had brought me here against my most fervent desire, but had kept this place from Fara, the one who dreamed only of it.

I was living a new existence, but it smelled of betrayal.

In the beginning, however, we had a favorable situation in the City of Thousands. Andriantsitoha immediately got along very well with his new benefactor, the royal wife.

This woman, one of the remaining former companions of the great King Nampoina, had lived alone since the monarch's death, having had no children. Rasoa, who'd had the idea to introduce her brother to her, seemed to bask in her affection. The royal wife generally looked favorably upon the Christians, although she was still very connected to ancestral values. She was a sharp-minded woman who did business with vazaha business-people in particular. Yet she was illiterate, and weary of being fleeced by the unscrupulous middlemen swarming the City, so she was looking for a trustworthy person to help her manage her estate.

Andriantsitoha was pleased to serve a sovereign's wife, even a little-known one—Nampoina had had over twenty of them, only a handful of whom had left their names to posterity. It was quite a respectable activity, especially since famous names still paid visits to the lady's home.

We made our first courtesy call to our benefactor with Rasoa.

Nenibe, as her neighbors called her, was an affectionate woman. She welcomed us informally and immediately started using Andriantsitoha's nickname, Tsifa. I introduced myself to the head household slave, an older man who answered to the extraordinary and uncommon name of Iarivolahimihaga. While the masters chatted, we served passion fruit juice—a fruit I hadn't known about before.

"I love this passion fruit's wild flavor!" said Andriantsitoha to our hostess. "How did you come by it, my lady?"

"Antalaotra traders sold me a few baskets. You wouldn't believe the range of amazing new things that they can bring to the kingdom! In fact, Tsifa, you'll have to negotiate with them often, since you'll be taking care of some little things for me . . . "

Squatting south of the hearth next to Iarivolahimihaga the slave, I flicked my eyes around the interior of Nenibe's hut. It was a sparse room, a little larger than average. At first glance, nothing indicated that a king had spent time there. But a large musket with a sculpted grip was nailed to the north wall, and two ivory powder horns hung below it. Elsewhere, all the utensils, from the serving fork to the pitcher, were arranged according to traditional rules. Impeccably clean and very sturdy in appearance, they nonetheless had the look of old things; I saw distinct marks on some of them, drawings or small nicks. I contemplated the stool north of the hearth and the raised bed in the northeast corner, imagining Nampoina relaxing here in between battles.

Iarivolahimihaga, the old slave, followed my gaze, smiled, and whispered, "Most of the objects you see here are what he used. We don't throw any of them out, and we only replace them when they get hopelessly worn. I was the one who loaded the musket when he went shooting."

The weapon had a name: Ihaoloahibefofonaina, the Breath of the Bull.

"Many people in my region are talking about Rainitsiandavana, the guardian of the talisman Zanaharitsimandry," said Andriantsitoha. "The one who converted to Christianity. What exactly has happened to him?"

"Oh yes, people in the City didn't talk about anything else back then! He was such a good man. Isn't that right, Rasoa my girl?"

"He was a saint! His light will always shine in our hearts."

"Really? But I heard he met a bad end."

"He never did anything bad at all, I'm sure," Nenibe snapped. "You know, Tsifa, some people here have the gall to sow fear and sorrow without reason the instant they acquire any bit of power. My husband never would have allowed that."

Andriantsitoha refrained from commenting. It seemed like the august lady didn't much like her late husband's daughter-in-law—the current Sovereign. My master looked around nervously, and I promised myself that I'd be careful to check if anyone was listening at Nenibe's door. I didn't have any desire to end up like Rainitsiandavana.

"Do you want a little rum in your passion fruit juice?" asked Nenibe. "It gives it a little kick. No? Are you sure? Right, I was telling you that this woman, this usurper—you know who I mean—she won't back down from anything . . . "

My master listened politely to the diatribe that followed, but was visibly worried. At one point, something pounded against the wooden side of the house. Andriantsitoha startled violently, and I jumped to my feet. But it was just a red rooster come to wander the room and peck at a few scattered grains of rice on the floor. I sat back down. We'd only been there for a short time, but already it felt too long.

However, the passion fruit rum seemed to inspire the mistress of the house: after knocking back a third glass, she lit a pipe and, in less time than it took to roast a grasshopper, started saying things that were serious enough to get an entire province exterminated. I remembered that the current Sovereign had wiped out the family of her late husband, King Radama, in order to ascend the throne.

I shivered at the thought. Andriantsitoha steered the conversation to business, as if he'd read my mind. He promised the old woman to keep precise records as well as a register of transactions, and offered to reorganize her network of intermediaries. After a few clarifications, she dissolved into grateful tears and embraced him warmly, moved by the rum.

When we left the royal wife's house, she was snoring on her mattress, a weak smile on her lips.

We still had to go to Mary the Christian woman's house with Rasoa. Soon afterward, I took over the bulk of the tasks writing and keeping accounts for Nenibe, leaving my master the time to cultivate his relationships with merchants and influential men, in which he excelled.

It was still fresh in people's minds, so we soon learned every last detail of the Rainitsiandavana incident, an epitome of those uncertain times. I don't know if Rainitsiandavana was truly a light for most people, as Rasoa had claimed, but he certainly altered the destinies of everyone around him.

Rainitsiandavana the holy man had been a poor farmer living in a northern district. Beset by great sorrow upon the death of his wife and son, he discovered Christianity one day. The man had been the talisman Zanaharitsimandry's guardian, but he'd felt personal loss as a failure of his ancestral sciences. He was illiterate but refused to educate himself, and he kept his talisman to serve the Holy Spirit from that point forward. He became a traveling preacher and attracted many disciples thanks to his oratorical skills. They said that everyone in the Mandiavato clan became his disciples. Rainitsiandavana wasn't worried about the fact that he'd never read the Holy Scriptures: God, he claimed, was teaching them directly to him, through dreams and inner revelations.

One day, after falling out with the missionaries, the preacher decided to bring the Good News directly to the kingdom's capital.

He arrived in the City of Thousands leading a procession of one thousand people arrayed in coral, gold, and silver. The Sovereign Queen, who'd caught wind of his reputation, dispatched messengers to receive the preacher at the entrance to the city. A crowd gathered, and Rainitsiandavana made a speech.

"This is what you must know, o my people. Nampoina and Radama live again. They crossed seven rivers and seven hills to return from the kingdom of the dead, thanks to the resurrection of the flesh. And by the grace of the Holy Spirit, rice will soon grow without you having to till the earth, and it will be the same for potatoes. You will no longer have to work, for this, the land of our ancestors, will become the land of paradise. And there will be no more war and no more suffering."

The Sovereign summoned him before her and asked him where Nampoina and Radama were, for she was eager to see them again. At his failure to make the former sovereigns of the kingdom appear, she rebuked him and threw him in prison to question him further. The next day, when the Queen asked him what the land of paradise was that he spoke of, Rainitsiandavana answered that it was the land of a couple named Adam and Eve, the father and mother of all men.

"Then I am of the same lineage as my slaves?!" cried the Queen .

"Yes, even the Queen," he replied.

She was furious, and the guards seized him. He was thrown headfirst into a pit with three of his companions, and the executioners filled it with boiling water. Seventeen of the preacher's other disciples were submitted to *tangena*. Eight of them died, and the survivors were thrown into slavery. His disciples were scattered, his village razed to the ground, and all the villagers' possessions split up among the Sovereign's officers.

20 *Fara*

HOW MANY MOONS, how many years have gone by since Tsito left? I don't know anymore. Time passes so quickly. What's he doing right now? How is his new life? What kind of work is he doing? It's weird, I miss the little slave. Sometimes in the evening I pick up the valiha and I pluck out a few notes in the silence. I remember the days we spent together in the fields, the games we played together. The fampitaha.

Sometimes I regret treating him so poorly. It was unfair. Why did I take pleasure in humiliating him? I don't really know, it was like I'd gone crazy. Fampitaha fever, probably. And Faly. Now I know that things were much better before. I have all kinds of memories of time with Tsito; even the most trifling details acquire new depth. I remember the *fampanononana* riddles we asked each other in the evening on our way back from school.

"Guess what I am: I've had my heart and guts taken out and it made me roll a little, but now it's easier to stay steady."

"Easy: a pirogue tree."

"I barely get wet in water and I never dry on land?"

"A shadow!"

When the weather was nice, we'd catch fish or crabs in creels in the river. Sometimes, we'd just sit in the grass on the highest point on a hill, watching the fields and rivers in the distance. We'd gaze out over the windswept expanse and squint at deserted and silent villages, looking for a familiar shape, whether human or zebu. When it rained, we'd cover ourselves with a woven square of bulrushes or a big palm-tree leaf. When the sun reappeared after the downpour, radiating heat through the shelter of leaves and tall grass, a light, earthy mist rose in the air, covering the ground and seeping into our clothes and hair.

I've realized that I almost don't think about Faly at all anymore. Faly let me down. He introduced me to love, but he scared me. There's a violence in him I don't understand. Would he have married me if we hadn't broken up? I'm don't even know that. I think I did the right thing, ending our relationship. At least failure at the fampitaha did something good. Faly is not your average boy, though, or common. His capacities, his strength, his courage, they all outstrip the men I've known since. But he's not a human being; he's a raging flood that sweeps away everything in its path. There's nothing restful in him, nothing reassuring. Everything is conflict, confrontation, challenge.

Still, I'll have to get married someday. I can't end up like my mother, can't be a forsaken woman, growing older and a little crazy. I won't stand for it. But I can't rush into something without thinking either. What happened the other day was a warning. By my father and mother! That's what's in store for me if I don't change something.

It was evening, I didn't hear them coming.

"Haody! Is anybody home?"

I'd been weaving quietly, leaning against the western wall, facing the hearth. I'd jumped, torn from my thoughts.

"I'm here! What can I do for you?"

"Are your parents here, my child?"

"My mother is stacking wood behind the house. My grandmother is resting in bed."

"Could you please call them?"

"Yes, sir."

I recognized the two men: the older was a rich farmer named Rafidy, and his companion, Laza, was a man known for his skill with words. My mother was surprised and a little intimidated. Bebe ignored her back pain and rose from the bed to pay the visitors her respects. I was asked to leave, which wasn't a good sign.

I stayed close enough to the family hut to grasp at least a little of what they were saying. "To begin with, I ask forgiveness from the elders present here for speaking my words before them. May resentment and disgrace vanish beneath seven mounds of earth and fall into the grave from which there is no return. Now: we have come to discuss a matter under the familial roof, and my kinsman here asked me to speak on his behalf."

But after a little while, I couldn't hear much more, since they lowered their voices.

Bao came out, emotional. "O apple of my eye, this is a marriage proposal!"

"What? He wants to marry you? I'm so happy for you!" I said, clapping my hands.

"Not me. You!"

The earth under my feet suddenly started burning like a bed of embers. A proposal! My heart started racing. My hand in marriage—but who was the suitor? Rafidy! The ground shifted again beneath my feet, this time slippery and treacherous as the foam-flecked stones sticking out of the water at the spring. Rafidy, the old farmer!

"But . . . I don't want to marry him!"

"Are you mad? You don't have a choice! You will prove yourself worthy of such an honor, do you hear me?"

"I don't wanna marry him! I don't wanna marry him!"

"Shut up, will you? How dare you say that to me! Do you want to live your life in disgrace?"

Bao slapped me and tried to gag me with her hand, but I wrenched myself free and dashed away.

Still, I had to know what was going on inside the hut. I crept back and slipped underneath the window to spy on them. They couldn't see me in the twilight.

Bebe, seeing Bao come back into the room looking defeated, knew instantly that things had gotten more complicated. But she probably expected that. I watched her rack her brains to come up with something, something to save the situation, preserve the family honor while not offending the visitors.

She had an idea. "You came knocking on our door with such boldness and fervor! We are overwhelmed, you have flattered our dignity. If it was for us alone to decide, Fara would be yours, but alas, we cannot act like she has been orphaned by her father. We cannot pretend that the wellspring from which her young existence spouted has dried up. Yes! Her father, the sun which saw her first stems and buds burst to life—he shines above our heads to this day, and we cannot give you consent that does not belong to us, nor approval that does not fall under our authority. That is why I will ask for your patience until we have had the chance to consult him."

The two men exchanged glances for a moment, unsure, before eventually taking their leave.

Satisfied with her performance, Bebe asked me to massage her back before going to sleep. Bao had already fallen asleep, still brimming with anger but exhausted from arguing with us.

My grandmother chuckled. "The father excuse was a little simplistic, but clever enough that no one can find fault with it. Men always have the last word in this community." Bebe groaned with pleasure from the pressure of my hands. She laughed again. "On the other hand, women's work does quite well on its own. I'll simply tell the suitor that the father has refused."

I dug out Tsito's farewell letter. There's a certain pleasure in reading it again, stroking the box sculpted from zafimaniry wood. The words are written in neat, tight rows all along an imaginary line. Tsito has always had a strong preference for things in the proper order.

The third day of the Alahasaty moon
My honorable mistress, Rafaramanorosoa,

I pray that you may reach an old age and that illness will stay away. I write to you on this day to express my devotion and unwavering loyalty to you, for the thought of you is as dear to me as my eyes, the windows of my soul, and that I wish for you to glide on sugar and swim in honey. I am your servant now and forevermore, even when I've grown up and accomplished my duty in the community.

For when I grow up, I will not forget you, and I will always kiss the soles of your feet. I will be your rock as Jehova was for David, and I will

*be the steadfast tree that accompanies your final days. As Kristy said, I
was thirsty and you gave me water to drink, I was hungry and you gave
me bread to eat. And I will be like him, you be sure of that.*

*For you are my only path and my only destiny, and you will never have
to be afraid, for I will always be there.*

*Your very devoted servant, and also a child who saw you bloom among
the most beautiful flowers in the Garden of Eden,*

Tsimatahobario Andriampanoha, known as Tsito

I know Tovo goes to the City of Thousands once or twice a year. I envy him.
He sees Tsito there. I wonder if they talk about me. Tovo kind of clams up
on the subject, oddly enough. He also doesn't talk about exactly what he
does with Andriantsitoha's servants. He tries not to associate himself with
them too much here, but I know he meets up with them all the time on
his way to the City. I think he's spying on the elders to report back to the
provincial lord. Why doesn't Andriantsitoha come back?

A toxic atmosphere hangs over the province. Two moons ago, someone set fire to the rice silo belonging to Andriamady. They breached the
trenches at night and spread oil, dried straw, and scraps of cloth. It went
up in flames in a few seconds. An entire harvest was lost. Andriamady
cried like a child. It was distressing. Who could have done such a thing?
Someone's trying to provoke something. There are more and more strangers
prowling the area. They even came to the Anativolo market one time. But
they might have accomplices.

Two weeks later, someone desecrated some Zafimanelo vaults, including Andriantsitoha's family's. We could barely believe it—wouldn't they
be scared of the ancestors' curse? They dug holes in the tombs, and went
inside and burned something, probably witch's incense; the odor spread for
three fields. Crocodile teeth and bird carcasses were found by the tombs.

And three days after that, we saw shadows dancing on the walls in
Tendroarivo. No one wanted to believe us, but we definitely saw them. It
was the middle of the night; my mother was unwell and we weren't sleeping. We can see Tendroarivo quite clearly from the northeast of the house.

The elders said that it wasn't possible, the sentries would have seen it, but there were shadows, I'm positive; they cut a clear figure in the full moon. They were dancing a grotesque, terrifying dance.

Andriamady and the elders have been arguing constantly since the vaults were desecrated. The influential men claim it was bandits or witches from a neighboring district; the Zafimanelos are crying a new conspiracy against their clan. Now, they've armed their slaves, which only exacerbates the tension.

Our land is becoming more and more inhospitable. I wonder if I'll live in the City someday.

21 *Tsito*

Gunpowder and the Torture of Cannons

THE SITUATION in our little community in the City soon started to deteriorate. It didn't come as much of a surprise, because the whole enterprise in itself was an enterprise born from a single man's mind. I now knew for sure that Andriantsitoha had long conceived of the project to establish himself in the City of Thousands. He'd already harbored the idea during King Radama's funeral. He never gave it up—and it was somehow to our great misfortune.

However, Andriantsitoha had enlarged his network of contacts since we'd arrived in the capital. My master had gained access to several sectors and strengthened friendly relationships or connections of convenience to a number of influential people. But he'd had only mitigated success and hadn't won any tangible advantage; powerful men didn't trust him and neglected to include him in their projects and plots. There was one essential reason for that: money. Our resources were vanishing before our very eyes.

Because of repeated shortages and poor harvests starting in the sixth year of our stay, yields from the Ambohimanelo province had been thinning out, compromising our means of sustenance. Nenibe was a charming woman, but she'd made her business prosper by paying a miser's wages to the people who helped her; we couldn't hope for anything from that angle. Some years, we survived only on the rice and grain fields my master had bought—Ibandro and I worked them doggedly, but had meager results.

"The poor are not friends of the affluent," the ancestral adage goes. Even his clan members started treating Andriantsitoha with tenser, slightly contemptuous manners.

Our initial decline was even crueler as negotiations for power and privilege intensified around us.

The privileged circles of the City, which we came to know from Nenibe, were driven by an intense hunger for change. The august lady opened her home to all that the kingdom had to offer of plotters and parasites. The kings' close relatives came to envision a kingdom in the image of vazaha monarchies, which they in truth only had a murky concept of. Some of them even made known their wishes for a foreign invasion. Others came to glorify secret associations with untold goals, whose ramifications spread beyond the seas, and whose gruesome initiation rites were cause for concern.

I fear that the frivolities of powerful men have persisted to this day.

Most people grumbling at Nenibe's house were rich men angling to get the best position for their interests, but a small number were motivated by the strength of their convictions, as in the case of the Christians. From Andriantsitoha's point of view, they had the potential to be even more dangerous. They had a particular talent for inciting crowds. And attracting the eye of the Bull.

"I will never worship the vazahas' ancestors!" exclaimed the Sovereign in a speech. "Out of the question! I am the keeper of the honor of the twelve sovereigns, and I intend to preserve it!"

In the City, we experienced these tensions almost daily. A woman called Rasalama had recently been speared, by order of the Palace, for having refused to renounce her rebellious beliefs. She had proclaimed defiant words until her death. After that first martyr, the converts' passions flared, and hostility toward them kept mounting. The relationship between Rasoa and Andriantsitoha suffered from it, to the brother's great consternation. His Christian sister was increasingly the target of her brother's distrust and disapproving remarks. She was starting to keep her distance.

In the winter of the seventh year, the darkness looming over us descended even further. I still remember perfectly what happened. It was an afternoon like any other: Ibandro and I were doing the impossible, wresting a few seeds from our field, despite the dry season. We'd managed to divert water in to irrigate the plants, thanks to long bamboo stalks and channels dug to adequate levels. Spades in hand and sweat on our foreheads, we surveyed our work with a glimmer of hope. Suddenly, we saw a group of children racing down the hill.

"Come quickly! The master is ill!"

As we ran toward Andriantsitoha's house, we saw him coming toward us, his face flushed. He wasn't sick; he was boiling over with rage. Storming out of his hut, he snapped his cane in frustration and stumbled, landing face first on the ground—the children were alarmed.

At first, we couldn't understand his ranting. "We must defend ourselves! It's all a huge plot. I've got it from a solid source now! Everything was set in motion a long time ago!"

My master had gotten much thinner and his eyes more hollow since Rasoa had started ignoring us. He wasn't sleeping much anymore.

"They want to strip us of everything. They're pressuring the Palace to make my province part of the royal domain!"

Andriantsitoha was shouting himself hoarse. Informants had revealed to him that Andriantsoly—the very same Palace officer who had wanted to sell him a customs post several years earlier—had set his sights on Ambohimanelo and a few neighboring territories.

If the province was transferred into the royal saddlebags, Andriantsitoha would lose not only his sovereignty, but all his resources as well, including the use of his ancestral lands. It would plunge him into poverty and destitution. Andriantsoly, the presumed architect of the conspiracy, had hauled himself up to a lofty rank within the military hierarchy since our last meeting with him: now he commanded an entire corps of the Sovereign's tax collectors. He received a share of every new contribution and, like many people, took a little extra for himself, too.

"The man asked about us after we met. He's been on our trail for a long time. He's circling above us like a vulture. He was behind the provocations in Ambohimanelo! He was behind the desecration of the vaults, too! He has accomplices on the ground there."

"Who do you think they are, my lord?" asked Ibandro.

"There's at least one we've sensed for a long time: Ranjato. Yes, Ranjato! That old rat, so quick to negotiate with thieves and assassins. But oh, he'll get what's coming to him!"

As for me, at first, I had doubts about the truth of where such a plot originated. Andriantsitoha was so obsessed with the idea for such a long time that I eventually grew suspicious. I wouldn't have disputed that there were enemies in Ambohimanelo, but I was inclined to think that his indecision and arbitrary projects explained a large part of the discontent. And that didn't take into account how he infringed upon the ancestral rules: How had he had money and crops collected beyond what he was due without prior authorization from the Sovereign, the sole mistress and owner of the land? Plus, I wasn't convinced that the elders could have stooped so low as to be traitors. There was a step between disapproval of a misguided lord and association with a horde of raging dogs to sell out their own community, a step that I didn't think they could make.

But while I was walking back to Nenibe's house a few days later, the sky suddenly caught fire above my head. I'd taken a shortcut, an isolated path withdrawn from residential areas. Terrified, convinced that the Perfumed Lord had chosen to burn up my miserable existence, I threw myself to the ground to avoid the fiery cinders falling on my hair and shoulders. My fear mutated into bewilderment, then anger as I heard the cackling, surging back from the past almost entirely intact.

"Well well well, little slave—he can grow as much as he wants, but his mind is still small, huh? Look at that! A little fire, nothing special: that's all it takes to scare him!"

"You? What are you doing here? And what is that sorcery?"

With mock concern, Faly showed me a small vial filled with a brown substance. He tapped a small trail out onto the ground and set fire to it with a flint striker. It screamed like an angry cat and cut a blackish scar into the clay.

"It's only powder, o my favored slave. Good black gunpowder, for cannons. It's very useful for sending chunks of scrap metal to pulverize the flesh of the kingdom's enemies."

He hadn't changed much. His tall figure was just a little more sunken. His grin was the same: fixed, sardonic, all violence and force. I got ready to defend myself. However, my old rival seemed to have other ideas.

"Didja know that Arabs lashed rebels across the mouth of a cannon to execute them? I'll have to save that torture for you someday. That'd teach you to think about breaking the ancestral rules of group separation. Anyway, has your master Andriantsitoha succeeded? Has he made a lord out of you now? If what I hear is right, you're still wallowing in mud in the rice fields, aren't you?"

"I don't have to waste my time talking to you. Continue along your way."

"Ooh, it's wild how bad-tempered these little animals get when they get bigger!"

"I already almost drowned you once. You remember that? I can still make you go laugh with the worms in a tomb."

He went pale. And he pulled a knife from a fold in his wrapper.

"Oh yeah? May I be cursed to the seventh generation if I don't slit your belly open first!"

I grabbed a large rock that I'd spotted off to the side. I felt sweat running down my forehead, and my ears were ringing. I was determined to kill him this time.

Faly saw that in my eyes, and it seemed to amuse him. And calm him down. He put his knife away coolly, and smiled.

"A man doesn't lower himself so much as to fight a slave. I have better things in mind for you. Did you know I'm working for the Sovereign now? Yeah, it's true: I'm working in the royal magazine. One of the Commander in Chief's aide-de-camps took me under his protection. Making gunpowder's a fascinating process!"

I chucked the rock into the bushes. "Get out of my way. I don't care what you're doing," I said, starting to walk away.

"But I'm doing other things that you might be interested in, too, regarding your master. Your destinies are tied together; it'll do you good to know it, too. You're dying to know more, aren't you?"

"No."

I watched him as I walked away. His last words snared me like a wild animal—growling, gnashing. "Hey, slave, your noble lord will soon be begging in the streets! It's over for him. You, too. If I were him, I'd start looking for some honest work to survive off of as soon as possible: a servant for a vazaha, maybe. Or a rich man's slave! You can give him advice, you've got experience at that!"

Tovo came to the City the next week. He hadn't made the trip for almost a year because of the problems undermining the province. He brought more bad news.

"Vero came back to Sahasoa a little over a moon ago. After more than four years away."

"I'm so happy for you! You don't look very happy about it, though."

"She's already left again. She only stayed for a brief time. Something happened while she was there . . . "

Vero didn't come back simply to see her family. Her visit to Sahasoa had an objective: to convert the population.

Ever since the Sovereign had prohibited their religion and ordered everyone who'd gotten baptized to turn themselves in under pain of death, countryside Christians had gone into hiding to practice their faith. Unlike their City brethren, who had some support, they were hunted relentlessly by the authorities. But instead of fizzling out after the missionaries left, their coalition had acquired new energy. Some of the faithful had converted their houses into secret meeting places. Others refused to burn their holy books and hid in caves or empty tombs in order to keep reading them. And, despite the danger, some had undertaken the task of spreading their faith.

Vero was among the latter—and it didn't surprise me either. It was just like her.

"She said that the days of the 'kingdom of darkness' are numbered," Tovo said. "And that several renowned seers had renounced their talismans and ancestral beliefs to join the Kristy movement. And that people who read the Baiboly now numbered in the tens of thousands."

When they'd tried to make her see reason, Vero had told them the story of Rasalama.

"Apparently, the woman went to her death praying and singing hymns! Can you believe it?"

"It's true. It strengthened their movement."

"But that's madness! Do they find joy in death, then?"

"Perhaps. Tell me exactly what happened in Sahasoa."

Going against her family and friends' advice, Vero went from house to house to preach her beliefs. At first, when people found out she'd returned, they welcomed her and listened to her. But as soon as they found out how contemptuously her group was viewed, they became terrified and threw her out. News of what she was trying to do had spread very quickly.

"She even tried to convert Andriamady!" said Tovo. "Can you imagine that?"

"Unbelievable! What did he say?"

"He cut her off after three sentences. 'Why would I care about this? Besides, a child's speech is not for lords to hear. Didn't your parents teach you anything?' I almost felt sorry for her."

"Don't feel bad for her. She's stronger than the rest of us."

"Manantsindry the seer and another elder came to chide my parents afterward. Manantsindry advised them to bathe Vero in the pond, as he said, to cleanse the vapors affecting her!"

The day before Vero left, she'd gone to see Fara. Tovo had gone with her to Bebe's house. Vero had begged her friends, "Come with me! Save your soul and leave this ungodly place! You have already heard the Truth! You're not like them!"

They had refused. Fara and Tovo had walked her to the entrance of the village early the next morning. Vero took off her sandals before the great rolling gate stone and shook the dust off of them.

"What are you doing?" Fara had asked.

"I'm doing what the Lord told us to do," she'd answered, and put her sandals back on her feet.

Vero's time in Sahasoa had had repercussions for the entire province. Before giving Andriantsitoha his report, Tovo got worried about my master's reaction. "Don't be scared," I told him. "None of this is your fault."

Ibandro was there, too. The provincial lord and his head slave listened to my friend's tale in silence.

"And Ranjato reported the incident regarding my sister directly on high, without going through Lord Andriamady."

"On high?" said Andriantsitoha. "What do you mean?"

"He sent a messenger here, to the City. His name is Rasendra—you remember, the one who spoke for the tomb repair?"

"I know him. Go on."

"He's supposed to go see a Palace dignitary, I don't know who. To inform the Queen that there are still insurrections going unpunished in your province. And that you, or your brother, are refusing to obey royal orders."

Andriantsitoha's hand spasmed uncontrollably and four deep furrows creased his forehead. Ibandro looked at me; we had the same thought. People here had lost their heads for less serious accusations.

And it didn't stop there. Ranjato hadn't waited for his messengers to come back from the Palace with an answer. He'd taken it upon himself to gather the population and demand that they obey the royal injunctions. "Our Sovereign, may she grow old safe from illness, has ordered those among us who were baptized or participated in a Christian service to turn themselves in, under penalty of death! Will we, the People Under the Day, betray the ancestors of our sovereigns? The spirits of the twelve kings of the twelve sacred hills live now in the body of our Sovereign, may she grow old alongside her grandchildren! Will we betray her trust? No, I say to you! I

177

would rather death take me this instant, along with all of my descendants, than disappoint our Sovereign!"

"What do you expect from us, Ranjato?" asked someone in the crowd. "I don't think there are hidden Christians among us. All these things happened in the City of Thousands, not here!"

"That's right! What do you want? And why isn't Lord Andriamady here? Are you speaking on his behalf?"

"I speak not on the behalf of a common lord but our Sovereign! Are you all deaf, or have you lost your minds, that you haven't heard her voice? The Sovereign is mistress of all words! Why do you think we're safe from opposition forces? What makes you think Christian vermin have overlooked our communities? Just this very morning, I've heard reports of their insidious attempts! Yes, even here in Sahasoa!"

"You mean that crazy girl, Randria's youngest? She couldn't even convert a fool! Besides, she left!"

"You talk so smoothly—what, did you get right up close and personal with her, to be so confident of her talents?" the village chief shot back. "Do you think that spitting out a few words here will be enough to establish your innocence? How do we know that you're telling the truth?"

The villagers exchanged glances. Ranjato's words were making them afraid.

"Our Sovereign expects us, collectively, to turn ourselves in. Even if there is but one guilty person in a thousand and five thousand, our villages must be purified! I have read the auspicious days in seeds! It must be done before this moon wanes!"

When Andriamady was finally alerted by the villagers, the crowd had already dispersed. Ranjato was summoned, but showed no remorse. "Yes, my lord," he said. "I took the initiative to summon the people, for these were our Sovereign's orders. And we cannot suffer any delay. I could not wait for your arrival."

"But I am the lord of this province!"

"Apologies, my lord, but I was not aware that your brother had died," said Ranjato.

"What are you saying? My brother is not dead; he is away. And in his absence, I am his replacement!"

"I was told that Lord Andriantsitoha was settling in the City. Absurd, isn't it? I'll have my servants punished for spreading such gossip, don't you worry, Andriamady. Forgive me for being so bold as to address you as such, but I was already on a first-name basis with your father. Anyway, do you think I was right or wrong to assemble the people to remind them of the Sovereign's word?"

"Uh, you were right, Chief Ranjato. But—"

"I appreciate your perceptiveness, Andriamady."

Andriantsitoha was livid.

Silence fell. I cleared my throat and spoke. "My lord, there's something else I must tell you."

I told him about my encounter with Faly and explained the kinship linking our old playmate with Ranjato.

Tovo wasn't surprised to learn that Faly was in the City. "It has been several moons since he disappeared. We were wondering where he'd gone. That explains everything."

Andriantsitoha stood up and started pacing around the room.

"He must have been sent here to spy on us. But the most pressing matter is to find that messenger. They're probably together, at any rate. Tsito, where does this Faly work, did you say?"

"At the magazine, my lord."

The building was on a ridge next to the royal hill. We were there less than an hour later. We stayed a short distance away at first; Andriantsitoha sent two men ahead to scout. But their investigation was in vain: neither Faly nor Rasendra the messenger could be found. The men in charge told them that Faly had been summoned to see his protector, an aide-de-camp to the Commander in Chief. As for Rasendra, they didn't know who he was.

"Alright, let's go to the Palace!" Andriantsitoha decided.

After a short search, Ibandro was the one to find the messenger, just outside the Palace. The man had requested to meet with a high judge who was close to the Sovereign, but the judge was occupied with other matters and told his men to have him wait. The atmosphere in the City had turned decidedly denunciatory: informants and other zealous assistants in the kingdom crowded into the outer courtyard, where the guards kept them waiting.

Ibandro hailed the one called Rasendra, who was gripped with fear, and led him behind a large tree, where Andriantsitoha was waiting.

"What are you doing here?" the lord of Ambohimanelo asked him.

"I came under Ranjato's orders, my lord."

"I've heard that you came to see a judge. What about?"

"There were Christians who came to Sahasoa to try and make the people rise up against our Sovereign, and Ranjato gave me the mission to alert the Palace and have them send they-who-call-forth-the-tangena-spirit."

"Christians? Which Christians?"

"We don't know exactly how many, my lord, but there had to be a lot of them. A woman even had the audacity to harass people in the streets."

"Tell me—how long has Ranjato been summoning the people in my place? Who is this taro root trying to rise above the banana tree? And why do you obey him, while my brother is the one in the province who stands for me? Are you a traitor? Trying to support a new lord?"

"He said that we had to obey orders from our Sovereign Mistress, my lord!" cried Rasendra, terrified.

For a moment, Andriantsitoha stared furiously at the man. Then, he beckoned to us and we walked away toward our residence, to Rasendra's immense relief. Ibandro alone stayed behind.

That evening, when my friend came back, I asked him what had become of Rasendra.

"I told him that the lord's orders were for him to leave immediately, without talking to anyone."

"Oh. And did he agree to?"

Ibandro shrugged. "You're kidding, right? The guy was all too happy to get off so lightly. Still, I escorted him to the city gates, to make sure he'd keep his word. I just told him that the next time, I'd rip his head off with my own bare hands. Sometimes you need to make a convincing argument."

I slept poorly that night. I dreamed that I was back in the village of my birth, deep in the forest. My father and mother were with me, reappeared from my long-ago past. Their faces were blurred. I embraced them in tears and promised never to leave them again, promised to protect them. Suddenly, there was an explosion, and soldiers attacked us. A soldier was shouting and running toward us, and I took aim with my gun and shot him. I knelt over the body and, despite the blood smeared on him, recognized Tovo's face . . .

A noise woke me up. There was someone outside. I rolled over, looking to where Ibandro slept, but saw that he wasn't there. I wasn't worried: he sometimes took nocturnal adventures to go on patrol or visit women. Even witches got out of his way. Still, I picked up the knife I always kept within arm's reach and stepped out into the night as silently as possible.

Andriantsitoha had gotten up. He was frozen, looking toward the royal hill. He wasn't alone. Half of the household had woken up and was looking in the same direction. A very bright light shone in the distance.

"What is that? A fire?" I asked one of the slaves there.

"I don't know. There was a huge explosion. That's what woke us up."

Andriantsitoha instructed his people to go back to sleep, then turned to me. I couldn't see the expression on his face in the dark.

"Tsito, I'm going to need you very early tomorrow morning. We have many things to do."

I went back to sleep and awoke to the crowing rooster. Ibandro had returned and was asleep. Outside, the housekeepers and other slaves were already discussing the news: a Palace gunpowder magazine had exploded. An accident. Five men lived and worked within its walls, and three carbonized bodies had been found. The other two had disappeared. Vaporized.

I washed my face with cool water and headed for Andriantsitoha's hut.

Word on the street was that the Sovereign was deeply distressed. It wasn't the first time an accident like that had happened. I grieved for the servants who had perished.

I'd be lying if I said that I was sad about Faly.

22

The Taro and
Banana Tree Meet

ANDRIANTSITOHA SENT ME to Ambohimanelo. Ibandro and I were charged with helping Andriamady put the province's affairs back in order. Thus, after many long years, I again saw the country where destiny's hand had once set me down. Again I saw the land that the joys of childhood had knit more strongly to my soul than any ancestral ties. When we came into view of Sahasoa, I couldn't keep the tears from coming. Nothing had changed: the terraced bluff of rice fields was still there, with the little valley and the pond.

Ibandro smiled and set his hand on my shoulder, and I was grateful to my friend at that moment. I couldn't look too closely to the southeast, where Bebe's house was. Luckily, we went straight to Ranjato's house, which was on the north side of the village.

Ibandro knocked roughly on the door, as usual. "Haody! Is anyone there?"

"Yes, who is it?"

An elderly woman appeared in the entrance. She recognized the head slave. "Ibandro? I didn't know that you were here! What news do you bring? What can I do for you, sir?"

The old woman was friendly and sweet. I suddenly felt awfully guilty: we'd come here to rebuke them. And give them dire news.

"We'd like to see *Ingahy* Ranjato, ma'am, thank you. We're here on behalf of the lord of Ambohimanelo."

"Of course. Please, come in. He's resting in bed. I'll call him."

But Ranjato had heard us and was already up, standing firm in the middle of the room, making us come to him, his expression severe and critical. Hardly affected by Ibandro's enormous build.

Ranjato was a very respected elder in the community. He was one of the richest men in the province. He owned a dozen rice fields, four or five houses, more than two thousand head of cattle. His clan was part of a venerable coalition that had helped establish King Nampoina's power. In their time, some of his ancestors had been on a first-name basis with the highland monarchs. This man had a certain distrust for the lords of provinces on the outskirts, who, like Andriantsitoha, were falling out of fashion—and he made no secret of it.

"What're you here for, Ibandro? If you've come here to my house to teach me some lesson on your master's behalf, you'd better leave now; I will not tolerate insolent words from a slave."

Ibandro smiled and spoke in his most humble voice. "My lord, I beg your pardon for having even thought of approaching your home without an invitation. Grant me your indulgence. I know that I am not worthy of speaking as I do in the presence of elders—"

"What's your master doing in the City? When are you coming back? If the lord has something to tell me, he should send his brother; I don't see how I can have anything to do with someone like you."

Ranjato's wife looked worried, glancing back and forth between her husband and the colossus.

Ibandro's smile broadened. "The fact of the matter is, I could not permit myself to have any semblance of a discussion with you, my lord. I have but two things to deliver to you from my master: a sign of his esteem and a message."

"A sign of what? You'd best not be mocking me, boy."

I watched Ibandro put his hand into his bag, my heart beating fast, and heard him reply in an even tone, as in a dream. "Mock you? What an idea! Far from it. Here, this is for you."

What he chucked to Ranjato struck him straight in his chest, and he yelped. His wife screamed as the round thing rolled to their feet. It was the messenger Rasendra's head.

The next instant, Ranjato had been swept off the ground: Ibandro was holding him in one hand by the collar of his garment, growling in his face. "Here's the message, old fool: the next time that the taro has fantasies of growing taller than the banana tree, it will be decimated like its messenger and ripped out of the ground by its very roots. As for your spy who worked in the gunpowder magazine, know this: he wasn't very lucky. He went up in smoke."

There was a dull thud: Ranjato's wife had fainted. Horrified, I bolted from the hut.

I had only one thought: to run away, as far as possible.

To flee from the confrontation, I wanted no part of it. Rasendra's head had traveled the whole way with us, packed neatly in my companion's bag. It made me nauseated. I left the village, taking the first path at random. I realized how naïve I'd been: How could I have believed for a single instant that the magazine explosion had been an accident? Deep down, I'd already known that it was Ibandro, but had refused to believe it. I laughed bitterly. What had I really hoped for? What had I come to do here, with Ibandro?

"Tsito?"

The woman's voice stopped me cold. I didn't recognize it, and yet there was something in the intonation, solid and deep—an inexplicable, familiar gentleness. It was her. I looked up; she was in front of me.

"Tsito?" she said again. "I didn't know you were back."

Fara was a mature woman now. She was coming back from the market; one of her hands held a basket with tufts of vegetables poking out, and the other balanced a small earthenware pot on her head, probably honey or a spice. Time had made her still more beautiful. Her silhouette, to my eyes that had embraced it a thousand times, still had an ethereal quality to it, calling to mind the fampitaha, slender adolescence. But childlike grace had relinquished its place to a full, shapely figure that pleased the eye, a lovely, blooming flower—intoxicating. I was dumb for a long time, and only recovered my senses when she narrowed her eyes with impatience.

"Tsito? What's wrong with you?"

"Uh . . . my apologies. Yes, ma'am, Andriantsitoha instructed us to deliver a . . . message. How have you been? Your mother and grandmother, are they well?"

I wanted desperately to take back those cold, formal words. I said such flat, insipid things while my entire soul was boiling over. But I tried to appear normal, afraid that if I let myself be conquered by my emotions, she'd take me for a madman.

"Why haven't you written to us this whole time? Bebe is very old now."

She stepped toward me, increasing my anxiety. She looked at me hard. "She thinks that you forgot us. That you don't love us anymore. What did we do to you to deserve that?"

Suddenly, I was flooded with remorse. The truth appeared to me, plain as day: in my blindness and hatred, I had cut all ties with those dearest to me. With superhuman effort, I held back the tears coming to my eyes; I didn't want to add ridicule to insult. Yes, I'd abandoned my wellspring, my hearth, my home, the most precious part of my existence. This much was clear now. I'd only been following my vanity. I was worse than Andriantsitoha. I'd been a coward, and all the regret in the world couldn't fix it. But Fara was here, in front of me. I opened my mouth to attempt the impossible, to redeem myself.

A man's voice interrupted, and I lost my momentum. "I've been looking for you everywhere, my friend. What got into you? I didn't know you were so sensitive."

Ibandro greeted Fara, giving her a big smile. She peered at us questioningly.

"What's going on?" she asked Ibandro.

"Nothing, mistress Fara," he laughed. "I just played a trick on our friend here; I can be pretty childish from time to time, you know. He seems to be too easily upset, though."

While Ibandro talked, a name crossed my mind: Faly. My old adversary was now in the kingdom of shadows. Did he deserve that? Did Fara still love him? Should I break the news to her of his death? She'd find out sooner or later. But I couldn't: speaking his name out loud, I felt, would erect a barrier between us. Another one. I couldn't think about it anymore. Even in death, Faly was a plague on my life.

"Fara. We have to go now," I finally said. "But I promise to come visit tomorrow. I have to see Bebe and Bao. We should talk."

She nodded her head—very well—but said not a word. After one final look, she continued down the path.

I didn't get a wink of sleep that night. My regrets and doubts only grew, and anxiety kept me awake until the rooster's crowing.

Ibandro and I had spent the rest of the day helping Andriamady rally his clan. The Zafimanelos had been arguing with the elders ever since the vaults were desecrated, and they'd foamed furiously when they learned how Ranjato had tried to condemn them. Exhausting, endless discussions had followed: people called for retribution and violent revenge, but no one followed through on anything. The clan was made up of farmers and craftsmen: they had only a weak force to deploy. And as for influence over the people? They had almost none, especially in Andriantsitoha's absence.

I went back to Sahasoa alone. The bright-orange morning light illuminated Bebe's hut from afar, with its woven palm-leaf roof with a thin white curl of smoke rising from it. The house looked smaller than I remembered it, and more run-down, slumped like an old woman under the weight of years. I stopped at the tall fig tree and traced my fingers over its familiar bark. I could still make out a few carvings: "Tsito . . . Fara, 1827." The roots were brown with dust; the earth around it, now almost bare, was red and cracked; a yellow-and-black spider had constructed its web over the opening at the tree's base, where we used to slip through as children.

Bao and Fara weren't there.

Bebe didn't recognize me at first. Her sole good eye couldn't make out much anymore, not even in front of her face. I also looked and sounded different. I had to speak my name right in her ear.

"Tsito? Is it true? You've come back, praise the Perfumed Lord!"

I gave her the presents that I'd bought the day before from the Zafimanelos: a new kitchen knife for her, an engraved pewter bracelet for Bao, and an embroidered lamba shawl for Fara.

She thanked me and kissed my hands. I was overwhelmed with sorrow and discomfort.

"Fara left early this morning to sell raffia garments at a market half a day's walk from here. Oh, but you know it: you went there yourself once. I remember now, she told me yesterday that you'd arrived. Oh, my boy, my memory is failing me terribly with my old age. I'd been trying to remember since this morning what Fara told me; she spoke of a happy event that would occur today, but what? And I'd promised myself I wouldn't forget it . . . Oh, my Creator, I prayed, what joy do you have reserved for me today, and why won't you give me a little memory, that I might be glad of it in advance? But the Creator is mischievous with the old! Anyway, here you are. Let me kiss you again, my child."

When our tears had dried, I asked Bebe if Fara had left a message for me. Again, the grandmother was unable to remember. But I hadn't hoped for much. Bao had been gone for several days, most likely still huddling in the arms of some temporary lover.

I had to leave that night. I didn't try to see Fara again. The truth was, she'd left an explicit message: her absence. It was perfectly clear. Our paths diverged anew.

Eight moons later, in the City, when Tovo told me that Fara had gotten together with a soldier and was expecting a child, I asked Andriantsitoha's permission to go to Mantasoa to hone my craft under Laborde. I'd made the acquaintance of an ironworker named Rainimahery, who did a lot of work in the Frenchman's workshops. Mostly, I wanted to try to fill the void that had opened up in me and get away from any violent plots.

My master resisted at first but eventually agreed. Laborde was the most influential man in the kingdom: the skills I could gain there—and the relationships, too—could only serve his interests.

23 *Fara*

CAN I EVER HAVE A TRUE HOME? Sometimes, I understand my mother's turmoil. Love is like rice, as the proverb says: when you transplant it, it grows, but never in the same way. It retains a bittersweet memory of its first soils. Every time it is uprooted, it dies a little; every time it is replanted, it loses a piece of its soul.

But it also bears fruit. I bore a daughter, my first child. She has no father, life is a rebirth. I named her Ravoromihanta, or Hanta. I see my destiny in that smooshed little face, that chubby body. Bebe kept a steamy heat in the family hut up until the birth. My grandmother also burned a torchwick tied to the trunk of a banana tree for the whole time, as the ancestral rules dictate. It was suffocating. I'm glad it's over.

One week after Hanta's birth, she was laden with bracelets and presented to the sun. Tovo was chosen to represent those whose father and mother are still living, and he carried the baby around the house several times, followed by a young girl carrying a basket. I watched them process from the doorway, still weak but happy to have produced a child.

"Hail to you! The Creator has given you a descendant!" people said.

I drank a broth of tiny shrimps to stimulate my milk. My breasts became hard and painful, like a cramped muscle. The pain fades as she suckles but comes back if the feedings happen too far apart.

Fortunately, Hanta has a good appetite: she greedily slurps down what gushes out. Sometimes she chokes and lets the tit drop, daubing milk onto her face. I love that. I give thanks to the Creator for letting me live with my family in this little hut, where milk flows in abundance.

"Did the Sovereign Queen also nurse her son in her Palace?" I asked my grandmother one evening.

Bebe put down the large spoon she'd been using to stir the rice in the large pot, and wiped away the drops of sweat glistening on her forehead. "Of course. Sovereigns don't burst out from inside the earth. Their wellspring, like ours, is in the family of mankind."

"But they must have power that we do not, otherwise why would they be holy?"

"The ancestors say, 'They can rise to the top as cream does, but milk will always reveal a common ancestor.'"

Sometimes I wonder what I can possibly offer this child.

I've never had a real home myself. I see my father every other year; my mother can't stay three days in a row in her own house. The man who gave Hanta life will probably never come back to Sahasoa.

I met Andrianarivo, Hanta's father, when celebrating the construction of a new tomb. Maybe that was a sign from our ancestors. He was going to join a commander at the fort; he'd been named aide-de-camp. That position gave him more freedom than his fellow soldiers had, so he was able to make a long supply stop in Tendroarivo. When the soldiers at the bivouac found out that we were getting ready for a party in Sahasoa, they decided to come visit the village.

I noticed him right away out of all the men in uniform. He wore slightly different clothes: his appearance was more carefully put together than his friends', whose clothes were red with dust. He was also younger than his brothers in arms, and he looked resolute, full of promise. He approached me, and his words seduced me from the first moment he spoke.

"I am a migratory bird," he breathed in my ear, "and never have I seen a pond so blue or flowers so lovely as here in Sahasoa."

"Oh? Passing thirst, a nomad's simple cravings. We don't lack water in this place."

"No, there are many swamps, but this one among the rest is more appealing. Never have I had such a desire to lay myself down among the water lilies, to grip their leaves between my toes and plunge my lips into their white corolla."

189

"Only to take wing once again?"

Bao stood a few feet away in the crowd, watching us, furrowing her brow ever so slightly. Despite her reckless life, or maybe because of it, my mother often proved quite prudish about everything regarding my love life. As for Bebe, she had given up nosing around my business a long time ago.

Soldiers have a good reputation for frippery. They're just below amboa-lambos, idle dogs who swagger down the street after girls instead of turning clods of earth in their ancestral rice fields.

I feigned indifference at first.

But yes, I'm convinced that the ancestors desired us to meet. Sometimes, at night and into the morning, I look back on all of the tiniest details of how it happened.

It was a gorgeous day in the moon of Asombola, and a joyful atmosphere hung over Sahasoa. A rich family had called the community together to repair their vaults. The village buzzed with energy, united to raise the flat rock.

He-who-provokes-the-rocks whirled around the procession like a furious bee. "*Maimbo olom-belona!*" he growled. "Human meat! I smell the scent of human meat!"

With a painted face and tattered clothes, the entertainer pretended to chase small children around with his booming voice, making scary faces. They laughed and shrieked, running through the crowd to hide under their mothers' skirts. He-who-provokes-the-rocks did it all, smacking the people who carried the rock and shoving onlookers.

Seeing him annoying the people, the soldiers nabbed the jester and hoisted him onto their shoulders, like a lord. The entertainer was thrilled and showed all his rotten teeth, scolding the crowd playfully.

But the troops threw him into the pond, to the immense joy of every-one. Then they danced a jig to the Sahasoa musicians. I clapped along with everyone else, thrilled to watch.

Andrianarivo took advantage of that to reenter the fray. "What do you say we go share a meal, take a break, solidify our friendship?" he asked with a wide smile.

The strongest men had dug the rock from the belly of the earth, and everyone else replaced them to pull the great sled along. The women clapped and sang while the men pulled. Many zebus had been sacrificed. Their meat would be shared by all, to bind the villagers together in solidarity.

"Sweet words make a meal," I replied. "But to be worthy of the flesh that seals friendship, you'll have to do some earnest work."

He immediately took off his uniform and boots to join the men pulling the rock. His arms were strong, and his enthusiasm equal to that of the most energetic villagers.

Our idyllic romance lasted for one season, like the great white bird and Itasy Lake. Three weeks after Andrianarivo left, I realized I was pregnant.

It's been over a year now since Faly died. I didn't love him anymore, but it was hard when I found out. I was mad at Tsito—why didn't he say anything the day we met on the road? Not a single word came from his mouth, even though Faly was a playmate. Was there that much hatred from childhood quarrels? I don't understand such lasting grudges.

Chief Ranjato's wife has fallen ill. She's barely gotten out of bed since her adopted son passed away. Her husband is livid; people are whispering that Andriantsitoha had one of his men killed. His disagreements with the Zafimanelo clan have morphed into outright hostility, and several elders have taken his side. These days, weapons leap out of their storage caches at the slightest provocation; the village chief of Tendroarivo, the oldest of the elders, is having trouble calming each side down. I wonder if Faly was involved in all of that.

Faly didn't like Andriantsitoha. To him, the provincial lord represented calculating cowardice, shirking responsibility.

"He trampled the sacred virtue of his own clan," he'd said. "How could he abandon his ancestral lands and give himself over in the City?"

"Every lord who goes to serve the Sovereign most likely does the same thing—"

"Andriantsitoha isn't serving the Sovereign, he's serving one of Nampoina's old wives! His words are wise and flowing, but his soul is as slippery as a frog's skin. He's pursuing goals that only he knows."

What part does Tsito play in Andriantsitoha's plots?

The slave boy has changed. The Tsito that I knew wasn't capable of doing any harm to others. Did this Tsito kill Faly? I didn't want to talk to him when he was here, I was afraid of finding out he was a selfish person, stripped of his conscience. It would have been devastating, I would have hated him. It would have been like losing a part of my childhood.

Everything around us is changing. The crowds at the Anativolo market are getting smaller every week. Andriantsitoha isn't the only one who's left: several families I know have left their rice fields behind to move to the capital or some other city.

Our district doesn't organize fampitaha competitions anymore. Bebe isn't telling her old stories with their wonderful characters anymore, she doesn't even recite her hainteny, which burst with such life.

Where is Tsito now?

24 *Tsito*

Don't Believe for a Moment that Laborde Is Not a Vazaha

IF ONE WORD could be used to describe the prevailing atmosphere on Laborde's construction sites in Mantasoa, it would be this: teeming. Even before reaching Mantasoa itself, you'd start stumbling over tree trunks lining the road. All around the work sites, the earth looked as if it had been moved by a giant's hands. Seen from a distance, the embankments and supporting ballasts looked like a long gash ripped open through the forest. Soldiers oversaw the laborers building the road that linked the new city with the capital, mostly slaves or clans who had fallen into disgrace. There were thousands of them.

My friend Rainimahery, who was escorting me, hailed one of the workers to ask if Laborde was in the area. He was told that Ramose Laborde had headed east that morning, and would either be in Mantasoa or the rum distillery.

A few hours later, we arrived in Mantasoa, a city rising from the ground by the will of a single individual and the industry of a multitude. Everywhere we looked bore the marks of human labor. The most arrogant of these was a hillock designed like the royal hill, except this one had concentric rings. It was crowned with a wooden residence for the Sovereign. Stone buildings peppered the surrounding area.

"Ramose Laborde formed this lake himself, using a system of canals," said Rainimahery.

"Is this vazaha a wizard, that he can bend the elements to his will?" I exclaimed.

"He's just clever. It works very much like the irrigation canals in our rice fields, only on a larger scale. Remember, Nampoina made a river deviate from its path to deprive enemy cities."

"What about that? What is it?" I asked, pointing at a building with a tall chimney.

"That's the intense flame. It melts metal for making cannons."

We went into the workshops, but the vazaha wasn't there either. Rainimahery introduced me to a foreman named Ratsimba, who asked what I could do. I gave him the letter of recommendation that Andriantsitoha had written. He placed it on the table without reading it.

"Ramose is the one who decides whether or not to take you on. The only thing I do is to see if you're good with your hands. Come with me."

He brought us to the carpentry shop. As I walked into the building, I was pleased to find myself in a familiar atmosphere. Two master builders were at work. There were some machines I didn't recognize, but I knew most of the parts lining the wall.

"I have lots of experience making framework and other structures," I said. "Allow me to show you."

He agreed, and I started working with the other carpenters. In the meantime, Ratsimba explained to Rainimahery that, in addition to metal tools and weapons, Laborde wanted to produce fabric, glass, paper, and jewelry here, along with terracotta products and musical instruments.

"Ramose went to supervise work at the sugar refinery," said the foreman. "He should be back soon."

Three hours later, the master of the city hadn't yet returned, but I'd finished part of a staircase and banister that I'd reproduced from existing models. Ratsimba seemed convinced.

"Good. We actually need a carpenter, because one of our master builders fell ill and had to return home. You'll be expected to do other things, though, too. Come back tomorrow around noon. If Ramose agrees to take you on, I'll show you where you can stay. Ramose built houses for his workers, and we have rice fields."

I never knew if the vazaha cared about Andriantsitoha's letter, or if he even read it. At any rate, I was assimilated into the mass of Ramose's thousands of workers and laborers the next day. My destiny overlapped with unknown men from every horizon, who had all washed up by choice or bad luck in Mantasoa, a city where the most useful—and useless—things were fashioned for the glory of the Sovereign.

I stayed in Laborde's workshops for a little over two years. I learned to make flutes and violins, melt minerals into metal, raise silkworms, fabricate dyes from tree bark, distill rum, and extract gunpowder from a mix of urine and animal entrails.

It was an exhilarating time in my life, with a flood of knowledge. Laborde himself could sometimes be seen turning to technical books that he'd had brought over from Europe, which I read surreptitiously when he left them lying around the workshop. *Roret* manuals and *Steelworking Lessons of Prof. Verbouks at the Polytechnic Institute.*

This vazaha had been shipwrecked on the island in a storm, and he was a complete mystery. Some admired him, some despised him, and everyone envied him. He'd become a favorite of the Sovereign and appointed himself master craftsman, wise ombiasy, dance instructor, and counselor to the princes, all at once. Mantasoa was equipped with private quarters for the Queen and the rest of the royal family—Laborde knew who provided for him.

But the people there weren't happy.

The laborers had the most terrible work in the entire realm. Twenty thousand men served Ramose day and night, reshaping the world in his image, according to his inspirations, ambitions, and fantasies: building roads, aqueducts, gardens, grand residences, or machines that would never actually be used. The labor was demanding, the pressure constant. All the wardens were merciless, especially the soldiers, who did their own reshaping of the ignorant masses with sticks, whips, and rifle butts. We were slaves to an invisible giant, tiny men in the jaws of the legendary *songomby* monster.

When Laborde's great wooden residence was finished, Ratsimba was named the foundry foreman in recognition of his work. I was transferred with him.

Every morning at exactly five o'clock, we started filling the shed next to the furnace with ore and charcoal. We used wooden wheelbarrows to transport the necessary materials for three firings per day. Not a single minute of delay was tolerated. At seven o'clock, everything had to be ready. Our boss stuck to procedure. "Fill your shovels! Fill your barrows! Move it! Shovel-barrow-move! Move move move! You think Laborde's not a true vazaha?"

Around eight, Laborde would arrive to oversee the first firing. Sometimes, his son or another white man would take his place instead. And we'd watch Ratsimba run from the shed up to the throat, from the throat back down to the shed, and from the shed to the bellows, always in the same order, while the vazaha gave him instructions.

One day, one of the workers came to Ratsimba.

"*Sefo*, there's something odd in the belly of the furnace. I think we have to stop the ignition. There might be too much waste left in the interior."

"Certainly not. Ramose inspected the cistern and the entire furnace yesterday. Everything is working perfectly. It's time now, and Ramose will be arriving. Ignition!"

"But, Sefo—"

"Move it! You think Laborde's not a true vazaha?"

The furnace was lit, but the heat wasn't transmitting properly—it hung down in the lower levels. Ratsimba got all worked up, running around and yelling. He climbed back up to the throat and pushed aside the worker who had been waiting for the temperature to rise before pouring in the ore. The foreman leaned over into the throat to see into the belly of the machine. In that instant, he slipped, and we watched in horror as he disappeared into the cistern, just as the furnace became unblocked and belched out a ball of flames.

We only found a small piece of Ratsimba's tibia bone and the iron frame of his glasses, which had fallen outside the furnace. We wrapped the relics reverently in a small silk shroud and sent them to his family.

I left Mantasoa a little while later, one morning in the moon of Adimizana. I hadn't found the salvation I'd hoped for there, but I had learned to fear the intense flame of knowledge.

My time at Mantasoa wasn't unfruitful. I spent a lot of time considering my situation while I was there. Living with Laborde's workers, I'd been subject to their difficult conditions and collective work. Sometimes we got up when the toads croaked and didn't stop working until our muscles and bones were about to dissolve into sweat and dust from the shed, after thirteen or fourteen hours of labor. Still, the work had a special quality: this new knowledge produced objects of portentous grandeur. I remember when the first large-bore cast-iron cannon was finally taken from its mold, as shiny and black as a giant's penis, and we were all seized with terrible fear. One of my fellow workers whispered a hoarse plea to the ancestors for protection: "*Io ny anareo ray razana! Mha hahamasina anareo anie fa tsy hihinana anay vahoaka!*"

This sacred power of objects spread among the people. Anyone in the City of Thousands who gained instruction with the vazahas' machines was sought after by men in high places, and if the most skilled of these new artisans made the mistake of forgetting to save the best of their inventions for the Palace, they risked disgrace or even death.

As for me, I had long kindled the project of my emancipation. The model of the servant's undivided piaster had not left my mind. Without meaning to, I quickly became a prominent craftsman when I returned to the City of Thousands. A general for whom I'd crafted a reproduction English love seat was so delighted that he gathered every last one of his relatives together to wax lyrical over the velvet upholstery. One month later, I repaired a marble clock topped with a sculpture of a woman in bronze—a royal princess had sent for it from France, but it had been damaged in a fall. Those two jobs earned me a client base and the foundations of a good reputation in less than a year.

It was the ideal opportunity to regain my freedom, but also the most improbable: my market value had just multiplied a hundredfold. Not a week went by without some influential figure reaching out to try to give me a job. However, as soon as I made the request for my emancipation, Andriantsitoha gracefully agreed, even as his own troubles were mounting and his fortune dissolving. He could have sold me for six hundred piasters, at the very least, but not only did he not sell me, but he also gave up the consistent revenue from selling my services, all for a simple undivided piaster.

This decision was characteristic of my master, a clear reflection of his personality. Ibandro, too, had brought all his influence to bear and made an impassioned plea in favor of my liberation. The head slave and I had broached the subject before I'd left for Mantasoa and discussed it numerous times since. He saw my career as a kind of recompense for his own destiny. He helped me as he had helped other slave children in the past, creating a defiant line of descendants to compensate for his own lack of offspring. Ibandro shared with me that Andriantsitoha had offered to emancipate him upon the death of Andriamaro, but the head slave had refused. He hadn't known where he would go, and didn't know how to do anything but serve: his destiny was fixed. Without Andriantsitoha, he would return to dust. Ibandro believed that I could achieve true liberty, something he could only dream of. And thus, working for my emancipation was, to him, a sacred duty.

But Ibandro could never have convinced Andriantsitoha alone. My master agreed to free me because he was driven by an inner fire, a hatred of his peers that the City only seemed to aggravate. Was that just a simple reaction to disappointment? An effect of his education? Had he taken getting rejected by the moneyed circle badly? Whatever it was, the lord of Ambohimanelo had a savage, acerbic rationality that made him hate almost everything that other people did, and sometimes do the opposite of what was in his interests.

"They're just conceited buffoons," he would say. "Three-quarters of the big names in this city swear only by the size of their house and the length of their litter chair. And how many slaves they own. They have less brains than a flock of sparrows, and yet they find comfort in their idiocy and revel in being around each other."

Ibandro shared his master's feelings and he laughed at these outbursts.

"The ancestors have a proverb to describe that sort of gathering, my lord: 'A meeting of dogs where they only sniff each other's asses.'"

"Yes, my friend! That's perfect. You see, Tsito, you're much too intelligent for them. I'd much prefer to lose you outright than to trade you to these gossipy dogs in golden plates and braiding, even for your weight in gold. They'd drown you in menial tasks unworthy of you, and humiliate you as punishment for being smarter than them."

He decided that my freedom would be returned to me on the first Friday of the next moon, Alahamady. That was the most auspicious day. In exchange, and as a token of my gratitude, I consented to keep working for Andriantsitoha for at least two more years.

In that, I promised myself to give him the best I had. The principle of the servant's piaster had worked both ways: as the years had passed, I'd come to respect my master and care about his fate even more.

25

Of Courageous Men
and Foolhardy Rats

I SOON DISCOVERED that from that point forward, wherever I went in the world, Blake's shadow would not be far away.

When winter came, the Sovereign decided to circumcise her son. Andriantsitoha began to hope that the royal festivities would give him a chance to regain a favorable position in the Palace, but when the time came, the dignitaries he contacted informed him that his clan could not make use of their usual privileges. The Zafimanelos were falling out of favor. They were even stripped of the right to attend the ceremony.

"I told you she was unpredictable!" Nenibe said. "She doesn't balk at betraying the words of Nampoina and Radama, at changing the traditions that have ruled this earth since the dawn of time!"

We were at our protector's house when the news came.

The royal wife poured herself another glass of rum and downed it in one swig. Her eyes were filled with both rage toward the usurping queen and tears of compassion for "her little Tsifa," as she called him.

"Could you get me an ember, my child?"

Andriantsitoha stood up, concern on his face, and took an ember from the hearth, passing it to the elderly lady. She relit her pipe as twitchy staccato sounds came from her mouth, all the while studying him out of the corner of her eye. I knew that Nenibe always did that when she had a favor to ask.

Andriantsitoha and I had known for a long time that our work for the royal wife wouldn't be restricted to trade and business. The elderly lady couldn't go out as frequently, so she depended on others to fulfill her many needs. She only went out in the City on important occasions, usually on a slave's back. She preferred to entice people to come to her.

"Do you know young A . . . , that charming young man?"

"Yes, my lady. I know him very well."

"They say that he's learned some secret ways of reading destiny in flying birds, passed down from the oldest ombiasy. I would very much like to speak with him."

"It will be his honor to receive an invitation to your home, Nenibe."

"I thank you for your devotion."

In addition to interesting young men, Nenibe was attracted to dishes from faraway countries. Ever since we'd found her a talented chef, we'd eaten foods at her table as rare as the great southern bat, striped eel, or smoked crocodile meat. Andriantsitoha had also procured a variety of imported tobacco for her, to her utmost delight. But none of that had brought us even a twelfth of a piaster, which enraged me. The City was a world where everyone tried to extract the maximum profit from his fellow man, without spending a single cent.

While I listened to the masters, though, I saw a glimmer of hope. I realized that even if Andriantsitoha's relationships had, up to this point, only worked to procure *tsindrifes*, leg-pressers for the royal wife's pleasure, there was at least one other person who could be of use, who'd already proven her usefulness. The same person who'd introduced us to Nenibe: Rasoa, the lord's Christian sister.

How great was my satisfaction, then, when my master informed me that we'd be going to a meeting of influential Christians with Rasoa that very evening.

Andriantsitoha and his sister felt great affection for each other, but had clashed once or twice on the battlefield of beliefs. My master was still skeptical; his natural suspicions were not at all compatible with the sometimes frenetic enthusiasm of Christian advancement. Rasoa couldn't understand it.

But the two had recently reconciled after a period of quarrels. It had been an affectionate meeting, and Andriantsitoha was still sailing on its wave of warmth. Besides, his house was teetering on the brink of the abyss, and he needed help urgently.

The meeting took place in a busy neighborhood, not far from the Commander in Chief's residence.

At first, it was quite pleasant. The owners of the barn where the Christians had their secret meeting were nice. Some of the faithful were already there when we arrived, and they were having discreet, dignified conversations. Andriantsitoha politely listened to them read their Baiboly. But the people who showed up later, when night fell, soon grated on my master's nerves.

The head of the Christians who regularly came to that place was named Rajohary. He was still a very young man, and his mother had been a confidant of one of the Sovereign's aunts. He orbited in circles close to the Palace. His words immediately struck Andriantsitoha as suspicious. The man had studied under the missionaries, like many who were there. But unlike the devotees who'd arrived earlier, he seemed to drop the names of well-known characters with ambiguous morals more readily and explicitly than the usual apostles of Kristy.

He even mentioned Laborde, whom everyone knew was plotting with vazahas beyond the seas. Rumor had it that the Frenchman had even smuggled some of them into the country illegally.

"Soon, we will organize a parade as a testament of our faith," Rajohary announced at the meeting. "We will praise our Savior before the people and proclaim his coming!"

The news was received with great enthusiasm.

"God bless you, Rajohary! Be our guide, we will follow you. Our duty is to be a light for the people, to show Kristy in all his glory!"

"I cannot yet give you a precise date, but it is coming soon. We will walk across the city. There's a chance that we will have a royal fanfare on that day. I've asked for soldiers to join with us. They will be attired in their parade uniforms and will lay their guns aside in exchange for bouquets of flowers."

Rasoa clapped.

"It will be a hymn to peace and love, we will sing our faith and hope! Oh, I can't wait for the day to come!"

But her brother was far from sharing her joy. I saw a catastrophe coming, and we hadn't even been introduced to the major players yet. Andriantsitoha stood up and strode over to the door of the barn where I stood guard with other servants.

"Are these people insane?" he murmured to me, looking stunned. "How can they be so excited about the possibility of facing the Sovereign's wrath?"

The lord of Ambohimanelo was so disoriented, I thought, because he was part of the old school; in Reverend Jones' classes that he'd attended, this type of zealousness had still been rare. It was easy to picture the missionaries' first students having more passion for science and grammar, in a world that didn't even have any churches yet. These Christians came from a different mold, a different time—that of missionaries like Blake. It made me think of Vero: What had become of her? I'd asked Rasoa if there were Sahasoa people among her acquaintances. She'd told me about crossing paths with a woman from our province who was carrying out an evangelical mission in the Vakinankaratra countryside. I recognized our friend from her description.

"Their unshakable faith is impressive, certainly, but it's distressing, the way they rejoice over anything and nothing," sighed Andriantsitoha.

He lowered his voice even more. "I'll tell you what: some people here seem to have less brains in their skulls than an *ambolobitaka* grasshopper."

"We will keep working," the members of the assembly repeated in a state of rapture. "We labor for a kingdom that is not of this world, but the kingdom of heaven! We must proclaim the coming of the Son of Man!"

Andriantsitoha went back to his seat, but in the end couldn't take it anymore, and asked, "But are you not afraid of being killed? You do know, don't you, that setting up another king is a most serious crime?"

There was a brief silence, then several people answered him at once, some with a gentle, self-assured smile, others with more vehemence.

"His kingdom is much larger than this one, my friend," said an older man. "From the highest clouds to the depths of the earth, there is nothing that doesn't belong to him."

"That's the truth!" cried a woman dressed in white. "He watches over his people, every single one of his subjects, with more love than the best of our shepherds has for his flock. He is the heavenly keeper. What have we to fear?"

"Yes, what are you afraid of?" demanded a bearded man. "Out path is clear: we will not hesitate to follow in our sister Rasalama's footsteps!"

"There are many dignitaries who stand with us, and the army would not dare make an outright attack against our congregations," said someone directly beside Andriantsitoha.

The last statement, the most outrageous one, was a sign of the times: ever since the Sovereign's speech against the vazahas, military officers had had orders to hunt down Christians, who would be put to death if they didn't renounce their practices. And yet some of the most active militants, well-known public faces, went unpunished, and meetings of converts continued unabated. Everything that had to do with the followers of Kristy became more ambiguous the closer you got to power.

The meeting that day was punctuated by hymns full of passion, echoing throughout the whole neighborhood. To Andriantsitoha's great discomfort.

At that time, we weren't yet fully aware of the coalitions trying to pull the strings in anticipation of the Sovereign's succession. No one believed that the Europeans could be driven away in any lasting way. And it was widely believed that the ones closest to the Christians would be the most likely to profit from their power.

Rasoa got involved in a project that night that couldn't have been more displeasing to her brother. The group meeting in the barn set a goal for themselves to have a worship service in the Palace itself and bring Prince Rakoto to take part in communion.

Andriantsitoha took his sister aside. "Madness!" he said. "Utter madness! You're not actually going to get involved with this, are you?"

"Tsifa! This is an extraordinary opportunity! A day in a hundred! A courageous act for the glory of Kristy!"

"Courageous? It's like a rat tarrying in the house of his worst enemy!"

"Why are you acting like this? Are you still a slave? Would you rather remain in darkness?"

They'd raised their voices. Every head turned toward them.

Angry and proud, Andriantsitoha wouldn't retreat. He spoke loud and clear. "Besides, I don't see what glory there is in converting a teenager; it's a victory over a bull without horns."

"He is the royal prince! He will be our next Sovereign," said the bearded man who'd spoken of Rasalama.

"And what do you know about it? I hear it will be Ramboasalama."

"No, Rakoto will soon be proclaimed the heir!" interjected Rajohary, the group's leader.

"Anyway, how Christian is it to meddle in Palace intrigues?" Andriantsitoha continued stubbornly. "I know some Scripture as well. I don't think that it says anything about—"

Rasoa cut him off: "It is written, 'He who is not with Me is against Me!'"

"Do not take that tone with me!" he screamed.

He leapt to his feet and pointed an accusatory finger at the crowd. I sighed—the break was complete.

"What the hell do you believe? The kingdom is not a pot of honey for every fool to dip their fingers in! It is a bull with large eyes, just waiting to charge. You are all lunatics!"

Everyone stood up in silence and left. Rasoa gave her brother the kind of pitying smile reserved for weak and ignorant minds. She walked up without a word and gave him back something that he'd given her as a gift that very morning. It was a beige-colored lamba with embroidered motifs, the kind that the seamstresses in the City of Thousands made most excellently in those days. Then she left, without looking back.

Following that, Andriantsitoha tried to track his sister down, but to no avail. Weeks passed. Prince Rakoto was circumcised and proclaimed heir to the throne, as Rajohary had predicted. The Christians' parade took place as planned, under the City's astonished eyes. No one was arrested, or even reprimanded.

But violence in the upper echelons of the kingdom was still increasing. Inter-faction fighting intensified; it had already led to the assassination of one of the Sovereign's favorites, Prince Rakoto's alleged father. Lines were being drawn in the sand.

Andriantsitoha spotted Rasoa by chance one time, on a Thursday just before Alahamady in the neighborhoods on the city's hills. He tried to catch up with her, but a friend stopped him and told him to calm down: she was with a group of people surrounding an adolescent, whose presence was alluring and full of vigor. The Crown Prince. Once the group had moved away, my master waved to his sister. She looked in our direction. I'm sure she saw us, but she turned her head and disappeared from view.

With her, our last hope to have even slightly influential allies disappeared as well.

The ancestors say, "Even when fate does not take its revenge, there will always be some backlash."

Things turned from bad to worse for Andriantsitoha the following year. I can still remember. I was coming back from Rainimahery's place. The kingdom's relations with foreigners had just been pushed to their limits. The latest news was rocking the City.

"Vazahas have shelled Toamasina! Vazahas have shelled Toamasina!"

Too accustomed to their unprecedented privileges, the Europeans had cried bloody murder the instant that three grains of rice were taken from their profits. The Sovereign had given foreign traitors her last warning to obey the kingdom's laws, and French and English ships had taken them on board. Not content just to come to the aid of those beyond the law, the ships had shelled the port in an act of defiance. White arrogance had gone too far. They'd even tried a landing attack but were rebuffed. The Sovereign flew into a rage. She had twenty vazaha heads planted on pikes along the shoreline, their faces turned out to sea.

I wondered to myself what kind of repercussions these clashes would have on the People Under the Sky. I was walking with one worried eye on the great Betsimitatatra plain, when I saw Ibandro coming down the path toward me. He was in tears.

"They've taken Ambohimanelo! This is the end! It's a curse, the ancestors have bestowed a curse on us!"

"What? Who? What got taken?" I cried.

The Palace had decided to transfer Ambohimanelo to the royal domain. For Andriantsitoha, it was falling into a bottomless abyss. He was nothing anymore, he no longer existed. Andriantsoly, the tax collector general and candy lover, had won. I'd never seen Ibandro cry before. In that moment, I realized just how close he was to his master.

Andriantsitoha didn't even look up when I walked into his house. He sat on his stool and stared at the meager field of dry seeds that would be his only fiefdom from then on. The former lord of Ambohimanelo had turned white as a ghost. I left when evening came, after silently placing on his bed an ivory-hilted dagger that I'd made.

We hadn't exchanged a single word.

BOOK 4

Ravinkazo nanintsana
Ka ny lasa tsy azo ahoana
Fa ny sisa ampanirina

Leaves falling
There's no protecting those that drop
But those that stay are made to grow

MALAGASY HAINTENY

26 *Fara*

THE SOVEREIGN RULER has issued a proclamation:

"To the People Under the Sky, I say to you: I will travel the land and visit the twelve sacred hills. I will do this to honor the tradition of my ancestors. I will circumcise my son. And thus I call upon you to cleanse the paths that I will be traveling. Mow the grass and widen the roads in anticipation of my arrival. Most importantly, I call upon you to kill all of the rats. You must hunt down every single rat, even if there are only two or three on each hill. All the rats must be exterminated."

When Ramanantsoavina, a ten-times-honored general from the Royal Army, delivered Ranavalona's words to the people in our province in the central square of Ambohimanelo in this, the fifteenth year of her reign, fear swept through all those gathered there.

Bebe heard the messenger, and she's still shaking. She rushed home in distress, trying to catch her breath. She's been sitting on her stool ever since.

"There will be a mass trial," she whispers, again.

"For the rats?" asks Hanta, squatting beside her.

My daughter has grown. People think she takes after me quite a bit. Her words are no longer just a child's babbling. She's four years old.

Prince Rakoto, heir to the throne, is of age to be circumcised. No shadow shall cast dark aspersions on a highland prince's passage to adulthood.

My mother is sifting seeds in the sahafa.

"Why are you afraid?" she asks Bebe. "There's nothing for us to be ashamed of."

Bao won't register bad news right now; she just got back together with Rainivonjy, one of her favorite lovers, after being apart for several moons.

He's dropping hints that he's ready to marry her, that he intends to dismiss his first wife.

"Why rats?" asks Hanta. "What're they going to do?"

"A rat is a sorcerer or rebel," says Bebe.

I look at Bebe. She doesn't say anything else; she looks down at her hands, which are old and dry, the nails have turned yellow. Rats must die. They-who-call-forth-the-tangena-spirit will descend upon our villages with the earth husbands, to purify the people. Judgment of the masses.

Bao tries to be reassuring. "They won't do a single thing. People will go lay their stones, one or two beggars will be judged, and everything will go back to normal."

Silence settles. I walk out of the hut and finish hanging the laundry in the yard to dry. I keep listening through the door, but no one speaks. I go back inside and sit behind Hanta, pulling her to my breast.

"This happens from time to time," I murmur gently, stroking her hair. "All boys of the proper age will be circumcised at the same time as Prince Rakoto. There's nothing to be afraid of."

"Let's hope you speak the truth," breathes Bebe.

At the hour of tying the calf to her stake, a neighbor brings us news: a judge has arrived in Sahasoa, flanked by two earth husbands. Ranjato offered them the use of his house for their preparations. Villagers will be called, starting at sunrise, to place their stones. They'll go off to collect stones in the fields and confer with each other. They will place one stone for each person they suspect of sorcery.

The people who receive the most stones are a danger to the community. They will be judged.

A day passes, but nothing happens.

Night falls again. A huge full moon rises on Sahasoa. The gate stone casts a round shadow into the village. The surrounding hills pulse with buzzing insects and screaming wildcats. Thin trails of white smoke rise here and there above thatched rooftops, and whispered conversations carry on the wind.

Packs of men roam the paths, empty of the usual traffic. Their noisy footsteps echo through the night. Worried villagers keep watch in their huts. Trickles of light filter weakly through the cracks of doors and windows.

"*Sarobabay, izay voa aza tezitra!*"

More footsteps echoing. Then, the echoes of stones being thrown onto rooftops.

"*Sarobabay!*"

The sentence of judgment. The call of tangena, that our fathers have passed down since the beginning. *Sarobabay*, a cry whose meaning has been lost to the endless string of tormented nights.

"What're they doing?" Hanta whispers.

"Quiet!" orders Bao. "Not a word. Not a sound."

The footsteps come closer. There is a silence in the night. Then they fade.

"They're leaving," I sigh in relief.

"Our ancestors have smiled on us," says Bao.

But they haven't gone. A stone falls on the roof of our house with a dull thud. Then a second. And a third. Soon, rocks are hailing down. Then another silence.

A knock at the door. Three times. *Bam bam bam.*

"Who's there?" Bebe tries to control the quiver in her voice.

"Rekindle the fire."

We blow to pull flames out of the hearth's slumbering embers. The dim hut emerges from shadows. Hanta starts to cry.

"Rabaovolamirindra! I name you a witch and a threat to a thousand men and a thousand women! You must purify your name, if you are able."

My mother screams and collapses unconscious to the floor.

We don't dare speak for a long time. My mind floods with swirling, piercing questions. What will we do?

"Who could have accused me?" asks my mother, holding back her tears. "This is a mistake, I'll tell them that it's just a mistake. Or spite. I'm not a witch!"

"Neny, please. We know that."

She doesn't hear me. "Someone made a mistake. They took me for someone else. They caught someone else dancing on a grave in the night, making cats and evil birds talk. They think it's me. I'll set them straight."

Bao wrings her hands. A terrible weight is constricting my chest. I stand up, trying to calm my pounding heart.

Hanta screams.

She's opened the door and lit the outside of the shutters with her lampwick.

The mark of infamy. They drew it on the door of our home with thick strokes of chalky earth.

Bebe is still kneeling in the northeast corner of the hut. She sighs sadly. "We ask that the outcome be favorable. We ask that the verdict be just."

Bao nearly faints again. We have to help her stand up. It's time to leave.

An idea comes to me, a hope. "We have to get word to my father! He can save us. Yes, Rado, he has influence."

"You think so?" asks Bao, weakly. "Why not Rainivonjy? He's a friend."

"No," says Bebe. "That may not help your case."

"Right. We have to let my father know." Now my heart beats with hope.

Bao looks at Bebe, who nods in agreement.

"She's right. We have to try everything. But who can take the message to him? We must not be separated right now. The four of us must stay together."

"I'll send Tovo. His home is not far from here. It won't take me long."

I run out to Tovo's house a little to the west. He's not sleeping either. Tovo agrees to go and leaves immediately.

When I return, Bao looks pitiful. She tries to act brave, but can't. She sits cross-legged near the hearth. Bebe is slowly braiding her hair, trying to hide her own emotions. She watches my mother's devastated face and sprinkles it with drops of fresh water to cool it. Her motions are imbued with rare tenderness. Bao knows it. She turns her large, dark eyes on Bebe.

"You must be strong," says my grandmother. "You must be beautiful, my daughter. Beauty is a type of strength, it can affect even the judges."

"I'll try."

"You can beat the tangena. Thousands of people have. You are innocent. We are easily delivered from what we are not guilty of."

"I'll try."

It's time. We set off.

Predawn is a dreadful, harsh glow. The paths are shadowed and silent. All the hearth-fires have been extinguished, but we know that the neighborhood is watching us leave. We hear, more than see, other families sneak out of their huts. Someone says, "We are easily delivered from what we are not guilty of," to give themselves courage. Families soon converge on the path, forming a procession on the road to judgment. We don't look at one another. Hanta clings to my hand, and I press her against my thigh. My eyes are so clouded with tears that I can barely see where I'm putting my feet. What will our lives be tomorrow? What will our lives be the day after? Will Rado save us?

Bao walks in front of us, her face wild, her eyes dead.

She is naked in the hut, which has been emptied of all household objects. A hole has been dug in the ground and a large wicker basket placed in it. She's sitting on a small cushion, facing the east, her legs stretched out. She is alone, but we are just a few steps away outside, with only the bamboo walls of the hut separating us. They permitted us to see her briefly before the trial starts. From where I stand, I can watch the entrance to the room where she sits.

We can hear the servants bustling next door.

Bebe, her forehead to the ground, murmurs, "We ask that the outcome be favorable. We ask that the verdict be just."

Soon, I see the two earth husbands enter. One of them is holding a pitcher. I know what they'll do. Bebe explained it to me. They'll make her drink water collected by cupped hands, then pour some on her head, her chest, and her feet. The water is cold. I think of her shivering, I hear a sob. They make her eat a bit of rice, laying a bed for the tangena.

In walks the judge, he-who-calls-forth-the-tangena-spirit. He goes straight to her and says, "Open your mouth."

Silence.

He places a patch of birdskin on her tongue, which he commands her to swallow. The action is repeated three times. The pieces of skin will testify to her ability to regurgitate the poison, and will decide her life or death.

The judge pours two spoonfuls of tangena into a cup. One of the earth husbands proclaims, "We have gathered here, inside and outside of this home. The time has come for Rabaovolamirindra to drink the tangena. May those whose only goal would be to denigrate her, or those who would wish her death out of pure spite, be struck down by this tangena in return."

"Open your mouth," says the judge again.

He pours the tangena into her mouth. It tastes slightly bitter. I hear her breathe deeply as she swallows the poison. He-who-calls-forth-the-tangena-spirit places resin from a banana leaf on her forehead and recites the incantation to the spirit of the tangena.

"Hear and attend, o Manamango, you are now in her belly, you are now infusing her bones, you see her now from the inside. If she is guilty of sorcery, if she has brought harm to children or if she has brought harm to adults, if she has trampled on a tomb or if she has sung with wildcats, if she has made use of harmful magic spells, then break her from the inside, ravage her entrails! But be wary, Manamango: like all ordinary folk, perhaps she has argued with others, perhaps she has taken the belongings of others. If that is all, if it is merely a crossroads, where one road must be chosen over the other; if it is merely the splitting of two streams, one of which serves to slake our thirst and the other to wash out feet; if this is the case, then let her live, let yourself be drawn out of her, for your task is to hunt down sorcery. Return and leave by the opening through which you entered."

Bebe, her forehead to the ground, murmurs, "We ask that the outcome be favorable. We ask that the verdict be just."

They take an entire pitcher of rice flour broth and make her drink it. A terrible weight is crushing my shoulders. She has to be feeling the tangena in her stomach now, spreading through her limbs. They make her drink another pitcher of broth. When the first wave of vomiting erupts, my mother lets out a long, painful groan. I break out into sobs, and Hanta sticks her fingers into her ears and buries her head in my clothes. The vomiting continues; the revolting sound of splatters in the wicker basket is her entire life hurtling out of her, expelled out from her mouth to meet its death in a foul hole.

One of the servants comes to the entrance of the hut. He takes a banana out from the folds of his wrapper, peels it, and starts to eat.

"How is she?" asks Bebe.

"Nothing's come out yet."

The sun has lifted over the horizon, bathing the edges of the trees in smoldering light. The great Sahasoa fields have emerged from the night, but the countryside is empty. The farmers would rather stay away from the chief's home today. The families of the accused, like us, are the only ones to witness this sad, majestic dawn.

Outside a nearby hut, a seer is busily undertaking the many rituals of pacification.

Another servant comes to the entrance.

"How is she?" asks Bebe again.

"One of the skins has come out. The rest have not."

I can barely hear Bao's groans anymore. I gnaw at my hand until it bleeds. "Why, oh why? Woe is us! Oh, woe is us!"

"We ask that the outcome be favorable. We ask that the verdict be just."

I finally calm down. I take Hanta's small hands in mine. Yes, we ask that the verdict be just. We are being judged not by men, but by our ancestors, by the Creator. Blessed are they who have given us life.

Bebe isn't praying out loud anymore, but her toothless mouth still moves. She looks down and contemplates her hands, her dry old hands with yellowed nails.

27

BLESSED BE OUR ANCESTORS who have given us life.

Bao surrendered to the tangena. She will never dance again.

One scene is forever etched into my mind. They had dragged her outside and thrown her into the yard. We ran over. Her long hair was spread in the dust, her finely sculpted dancer's arms lay unmoving on either side of her torso. At this memory—even today, still—a silent sob climbs inside me, moving toward my throat and my eyes. Bao's face was a mask of pain.

When Rado and Tovo got close enough to see the place of judgment, the sun was already low in the sky. Groups of villagers sat silently on the hills. They knew that the trial was over even before they saw the long ropes pulled by strong men. But they still had hope—at first, they didn't see us among the mourning families following the rope-pullers. Rado came closer to be sure. For a second time, he looked around the group of people following the bodies being dragged by their feet. Not seeing us among them, he was about to run to our home, when he recognized the last body, the one still waiting to be pulled.

After the trial, Bebe yanked us behind one of the houses. My grandmother held me against the wall, gagging me with one startlingly forceful hand. My body shook with spasms, and a flood of tears streamed from my eyes. I wanted to die. Hanta watched, frozen, terrified.

Rado found us and took control of the situation. Bebe couldn't have managed without him.

He said to me, gently, "You're not allowed to cry during the procession."

"But . . . how? You?" I stammered.

"First, you must stop crying," he said, more sternly. "You're putting everyone in danger."

"Iada! We have lost her! She's—"

"Quiet. This is not the right time. If they see a single tear on your cheeks, they'll fall upon you, too."

"But I am so sad!"

"Do you want your daughter to be an orphan?"

"No!"

"Then pull yourself together."

We followed the inglorious procession without a word, our eyes to the ground. The bodies can't be carried. They have to be dragged along the ground so they never come above our knees. The judge and the earth husbands examined the followers' faces carefully. Any excessive emotion can be interpreted as a sign of collusion, and anyone who draws attention to themselves might be seized and judged as well. It is forbidden to bury the bodies of witches in ancestral tombs. They must be pulled at the end of a rope and thrown together into a pit.

Weeks have gone by. Sadness has covered our home like a shell of gray sky above the bare hills in the dry season. The mass trial left a festering gash on the face of this community.

In Ambohimanelo, the usual festivities for the circumcision of young boys came to pass, for the People Under the Sky must emerge purified and stronger from the trial. But joy shared the space with tears and anguish. Those who lost someone dear to them still had to endure disgrace and be marked as friends to evildoers, protectors of tangled nests of spells.

Yet our grief helped me grow closer to my father. All these years, he'd only ever passed through with the changing seasons, like a migrating bird. In mourning, I discovered more of his presence, his voice.

"We must learn to accept this. Death is a solitary path that everyone will take someday. But this is not just one person's destiny: all the People Under the Sky share it. Bao simply went down this communal road before any of us did."

Rado confided to me that he'd left the zebu trade to focus on other business, but he'd had trouble adjusting to his new activities. He told me that sometimes he felt he was belittling himself with such base things. He'd driven herds on the steep zebu paths all his life, he'd climbed the most untamed hills, crossed chasms littered with boulders, forded crocodile-infested waters. My father had risked his life among the bloodsuckers of the swamps and the extortionists of the open roads, and he had never sold off the honor of his family and clan. Today, that trade—in his eyes, the only one worthy of noble efforts—was forbidden to him. A core group of the kingdom's dignitaries had taken over. And he, Rado, had to scramble through odd jobs to survive. Pushed out of the market and threatened by a swarm of new predators, he had to defend his interests constantly.

The changes happening at the heart of the kingdom hadn't just cost him his commercial connections; they'd also cost him his rice fields.

"People came one day with royal mandates. They took over the most fertile plots in the region under the most outlandish pretexts. They barely even tried to disguise their strong-armed takeover. A small-time despot moved near my house, and he was insolent enough to hire laborers to work on his new fields." My father had tried to call on his network of friends, but to no avail: the people behind the faction that had pounced on them were too powerful.

Rado has his own family; I can't blame him for leaving. He told me about his firstborn son, Renja, a hard worker who'd never let him down. He'd overhauled what was left of the family's estate doggedly, while still providing for his wives and children. His first wife, though, Vololona—her health was fragile. He had another son that his second wife, Raivo, had given him. He had a more adventurous spirit and had decided to try his luck in Mojanga, the large northern port city, where he'd served the last governor. The latest news was that he'd left for the Comoros Islands.

"Tell me one more time how you dreamed of Neny," I asked Rado before he left.

"It was no dream. I was not sleeping. It was just before Tovo arrived. A memory, a fleeting image suddenly flashed across my mind. I looked out at the rice fields and thought: Bao. It was something about Bao. But what was it? I searched my memory, which is usually very good. I found nothing there."

"It was her, a message. She was departing for the market of no return."

"A woman passed by our home, and suddenly I had the vision. That hadn't happened to me since my youth, since the time she filled my whole mind, the day after the royal fampitaha. The details were unclear, but I knew right away that our ancestors were trying to tell me something: a distinctive sorrow weighed heavily over the waking dream. Then, my thoughts gained clarity. She offered me water and rice. She had a particular way of doing it, with intimacy and respect. It sent me back, briefly, to our early years. I felt intense emotion: What was the meaning of this image? What evil had occurred?"

"And that's when Tovo arrived."

"Yes. For some reason, I was not the least bit surprised when I was told that a young man from Sahasoa was waiting. I think I was expecting it."

After doing his best to comfort us, Rado continued down his own path. Bao's death seemed to have pushed him to make a difficult decision. But I wasn't about to ask him about it.

"I must leave you," he said gravely. "I would rather have stayed, but I have obligations: friends have asked me to stand with them. Our ancestors say, 'Those who are unified are like a rock, those who are divided are like sand.' We're gathering our forces."

Nine moons have passed. Everything we do is still haunted by the loss. Bao is not even a shadow, because we were not allowed to mourn her and weep for her. We didn't even have the consolation of giving her a decent burial. She is an absence: permanent, unjust, incomprehensible.

Bebe has stopped talking. She had already stopped telling stories, and now her very words have stopped flowing, like a dried-up spring. She sits on the doorstep from morning to night, her eyes unfocused. The only proof of her presence is a weak chewing sound every so often. As for me, when I'm not working the fields, I spend most of my time in bed, broken, lifeless. The morning sun has become a burden since the night of tangena, the moonlight a continual curse.

We avoid village life. We feel malice toward the ones who laid their accusing stones for Bao. Tovo sometimes comes to comfort us; he brings vegetables, herbs, some fruit. He's the only tie to the community we have left.

The rice harvest has been cut in half. Times have become hard. The rain has not arrived when it should, and locusts have struck. The sky has become stingy. Drought is settling in.

Another year goes by, hollow and monotonous.

Our ordinary yields have become practically nonexistent. Only the off-season rice still produces small seeds, under the weather's whims. It's not enough to live off of. Famine has already hit the West and casts its shadow over all the surrounding regions, like a huge specter. Starving people wander the streets.

The district has been placed under shortage rations. We don't have the excess unmilled rice that we used to sell at the Anativolo market. No one is buying the woven baskets and garments we make anymore. Even raffia clothes don't have any takers anymore. Some destitute villagers walk around entirely naked.

The moon is in its third quarter. We're running out of resources. Tovo's also hit hard times, he doesn't bring us extra food like he used to.

The other day, a farmer woman from a neighboring district pushed into the market and collapsed at the feet of the village chief. Her skin hung off her bones, and her eyes had disappeared into their sockets. Unable to speak, she raised her hands up to Ranjato, imploring. A child, a little skeleton with a head larger than its body, was latched onto her breast, sucking obstinately from a crumpled, dried up nipple. The villagers did what they could to save them, but the mother and child perished shortly afterward. They were buried together in a makeshift grave.

"Bebe, we have to find something to eat!" I say.

The elderly woman looks at me, then at her great-granddaughter, Hanta, whose ribs and cheekbones are starting to stick out.

"Yes. What do you intend to do?"

I don't answer. But I look at myself in Bao's mirror; my face is worn with fatigue, and the hand holding the mirror is shaking. I don't have enough strength to think. We don't have much choice anymore.

When the sun brushes the ridge of the rooftops, I leave the village and head for Tendroarivo. Once there, I make a call to a house on the east side of the hill, facing the forest. It's a large house fenced in by a low wall. I see a large cattle pasture slightly below, and further on still, a group of very green rice fields. The estate drips with opulence: a costly cistern-based irrigation system runs along the fields, and they must use imported fertilizer. The slaves announce my arrival to the masters of the house, and I make a superhuman effort to ignore the intoxicating smells of food emanating from the kitchens.

A few moments later, I leave and take the road toward the Anativolo market.

When I return to the house, Bebe is sitting on the doorstep. Hanta is playing alone in the dust.

"No point in asking where you were," she says, pointing at the basket of food in my hand. "I know you went to the usurers."

"Yes," I say. "What else could I do? Don't worry; I'm going to start turning the earth today, so that the rice field is ready. We'll make our way out of this. It will rain soon, I'm sure of it."

But the moons pass, and the rain does not come. I go back to Tendroarivo a second time. More moons pass. The sky is still empty and the soil remains dry and hard as a rock. Even the mountain rice is spoiled now. Losing hope, I send Tovo to look for Rado, but the trader is nowhere to be found. Tovo explains the situation to his second wife, who whimpers that her husband is leaving twice as often as before, for much longer stretches of time. His business has changed; no one knows exactly what he's doing. She promises to send him to Sahasoa as soon as he returns.

One morning, four men appear in front of our house. It's Ranjato with Rahidy, the usurer, and two witnesses.

"Rafaramanorosoa, this man tells me that you owe him money," says Ranjato. "Is that a fact?"

"My lord Rahidy, I must appeal to your compassion," I say. "We just need a little time—"

Ranjato interrupts. "Do you have possessions that can serve as compensation for Sir Rahidy?"

Without waiting for an answer, Rahidy walks into the hut, then strides back out and does a quick lap outside. He shakes his head. Ranjato approaches him and they have a quiet discussion. "I know their rice field, it's over by . . . and it's about . . . and you could get . . . " "No." "Really? Think about it . . . "

Then, Ranjato looks very serious and frustrated, saying, "Rafaramanorosoa, I'm afraid that you may be obligated to pay with your person."

Bebe and I cry out at the same time. Hanta hides behind the elderly woman. My grandmother, who herself has almost fainted, picks her up and holds her.

"Be a slave?" a voice inside me screams. "Never! That must never happen to me!"

I throw myself at the four men's feet. "My lords, give me two days, please. I only ask two days of you, and I will reimburse the entire sum. I'll pay interest!"

"Come on, let's not split hairs over days; I already gave you several moons' grace," says Rahidy.

"He's right," says Ranjato. "How do you think you can find in two days what you haven't managed to earn in several moons?"

"I can! My father is a rich trader. He will save me!"

"How rich?" asks Rahidy.

"Richer than you," lies Bebe, sensing a crack, a way in. "And an uncompromising businessman. Especially merciless toward people who have no honor."

They have another private conversation, Ranjato gesticulating wildly. Rahidy withdraws. They leave but promise to come back if the money is not paid back with interest.

Several days have passed. Bebe is pensive, sitting on the threshold.

"It was not yet your destiny," she says, "but that was a warning from our ancestors. What do they want us to know?"

I don't try to answer the question, and Bebe sighs. Ever since Bao's death, there has been silence between us imbued with meaning and emotion.

I'm still free because Rado eventually came back. Tovo had left to find him, based on information that a zebu dealer provided. My father went to see Rahidy as soon as he arrived and cleared my debt. Bebe and I were worried about how much he had to pay, but he didn't hesitate: he paid it all, down to the last fraction of a piaster. And he left again, taking Tovo with him.

"Could he have gotten rich?" asks Bebe

28 *Tsito*

Of a Man's Honor and Everyday Fare for Pigs

I WAS WORKING in Rainimahery's workshop one morning in Adijady when I heard someone knock. I set down the table leg I'd been polishing and opened the door. It was Tovo.

"When did you get in?" I asked.

"Two hours ago. Ibandro told me I'd find you here. I hear you're no longer a slave?"

I studied my friend. He was thin and haggard, and his clothes were dirty and torn. I saw bloodstains. He looked feverish.

"You look like a bearer of bad news," I said.

"Yes. Is there any food in this workshop? Even a pitcher of water would be wonderful."

I gave him the herb rice that I'd brought for my lunch and drew a bowl of water.

I waited silently until he'd recovered his strength. I was worried: I knew there was some misfortune, but I couldn't press him. Dire news is never shared as you walk in.

When he told me of Bao's death, I wept long and hard. The regret that had filled my heart when I'd last seen Fara rushed back to me. I felt the same grief in my soul that must have flooded Bebe and Fara. I felt guilty for not having been there to help them, to comfort them.

"Like I told Andriantsitoha, famine has struck the province, too. Everyone has fallen into terrible poverty. Some days, we only have roots to chew; they scrape the inside of your stomach and don't give you any energy, but at least you feel like you've eaten."

Thus, my worst fears had come true. My home, which had held me like a nurturing mother, had been decimated; the land of my youth had been devastated.

"That's not all," said Tovo. "After paying Bebe and Fara's debt, Rado took me with him. I was looking for my way in life, and your former master agreed to include me in his new line of work, but things went badly."

Rado had not crossed my thoughts for a long time. The image I had kept of him was of a man skilled in his work and fair in his actions. I never forgot that he'd taught me the fundamentals of the art of survival, on pathways across the kingdom and through life. The story Tovo told me both enlightened me on how things were evolving in the kingdom and shook me to the core, but it wasn't truly surprising—it merely illuminated the slow decline of areas that had once held power.

After a royal decree granted a small group of noblemen and generals the exclusive right to export rice and zebu meat, Rado and his friends scrambled to reinvent themselves. Some of them had tried their luck in new commercial pursuits, like silk or honey. Others had relied on their physical prowess and knowledge of faraway lands to serve powerful lords, but that could be risky: one of Rado's colleagues had underestimated the hatred that many regions felt for his new master, a general who'd become skilled at massive treachery, and was executed by a group he thought were his allies. Some of the army officers used military campaigns as an instrument for pillaging.

Ndriana, the leader of Rado's fraternity, had gone into hiding. But first he'd accepted a modest role as a protector of sacred lands, resigning himself to his fate.

"And this was a man who'd been a trailblazer for many of King Radama's campaigns!" exclaimed Tovo. "He negotiated two major alliances for the Sovereign. But the Queen's entourage distrusts the former King's closest advisers in particular."

Things had turned bad when a dignitary had gotten it into his head to force Ndriana to oversee his pig farm. The man, called Rakatavy, had vast pastures just outside the capital and exported pork to the Île Bourbon. The farm was located beyond the city walls because the Sovereign Queen had banned pork meat in the City. Rakatavy needed men to feed his pigs and protect them against prowling thieves. At Ndriana's refusal, the dignitary flew into a rage and threatened to throw his wives and children into slavery.

The trader pretended to bend and accept the offer, but when Rakatavy, his face struck through with a huge, satisfied smile, went to visit the new pork facilities, Ndriana lured him into the shed and slit his throat. He then cut the body into pieces and threw them to the pigs—a vast improvement on their everyday fare.

Ndriana then called Rado, who'd been brought to the brink of collapse after being dispossessed of his lands and finding no success in his new ventures. Ndriana's idea was simple: since these men had stolen their trade from them, they'd pay them back in kind, by targeting their herds.

Tovo laughed. "Rado said it would be smooth and easy; they already had all the experience and know-how. All they had to do was get back on track."

From the very first moons, Rado and his friends sowed terror in the main regions to the south and east. They attacked not the cattle on farms, but the recent purchases made by the trade's new masters—they divided up their spoils, offloading it in far-flung districts or outside the kingdom's borders. Their unrivaled knowledge of the terrain and secret paths made them untouchable.

"I took part in two of those operations," said Tovo. "They were risky but offered clear, tangible benefits. Our end customers were sometimes even vazahas, all too happy to secure extra supplies at a third of market price."

But attacking governmental convoys couldn't last: the interests involved were too significant.

Palace dignitaries invested huge sums of money to suppress the highwaymen. They promised fortunes to zealous subjects and impunity to reformed brigands. The number of traitors grew, and spies abounded.

Ndriana and Rado twice fell into an ambush, but got out without much hassle. The third time, two detachments of soldiers blocked their way to the south and east, and they had to retreat back to the cliffs outside of Imerimandroso. Cornered, they had no other choice but to scale the rocks without cover. Seeing that, the soldiers took a battery of cannons three field-lengths away and fired on them. Meanwhile, one detachment started climbing the more forgiving slope on the western side.

Tovo's voice was husky with emotion.

"We'd lost half of our men. Only the strongest reached the top. The ones that fell were literally impaled on bayonets. Some tried to flee to the west, but were gunned down one by one. Ndriana got wounded trying to help three men trapped on a ridge. Rado and two companions managed to get his bloodied body up to the summit, but only with great difficulty."

The survivors scattered into the forested area on the northern side, the most suitable place for a retreat. It took them three days to regroup and tend their wounds. But they knew that the soldiers wouldn't let them go. Whole populations fled before them, and they could barely find enough food and water.

Their final refuge was a deep valley. Tovo cleared his throat, took a long draft of water, and sat silently for a moment, eyes in the distance, before he continued.

"I'll never forget that night. We were in a deserted little hamlet of about twenty huts. We knew the soldiers were there, surrounding us, but we didn't see them—none of our lookouts had raised the alarm. Rado and I had carried Ndriana into a house to care for him. Rado got up and picked up the candle to cast light on the wounded man's face. His breathing was weak and his forehead covered in sweat. His eyes were glassy, half-open, as if death had already taken him.

"'He's not going to survive,' I whispered.

"Rado smiled. 'With a little luck, though, he'll outlive the rest of us.'

"He set the candle down and picked up Ndriana's gun. We walked out into the yard.

"It was a magnificent night outside. I hadn't seen such a beautiful night since I'd left the village.

"Then we saw them.

"They'd spread out all around the rim of the basin, in torchlight. There were at least ten columns snaking rapidly out of the darkness. The soldiers had taken no chances; there was no way out.

"'Rado, we're ready,' someone said.

"The rest of the men were outside, too, silently watching the soldiers advance. Rado spat on the ground and checked one last time to make sure the gun was loaded. We didn't have many guns. One of the fighters put a necklace of crocodile teeth around his neck. A bottle of barandro mixed with sacred earth was passed quickly around from hand to hand. Rado drank a mouthful and wiped his lips.

"'Good. Well, let's go, then.'

"The soldiers started screaming like they were possessed, like they did every time they charged. We saw our outposts fall one by one. They set fire to all the farmers' huts as they passed, just as a precaution. The columns all got into firing range quickly. Civilian scouts carried torches to help the soldiers' advance. Rado gave the order to cut them down first.

"At a certain point, all the scouts disappeared and darkness fell again. We heard the officers give the order to halt the attack. Then, new torches were lit, and the assault continued. The same scene played out four times. Toward the end, Rado ordered his most courageous men to crawl into the shadows up to the first line of torch-bearing soldiers, take them by surprise, and run them through. His tactics worked: the soldiers' morale dropped every time they were plunged into darkness.

"But just as we started to think we had a chance, Rado took me by the shoulder. 'You have to leave, now, before the sun rises,' he said. 'Crawl into the wounded and the dead. Smear your face and head with blood. Don't move when the troops pass you. They'll be too preoccupied with driving us out.'

"'But why?'

"'You dying here wouldn't mean anything. You're young, and you still need to find your path. Also, I have a favor to ask of you.'

"He rooted through his clothes and gave me a purse. 'You know that Vololona, my first wife, recently died. Give this to Raivo, my second. Keep fifty piasters for Fara, and take twenty for yourself. Now go!'

"I did as he said and managed to crawl into the woods halfway up the hill. From there, I watched the end of the battle.

"There were too many soldiers, and they moved too fast. Rado and his companions gave their positions away by their muzzle flashes, and they soon came under fire. Then the sun started to rise, and we were able to see faces across the distance. The soldiers were as terrified as Rado's men were; they screamed to give themselves courage. I watched Rado take easy aim at two of them before tossing his gun aside and drawing his machete.

"He waited until his friends, too, had used up their last bullets and picked up their swords and assegai spears. When the first soldier's shadow appeared from around the bend in a hill, Rado rushed at the enemy, the very front line of the troops. I fled into the woods and heard the cannons firing as I ran."

Tovo hadn't yet brought the money to Rado's wife. He hadn't returned to Sahasoa yet either. He'd been afraid of making an easy target for the fahavalo, or of dying of exhaustion on the road. He came first to the City, a much closer destination.

Rainimahery arrived while we were talking, all excited. He greeted Tovo without noticing the awful state my friend was in.

"I have some amazing projects for you," he said. "A new world is opening up to you, possibilities you'd never even dreamed of! I'm going to introduce you to some friends first. I didn't talk to you about this sooner because I wanted to be sure of your virtue. I hope you won't hold it against me."

"Of course not, don't worry about it. I'm quite honored. But look, my friend Tovo here has just given me some bad news."

"Sorry to hear that. But I wanted to tell you this: we're going to introduce you to Prince Rakoto. He agreed to meet you!"

"What?"

"Yes, the Crown Prince! He's formed a brotherhood to benefit the people. He's calling us his *mpanasoas*, his philanthropists. You will be one of us."

29 *Fara*

"LOVE IS LIKE THE SILKWORM in winter: touching it makes its eyes open wide."

Our ancestors were right—love does not have eyes. Or if it does, they're a blind man's eyes, like a caterpillar's. One day this winter, Hanta was carrying a little kite when she came back from the water run at the spring.

"Look, a man gave me this!" she said.

I was alarmed; giving children presents is a common practice among kidnappers.

"Who gave you that? You should never take anything from a stranger!"

"He's not a stranger, he knows the whole family!"

"What? What did he look like?"

"He also gave me this, for you."

I took what she was holding out for me. I studied it, perplexed—a miniature valiha. My heart started beating faster.

"What did he say to you? What did he look like? Tell me!"

"He's outside. He wants to talk to you."

I flew out of the house and stopped dead at the sight of the stranger. I didn't recognize him right away; undoubtedly, my eyes were not yet open wide. He was a tall man, dressed like the well-off young people in the City. But his build belied hard labor. His face, its edges sharpened since we saw each other last, was crowned by a wide, resolute forehead. His eyes had stayed the same.

Tsito looked at me intensely, then lowered his eyes. He seemed upset, but with himself. We remained mute for a moment, facing each other.

"May I ask, did you receive my first gift?" he said with respect, finally, his eyes still lowered.

"Yes, my daughter just gave it to me. Thank you very much."

"That is not the gift I mean: the first gift, the jewelry box. With the letter."

"Yes . . . yes. You want to— Would you care to come inside?"

"You have a very lovely daughter."

"Thank you."

"I brought this as well, for your mother."

He took a silken lamba from a basket and held it out to me.

"She's . . . I'm afraid I must tell you . . . " I stuttered, tears springing to my eyes.

"I know. I only recently heard. I came as soon as I could. I would be honored if you accepted this lamba for yourself. You would do her a great honor to accept it."

"Oh, yes. Thank you! Thank you."

Tears were streaming down my cheeks, but he turned away and pretended not to notice them.

I went inside, and he followed. He had to bow his head to get through the door. Bebe was in bed. Hearing us, she said, "Who is it?" He answered, "It's me, Nenibe!" Not knowing what to do, I tried hurriedly to reorganize the house a little bit. It was still early, and I hadn't had time to put away the utensils.

"What fruit have you brought us from your outing, my boy?" asked my grandmother sweetly.

I think that moment was Bebe reliving the past. It sometimes happens to her. She forgets the passing of time. She must have thought that Tsito was coming back from the market or the spring. That we were still children. Tsito always brought her fruit back then. I squatted to the west of the hearth and started to revive the fire.

I thought he was going to sit down south of the hearth, but he stayed standing, in the middle of the room, while Bebe eased herself slowly onto her stool. The air felt strange.

Tsito took a bunch of bananas and a large pot of wild honey out from his bag and presented it all to Bebe with a big smile. I'd forgotten his wide, kind smile. My grandmother smiled, too, for the first time in perhaps several years.

"Bananas on your back and honey on your head—one sweet thing on top of another. May our ancestors bless you for your intent."

Tsito waited until she was sitting sturdily on her stool, with the fruit and honey at her feet. Then he turned to me and his face became somber again, almost severe. He leaned closer.

He looked carefully at me. "How are you faring?" he asked.

I didn't understand. Why such old-fashioned words? I hesitated. Did I seem ill? Had I really gotten that much older?

Then, he touched me. He placed his hand on my shoulder and looked at me again, intensely. I saw mercy in his eyes. I trembled. His touch was gentle and burning all at the same time.

"Fara. Rado left this for you. You have to be strong and accept it."

I looked at the coin-filled purse that he set on my knees. I didn't grasp the meaning of his words. I simply thought about how he'd said my name . . .

"Rado has left for the market of no return," he said.

Finally, I understood. The room started to spin, and I fainted.

When I came to, I was lying on the bed and Bebe was dabbing my forehead with a damp cloth. I sat up right away; I had to unload the weight squeezing my chest.

We spent the next hour sitting in a circle around the hearth.

I told Tsito about our lives over the past three years: the fear, the despair. I didn't hold anything back, I mourned and cried. I was ashamed of acting that way, but it eased my pain. I could finally breathe. Why did I lose my father at the exact moment I'd found him again? Why wasn't I able to lay my father or my mother in the ground? Tsito was there. He listened. He held my hand. He saw the pain that had stayed buried in me, he saw the tragedy that still prowled around the house. He had come back. One room of my palace was collapsing, another was being miraculously rebuilt from a landscape of ruins.

Then, suddenly, Bebe was also among us again. My grandmother pushes further and further into a world of confusion, a broken, opaque world, but emotion restores her clarity of mind. She recognized Tsito, an adult, and remembered his last visit. She'd always loved him and thought of him as her own descendant. She saw a favorable wind blowing in his return. A dawn that would dispel our misfortune.

At the hour of the Creator's high sun, someone knocked at the door. It was Tovo. He'd just returned bringing Raivo the money left by her husband, as well as his final instructions.

When we were all sitting on the mat to eat the midday rice, Bebe poured a little rum into a mug and threw it out toward the northeast with all her might.

"May all misfortunes be now in the past!"

After Tsito and Tovo had finished regaining their strength, we showered them with questions. Tsito's too-large body didn't bother us anymore, and we got used to his booming voice. He eased into the familiar household universe once more. He laughed the same way as adolescent Tsito.

"So, you left Andriantsitoha to work for Laborde?" asked Bebe.

"Yes, for a bit. I helped build the intense flame where metals are melted to make cannons."

"You've become . . . " I said, and then his name got more comfortable on my lips: "Tsito, you've become a wise man, an ombiasy! Laborde is quite a formidable character; we even know of his renown in Sahasoa."

"I never collaborated with Laborde closely. I was a smith. And don't forget that Laborde is, above all, a vazaha. He wants superiority over other men, he wants to dominate his world."

"But they say that he's built wondrous things!"

"Well, yes. He works men to death for those things. Six thousand men were required to transport the central pillar for the Sovereign's new Palace. Three thousand of them died. In Mantasoa, his lieutenants sometimes whipped us until we bled."

"Wouldn't that be more of the Sovereign's wishes?" asked Bebe.

"No difference. One is a musician, the other a patron. As the ancestors say, they profit from the same art."

Tovo set down his mug of rum and butted in. "I've got news for you, you'll never guess: Tsito was introduced to the Crown Prince!"

Tsito glared angrily at Tovo; he'd wanted to keep that from us. He'd also kept what he was doing with Andriantsitoha from us, at the beginning. And when we were children, he'd kept from us that he had a gold coin. For Tsito, the world is a hostile place where all men are powerful enemies. You must not yield a scrap to them. But I don't blame him. Now I understand a little better what it means to be a slave.

He eventually explained to us that he was going to join a brotherhood formed by Prince Rakoto, which had the secret goal of surpassing vazahas in the arts. Tsito is a little older than most of the Prince's companions, but Rakoto had heard of his talents and made sure to include him in the group. They're building bridges, terracing plains. Fabricating all sorts of things. The Prince calls them his mpanasoas. People have given their association a strange moniker: the Menamasos. Men-with-red-eyes, or those-who-do-not-fear-challenge.

"Surpassing vazahas in the arts? Now, what kind of joke is that?" asked Bebe, intrigued.

Ever since Rahidy the usurer tried to make me a slave, I look at lost men in a different way. I know that Tsito's family had been crushed by the trade of human beings, like a palm nut under a pestle. They were treated like livestock, shown at market, abandoned to their excrement. I could have ended up like them. And when the tangena took my mother, I experienced my first tragedy without explanation or some sense of justice. Even Bao's body was lost. Her bones are in a pit, among animal carcasses. What are we?

"The things that I learned in Blake's classes were of great help to me," said Tsito. "My time with Laborde was also fruitful."

"So how are you going to surpass the vazahas?"

"I've only met two or three people in the association. I was brought into the circle by a remarkable man named Rainimahery. He's kin to the Prince. He says we'll soon be able to build our own ships, our own locomotives. I have great faith in him."

"You're going to live among the kingdom's high-class people!" said Tovo.

236

"I doubt that it will extend my days or give me better health. But I'll try to make something useful of it."

"Will you remember us, if destiny is not favorable to us?" I asked.

"Why would you ask that?"

"Because ever since my mother died, all I think about is tragedy. Sleep has abandoned me."

I regretted the words as soon as they'd come out. I didn't want to complain. But they expressed my exact feelings.

Bebe laughed. "The best thing is to be like me: be satisfied by an old woman's naps, that you take while the herbs are cooking."

Tsito stayed in Sahasoa for a full moon.

We slipped back into our old relationship, walking in the rice fields and down by the pond. And through memories. Since the infamous tangena episode, Bebe, Hanta, and I had lived a distance apart from the rest of the community, which had also revealed to me just how precious it was to have the support of a close friend or relative. My relationship with Tsito, both old and new, became as strong as the bond between water and rice: inseparable in the fields and companions in the city. I felt as if life had extended its arms out to me again, and I was grateful to Tsito for it. His presence renewed my strength and reminded me of the security of my childhood.

I remembered the first present, the small box and the letter. One day, I asked him why he'd come back.

"There are many trees," he answered, "but only sugarcane is sweet."

I looked at my former slave. It had been over ten years since he'd left our home. He was the same person and a different person all at once. Tsito was now a free man. The experience that he'd acquired in faraway lands, the trials that he'd lived through—they showed in his habits. His speech was distinctive, different from normal, everyday language, and despite his shyness, he'd gained a commanding maturity of mind. He'd earned a privileged place in the community and held a position that stretched beyond the scope of a little town like Sahasoa. Yet at the same time, I saw a familiar gentleness in his eyes that had been with me throughout my childhood. And in his words, the flavor of our games of old.

"And how will you love me?"

"I will love you like my eyes, the windows of my soul: without them, I am weak as a child, but with them, the world smiles at me."

"Then you do not love me, for I will be of no use to you in the darkness."

"I will love you like the door to my home, protecting me from enemies and keeping the hearth warm."

"Then you do not love me, for you push through me without shame to achieve your ends."

"I will love you like the Sovereign of this realm, mistress of our lives and our destiny."

He was firm without pushing me. He took me to the caves that we'd explored a dozen years earlier, when our adolescent selves craved adventure. The other kids believed that songombys lived in the caverns, and had been afraid. We fished for crabs in the same waters, splashing and laughing together. We wove a huge net of dry grass and baited it with dragonfly larvae to catch fish and eels.

He wanted to go back to the valley we'd discovered with Vero. He took my hand and told me stories of kalanoros, faraway lands, and fantastical worlds, just to tease me. He used the same inflections as Bebe did. We stopped at a huge moss-covered rock at the forest's edge, to pray to the vazimbas.

When we stood back up, I took his arm to stop him and sank my eyes into his. He did not lower his gaze.

"Alright. But I do not want a partially shadowed union," I told him. "I want a love under the full moon. Nothing less than the full moon."

Tsito left. He'll come back. We loved each other with a serene love. Our love is as solid as the high hills that surround Sahasoa. It is as vast as the lake of islets that black kite birds fish in. As deep as the kalanoro valley. Tsito wanted to stay longer, but I sent him off; he has to keep the promises he made to Rainimahery. And to Andriantsitoha. I know that our future depends on that, somehow.

We parted with the promise to see each other again as soon as he solidifies his standing in the City of Thousands.

30 *Tsito*

God Save Ranavalomanjaka

I HADN'T BEEN BACK in the City more than a week when Ibandro came and knocked at my door. His eyes were damp and he was breathing heavily, as if he was trying to expel poisonous vapors.

"I came to ask you to watch over our master. I have to go back to Ambohimanelo."

I made him sit down first and catch his breath. To give him comfort, I offered him a plate of boiled taro with honey, one of his favorite dishes. White hair covered Ibandro's head now. His open features had gone hollow, his posture slightly hunched. Bringing the taro root to his mouth, his enormous hand trembled. I was afraid for my friend.

"Ibandro, what's happening?"

"It's not me. It's the Bull with Large Eyes. He has pointed his horns toward us."

Andriantsitoha had always been convinced that the Zafimanelo clan had a sufficiently solid place to stand fast against the kingdom's upheavals. There were illustrious elders on his branch of parentage who had fought alongside King Nampoina. Many of the other, more local lords had contributed to the glory of the highland princes, mustering troops for the sovereigns' unending conquests or providing laborers for the major works undertaken by the Palace.

Andriantsitoha spoke of his ancestral tree with pride. The Zafimanelos had traditional privileges, one of which was to recite the *kabary* that concluded the mass purification upon the death of a sovereign or a royal family member. They'd held that privilege since time immemorial, and the royal family had never failed to accord them precedence for those words. It was said that Zafimanelo speech was the wellspring of the bull's second life when departing for the market of no return. It was the mortuary bed the descendants of kings lay upon before they took the path toward the kingdom of the ancestors. The appropriate spring for midland monarchs to purify themselves in before continuing their long journey.

That edifice had crumbled. The Palace had proclaimed the disgrace of the Zafimanelos. The Queen had pushed them down to the level of beggars. Worse still, she'd set her hordes against them.

"But why?" I said. "What crime have they committed?"

"You remember the incident with the circumcision? We were forbidden entrance to the Palace, for the first time in memory. Then, our province was annexed. That should have been our warning. It was only the beginning. They were looking for some pretext."

They found their pretext.

As always happens in such cases, the improbability of the motive dictated the measure of disgrace. The opportunity presented itself with the passing of a kinsman to the Sovereign Queen, someone well known for clashing with the coalition in power; this individual was viewed very poorly, and the Sovereign had publicly admonished and exiled him to a distant province the year before. People suspected that the Palace had secretly had him poisoned, too. So, as misfortune would have it, the exile's provincial lord, a Zafimanelo, was an overzealous or perhaps too stupid young man, and he refrained from reciting the funereal kabary as the rebel was buried in a temporary tomb—most likely out of fear of implicating himself in the dissident, or in the hopes of being well-viewed by the Palace. A fatal error.

The Sovereign declared that it was an insult to her family and immediately ordered reprisals against the entire Zafimanelo clan.

Andriambelo the patriarch was publicly stripped of all his military honors. The same day, two hundred clan members living in the City were arrested and sold as slaves in the public square. Others were driven from their homes, dispossessed of their belongings, and either imprisoned or assigned to humiliating labor. It was a disaster, a fall into the bottomless abyss of dishonor.

Andriantsitoha and his family were on the run.

Ibandro was too noticeable, too visible; he couldn't stay in the City. He couldn't be of any more use there. Andriantstitoha, on the other hand, had decided to stay in the capital. He remained convinced that the hostile forces pursuing him would not stop until he was utterly annihilated. That his only chance of not being killed or thrown into slavery was to keep hiding in the big city.

"Returning to Ambohimanelo would make my enemies' task easier: that's the first place they'll go to find me. I'm sure of it, I can feel it. Here, the storm will eventually pass."

We managed to harbor him with one of Nenibe's influential relations. The man, an artisan, agreed to house my former master on our protector's recommendation, under the condition that Andriantsitoha conceal his identity. Andriantsitoha wasn't the only one in that situation. The few clan members still living in the city had also melded into the general population and were waiting for the ancestors to show them mercy. But to make matters worse, the authorities had revealed that Zafimanelo lords had been infiltrated by more Christians than almost any other clan. The situation couldn't have been worse.

The other members of Andriantsitoha's family had to leave. There were too many of them. They'd already just narrowly escaped the raiding party of soldiers who'd swept through the Zafimanelos' puny City domain, where they'd been living. They'd escaped into the surrounding woods, sleeping under leafy shrubs, lying exposed to rain and wild dogs. At least in Ambohimanelo they could hold onto hope that the storm wouldn't reach them.

I said farewell to Ibandro and the little colony one dark morning on the edge of the city, my heart aching. Vola, Andriantsitoha's second wife, was crying. The children sobbed, and the servants were despondent.

"Veloma zandry kely!" Ibandro called to me, one last time. "Farewell, little brother! Remember what the ancestors say: only halfwits have less ambition than their fathers!"

Several days later, I went with Andriantsitoha to the house of Mary the Christian, in spite of the danger. He wanted news of Rasoa. We were rather surprised to learn that Mary held no grudges against us; she was too excited about how the Christians' projects had been coming along.

"Everything is happening according to our plans, by the grace of our Lord Jesosy Kristy," she said. "Prince Rakoto and Prince Ramonja have converted! Praise God! Our cause is reaching very far now, nothing else will stop our progress. We'll soon spread the Gospel over the whole island!"

"But Rakoto isn't king yet, and there have been reprisals ordered against you!"

"Like Peter, like all those who have suffered in His name, we are prepared for martyrdom. We will die praising Him!"

The convert's words confirmed Andriantsitoha's deepest fears: his sister was going to make herself a target for both his clan's enemies and the ones who sought to destroy Christianity. Leaving Mary's house, Andriantsitoha was sober, lost in thought.

"Do you think we're cursed?" he asked.

I didn't really know how to answer.

Truth be told, that era didn't lend itself to optimism. Several provinces were close to a rebellion. The conquests undertaken by Merina sovereigns decades before had sown hatred and a thirst for revenge in all eight corners of the great island.

"I'm afraid that the water in the rice fields is about to burst its banks," I said.

My former master sighed. "I despise uncertainty above all. But what can I do? I don't even know where my sister is. Now I myself am in exile."

We knew that the judges were putting many Christians on trial. Mary couldn't tell us where Rasoa was. Up to that point, the Kristy movement hadn't been as brutally suppressed as other rebellions, but it was gaining more and more attention. The answers of the accused to judges' questions fueled conversations throughout the City. People said that they were defying authorities: they claimed, "We would rather die than renounce our prayers." They readily admitted to having renounced praying to the sovereigns of the twelve sacred hills.

Everyone knew that a wave of repression would soon be rising. But no one knew what it would look like as it crested. Wasn't the Crown Prince himself a Christian?

In the weeks that followed, fear caused the powerful to commit the most awful abuses. Bloody suppression campaigns were begun in the provinces. In the City itself, Rainimahery and I witnessed awful scenes. One day, several hundred captives from the coastal regions—which had surrendered to military rule—were exhibited in the public square, bound together by their hands and feet. They were hemmed in by a large death squad. A signal sounded, and under the crowd's horrified eyes the soldiers set upon the defenseless prisoners with their sabers and bayonets, exterminating them down to the last man.

This was not the time to have Fara come, I thought.

One moon after that, my Menamaso friend sent me an emergency messenger to tell me not to leave my house until further notice. I'd intended to leave for Sahasoa and had to cancel my trip. The Palace had given the order to put to tangena a large number of slaves, most of them from the coast. They weren't daring enough to go after the Prince's companions, but others died by the dozens.

Yet it was in this poisonous atmosphere that Rainimahery mounted his most ambitious project, which included me.

One morning, he came to my house with a very young man whom he introduced as Randriamahita. He was one of the Crown Prince's cousins.

"Do you understand this?" asked Rainimahery, holding a book out to me.

The work was *Directions for Laying Off Ships on the Mould Loft Floor*, by John Fincham. It was an instruction manual for naval construction, written by a master naval carpenter who worked in a place called Chatham. I paged through it, but the material was so new to me that I didn't grasp much of it at first. Rainimahery was bursting with excitement and tapped the open book.

"Here's what's going to happen: You and Randriamahita are going to build me a scale model boat from this manual. I want it done within a week. I've gathered all the wood and metal that you'll need in my workshop. Work on it day and night. You'll find that our young friend here has lots of knowledge in this area, too."

He didn't want to say anything further, and we got to work right away.

Randriamahita was a gifted young man, and I took an immediate liking to his skills and intuition. Fincham's manual proved to be far from perfect, and the scale conversions were difficult, but Randriamahita and I complemented each other perfectly: when the book's methods didn't apply to what we were doing, my young friend's imagination helped him find another approach, and when the structures didn't fit together, I invented whatever joining part that would fix the problem. After four days of trial and error, we had the frame. The rest of the hull was only a matter of filling things in.

On the sixth day, at the hour of serving the evening rice, all the elements were in place. We only had a bit of paint left to touch up.

Exhausted, but proud of our work, we decided to celebrate our accomplishment. We bought bottles of rum from one of Randriamahita's friends, and I grilled zebu meat in the courtyard outside the workshop.

"Hey, so get this, Tsito," Randriamahita revealed as we drank. "I've picked my future wife, and I'm going to get married soon."

I felt instant fondness for my colleague. I thought of Fara: our happiness was so new and intense that I was sometimes beset by fear. Fear of losing everything, all at once, in a cruel twist of fate. Was it all real? It wasn't just a dream?

I studied my new friend's delicate features. Despite his manly body, he barely seemed old enough to go out with girls. There was a sweetness in him; he was affectionate and likable.

"I'm thrilled for you!" I said. "Would you have guessed that I have similar plans? I'm getting really restless about it, to be honest with you."

He raised his glass. "To our plans, then. To our work. And to our Sovereign Mistress's health!"

"May she grow old alongside her grandchildren!"

We left two hours later, after drinking very well. Randriamahita wanted to go back to his place. I was also wishing for a very well-deserved rest. We walked part of the way together in the night, swaying slightly. All of a sudden, I was optimistic about the world. I was happy with myself, my work. I felt strong, capable of overcoming all trials. I thought that Ibandro would be proud of me.

"C'mere, I want to stop by a friend's house first," said Randriamahita.

I went along with him, too proud of myself to think it inconvenient. When we reached a huge compound, Randriamahita started kicking the gate. I thought that his friend was either sound asleep or hard of hearing. But then my young partner started shouting, his face convulsing with rage.

"Andriamifidy! Son of dogs! Come out of there, you degenerate piece of crap, come out here or I'll come in and pull you out myself! If I have to come in there, I swear to the ancestors that I'll drag out that legion of pigs you call your family, too!"

My jaw dropped, and I watched him scale the wall of the property, as voices rose and shadows moved around us. I managed to grab his legs just before he got over to the other side.

"Calm down!" I told him. "Are you crazy? We're going to get ourselves killed!"

But he'd already unleashed his anger, and light came on in the house. His eyes bulged; he was a different man.

"Andriamifidy! Your house is nothing but a nest for evil birds! A hole for giant rats!"

"Stop it!" I said, trying to drag the drunkard away. "That's enough! Let's go."

"Let go of me, you filthy slave! Don't mess around in this! Andriamifidy! I know you can hear me! So listen up. Did you know your mother was a bitch? Huh? Did you?"

I pulled him sharply, but it was too late. An instant later, we were surrounded by a dozen rough-faced men armed with knives, sabers, and spears. Two torches projected their muscled shadows onto the ground.

People say that slaves have very powerful voices, for lack of melodiousness. Perhaps they're right. I started screaming with all the strength I had; I screamed like never before. My voice resounded through the streets, a piercing echo that rolled three field-lengths away.

"Stop! This is a child of the Queen's house! Stop in the name of the Sovereign Queen! In the name of Ranavalomanjaka!"

We were at the Palace the next day.

Randriamahita and I were on our knees, facing the Sovereign Queen, backs bowed. At Ranavalona's right sat the Prime Minister, Commander in Chief. At her left, a group of men, including Rainimahery. Standing next to his mother, the Crown Prince. In the middle, on the ground, between us and the Queen, a scale model of the sailing ship. The fruits of our labor.

"What you've done is very serious, Ndriamahita," the Sovereign said. "Are you aware of that?"

"Yes, Your Majesty. I ask your forgiveness. I also ask forgiveness from all the elders present here."

"Who is this Andriamifidy that you insulted? His clan has made it a state matter!"

"I don't know, Mistress."

"What?"

"I came across him that day. He seemed conceited and self-righteous. I felt he was eying me with scorn."

"Unbelievable. You realize that without your slave's presence of mind— what's his name, again?"

"Tsito, Mistress," said Rainimahery.

"Yes, Tsito. Without his presence of mind, you both would have been killed. What punishment shall I assign for this crime?"

Randriamahita started to cry. "Your Majesty, I deserve the most severe of punishments. Do with our lives what you will. They belong to you.

Take them, if it pleases you, and we will bless your name as the executioner strikes his blows."

The Sovereign burst out laughing.

"So, in order to punish you for nearly getting yourself killed, I'm supposed to have you put to death? You're certainly not helping your case, you take me for a halfwit. Oh, my child, will you never grow up?"

All the men in attendance guffawed. Even the Prime Minister laughed.

The Queen paused, and the laughter stopped. She looked pensively at the boat. After a moment, she turned to her son.

"Well then. Koto, explain your project to us. What exactly are you and your friend Rainimahery preparing? What can we expect from this ... toy?"

To punish Randriamahita, the Queen confiscated his most treasured possessions until further notice: his violin, his billiard table, and his horse. She also had his entire alcohol reserve destroyed. The Palace paid Andriamifidy's clan a hundred piasters to make up for the affront

As for Rainimahery's plans, they were simple: he wanted to send us to Chatham to learn how to build boats.

Despite the disputes she'd had with the vazahas, the Sovereign had never completely severed her relationships with the foreign world. She'd publicly informed the Europeans that they were unwelcome, but had continued to receive people she judged interesting, especially at Laborde's suggestion. The Palace had even sent ambassadors to England and France.

Sending young apprentices abroad was the continuation of a policy set in place by the great Radama, the Sovereign Queen's late husband; it was just being carried out more covertly. The memory of the Franco-English squadron's aggressions at Toamasina had pushed the Queen to consider the project seriously.

Spurred on by her son, with our scale model in her hands, she gave her final consent that day. It was time for the kingdom to build itself a fleet.

We left the following Friday.

Rainimahery had already planned everything in advance, and the whole royal machine was mobilized. I had just enough time to entrust Rainimahery with a letter for Fara, which he promised to give to Andriantsitoha.

A schooner brought Randriamahita and me from Toamasina to the island of Mauritius, where we stayed for a few weeks. On a beautiful day in Adaoro, a large four-masted ship raised anchor and sailed for Europe. Two months later, weakened by the journey and seasickness, we reached Chatham, in the county of Kent, in the southeast of England.

31 *Fara*

ANDRIAMADY RECEIVED A VISIT from a group of dignitaries from the capital. They're looking for the former lord, but no one knows where he is. His family has come back, though, and they're almost as poor as we are now. Most of their lands have been reclaimed. I hope that Tsito isn't in danger. He's no longer attached to Andriantsitoha's house, but I'm still worried.

Tovo has stopped making trips to the City. We don't get any news from the capital anymore. We live off of rumors now. The Zafimanelos fell out of the Palace's good graces. The clan's historic chief, a high-ranking old officer, was publicly debased by the Queen and condemned to servitude.

One of the men from the City is a high judge, a kinsman of the sovereigns. He bullied Andriamady. We've heard that a seer with a fearsome face has interrogated several families in the province. It's causing lots of worry. Tovo, who's occasionally been working for Andriamady since he came back, was present when the high judge questioned Andriamady.

"Where is your brother, Andriantsitoha? He must surrender himself and ask the Sovereign's pardon."

"I'm unaware of his whereabouts, my lord."

"Don't lie. We have reason to believe that he's here."

"If he were here, I would have delivered him to our Sovereign Mistress bound hand and foot, since that is her wish."

"We're not convinced. We have serious concerns regarding this province."

"What crime is my brother guilty of?"

"He incriminated himself in the City in the company of Christians who are conspiring against the kingdom's interests. We have suspicions about other members of your clan as well. We heard that you acted against our Sovereign Mistress's orders a while back. You banned citizens from denouncing their crimes themselves, you banned purification?"

"May the Sovereign have me killed if that is her wish, my lord. May she take my life, for she is the mistress of it. I had thought it proper to forbid such a thing, for, in all honesty, there are fewer Christians in this province than lice on a bald man's head."

The group of dignitaries left, but they're gathering in a town on the edge of the province.

What will happen now?

When I was little, I often thought about the sky princesses. I liked pretending I was one of them, living above the clouds and lightning, a woman whose beauty would drive men below the heavenly world mad. In my dreams, the one character who tore me away from the affection of my father, the master of the sky kingdom, was a prince of the highest family of the earthly highlands. I'd picture many boys in that role, but Tsito's face never showed up in the fantasy. Tsito was a slave, a forbidden love. There were a few rare legends that I occasionally gave him a place in, but they were weird, supernatural stories, like the legend of the Tritriva lovers. There's something I never told him: even on the banks of the pond, when we played Princess Ifaravavy and Prince Andrianoro, he was not the one I saw and heard. It was Faly.

I'm expecting a child from Tsito. I haven't told anyone apart from Bebe. I'm afraid that the child will have an unfavorable destiny. I confided my fears to my grandmother, one day when illness stayed away from her mind.

"Why such fear?" she'd asked.

"Tsito is a slave. Our union is forbidden. I'm afraid of our ancestors' wrath."

"He's not a slave anymore. He emancipated himself. And our ancestors have better things to do than worrying about these types of things." Bebe paused, then laughed. "And remember, you almost became a slave yourself!"

"That's not the same thing."

"Yes, it is."

I fell silent. The worry did not leave my mind.

"My mother died because an evil sign hangs over our family," I said. "Why would our ancestors be more lenient with Tsito and me? My mother suffered her whole life. And you were the one who told me that some evil part in my own destiny also affected her, something that grew while I was still in her womb."

"I didn't think that. That was Ranaka."

"So maybe he was right! Otherwise, why did my mother die?"

"Bring me something to drink, I'm thirsty."

Bebe sat on the doorstep and ran her hand through her thin white hair. I gave her a pitcher of water. She took a few sips and handed the pitcher back to me.

"The ancestors say, 'The soul is what makes us human.' They also say, 'Everyone is in himself a nobleman.' So tell me: What are you looking for in Tsito? The cloud prince you'll never reach, or the precious slave you might be losing?"

Andriamady didn't have the last word.

The high judge came back with half the initial group but more armed men. He summoned the people to tell them to follow the Sovereign's will and expel harmful elements.

The farmers gathered together in groups. Vero's family was one of the first to turn themselves in. The whole village still remembered Vero's visit; not turning themselves in would have been suicide. "As for those who inspire suspicion," the Sovereign Queen had said, "let them impugn themselves and I will not extinguish their lives. But if they do not turn themselves in, I will surely extinguish their lives."

Vero's parents are modest farmers who obey the kingdom's laws. Three days after the high judge's call to turn themselves in, the whole family appeared before the earth husbands. In addition to Tovo, Fidy and Lanto, children of her father's first wife, answered the call. The judge questioned them carefully. He also heard testimonies from several others from outside the family. On the third day, the judge declared that only tangena, a judgment of last resort, could determine their innocence or guilt.

"We know from a credible source that one member of your family belongs to the most impertinent and extremist sect of Kristy worshippers. We are actively seeking this person, along with twelve other Christians guilty of subversive plots across several districts. Some of them are currently trying to escape to Mauritius. You must purify your name."

They were submitted to the trial the next day, in three adjoining houses that the visitors had requisitioned. None of their relatives came to their aid in prayer, for fear of being accused of collusion. Bebe, Hanta, and I were the only ones to support them. Andriamady sent a seer who agreed to perform the rituals of pacification with us.

When will this end?

The mother died first. She had her youngest child's delicate constitution. Her limbs started shaking just after the poison was administered. That's "spinning silk," one of the most blatant signs of guilt. They grabbed her and strangled her with a rope.

The oldest daughter, Lanto, was felled by the tangena before the sun had even reached the rooftops.

The father regurgitated the first two birdskins but, too weakened by the poison, couldn't get rid of the third. They finished him off at sunset.

Fidy, the eldest of the boys, succeeded in getting the three skins out. They dressed him again and gave him his freedom. But his stomach was still bothered by the three pitchers of rice flour broth that they'd had him swallow, and as he walked outside, he let a little bit of vomit escape on the doorstep. It was the "splash," a mortal failure. They dragged him back into the hut and crushed his head with a pestle.

Thanks be to the Creator, Tovo survived. We brought him home with us and cared for him. On Monday, we joined with Lanto and Fidy's families to bring him to his parents' home. The children waved white lilies and sang.

Here we are! Yes, we're here!
The righteous cannot lie!

Yes, we are happy!
For the righteous cannot lie!

The extended family sacrificed a cow, and the survivor was bathed in purifying water. The villagers hurried to congratulate him.

"Hail to you! The Perfumed Lord has brought you justice!"

"Yes, it was not strength, but justice that prevailed. We are easily delivered from what we are not guilty of!"

As soon as he'd regained enough strength, Tovo departed Sahasoa, slipping away in the night. He was afraid of getting accused of being Andriantsitoha's informant. He came to see us just before he left, giving me only just enough time to scribble a quick note for Tsito, to tell him to come back as soon as possible.

Some other families were submitted to the truth trials in Sahasoa, then the high judge and servants disappeared. A Palace messenger had arrived in Ambohimanelo the night before; rumor had it that they'd gotten orders to leave immediately for a more populous province on the edge of the kingdom. The farmers were relieved. Some even believed they saw one of Andriantsitoha's clever maneuvers in it.

Whatever it was, the Bull with Large Eyes has withdrawn. For now.

Praise the Creator. I gave birth to a son, whom I named Tsitohampanarivo, or Manarivo. My fears have vanished. I'm proud of him. He has his father's wide, rounded forehead. On Ibandro's recommendation, one of Andriantsitoha's young sons agreed to represent those whose father and mother are alive in the newborn welcome procession among the highland people. He was followed by a boy this time, who carried a spade, a thick rope, and a scale, as tradition dictates.

My parents' death has strengthened my relationship with Rado's family. Raivo got over her disapproval of me and gladly joined us to honor the newest birth in the family. Ibandro stayed for the entirety of the festivities, clapping his hands. We killed a fatted goat and two chickens in honor of our guests.

"Fara lost two people dear to her," Bebe told them, "but in you, she has found a real family."

Still, I'm worried. I haven't heard any news from Tsito since he left. Has he forgotten me? Has he seen Tovo? Did he ever reach the City of Thousands? Is he even alive? Black images and a mess of questions rush through my head and fall unanswered in a heap of thoughts.

One morning, I decided to write to him again. To tell him, finally, that I had his child.

Among our old school things, I found an old pen that seemed in fairly good shape but only yellowed, brittle paper. I procured paper of passable quality from the village chief's wife, along with ink. As a desk, I used the wooden board that we'd once written our words on. Fully equipped, I sat down at the foot of the old fig tree and wrote, long and diligently. I raised my head every so often to watch Hanta, who was rocking the newborn gently in her arms.

When I finished, I folded the letter carefully and wrote a note on the back.

Dear Sir Rainimahery,

You do not know me, but I am the fiancée of Tsimatahobario Andriampanoha and I am also now the mother of his child. If the Perfumed Lord wills that this letter reach you, I would lick the soles of your feet, good sir, and request that you deliver it to him so that he knows how alone and abandoned we feel this far from him.

Your devoted servant, Rafaramanorosoa

It was better to send the letter to Rainimahery instead of Andriantsitoha, who might have changed where he was living again. A traveling merchant agreed to take it. Ibandro gave him instructions on how to find the Menamaso's residence. I prayed for our ancestors to guide his path.

The craziest rumors are swirling about what's happening in the kingdom. They say that the Sovereign lost sleep over a challenge issued to her by a missionary on the sacred hill of Ambohimanga. People coming from

BEYOND THE RICE FIELDS

the capital claim that she hasn't calmed at all since the vazahas attacked Toamasina. They're still causing trouble and plotting new schemes. There are reports of Christians—considered no better than the vazahas—who organized a brazen procession of soldiers, royal princes, and female slaves. The Christians and their coalition crossed from one end of the City to the other, singing and dancing under the people's stunned eyes. The parade had been organized to commemorate the birth of Kristy. Some people thought they recognized missionaries and priests disguised as Arab women in the parade. It made me think of Vero.

People's respect for the Sovereign is only growing; farmers are coming in droves to publicly swear loyalty to their Mistress. She is the chosen one of the great Nampoina, he who never allowed vazahas to approach the sacred hills.

In Sahasoa, Ranjato requested to undergo the trial of tangena as a sign of his allegiance, and he survived. Hotheaded young men had the idea to go hunt for the Wandering White Man. They were going to hack him into pieces and hang his head at the entrance to the village, but they found only a bony carcass in a cave—he'd died of old age, all alone in his den, taking his mystery and legend with him.

Moons pass. Manarivo will soon be a year old. We still haven't heard from Tsito. I find I'm dreaming about him more and more often. In my world of dreams, I scour the City of Thousands looking for him. His tall shadow sometimes appears around the corner of an alley, and I call out for him with all my might. But he can't hear my voice through the noise and disappears without seeing me. I run in his direction, but the crowd slows my progress. "Where are you going? That street is off-limits! Come back!" People try to stop me, but Tsito is so close. I have to talk to him, I have to get to him. Someone tugs on the hem of my dress, and I hear crying. It's Manarivo. I realize that we're surrounded by heads, cut off and stuck on bamboo pikes. I want to take my son into my arms, but he's sitting astride a gigantic dog, which is baring its sharp teeth at me. I wake up in a cold sweat, in the dark, my heart pounding.

Another time, Hanta was trying to undo a pile of stones.

"Come here, Neny!" she said. "Come quick! He's buried here!"

"In the Creator's name!" I screamed, running over. "Who is? Who's buried here?"

"My grandmother's talisman! She buried it here before leaving for the judgment!"

"What? What is this tale? Who told you that?"

Then the stones started to move, and a white and black calf came out of the tomb. I broke down sobbing, convinced that Tsito had died. I fell to my knees and cried bitterly, "The ark is gone! The ark left without bringing the calf along! Tragedy is here with us!"

Bebe shook me gently by the shoulder, worried. I was screaming in my sleep. I told my grandmother about my dream, still hiccupping.

"I'm worried that your brain might be turning inside out in your skull," said Bebe.

"But it seemed to be so real! I thought I was going to die of sorrow!"

"It's probably just roaming spirits causing you misery. I know what to do."

Bebe cut a lock of my hair and mixed it with a little fat, which she burned in the threshold. The nightmares didn't come back.

The day after, I wrote Tsito a third letter.

The letter is still here. I'm waiting for someone who will agree to carry it to leave for the City of Thousands.

Waiting is a terrible thing.

32 *Tsito*

God Save the Queen

IN THE COMMISSIONER'S HOUSE of the Chatham Royal Dockyard, an artist had painted a vast allegory on the ceiling over the grand staircase. The Baroque painting from 1705 shows the god Mars receiving a crown made of shells from the hands of the god Neptune. The majestic Neptune represents the all-powerful fleet of Great Britain.

"Do you think the strength from their gods is what's helped them build all of this?" asked Randriamahita as we walked out of the building.

A few gray clouds slipped lazily across the Chatham sky. It was a small town, it didn't look like much, yet it housed one of the nerve centers of the British Empire. As we walked, I looked at the pointed spine of masts, which made the dockyards look like a forest devastated by cyclone winds.

"This Neptune scares me," I said. "He has a furious face. Those churning waves look like harbingers of evil to me. My time with Laborde taught me that if you try too hard to master the elements, some sort of ill will befall you sooner or later."

"See that?" my friend exclaimed. "It's monstrous!"

He was pointing at a seventy-four-gun vessel in the center of the space. The ship's hull was almost finished, and the interior work was underway. Workers swarmed around the vessel like a colony of termites. On either side, other frames sat at various heights, most of them still bare, like gigantic skeletons.

We followed a long row of low, almost identical brown brick buildings: the sail lofts. To our left ran the River Medway. There were many boats tied up there, most of them three-masts. Work sites stretched out in front of us into a swampy terrain. A drab, colorless landscape.

"Come on, let's go back," I said. "I want to breathe purer air."

A few moments later, we were climbing the gentle slope that led to the top of the hill. The incline got steeper, then we reached a plateau where we found a cattle pasture. The animals were massive compared to the ones at home; they looked like they had more fat than meat, and their horns were much shorter. Still, inhaling the animal ferment made me very happy: for a brief instant, the smell reconnected me, like a celestial umbilical cord, to my island and its rice fields, lost thousands of miles away from here. On the road, people passing by in carts and on horseback stared at us curiously. I saw a small squad of soldiers wearing tall fur hats marching in rhythm to the west. We hurried onward.

We crossed through a small wood and finally reached the top of the hill, crowned by a structure called Fort Pitt. It was one of several fortifications that the English had built around their industrial center. This one had been converted into a hospital, treating mostly construction-related injuries, which seemed like a bad sign to me. Man pays an ever-increasing cost to rise to power, no?

We sat in the grass, surveying the landscape, near a few patients who paid no attention to us. I was grateful to our mentor, Foreman Brown, a short, heavyset, and half-bald Englishman in his forties. After a few formalities with the Commissioner, he'd given us the day to explore the area at our own pace.

"Welcome to England!" the vazaha had said on our arrival. "I don't know what you came looking for in Chatham, but I can tell you what you'll find: boats, more boats, nothing but boats! Little ones, big ones, long ones, and wide ones!"

Outside of Fort Pitt, my friend Randriamahita rattled on enthusiastically as we rested from our climb.

"Didja know that England's fleet has over a hundred twenty ships in it, the biggest one in the world? I read it in a book."

I knew that, too, but I didn't answer. I was preoccupied with tracing the winding River Medway with my eyes. It arrived from the west, to our left, and snaked around to where the dockyard was, before climbing back north and flowing that way somewhere, out into the ocean. Within it, every kind of boat imaginable, stretching toward the horizon, and the enormous navy yard buildings and the bastions built around them looked like boulders extracted from the belly of the earth itself and hewn by giants' hands. I thought of my friend Rainimahery: Had he seen at least pictures, or drawings, of what our eyes were seeing? How could he have thought that two creatures as minuscule as us could grasp a world with such inhuman dimensions?

Chatham. It was, in some ways, a cradle of power and knowledge. It was paradise on earth for all souls who still felt young, ambitious, in love with naval sciences.

But Randriamahita and I were unprepared to grasp the implications of this art. I don't think anyone could be prepared for such a thing. Such an ebullient display of knowledge fascinated us. And crushed us.

When the vazahas accepted Ranavalona's request, in exchange for secrets and shadowy favors, they must have chuckled to themselves.

One of the Englishmen we met, Chester, was a jovial, inexhaustible man who never seemed to sleep, or indeed to rest. He was a server in an establishment called The Auld Simpson's Tavern, where we'd have something to eat after working at the dockyard. The other Englishman we saw most often, Eglington, was much younger and very talkative. He was an apprentice, like us; we'd met him in a workshop on fitting rigging elements.

I liked the noisy, hazy, smoky atmosphere in Auld Simpson's. We'd sit at a table in the back room where we could hear each other better, Chester would bring us beer and food, and we'd talk until late in the evening. Eglington usually joined us after going out with his pretty fiancée and bringing her back home; the young apprentice had very kindly agreed to help us learn the language, and he showed some interest in what he called "the Colonies." One day, his fiancée asked us, "Is it true that the Negroes also have kings?"

I told them about how anytime the sovereigns appeared in our country, they were announced with a tune that we called *sidikina*, from the English "God Save the King." He seemed pleased by that.

"And are there still slaves in your country?" he asked.

Randriamahita pointed at me. "He's a slave, actually!"

"Whose slave are you?" our friend spluttered.

"I bought my freedom back. I was emancipated by my master."

"That doesn't seem like the same thing, does it?"

"His master emancipated him because he proved his worth," said Randriamahita. "He paid him a symbolic amount, a *hasina*, as a sign of appreciation."

My Menamaso friend took a long draft of beer, set his tankard down with a clatter, and wiped the corner of his mouth, glancing around the room. I was getting a little tired of hearing him always explain things to white men, obvious things. Every time we did that, I felt like we had to use a bit of lie and imprecision to make the vazaha words fit, whether we wanted to or not.

I was and was not a slave. I'd paid an undivided piaster, but it wasn't a symbolic amount: it was hard-won money that I'd earned and deserved. And I never would have been able to "prove my worth" to Andriantsitoha if he hadn't already decided, long before, deep in his soul, that I could one day be accepted in the community. The undivided piaster was a way of complementing my master's hasina. What could a vazaha understand of the hasina of people and things, of their sacred virtue? For me, the vazaha world was an immense structure of rocks, fire, and metal, a mechanical world that relentlessly shaped all minds within it.

I missed Fara dearly. Andriantsitoha hadn't been the one to give me my freedom—she had. I would become worthy not from the skills that I could acquire with the vazahas, but from the affection and respect that defined her soul, and shook mine. Where was she right now? What was she doing?

"Tsito is homesick," said Randriamahita, clasping Eglington's arm.

"That, I understand. I would die if I was away from Chatham for too long. What's the city called where you live? I assume there are cities over there."

"Yes, we have a palace! The central wooden pillar is ninety feet tall and three feet in diameter. They needed five thousand men to transport it. There are lots of big brick buildings, too, like you have here. We even have a real industrial city, almost as big as Chatham, that we named The Eternal Beauty. But all of that is so mundane! Tsito, now, he comes from the country. I have to confess, I envy him."

"Why is that?"

"Life is so much calmer there. Time unrolls gently, in sweet peace. Two hours of work are enough to feed you for a week. They're overflowing with food. All the women there are nice and fat, and the children are as strong and clever as monkeys, from eating bananas."

"Really?"

"Yeah. The day I've had enough of city life, I'll go live in the country, too. If lice and rats don't scare you, there's nothing better than our farmers' lives."

They drank again. Randriamahita finished his tankard.

"Do you go there often, to the countryside?" the Englishman asked my friend.

"Not as much as I'd like, because of all my responsibilities. Just once or twice a year, to see my ancestral lands. Where would the kingdom be heading, really, if some denizens of the city didn't spend a little time thinking about the future? But our people are so precious: they bring us their harvests, their animals—" he leaned toward the Englishman "—and even their women and girls, for the night, you know?"

Eglington, who was also getting very drunk, seized Randriamahita's hand and pumped it vigorously. "I'm going to come and visit your island! Count on it, old fellow! Yes, I will!"

"You are most welcome there!" my friend roared, using one of his new English phrases.

I got up and walked out to get some air while they ordered more beer. Outside, I watched a bogie pass, pulled by two horses.

The apprenticeship was pure joy, like the time at Laborde's had been. I'd been captivated by the ingeniousness of the machinery that the Europeans had invented to move and steer their marine monsters—by the quality of metal, the sturdiness of the ironwork. In the workshops, among the gauges, half-hulls, the deft grid-work of sterns and strop blocks, I never felt the time pass.

But the tall buildings in the English town were dull and cold, and the streets forbidding. The houses lacked the proper orientation; they were just plopped down chaotically, like a permanent insult to the solar star. There weren't any zebus in the city; that essential animal, with its warm, reassuring shape, was unknown in Queen Victoria's country. There were only horses, sad and inelegant creatures, most often hitched up to cars. No one made kabary speeches in public places in Chatham, and no one listened. People normally only got together to drink and eat. Words seemed to have no sacred virtue.

When I went back into the tavern, Randriamahita was dancing on a table, a bottle in hand, and the Englishmen were singing, laughing, clapping.

"I think our young fellow here is well and truly gone again today!" Chester, the server, said to me, stroking his mustache.

I made a perfunctory excuse to our server friend, but unlike me, he was used to such outbursts. I was amazed by the English capacity for progress in such a tumultuous universe, where people bellowed like cows and fell down, knocking tables over. Women cackled with laughter, pursued by men with flushed faces. And yet I never saw Chester spill a single drop of liquor or lose his smile as he held his tray, his outstretched arm above the fray.

"I heard you were a slave once?" he said to me.

"That's correct."

"Shake my right hand, it'll bring you good luck. You know why?" I shook his hand. "This hand shook the hand of Willian Wilberforce. Do you know who he is?"

"No."

"Alright, come with me, I have to tell you this."

He set down his tray—for once—and we sat down. He told me that he'd taken part in the movement to abolish slavery in England. Wilberforce had been their figurehead. They'd gotten assent from England's assembly of wise men, which they call the House of Commons, then collected more than a million signatures to force the government to put pressure on merchants and major agricultural interests.

"One day, it will also be abolished in your country!" he said, getting to his feet. "It's inevitable, it's the destiny of the world."

That night, when all the customers had deserted the tavern, Chester hailed a cart and, as usual, helped me carry Randriamahita, who had been snoring loudly on a bench. The Menamaso's drunken behavior betrayed a combination of pride and childish innocence.

In Chester, I had seen a little of the best part of the English mind, beyond the machines of war and destruction.

I wondered what the destiny of our world was, the world of our ancestors.

I had a dream.

I was in a house and I heard the sound of the sea outside. I opened the door and saw enormous waves, brown and hairy like animals, coming toward the land. They crashed on the rocks with a hellish din and spewed spray high. In the distance, the hills were bare, deserted.

Then there was a lull, and the sea subsided. The silence on the coast was cut only by the sound of a whirlpool churning on the water's surface fifty paces east of the shore. A thin column of white and black particulates writhed above the swirling waters, growing wider as it climbed. The column leaned toward the houses, like a colossus bending over the world of man.

I cried out in fear as everything around me rumbled and shook. The top of the tornado was like a gigantic eye, watching me. I fled back into the house, which seemed to sink into the depths of the earth, and I thought I saw a trident emerging from the ocean behind me. I ran down an endless staircase. In my flight, I passed shadowy, blackish creatures. "Damned souls!" I thought. Along the sides, more rooms, bordered by decrepit walls, with foul things and vile creatures lying at their base.

Far away, at the back of a cave that sunk farther down still, I saw the outline of Fara, who was also running.

33 *Fara*

THE CREATOR and our ancestors have given us life; our destiny resides in them.

They came back.

Seven judges and earth husbands arrived in Ambohimanelo with a hundred armed men one Thursday night. They requisitioned the former lord's house and summoned the village chiefs. The Zafimanelos were rounded up first. They gathered them in a courtyard and tied them up in the heat of the day. Andriamady watched the fall of his relatives, powerless.

The judges ordered the villagers of the four towns to get together in groups of a hundred and retract all their wrongdoings. The stunned farmers wondered what there still was to confess. But the earth husbands and soldiers circulated among the people to ask questions and incite more zealousness in the trial of purification demanded by the Sovereign.

The judges themselves questioned everyone at length. All guilty people had to turn themselves in and ask forgiveness. They said that any guilty person who did not turn themselves in would be put to death on the spot. They asked people to confess their connections to Christians, their acts of sorcery, their conspiracies with vazahas or rebels. They encouraged villages to turn in any chiefs lenient with opposition parties, to identify those who evaded the conscription of laborers or soldiers or refused to obey the traditions of the twelve sacred hills.

The head judge issued a proclamation:

Here, then, is the reason that our Sovereign Mistress has sent us among you. She sent us to purge the belly of Imerina and drive out evil subjects.

Each one of you must tell us everyone whose actions have stolen sleep from your nights: those who steal, who attack houses, who wait in ambush on the paths, who bar the way of People Under the Sky, who speak ill of the kingdom, and who take action against the sovereignty of Our Majesty. You must turn them in to the earth husbands so that they can tell our Sovereign. If you do not do this thing, if you do not drive out the evil spirits and wrongdoers—including those in your clan and family—then you will have shared a criminal's burden, and you, too, will be guilty in the eyes of our Sovereign.

The judgments started on the second day. The invocations of Manamango, the tangena spirit, echoed through the streets.

A squad of soldiers came and took away the Zafimanelos. They were forced to abandon everything: rice fields, houses, slaves, and livestock. They were to be sent off with other laborers, people said, to the kingdom's construction sites.

The day after they left, an earth husband and seven servants knocked on Ibandro's door. They wanted to know if he was still in contact with Andriantsitoha. They asked him if he mourned the Zafinamelos' removal. Unable to lie, he told them what he thought. The visitors remained cordial and inquired after his health and his family, pretending not to know that he'd always lived alone.

But they'd learned everything about him and collected testimonies from everyone who didn't like him. He was summoned the next day to be put to the trial of tangena. He was accused of conspiring with insurrectionary sects and plotting against the kingdom's interests.

Ibandro appeared before the judge at the appointed hour. He was respectful and did everything he was asked to do. They had him drink a dose of tangena large enough to bring down a bull. But Ibandro was the strongest man in the province. Able to drink an entire pitcher of barandro without flinching. He regurgitated the poison and the three skins in less time than it takes to cook a pot of rice. His disconcerted executioners

265

conferred. They called another judge to aid them and accused Ibandro of having signed a blood pact with the tangena spirit.

The slave was thus put to the trial again, to see if he could survive once more. He did. So they found him guilty of making a pact with tangena and trying to pervert the course of justice. Four men chained him up by his hands and feet; he did not struggle. They put him to death by spearing, but needed to spear him thirty-nine times to kill him. He roared like a bull each time he was pierced. It could be heard from far away; children cried. His body was hacked into pieces and thrown to the dogs. The two who-call-forth-the-tangena-spirit and their servants received half of his fortune, as the law states.

Blessed be our ancestors who have given us life, in this, the twenty-first year of the Sovereign Queen's reign.

In Sahasoa, Ranjato spared no effort to expedite the Queen's requested purification. He personally went from house to house to encourage the people to go before the judges, he urged everyone to turn themselves in or inform on a suspicious neighbor.

"The kingdom's hasina is being restored!" he said. "What happened to the Zafimanelo clan is proof of the Sovereign's clairvoyance! They were plotting with the missionaries to set up a kingdom of disorder and dishonor, like the infamous Baroa kingdom. The vazahas lure in their followers with the idea of a world where a slave can insult his master, where kings bow to some other king who takes pleasure in washing the feet of bandits and beggars. What kind of madness is this?"

Ranjato praised the laws established by the great and wise Nampoina, which would secure the kingdom's greatness and prosperity for all time, which should never be changed or violated. No matter the cost. "Justice is like a stone thrown at a red bird," he kept telling the villagers. "Woe to the ears of rice in its path."

Two earth husbands came for him one morning when the toads croaked.

"The judge said that you must undergo the trial of tangena," announced one of the men.

"But I already did, and I was cleansed of all suspicion!"

"Those are the judge's orders. Purify your name, if you are able."

The dazed village chief followed the two servants into the dark morning. "This is a mistake," he told them. "I'm not a traitor. I don't need to do anything in there. I'm one of the ones who want to purge the kingdom of all harmful elements." He tried to console his wives and children, who had come with him: he would explain everything to the judges and everything would go back to normal.

Ranjato was put to tangena. Despite his age and weakness from a recent bout with marsh fever, he resisted the poison for hours, and succeeded in getting the first two skins out. But the third took a long time, and exhaustion seized him while the sun was already glowing behind the hills.

The earth husbands looked questioningly at he-who-calls-forth-the-tangena-spirit, then picked up the slipknotted rope lying in a corner of the room and approached him. He hung his head and wept.

They had us dig a pit with the other villagers in the heart of the valley, below the Sahasoa spring. A substantial number of bodies was already heaped up there at the end of the first three days of judgment. Small macabre processions spread out along the valley, continually pulling more bodies toward the excavated site.

Most of the slaves had been put to the tangena very quickly. Many died. Then, the first citizens who turned themselves in were interrogated. Their families were also arrested as a precautionary measure. Some of the villagers with connections to the convicts panicked and tried to escape, but they were caught by armed servants and executed on the spot.

The ones who survived the tangena thanked the Creator and their ancestors for their good fortune and either laid low with friends or left their village.

Silence lay like a blanket over the community in Sahasoa. Children no longer played in their yards, and the paths were empty. Many farmers had suspended all work. Every day, we waited anxiously to hear the outcomes of the judgments. New names of victims came out every evening.

We didn't dare speak in public to the families of arrested criminals. At night, everyone wondered which doors the servants would knock on before sunrise.

More strangers were arriving in the province, too, adding to the fear and confusion. People said that powerful seers had come to assist the executioners, that they were driven by relentless hatred. Others claimed that there had been dissent in the ranks of magistrates regarding Ranjato's judgment.

After Ranjato, many other well-known and respected figures in Sahasoa disappeared as well. Ramaro's family, who had entertained the neighborhood so much with their thundering quarrels, was decimated. Of the threefold house's thirteen brothers and sisters, seven died in one day. Doda, the hardiest son, perished first, because they doubled his dose. His wife, Saholy, was pregnant; she miscarried during the trial and died of hemorrhaging. The mother and youngest daughter couldn't hold back their tears as they pulled the bodies, and they were arrested, too. The old father threw himself on one of the tangena servants and tried to strangle him. They displayed his head at the village entrance as an example.

Ratefy, the carpenter, watched his wife's judgment in horror. They'd accused her of bringing forbidden fruits into the region, as well as other plants within the royal family's prerogative. They set fire to her orchard and confiscated her tools. Ravao survived the trial, but was so weakened by the ordeal that she died two weeks later. Ratefy laid her in earth and took his children away, leaving the village for good.

The morning of the fourth day after the judges arrived, the servants came and knocked at our door. Hanta and Manarivo didn't hear the executioners order me to go with them, and I decided to let them sleep. Bebe and I had prepared for this possibility and had agreed that whichever of us was not called would stay to protect them.

Ever since my mother's death, we'd obsessed over the memory of tangena. We'd turned over the details of that grim day so many times that this time, when tragedy had knocked on our door again, we mostly greeted it with detachment. We were much more afraid for the children than for ourselves. We prayed together and asked Bao to watch over the family, now that she was in the kingdom of shadows with the rest of our ancestors.

"We are easily delivered from what we are not guilty of," said Bebe.

"Take care of the children and pray for me," I said.

"Do not be afraid, o piece of my soul," said Bebe, although she could not stop a tear from running down her wrinkled face.

I learned that I was being rebuked for shunning the honest matches proposed to me by the authorities and instead associating with vagabonds and enemies of the kingdom. I was also accused of breaking the group-separation laws established under King Nampoina and of openly compromising myself with a slave.

When I was alone and naked in the room of judgment, I thought of my mother, and I felt like I'd already undergone the trial myself. Yes, this austere room was familiar. It seemed that even the hole dug in the ground, which I sat beside with legs outstretched, was not a stranger to me.

"My stomach will prove the truth," I thought.

I didn't wince when the tangena servants came in and poured cold water over my head, then my chest and feet. Two judges entered, and one of them approached and had me swallow three pieces of skin, one after the other. The other judge stood at the window, a backlit black silhouette. His partner told me to open my mouth, and I swallowed the poison, trying to keep my face expressionless. I swore to myself that this would not be the day that I joined my ancestors.

The judge told me to open my mouth again and peered at my face.

I was afraid not of him, but of the other one, watching us. He was different, wore an unfamiliar hat, and I realized that he was one of the seers that people were talking about. I couldn't make out his whole face in the twilight, but his intense eyes caught my attention. His hand was deformed, like a leper's, curled around a gnarled wooden stick. For a moment, I felt like a tiny animal facing a predator, and I shivered. But I overcame my fear.

I gulped down the rice flour broth quickly enough to surprise my executioner. Bebe had explained the whole ritual to me at length, telling me stories from those who had vanquished the tangena and its servants.

"Don't rush yourself to vomit. Drink, drink as much as you can, and wait for the last second. Resist until the very end. You have to vomit just before the poison passes into your intestines, but not before your stomach is bothered enough by the rice flour. You have to have a contraction violent enough for you to regurgitate the tangena and its bed at the same time."

Nausea overcame me in waves, but I held myself together with all my strength. I felt like my stomach wasn't strong enough to throw up the skins yet. I tried to breathe deeply and as steadily as I could.

A moment passed, and I felt the pinpricks coming into the ends of my fingers and toes. The poison was starting to clear its way through my body. No more delay, I had to throw it up now. I stopped holding myself back and my stomach contracted so strongly that I screamed in pain.

The servants came running over; they thought I was about to "spin silk." But the seer raised his hand and they stopped in their tracks—I was not shaking. I pointed to the broth pitcher. Two of the skins had come out. I only had the third piece to vanquish. And the tangena.

"Hail to you," said Bebe as she opened the door to me. "The Creator has delivered justice to you."

"We are easily delivered from what we are not guilty of," I said. "My day to join my ancestors has not yet come."

"I had no doubts about that," said Bebe, hugging me. "But tell me how you reached the favorable outcome."

Before I answered, I took my children into my arms and I prayed. Blessed be our ancestors who have given us life. Then, with my children still pressed to me, I drank milk that Bebe had poured into a bowl and sat on the threshold of the hut. I thought back to the tangena.

I'd had to get myself under control three times, but I'd eventually gotten the third piece of skin out. The judge and servants had then examined my limbs carefully, but found no trace of bruises or shakes. They'd given me back my clothes and followed me to the door, still suspicious. But I had conserved enough strength to avoid fainting and master my nausea.

Then, the shadow-faced seer had spoken to me from across the room. "Hail to you. Justice has been delivered to you. Now what will you do?"

I'd jumped. His voice was like an animal growl. I couldn't bring myself to look at his face in the dim light. There was something horrifying about that man.

"Truly it was justice, not strength, which prevailed. I will serve my Sovereign Mistress for the rest of my days and nights."

"Yes, yes. Well done. Thank you for your devotion to our Mistress."

"Long may she live."

The seer's question made me think. Ranjato died from tangena, even though he'd already been proven innocent. Many other villagers had already fallen victim to the seers. No one was safe, no one could be sure that their name was purified.

I finished the milk, handed Bebe the empty bowl, and clutched my children to me a little harder.

"Bebe, we have to leave."

"Where?"

"The City of Thousands. We have to get out of this hostile place. Too many people are dead. We can't stay here anymore. We have to find Tsito."

"You have my blessing."

"But you'll come with us, right? Without you, we'll only be wandering orphans!"

"I'm too old to make the journey. I would die on the way and be fodder for dogs. No. You have my blessing. You are strong enough now. You have vanquished the tangena!"

34 Tsito

Chatham, October 12, 1848

Rafara,

At this moment, my mind has still not yet been fully restored to me.
Your love, is it really real? It is like a dream that I do not want to see fade.
Yet here I am, having traveled so far away. The mere sound of your voice
cradles me still. It is sweet as honey. For you are my choice, and that will
never change for all of eternity.

Every strand of my hair desires you, everything in me longs for you.
Did you receive my first letter?

Rainimahery is a knowledgeable man. But how dumbstruck and astonished he would be if he could lay eyes upon all that is here. The Anglisy
have more ships than Ranjato has zebus. They raise a flag to honor their
Sovereign Queen, like us. Or is it we who do like they do?

I have to tell you about this. As we just arrived two days ago, we paid a
visit to Brown's family, our Sefo, out of respect. We'd purchased a chicken
and some fruit at the market to present him with an offering. A dog tied to
a tree started barking, and a woman appeared at the window. She stared
at us with a look of fear, then quickly pulled the curtains closed. Brown
hurried out, red as a tomato. He accepted the gifts awkwardly, but said,
"Sorry, boys, you know . . . The children might get frightened . . . They're
not used to . . . But thank you, boys, thank you again!"

He did not invite us inside.

I'm rather fed up with this Randriamahita boy. There's always something going on with him. I have to carry the man home every night because
he's pass-out drunk. Yesterday, he fell flat on his face in the street and was
almost crushed by a horse. I must say, I'm quite surprised that he's a royal

kinsman with sacred virtue. When he's not drinking, though, he really is a rather nice young man. What would I have done if he'd been trampled? I'm having nightmares from the noise in this town. The clamor from the forge where they make the metal pieces for ships is dreadful, loud enough to make you go deaf. I think even Rainimahery would go crazy. I like our little workshops better. Here, it's just endless noise. Sometimes I still hear the drop-forge hammers at night. But the vazahas do know how to make things: the ropes they manufacture here for their ships could run from Suhasoa to Anativolo or Tendroarivo, and some are as thick as tree trunks. And speaking of trees, there's an enormous machine here to slice them that's fed by underground canals and railroads. Even Laborde's tools can't compare to that. But how can anyone learn all of this?

Randriamahita is becoming Anglisy. He learns all things vazaha so quickly that the sefo in his workshop has congratulated him. People know he's from the Queen's family. The words he uses now are mostly vazaha. He was a student of Laborde's, and his father is a very educated man who knows the Anglisy language as well as Frantsay. But what I find bizarre is that he doesn't know what normal things mean anymore, not even vary vaky ambiaty. He's never worked a rice field, and he tells me that his house has a collection of seventeen clocks, twelve gas lamps, and a hundred billiard balls. His great-grandfather is still alive. Randriamahita says that believing in the ancestors' benevolence is stupid. He bought a bicorn hat for his elder, and a cane with a golden pommel that looks like a lion. He reads scholarly books and dances the polka and mazurka and other vazaha dances. The vazahas clap their hands and laugh at him—not meanly, I don't think—when he dances like that, and their laughter seems to give him more energy and make him dance even faster. One time he danced all the way until morning like that and then collapsed from exhaustion in the middle of the crowd. We had to call a doctor, who said that he was ill and couldn't work that day, which made his sefo very angry.

But for you, for us, I'm prepared to learn all the knowledge of the vazahas.

I went for a walk the other evening and thought very hard about you. I was coming back from the work site and felt that my soul was homesick. I walked by a neighborhood with little houses in a row—when I say little, it's still twice the size of Ranjato's hut, but you know, everything is so big here! But I'm digressing: I wanted to tell you that I tried, as I was walking, to imagine what the lives of people might be like here. I tried to peep through windows, and I discovered a little bit of the private lives of the Anglisy—a woman at her stove, a young man washing up—and it moved me. For once, I felt an affinity with these people.

But what made me truly homesick and made my heart beat so fast was when I saw an enclosed backyard. There was a little wood stove and a young servant girl fanning it. She was squatting on her heels, and there was an old woman standing and looking out through an open door, lost in thought. I saw the girl's black hair and I cried. It was you, it was us!

When will I come back? Where are you, my home? Where are you, my life? Where are you, my beloved? I've smelled the perfume of love.

But don't be afraid: I will be strong and we will find happiness. For you, I will be the great salt that comes from the West and the thick honey that comes from the East. My hands are buttresses. My heart is as solid as a shield. I am no longer the white rice that does not produce seed, or the zebu pen without a bull. I am the rock thrown at the red bird, which is not afraid of disturbing the grains of rice.

Yours: *Tsito, who loves you for all of eternity.*

BOOK 5

Teny arivo
Kabary zato
Faran'ny teny
Ifanatrehana

A thousand words
A hundred stories
But all talk ends
At the hour of confrontation

MALAGASY HAINTENY

35 *Fara*

THE CITY LOOKS DIFFERENT.

Most of the construction underway when I came here for the first time is now complete. Other work projects were added, and the Blue Forest has receded from the grand houses pushing relentlessly forward. The Palace's new look is flamboyant and mesmerizing. Under the purple sky on this gorgeous day of the last rains, the city is dazzlingly beautiful, but sad, as if some secret tragedy were weighing it down.

When we arrived at the gates to the City, I looked for the old woman who had taken us in when I journeyed here with Rado and Tsito—she reminded me a little of Bebe. But her hut had been knocked down. All the villages along the way seemed to be in mourning, people were talking of ordeals, judgments.

We have to find somewhere to stay quickly, so we're not taken for beggars. But where? We don't know anyone in this vast city. I don't know where Andriantsitoha is. Ibandro is dead; he's the only one who could have told me where Rainimahery lives. I shouldn't approach people directly, for fear of drawing attention. I feel a little awkward, and I might be lost. But we must not get discouraged. We decide to go to the riverbank first, to wash our clothes, which have turned red with dust. With a little luck, that will give us an opportunity to make friends with some people here.

"Neny, look!" says Hanta.

I look and am left speechless by the sight of the washwomen of the City of Thousands. The wide river hums with bustling life; its lazily winding waters ring out with the voices of women calling to each other from one bank to the other. There look to be a thousand of them, beating laundry vigorously against the Ikopa's rocks. Most of them are probably slaves or lower-class women, who do laundering for the City's prominent and well-off families.

"Come on, let's go down to the water."

I'm proud of myself for coming here. We're welcomed by the women, and they very quickly get us up to speed on life in the City. The women there come from every part of the city. Nothing escapes them—no event, no story.

"So you've come from Ambohimanelo, have you? I've heard that the rice fields there are lush and the lemons juicy. And how is the mountain rice growing in your lands?"

The washwomen are warm and very curious. They tickle the baby, who peals with laughter, and pass him around to admire and coo over him. Some of them, like us, came from deep in the countryside. I offer to work in exchange for a little food, but once they hear that we're hungry, they all go find their little lunch baskets. We attack the food like young crickets on a tender bamboo shoot. They watch us and laugh.

I finally learn more about the Menamasos.

Ever since Prince Rakoto marched with them in the parade organized by Christians, the reputation of the brotherhood of young philanthropists has grown.

People say that the Prince's big-hearted nature often compels him to save victims of persecution. He's intervened to save people from judges or to protect ones who've been unjustly arrested. He and his companions, who guard him in every situation, regularly ride around on horseback, which has helped them become even more fantastical characters in people's imagination.

"They're swifter than the wind!" they say. "The breath of their horses is stronger than Darafify the Giant's!"

The Menamasos have a good number of construction projects to their name, all built for the people's benefit. The washwomen have a particularly favorable opinion of them for having constructed a series of bridges over the river; many people used to drown from trying to ford it. The laundresses' praise runs as unendingly as the great river itself when it comes to Rakoto and his companions.

"He can bring a bull down with his bare hands," they say about the Prince. "He was playing with crocodiles at just fourteen. His shoulder is as hard as rock, and his arms are sturdier than hundred-year-old trees."

"I've seen him best ten wrestling opponents and carry two adult slaves on his back!"

"He's as strong as a shield and swifter than an eagle! He'll be a valorous Sovereign, a worthy substitute for the Bull with Large Eyes. The heavens will rend in two when he ascends the throne, and the earth tremble below his feet!"

"He is handsome, with such a captivating gaze. Witches and wild animals come to lick his hand. A great flame dances in his eyes!"

Listening to these words, we feel a rush of joy. I'm so thankful to the Creator for giving us such a loving and courageous Prince. From afar, above the ocean of rice fields, the sovereigns' hill seems to look down on us and smile in welcome.

A washwoman named Voahangy offers to introduce us to a family who has connections with the Menamasos. I'm flooded with hope.

"Come spend the night with me," says Voahangy. "It's late now, and you must be tired after such a long journey."

"May the Creator and our ancestors bless you for your hospitality!"

Voahangy's house is in the higher part of the city, in a place called Ambanidia. To get there, we cross a fragrant field, named Antsahamanitra, where a huge variety of plants grow. Higher up, on the plateau, piled-up boulders are cut through by thick clusters of trees. The place is unexpectedly lively. Kids and teenagers seem to be chasing each other through the tall grass with joyous shouts. I'm intrigued by such strange behavior.

"They're hunting wild guinea fowl," explains Voahangy. "There are a lot of them here, which is why this place is called Ambatonakanga, the Guinea Fowl Rocks."

A short distance away, a pretty wooden building is set on a little raised path. Hanta asks our new friend what it is.

"That's a Christian temple that the missionaries built. Lots of people used to go there to pray. Now, it's forbidden."

We keep climbing, and my limbs grow heavy with fatigue. The road seems unending. Hanta's so exhausted that she's not talking.

Eventually, she can't take it anymore. "I'm hungry. I'm so hungry I'd eat a guinea fowl."

"I'll make you Imerina cabbage," says Voahangy. "It's the best in the city, perhaps in the whole kingdom. But we only eat it in small quantities, with rice."

"Why?" I ask, curious. "It's not food for a large family?"

"No, not really. The plants are fairly rare," says Voahangy, smiling. "The proverb says, 'Imerina cabbage from Ambanidia: only by bartering will you get any.' What do you eat in Sahasoa?"

"Porcupines," says Hanta.

"Oh, hush, you!" I growl at her, feeling shame flush my face red.

Voahangy laughs. "Never you mind! Every child in the kingdom has cooked a porcupine at least once in their life."

I remember spring for the children of Sahasoa. Pretend picnics in the center of town. Is Tsito close? He must know this vast city as well as Sahasoa by now. Maybe he's also learned how to ride a horse. Could he hunt the humpless wild zebus in the forests with the Queen's retinue, too? Why hasn't he sent a messenger to the village? Why hasn't he showed us any sign of life?

"We eat eel with fried dragonfly eggs," I say.

"Really? Isn't that strange?"

"It tastes like the best of our ponds and smells like our forests. The proverb says, 'A delicacy like the Sahasoa eel, only lured by dragonfly eggs.'"

We finally get to Ambanidia, where we get our strength back. The Imerina cabbage is delicious and our hosts are especially friendly. "Our ancestors are watching over us," I realize, thinking back to the nights we spent in the forest.

Voahangy's house is nice and clean. Eight people live there: the wash-woman shares the house with one of her sisters, who has two children. It's a small blue bamboo hut with a straw roof and long, beautiful horns; there are fewer and fewer of these in the city. Andry, Voahangy's husband, is a cook for a vazaha who catches butterflies and all sorts of other insects and then spends long hours studying them. Voahangy sometimes does the white man's cleaning ever since the other servants ran off, scared of the huge black butterflies hung in his room. Voahangy says that even she is uncomfortable in the vazaha's big brick house; it's as cold as a tomb inside.

As we rest and start dozing off on the new mat that Voahangy unrolled in our honor, the sky cracks in half. Explosions pierce the walls of the hut. It's the end of the world. I throw myself on my children.

"Oh, that's right, you're not used to this!" Andry apologizes. "It's only the cannon."

"The cannon?"

Our hosts' children explode with laughter as they watch us, but Voahangy smacks their hands sharply with a thin bamboo rod and they stop.

"The City of Thousands falls asleep to the cannon sound," Voahangy says, as the blasts continue.

"And these days," adds her husband with a sigh, "we wake every morning to the call to arms from the *antsiva* shell."

Outside the hut, we see lights appearing here and there in the valley, and thin curls of smoke rising over the houses toward the darkness. We can't make out the hills in the distance anymore. The city purrs like a huge animal at rest.

The next day, after our first calm night in weeks, we set off for the residence of the Andrianonys, the family with ties to the Menamasos.

"These people have righteous souls," says Voahangy. "They help the poor and downtrodden. One day, my last-born was very sick, and they got a learned man they know to care for him; he saved his life."

"They're an influential family?"

"They're Christians. They all stand in tight solidarity with each other."

"Christians? But those are lawless people!"

"Some of the Menamasos are Christians; a large part of their education comes from the Europeans."

"I thought the Christians were in hiding."

"They try to be discreet, but there are those who are protected on high and do not fear persecution."

The family lives in Isotry, a neighborhood not far from Anosy Lake, northwest of the royal hill. Voahangy leads us through a maze of paths that cut through swamps and dense woods and run past the little markets that ring the capital. On the outskirts of another neighborhood known as The King's Rice Field, we see royal slaves working the fields, singing in unison. They're dressed in richly colored fabrics, decorating the rice field like dazzling flowers. Their voices carry beyond the valley. The Sovereign's will is that all occupations connected with the Palace reflect the grandeur of her realm. Thousands of people escort her on her personal outings, and every royal ceremony is accompanied by a feast.

But there's an unusual commotion in Isotry. The people have gathered in public squares.

Several groups are bound together and wait to be interrogated or put through some ordeal. The prisoners are all weirdly calm, as if resigned to their fates. I can't help but shiver. I ask Voahangy what they're accused of.

"Some are Christians," whispers the washwoman. "Others are suspected of crimes against the kingdom. But we don't have to be afraid of anything: the people we're looking for are not among them."

I can't keep myself from staring at the captives, overwhelmed by a deep sense of pity as I remember my own ordeal. There are people of every age and social status. Some are already wearing the heavy iron shackles of convicts, others have cuts and bruises. Entire families silently await their fates.

I think I recognize one of the tied-up women, and I feel my stomach seize up. I rush forward to see better, shaking, but soldiers surrounding the prisoners give the order to march at that very moment. I lose sight of her.

"Vero!" I yell.

"What is it?" Voahangy cries in alarm.

"I thought I saw someone from my village!" I tell her.

"It's best if we leave," she says. "The house we're looking for isn't far now."

My washwoman friend jerks me back: people have noticed us, and one of the soldiers is looking in our direction. I reluctantly let myself be pulled away from the captives, my chest constricted, as if one of destiny's doors had, for a moment, been left open a crack.

The Andrianony family lives in a large house with a veranda that overlooks the thick Isotry marshes. Voahangy introduces us and tells them that a Menamaso had promised to take us under his protection.

"And what is the name of the Menamaso you seek?"

"His name is Tsimatahobario Andriampanoha."

"Where is he from?"

"He comes from Sahasoa, near Ambohimanelo. But his father and mother were of the forest people. We call him Tsito."

"Oh, Rakoto really is encircling himself with people of so many different descents! Alright, we can have a friend ask around about him."

"Thank you very much."

I feel my entire being beating with my heart. We're so close! Soon, we'll be able to see Tsito again, after so many years. But now I feel more doubt. What if he's changed? What if he finds us undesirable now? I wring my hands in anguish and trepidation.

Andrianony's wife notices my distress and smiles compassionately at me. She probably doesn't understand the mix of sorrow and joy I'm experiencing.

"Why, whatever is the matter? You seem upset!"

My mind and body have been subjected to dreadful trials since my judgment in Sahasoa. I want to give myself over to this friendly voice. I tell her our entire story, I leave nothing out.

As I speak, the Christian woman reacts with emotion. Seeing tears streaking my cheeks, she takes my hands in hers.

"Don't fret, o piece of my soul. The God I believe in knows your suffering, and He will guide your path. I'm sure that if your description is accurate, the man you seek is an honest man, and he will not leave you destitute."

Andrianony's wife tells me that she and her husband were converted by a woman named Rafaravavy, whom Kristy twice saved from a death sentence pronounced by the Queen herself. Rafaravavy escaped to Île Maurice, throwing the Palace's best bloodhounds off her scent and even standing up to Tsitialainga, the royal talisman tasked with unmasking traitors and pursuing fugitives. Rasalama, the first Christian martyr, the one who sang hymns to Kristy with her last breath, was part of their group.

"The evangelist *Marka* says, 'Do not be afraid; only believe.' It will give you strength."

I snap my head up, coming back to the present.

"Ma'am! Tsito told me of another man, his friend—his name is Rainimahery."

"Really? We know Rainimahery very well!"

"Praise the ancestors for their compassion, our road is finally at its end!" I say, my heart pounding.

"He's a very skilled man," the woman continues. "He's crafted some extraordinary things with his hands. The Prince is very fond of him."

She immediately sends a messenger to Rainimahery's house to tell him to come to Isotry as soon as he can. So intense is my joy that I have trouble breathing. Since the sun is nearing the rooftops, the family offers to share their meal with us, which we accept gladly. I watch my hosts serving the rice, my chest full of gratitude.

The murmur of the whole vast city comes through the window. A nearby market quivers with children's voices and merchants' calls. Andrianony, the head of the family, speaks.

"Let us pray before eating, please. Lord, we are gathered here today around this simple meal . . . "

As the master of the house speaks, a thin ray of sun streams through a crack in the eastern wall just below the roof. It licks my feet in a bright square, and I see it as a sign from the Creator, thinking, "I will have my piece of the sun!"

The Christians don't observe the order of birthright when they eat. Once the prayer is over, everyone serves themselves at the same time, slaves included. Hanta and I refuse to touch the food until Andrianony has raised his spoon to his mouth. This makes our hosts laugh; they don't look like they're used to the way of the Ancient Ones anymore. I think of Blake.

The vazaha must be back in his country by now, across the seas, in faraway England. This English missionary, he saved my life. If he hadn't confronted Ranaka the seer, I wouldn't have been of this world anymore. My tiny corpse would have been thrown into a pit, and wild animals would have divided up my flesh. How many lives did he change by that, for good or ill, during his time among the People Under the Sky?

"What's happening? Do you hear that?"

The murmurs from the street are swelling. Children are screaming, and we hear a crowd forming. Andrianony is worried, he goes up to the westward-facing window to take a look, but at the same moment, someone knocks at the door. The whole household jumps.

"My lord," says one of the family slaves, "someone is asking to see you!"

"Who is it?"

"I'm not sure, but they're wearing a uniform!"

"Bring them in."

The officer in command of the little troop comes inside, alone. He is very polite.

"Our Sovereign Mistress desires that all those who seek to tarnish her reign and the memory of the twelve sovereigns be sought out and punished. She is the agent of Nampoina and Radama's will. Your household must prove its commitment to the Queen. I have earth husbands with me who will lead us to the place where you might purify your name."

I don't breathe. Andrianony asks for some time for his family to gather a few personal effects. It seems clear that they'll be leaving for a while.

The converts' faces are serene, but we are terrified, and Andrianony notices.

"Those three are not part of my family," he tells the officer. "They are just visitors."

"I must bring all people present in the house."

"But they have nothing to do with us!"

"If that is the case, they will be released later. For now, they must come with us."

A group of other prisoners waits outside, guarded by soldiers. All around them presses a tight crowd made up of curious residents, passersby, and families alarmed by the uniforms. When we walk out of Andrianony's house, all eyes fix on us. I am gripped by dizziness. All the eyes staring at us squeeze my mind. I feel like I've been thrown back into the public infamy of tangena. What will become of us? Plucking up my courage, I try to explain our case to the head officer myself, but he rebuffs me without listening to a word.

"Don't fret," Andrianony whispers to me reassuringly as they take me away. "I'll get you out of this mess."

They bind our hands and tie us to the other captives with a long rope. I still have my baby on my back. As our group sets off, a whisper rushes through the crowd. People form a line. Children walk alongside us for part of the way, their faces sober and full of questions. Dogs bark.

The trek seems unending. The soldiers make detours to take other people. We round Anosy Lake, a body of water that the previous sovereign had had set up to feed a gunpowder magazine. The surrounding area is very swampy. We have trouble keeping pace as the group climbs Larks' Hill; the summit is surrounded by a defensive trench and crowned with imposing trees filled with colonies of birds. Once we arrive at the top of the hill, we walk through some tall grass standing between the scattered houses, then we climb down the other side that leads to Analakely, "The Little Woods."

The procession of captives is led down the slope toward Analakely's spring. The woods are dense, and the air is thick with wildflower scent.

"That's where they're bringing us," says one of the prisoners.

Not far away, toward the base of the valley fading into the marsh, stands a group of huts. Part of the fields has been backfilled to host military parades. A row of buildings has been erected slightly aside to the north, using materials meant to last.

I see that other processions like ours are converging on these buildings.

Tangena is once again siphoning masses of victims into its stinking graves and poisoned feasts.

36 *Tsito*

I COULD SEE Rainimahery was irritated. He didn't understand my insistence on setting off immediately for Sahasoa. I'd been fidgety ever since I'd returned from my voyage. My extended time away from the island and the highlands had pressed into me a profound longing for my roots. I had to see Fara.

"I'm sorry I couldn't pass on your letters; Andriantsitoha has completely vanished. No one knows where he is. I know you want to see your hometown, but—"

"Sahasoa isn't my hometown. It's where I spent the best and brightest time of my childhood after being sold as a slave. I was born among the forest people, but my roots are forevermore in Sahasoa, and my fiancée is waiting for me there."

"Very true, my apologies, I remember. But I'd imagine that your fiancée has already waited several years. Can't she wait a few more days? The Sovereign could call upon us any day now, and I don't want to disappoint her. You know how important this is to us!"

I tried to calm my nerves. I looked around me: Rainimahery had moved into a new house, where he'd built a much larger workshop. He'd shown me many new tools. He was very proud.

"You haven't received any letters for me at all?"

"No, none. Tsito, you can't leave us now—this is a crucial moment for our brotherhood. We have a delicate part to play in these troubled times. We have enemies. We have to keep a low profile, make no mistakes."

"I'll only be making a quick trip. I'll be back before the moon finishes its cycle. I fear that something may have happened to her."

The letters. I no longer knew exactly how many. I'd written passion into each one during my exile; I'd poured all my love, all my hopes into each of them. Where was Fara now, what did she think of me? Perhaps she'd started a new life? I had a moment of despair.

My trip across the oceans had given me a bitter taste of empty promises. Besides the awful journey and those countries' wintry climate, the Europeans' strange morals had caused me to be scorned in such a myriad of ways that I'd felt almost violently homesick for my native island. The naïve dreams that white men's knowledge had planted in me had shattered upon contact with a world whose meaning—if it had one—remained a thickly veiled mystery. Randriamahita, my young colleague in exile, and I had learned many things, had passionate discussions, and changed the world in thought and word. But the memory of Fara had never left me during those long years. Even in far-off Europe, my mind had stayed close to her, just as the ancestors said, like the great vessel in the home that knows only water, and yearns only for water.

"You must have realized that the kingdom is working through a great crisis," continued Rainimahery. "Many of our friends and connections are being threatened, and your presence here will be very valuable to us. I receive daily requests for aid."

When I'd come back, it had seemed that the City of Thousands had changed, like someone whose features had been altered by an unseen illness. The people were in desperate straits, living to the rhythm of the waves of repression washing over the whole island. I'd never before felt such high tension in the streets.

"I have to go. I feel a horrible destiny weighing on my Sahasoa family. But I promise to be back before the next moon, to bring aid to our companions."

A messenger appeared at the door, interrupting Rainimahery just as he was about to reply. People were being persecuted and asking the Menamasos to intervene on their behalf.

"See," said Rainimahery, "it doesn't stop. This, again, is an urgent matter: people are being judged as we speak. Christians. I have to go immediately."

We went out to the street together.

"Please reconsider," he said, before hurrying toward the center of the City.

I hesitated for an instant, watching my friend set off with the messenger. I turned and walked quickly toward my house, in the mad hope of finding a messenger from Sahasoa, or a letter. I didn't know what to think anymore. No, I had to leave right away. I couldn't bear this uncertainty any longer. I decided to get on the road that very day: the earlier I got going, the better it would be for everyone.

Lost in thought, I at first didn't see the crowds spilling onto the streets of the City, unusual for that time of day. I got to my place and, to no surprise, found no messenger or letter there. Apparently, Fara didn't even know where I lived. The sun was already high in the sky. If I wanted to leave, I had to make my preparations as quickly as possible.

I opened my wooden trunk and took out pen and paper: I had to give Rainimahery a detailed explanation. He had done so much for me that I didn't want to disappoint or disrespect him. I didn't want my friend to take me for a man engaged only in his own interests. I had to tell him that my plans for the future and my life itself were in jeopardy. I could not risk a life without Fara, the sky princess who had brightened my childhood and completed my youth. A complete apology to him knocked around in my head, but no words came out onto the paper. I was too manic.

I gave up on writing and knelt in the northeast corner to call upon our ancestors. But it returned no feeling of peace to my soul.

Finally, I sat and tried to meditate, my thoughts racing feverishly.

No. First, I had to find Andriantsitoha again. He would definitely have news from Sahasoa.

I went to see Nenibe, the royal wife.

"The last I heard, he was hiding in Amboditsiry, with one of the Prime Minister's doctors," she told me. "But he must have more freedom to move about now—the storm brewing against his clan finally died down. The Palace found other people to persecute."

"Thank you very much, ma'am. May the Creator guard you and keep you."

Outside, soldiers were marching through the streets. I hurried toward Amboditsiry.

37 *Fara*

"**AND I SAY TO YOU:** if tangena does not purify you, it means the White Man's world has poisoned your blood and your mind and will make cowards and slaves of your descendants unto the twelfth generation," the earth husband intones in a leaden voice.

We've been gathered in a large open space under the beating sun. Only my hands have been untied, so I can take care of my baby. I give him my breast and cover his head with part of my lamba. One after another, dignitaries give short addresses. White clusters are scattered over the hills, on the outskirts of the square: the City's population has been called to attend the investigation of Christians and enemies of the kingdom, and many have come. The hills form a basin and have very few trees, so the addresses can be heard from far away.

The authorities intend to make each case an example for the highland people and generations to come. The number of convicts increases along with the spectators, fed by processions of prisoners.

"Some among you have been seduced by the vazaha missionaries' honeyed words. To those, I must ask: What do the ancestors of these foreigners offer you that you thus deny the word of your fathers and mothers, that you thus trample the honor of the kings of the twelve sacred hills below your feet? Have they promised you riches? Have they tempted you with power? Have you been so intoxicated by their obscene practices that you have forgotten even the mistress of your life, our Sovereign Queen? Have their incestuous caresses pulled you from the true way? And I say to you: even if we must destroy two-thirds of the population, we will not flinch before traitors, witches, and defilers!"

In this moment, among this crowd of unfamiliar faces, my love for Tsito is stronger than ever. Yes, I will have my piece of the sun! I recall the thin ray

of sunlight that came to lick my feet in Andrianony's house. The Prince is a
gentle man who sees good in his subjects beyond the prohibitions of social
status. He will be like Ralambo, the first Bull of the highland dynasty, whose
clarity of sight shaped the grand sanctifying rituals that ensure the goodness
and integrity of the people. As Sovereign and master of customs, Rakoto
will authorize my marriage to Tsito, the former slave. I will be the wife of
a Menamaso, and I will reside in the City of Thousands! My house will be
the home of all that is beautiful and good. I will be the friend-wife, keeper
of hearth and bed, and our children will be budding heirs to the forest.

"Our Mistress, in her infinite mercy, asked that all those who had been
baptized or taken part in a Christian service to turn themselves in for their
wrongdoings. She offered an opportunity for all those who, in a moment
of waywardness, shared a burden with enemies of the realm, to repent and
return to her. But to no avail! They would rather continue their lies and
fraud, they chose to keep supporting these evil creatures' fatal tricks and
traps. They shall perish today! The only survivors will be those whose names
are truly purified, those whose stomachs reveal the truth and innocence
that their lips were unable to proclaim!"

Never before have I found it so sweet to remember our common course.
Tsito's voice, his very presence, still echo throughout my being. His determined features are food for the eyes and the mind, and his unfailing
shoulders form the pillar of a home that will shelter many generations. I
squeeze Manarivo more tightly to my chest.

There will be no more slavery! There will be no more tangena!

I will no longer be the unmarried's child, the almost-child, I will instead
become mistress of a happy hearth. I will be the tree of multiple branches,
the tree with countless fruits! I can still hear the promises that we exchanged
in the kalanoro valley, I can still feel his words enveloping me like a precious
garment. Tsito. Yes, I will serve him and cherish him like the sovereigns of
this earth—I, the orphan of the ten hills, and him, the emancipated slave!

"The vazahas want to subjugate the people of this sacred land to their
desires and their unwholesome order, where mankind loses his honor and
revels in indignity. And I say to you: there is no place in this kingdom for

those who prostrate themselves before the Whites' ancestors. There is no place in this kingdom for those who have turned their back on the wisdom of Nampoina and Radama, for those who have rejected the word of the fathers and mothers who begat the thousand generations for as long as these hills have existed. And I say to you: they will perish, and their flesh be food for the dogs!"

And my children, they're guaranteed an honorable destiny. Hanta is a child of departure conceived on the hill of Tendroarivo. The soldier who gave her life meant little to me, but his seed bore bountiful fruit. I was looking for a bit of my father in those men of travel and passing-through, brought to me like migratory birds on the wind, only to be swept away soon after. Manarivo is still just a man-to-be, but his father's wisdom will one day express itself in his features and his manner.

"Soldiers and earth husbands will bring each one of you into these houses to the north, where you will be able to clear the suspicion that weighs on your person or your descendants. They will be the father and mother in whom you must confide, the small trickles in the crashing waterfall of purification."

The soldiers use the butt ends of their rifles to force the captives onto the dusty ground. We're still bound together by the neck and feet. Several prisoners are taken by surprise and fall hard. I hold my children tightly to me and try to locate Andrianony and his family. The soldiers start to untie those to be interrogated by the earth husbands. I finally see Andrianony and wave to him, but he doesn't see me. As I shake a cloth to try to get his attention, someone tugs at my clothes. I start and stare at the stranger sitting next to me—he, too, bound by the neck and feet.

"Someone's looking to speak with you," says the man.

"Who?"

"I don't know, I was just passed a message," he says, waving an arm vaguely off in one direction.

There are several hundred people there, and I can't pick out a familiar face among them. Dozens of prisoners are trying, like me, to communicate with people they know. Another message soon arrives through a network of captives: "The person who wants to talk to you is off to the northwest, next to a woman dressed in red raffia."

I turn in that direction and see the woman in red. Next to her, a fragile figure.

"Vero!"

It's really her. She's smiling and beckons to me. I feel immense joy, seeing my friend. So I wasn't wrong this morning, thinking I recognized her in a group of Christians. But in the same moment, I have misgivings, and I can't help feeling distrustful of Vero: Wasn't she the one who brought the wave of judgments onto Sahasoa? What harm could she bring me here? She's probably the last person I should be talking to right now. But she's my childhood friend—we were once young crickets together, should we now part fully grown?

Moving through groups of people, we find ourselves side by side before the sun sets.

We can't stop talking. Words flow through us like relief and enchantment. We hold each other's hands and briefly recover the innocence of when we shared every childhood joy. I've forgotten the reservations I had about my friend. For an instant, Vero has the same exuberant laugh as the mischievous little girl she once was. She's enamored with the baby and covers his face with kisses.

Evening falls with a dark-blue hue on the high roofs of the great city. No clouds come to hide the stars. It's as if the Perfumed Lord wants to spare us from rain, which can still fall torrentially in this season. No more ordeals or executions will happen today. The prisoners let go of their fear a little, breathing and talking among themselves. Even the soldiers guarding us are more relaxed. Guard fires have already been lit in the four corners of the wide basin.

Vero is even thinner than when I'd seen her in Sahasoa for the last time. I realize that my friend might not know what happened to her family. No. Impossible. But her next question confirms my worst fears.

"How are my parents? Have you seen them recently? And how's Tovo?"

I'm afraid. I'm terrified of having to answer the question, but also of realizing just how completely the passion that drives Vero—and all the converts—can sever the deepest family ties. How could she live so many years without coming back to her wellspring, without at the very least trying to find out about her family's destiny, her father and mother, her brothers and sisters? In her eyes burns a fire that seems to consume her from the inside.

"Tovo is well," I say.

I stop. My voice breaks.

"And everyone else? My father and mother?"

I look her right in the eyes, my own filled with tears of compassion. Vero's face is undone.

"Tell me!" she says.

"May they be blessed, they have returned to live with our ancestors."

"Both . . . both of them?" Her voice wavers.

"Yes. From tangena."

"Who else?"

After hearing the entire story, Vero cries softly against my chest. Her eyes have lost their serene glow. I can tell that she's working through a moment of doubt, turmoil. I want to turn her mind away from the horrible luck that haunts her.

"I'm looking for Tsito," I say. "He's Manarivo's father."

"Your children are beautiful," Vero says gently. "May they have a long and prosperous life."

"Thank you."

"Fara, please excuse me, but I have to pray."

"May your prayer ease your sorrow."

Before dawn, two soldiers come to undo my bonds and take me into one of the brick houses where I'm to be interrogated. I only just have time to give the baby to Hanta. The room is empty except for two stools and a candle that casts a weak light over the pounded dirt ground and silver-coated walls. One earth husband is sitting on a stool, with an officer standing next to him. It's the same soldier who took us from Andrianony's house.

"Sit down facing me," says the judge.

The officer leans down to the magistrate's ear, and I catch snippets of him explaining my case. The earth husband nods.

"What is your name?" he asks.

"Rafaramanorosoa, my lord."

"And where are you from?"

"Sahasoa, near Ambohimanelo."

"Have you been baptized? Have you ever attended a Christian service?"

"No, my lord."

"If the kingdom's enemies tried to win you over to their unwholesome cause, what would you do?"

"I would deliver them with their feet and hands bound to our Sovereign Mistress."

"I thank you for your devotion to our Mistress. Now, tell me what you were doing in that Christian's home."

I tell him my story, only omitting the ordeal that I endured in Sahasoa. I also neglect to mention that Tsito, the father of my youngest, is part of the Menamaso brotherhood. The earth husband chooses to consider my case more carefully, and he sends me back among the other prisoners to await a decision.

"Someone asked after you," says Vero as I return to my place.

A wild hope rises in me.

"Who?"

"A brother in Christ, named Andrianony."

I'm a little disappointed.

"What did he say?"

"That you shouldn't worry. He has friends who will intervene on your behalf."

I look carefully at my friend. Vero has regained her resolute face and the calm, inhuman look that she'd had during her last visit to Sahasoa. She did spend almost all night in prayer and silent incantations. Before dawn, when wild cats lick themselves clean, I heard her say, very distinctly, "I am ready."

That's a bad sign—there's nothing more dangerous than having a defiant spirit these days. Yet, ever since the time of Blake, I have known how easily converts can be pushed to provocation.

"Vero," I say gently, "when they interrogate you, you have to restrain yourself. Dying will not help your cause."

"I don't serve a cause. I obey the teachings of Christ, who is the Lord our God."

"Justice will not be delivered to you like that. Our ancestors say, 'An angered heart only causes prejudice, and anger only worsens pain.'"

"I'm not angry. Even if my family was destroyed by the forces of darkness. We must all suffer in order to get out from under the shadows, to travel toward the light. The suffering of my family is part of the price for our Redemption. I trust in Jesus Christ. I will follow him until the end. I'm not afraid!"

"But do you really have to go poke serpents in their den? You sound like Rose, or even Blake."

I glance around us. I have to calm down. I lower my voice.

"Vero, this land is sacred, it has been made by the very flesh of our ancestors. No one gets away with desecrating it."

She peers at me. I already know what's coming next. "You heard the Good Word, too. The Truth was revealed to you as well. Open your eyes and your heart! Turn your mind over to the Lord, save your soul!"

She hasn't changed since Sahasoa. A wave of anger crashes over me. "By my father's incest! Will you stop it with this foolishness? Is this Christ one of your ancestors? Is he buried in the City of Thousands? Under one of the twelve sacred hills? Did he preach in the holy city of Ambohimanga? How can you be proud of venerating the ancestors of another people, when you don't even know the first three words of their language? 'Do not fan the flames under another's cauldron, for only the owner will enjoy it,' our ancestors say. And they say this, too: 'Let each person be sacred in his own domain!'"

We talk at each other without listening. Vero presses on, her voice monotonic. "He is God become flesh. He died on the Cross to save all people of the earth. When He returns, He will open the doors of New Jerusalem to us! But cowards, skeptics, philanderers, murderers, libertines, witches, talisman worshippers, and all the liars will be thrown into the lake of fire and suffering!"

I jeer. "A lake of fire? My poor girl, you're stark raving mad!"

But then despair overtakes me, and I burst into tears. I nestle up to my children. I'm exhausted. I glance up at her through my tears. Her face looks possessed, her eyes glow as if feverish. I can't take it anymore, I don't know what will happen to us.

The cannon wakes us at daybreak. The crowd at Analakely is becoming denser and denser. People have been alerted, they flock from everywhere to this place.

At the hour of the sun streaming golden onto the undersides of the leaves, a soldier comes to bring me for further interrogation. Almost at the same time, two other soldiers take Vero away. I watch nervously as they head for another building a little to the west.

This time, two earth husbands are there to record my words.

"Will you call upon the twelve hills, the sacred power of the twelve sovereigns, and the talismans, Kelimalaza and Mahavaly?"

"I will call upon them day and night, as long as I live on this earth. I also pray that they bless the reign of our beloved Sovereign, the heir of Nampoina and Radama."

"So you will not call upon vazaha gods and vazaha ancestors? You will not observe Sunday as a day of rest, like the vazahas, instead of consecrating them to your sovereigns, as Nampoina and Radama wished?"

"I will never call upon the ancestors of the vazahas and I will never call upon their gods, whatever gods they may have. On Sundays, I will work for our Sovereign Mistress and for the grandeur of her realm, so that the world and other nations may be impressed and amazed by her countless good works."

"We thank you for your devotion to our Mistress."

"She is the sole mistress of my life. May she end it if it pleases her, or may she continue to allow me the benefit of it, if that brings her pleasure."

My bonds are untied and I am freed. I glance to the west as I leave, but I do not see Vero.

We find the Andrianonys, who have also been allowed to leave, on the edge of the large dais, where they've been waiting. The Christian man and his wife have large iron collars around their necks as punishment. But justice has been lenient with them—they haven't been thrown into slavery. I see Voahangy there, too, and I hug the washwoman in gratitude.

"Our friend Rainimahery is here," says Andrianony. "We owe our freedom to him today. He's waiting for us a little ways away; he mustn't be seen in public with arrested criminals."

I press my children against my chest. I thank the Creator for granting me this sweetness and warmth. "May our ancestors bless him and his descendants."

So, my wishes have been granted. Our journey is at an end, and our trials are over. I breathe deep of this air, so pure with the coming happiness. The great city, humming now with vigorous life, is showing us its friendliest side.

As we start to leave, the crowd shifts and blocks us. A regiment of soldiers is arriving at the wide basin, led by an officer on horseback, followed by a train of children and onlookers. The regiment stations itself in front of the buildings and awaits the officer's orders. The officer dismounts and storms into a house.

"Come on, let's go," says Andrianony, his voice cracking.

I hear the sadness in the convert's voice. Others will have a much less enviable fate than ours. What about Vero?

"Could I entrust my children you to, sir?" I ask. "My heart is too heavy and my mind will never find rest without at least trying to know my friend's fate. Voahangy, could you come with me?"

"Yes," says the washwoman. "I understand your sorrow."

"I have to see her, I have to know what they're going to do to her. She's just a little girl whose brain got turned inside out." I put Manarivo in Hanta's arms and address the Christian. "We'll be back at your house before the sun sets."

"Your concern does you much honor. May God guide your feet. If we're not at home when you arrive, a slave will be there waiting for you, to tell you where to find us."

As we start back down the path to Analakely, all the Ambodinandohalo cannons fire at once. Something is happening.

"Be careful!" Andrianony shouts in the distance. "Come back to us in Isotry before the night falls!"

38 *Tsito*

I FOUND MY FORMER MASTER as he was leaving the doctor's house in Amboditsiry. Andriantsitoha was greatly troubled. He'd grown older and thinner, but was dressed more richly than usual. Probably to inspire fear and respect.

"Tsito, you've come back! Come quickly, there's no time to lose. My informants have just told me that four pyres have been built in Faravohitra. I'm trying to find out where Rasoa is. I don't think she's really in danger, she's too clever for them. But I can't overlook anything."

While we hurried along, he told me about Tovo, who was still in his service. More mass trials had taken place in Ambohimanelo, and Tovo's family had been massacred. This caused me great sorrow.

"But the old traitor Ranjato fell as well. I got him in the end. I'd had rumors spread about him before the judges came. In this day and age, there is no pardon for such things. The earth husbands never overlook that kind of information. Ranjato was caught by his own trap."

He didn't know if Tovo had any news from Fara. My heart was seized with anxiety. I had to talk to my friend.

Andriantsitoha had located his family members, whom soldiers had brought to a labor camp one day's journey to the south. He'd just recently managed to free his wives and children, with support from other clan members who, like him, had been smart enough to recede from public memory and start to rebuild their lives. Rasoa was the only one who was still in danger.

"I sent Tovo to follow some of those bloodhounds from the Palace that hunt Christians. He's passing himself off as an enforcer for the Ancestral Coalition. That's the only way to beat them to their marks. He's looking for Vero, who may have been captured."

Things had evolved quickly over the last several months. Persecutions of Christians were rising. Lists of converts were circulating, and the kingdom's masters would fall upon them. The Crown Prince had intervened a few moons earlier on behalf of a group of Christians in prayer that the Sovereign had wanted to execute. Nine of them were eventually put to tangena. One man died, and five others were enslaved. Two captives managed to escape, and the last was clapped in irons. Word had it that the worst was yet to come for the converts.

The Queen was less and less tolerant, and a few days earlier had ordered the destruction of two houses belonging to a member of her own family, Prince Ramonja, because they'd been used for Christian services. Rakoto, the Crown Prince himself, was keeping a low profile: the Prime Minister had accused him in front of his mother of reading the Bible and pledging service to Christians.

Andriantsitoha had heard that converts closest to the Palace, or who were related to important individuals, usually had nothing to fear. They'd only receive mild sentences and would be placed under their powerful relatives' protection. The persecution of Christians from the lower classes or far-flung districts, on the other hand, was becoming brutal. Where did Rasoa and Vero fall into all of that? I wasn't nearly as confident as Andriantsitoha.

"I've prayed to our ancestors that they might look favorably on us," said my former master. "I've just been meditating on the tombs of Rangita and Rafohy, the vazimba princesses who birthed the highland dynasty. On my way back, I found out that a trial had happened at Analakely and that some Christians had been given severe sentences this time. Some of the names mentioned were very well known. But nothing is certain."

According to his informants, a dozen apostates were also going to be thrown off the ramparts of the royal hill. Women were part of the new batch of condemned converts. Where was Tovo?

Faravohitra soon came into view. As we arrived, I stifled a shout: Rasoa was among the converts about to be burned alive. I looked at Andriantsitoha:

his entire person seemed to have swelled with anguish. His veins looked as if they wanted to burst and pour his blood out of his body. She'd been bound to her martyr companions a few paces away from the pyres. She'd gotten thin, and her clothes were tattered, but it was definitely her. It was a dense crowd, and Andriantsitoha, struck with vertigo, had to sit on a mound of earth until he recovered.

"We must act quickly," he said, leaping to his feet and dragging me after him. "Don't forget, you're one of the Crown Prince's companions."

Seeing that the dignitaries and high judges who were supposed to be at the execution hadn't yet arrived, we went straight for the chief executioner.

"This girl shouldn't be here," said Andriantsitoha brusquely. "You've made an error, sir."

The man was taken aback. "Excuse me, my lord?"

"Why must I repeat myself, man? A different punishment awaits this girl. What's your problem, that you always misunderstand everything like that?"

The man, a member of the royal guard, was tall and solidly built. But he was only an executioner, easily impressed by the former lord of Ambohimanelo's self-assuredness. He looked as us, confused, and I congratulated myself on not yet shedding my European clothes. A worried shadow fell over his eyes, and he turned to look over the convicts.

Andriantsitoha didn't give him time to think. "Go untie her and give me two of your men to escort her," he demanded.

"But . . . the judge did say to bring her here, my lord—"

"I am a judge," interrupted Andriantsitoha, "and I tell you that this girl should not have been brought here. She is kin to Rakoto. Do you ever stop to think about what you're doing?"

The scared guard called two of his men and consulted with them briefly. Andriantsitoha saw Rasoa looking at him. His voice turned hard and sharp as ice.

"Do I need to have someone's head here? What do you have to chit-chat about? I told you to untie her!"

The men complied, and Rasoa was untied. A murmur swept through the crowd. People wondered aloud who this important person was, intervening on behalf of a Christian. We watched with satisfaction as the guards heard what was being said, wondering without daring to ask out loud and cause offense. They were supposed to know all the Palace dignitaries.

Rasoa was ready to go. She was calm, but her eyes were blazing. The guards waited at a respectful distance. We believed for a moment that we would leave, that we would win.

"Don't be afraid," said Andriantsitoha to Rasoa.

"I'm not afraid. I know that Kristy protects me."

"I'm going to take you with me. We'll leave. But you must not say anything around the guards. Don't speak, don't draw attention to yourself, don't answer any questions—"

"I will not renounce His name."

"Rasoa, please!"

"Excuse me, my lords," said a voice, "but who are you?"

For a moment, I felt like I'd tumbled into an abyss, but Andriantsitoha would not be flustered. We hadn't seen this man arrive, but he was clearly a judge; Rasoa seemed to recognize him. Both guards had come back as well. Andriantsitoha peered leisurely at his counterpart. I took a deep breath. We could not appear rushed, or worried.

"Allow me to ask you the same question, my lord," said Andriantsitoha. "Who might you be?"

"My name is Andrianasy, and I am one of the judges named by our Sovereign Mistress to handle the cases of these four criminals."

"Yes, your name is not unknown to me. Might it be possible that our message did not reach you?"

"What message?"

"Look, we must talk, this is becoming rather awkward," said my former master, taking him congenially by the arm and leading him off to the side.

We didn't have much time. But the new arrival was a shrewd man, not easily fooled. Andriantsitoha introduced himself with his real name, perhaps knowing that it wouldn't mean much to the judge as it was, and murmured confidentially.

"Let's get right to it: You know as well as I do that some of these converts are none other than our own children, our own descendants, that they were pressured by those Christian apostates to renounce the heritage of Nampoina and Radama. This woman is an especially difficult and cruel case, my lord, because she has strong ties to Prince Rakoto."

"I know. But our Majesty herself ordered her to be put to death."

"Well, she's changed her mind."

"What?"

"I told you. Our Prince, a close companion of my friend here, fell into deep sorrow at the thought of seeing this girl die. And his mother, our Sovereign, could not bear to see her child endure such torment. That's why we are here, and it seems that we arrived just in time."

"But we did not receive any messenger from the Palace!"

"Really? That surprises me, seeing as we sent one. In that case, you're quite fortunate that we came ourselves! Can you imagine what would have happened if you'd committed such a grave error?"

It seemed that Andriantsitoha's boldness was paying off. The other man looked shaken, torn between suspicion and the fear of doing something wrong. This era, and the reigning atmosphere at the Palace, did not allow for mistakes. Determining verdicts for influential Christians could be a nightmare for judges sometimes. They may well have been judges, but they could lose their heads, too, for not being able to correctly untangle the web of influences. Rumor even had it that one of the Commander in Chief's wives was hiding and protecting converts.

But suspicion won out within Andrianasy. The magistrate said that he couldn't make a decision without receiving direct orders from the Palace. He decided to go to the Sovereign's residence and suspend the execution until his return. They wouldn't dare proceed with the execution without having consulted the Palace again.

Acting insulted by the lack of trust, Andriantsitoha cut off his conversation with Andrianasy with a few choice words. It was time: I'd seen other dignitaries arriving in the distance, a group that could include someone who might recognize us. We hurried away. We had to act fast.

. . .

But what could we do? Where could we go? The situation was urgent enough to necessitate a quick selection. Andriantsitoha had a few high-placed contacts who could intervene. I myself had some openings to the Crown Prince, but I knew I couldn't persuade him without Rainimahery's help. We didn't have time to look for the Menamaso. No, we needed someone with direct access to the Palace or the Prime Minister's office. That only left us with two or three possibilities.

We ran toward Anosy.

Prince R . . .'s house was hopelessly empty. We yelled at the entrance to get someone's attention, but got no response. The backyard was deserted; even the slaves appeared to have abandoned the house. A neighbor informed us that the prince, a kinsman of the royal family who was known for his affection for Christians, had moved to the eastern side of the city. He said that the prince had been disgusted by the recent events in the City. Andriantsitoha roared in frustration.

Next, we knocked on the door of a high-ranking military officer in Isoraka. Andriantsitoha knew the man because he'd married a Zafimanelo woman. His wife, related to one of the Queen's old favorites and very close to the Prime Minister, told us that he was on his way to the Palace. We sprinted after him.

We spied his cortege as the sun's rays were already shining full onto the city. My heart was pounding so hard that it seemed about to burst in my chest, as a fruit splits under an ax. The general almost didn't recognize Andriantsitoha, and his men tried to block our way, taking us for brigands—we were sweaty, disheveled. Andriantsitoha shook with emotion.

"What in the world has happened to you, my friend?" asked the astonished general.

Andriantsitoha explained the situation and asked him to save his sister's life. He was prepared to sacrifice everything.

"Myself and my descendants will be eternally grateful to you, my general. I'll bring my men, my fortune, and the support of my entire

306

clan to support your ambitions. Save her! Bring me to our Sovereign Mistress."

The man was a sharp politician, well known for his innovative ideas and commitment to the kingdom's values. But his coalition had been ousted by an opposition group after the assassination of its figurehead, one of the Queen's favorites named Andriamihaja. He was not unaffected by promises of rallying support, and he had some respect for Christians.

"I think she still harbors a bit of ill favor against your clan, my friend," he said. "It would be difficult for me to get you into the Palace. But I promise you that I'll go there directly and try to be received by the Queen, I'll do everything that I can."

Andriantsitoha thanked the general profusely and watched him leave with his little cortege, his heart in his throat. We felt the sinking feeling of having done everything we could without actually increasing our chances of success. I decided to risk it all to see Prince Rakoto.

We set off immediately, but destiny was against us.

The clamor from the crowd came like thunder as we hurried toward the royal hill.

"They're burning the Christians!"

We turned toward Faravohitra and watched, as smoke rose into the air.

But all of a sudden, it started to rain, and the roaring of voices receded to a loud murmur. People were saying that the Perfumed Lord was intervening to save the Christians. Andriantsitoha stifled a cry and took off for the hills. I ran after him.

We slipped and skinned our knees on the sharp rocks but felt nothing. The rain reinvigorated us, breathed a fool's hope into us. Then, the downpour stopped, and we felt heat on our arms and shoulders again. Andriantsitoha lifted his head in terror. The sun. Rays streaming through the clouds. The wind was blowing the clouds toward the great plains.

We arrived at the site of torture, stunned and spent, as the columns of smoke rose again toward the sky, thickening. The flames spread rapidly, and we heard the convicts begin to scream. The crowd had compacted, and we could only move forward slowly. Women wept, and men lost their temper with the children shoving behind them. There was a great cry and the crowd stepped back as one: a pyre had caught fire. The tortured soul's despairing screams rose above all the other sounds for many long seconds, then stopped.

Andriantsitoha pushed through the crowd, swearing and screaming. He got smacked in return but didn't seem to feel a thing.

We saw her. She was tied to the second pyre from the left. She was trying to keep calm, but her lips trembled and tears streamed down her cheeks. The fire roared, enveloping her up to her waist, and she let out a long scream, an unending sob. Andriantsitoha tried to run to her, but a forest of bodies, arms, and heads kept them apart. He stretched helpless hands out to her, his eyes bulging. The flames flared up anew and covered her to her neck in a fiery gown.

Rasoa's hair caught fire, then her face became a black mask, frozen around a gaping, voiceless mouth, and Andriantsitoha lost consciousness.

As he came to, Andriantsitoha looked around himself as if pondering a dark world of evil creatures. I'd been trying to revive him for a while. My heart broke to see him like that. His piercing cry watching his sister burn, that of a trapped animal, still prickled my senses.

The only thing left on the pyre was a bent, black thing only vaguely resembling a human being. The former lord of Ambohimanelo, on the ground, unable to stand, looked at the thing that had been his younger sister, without understanding. People watched him in silence. I tried to help him up, but he shoved my hand away. He tore his clothes with both hands and growled in rage. A long moan came from his chest, growing to a wild shriek as he thrashed his fist toward the sky.

"What's wrong with that one?" someone cried. "He's probably one of them!"

Andriantsitoha looked at them, then turned like a frightened animal. Before I could catch him, he leapt to his feet and raced through the swarming City, spewing curses.

"He's mad! He's a madman! Look out!"

He tore down the slope, half-naked and roaring like a devil. The crowd parted before him, children fled when they saw him. I took off but stumbled and fell. I lost him.

The stupefied crowd watched as a huge rainbow arched above the royal hill. It was so huge as to be terrifying. I raced down to the plain, but couldn't find Andriantsitoha.

I couldn't waste time looking for him; I couldn't do much for him, as it was. I decided to return to my house, near Mahamasina. It was a shame, I was probably going to have to leave without seeing Tovo.

I stumbled across my Sahasoan friend on the little path to my house.

He had been looking for me. "Where were you?" he cried in agitation. "I heard you were with Andriantsitoha! I've been trying to find you for hours! It's too late now, Rasoa is dead!"

"How is Fara?" I asked. "Have you seen her?"

He hadn't seen her since he'd left the village two years earlier. He'd kept a quick note she'd written:

Tsito: Tovo's family is dead. We're frightened. There's something I have to tell you. Our lives could change. We must pray to our ancestors. Come quickly. Apart from you, we're like orphans. Fara.

Tovo was deathly afraid, too. He couldn't find Vero. The city's cannons suddenly fired again.

39 *Fara*

STILL NO SIGN of Vero. A bigger and bigger crowd presses its way into the wide basin at Analakely. Voahangy and I hold hands so we don't lose each other.

Rumors are flying, feeding conversations. We hear that the Sovereign will be making a proclamation, that the Prime Minister will address the convicts before they undergo an ordeal. They-who-call-forth-the-tangena-spirit, famous ones, have been spotted with the earth husbands who interrogate the accused. But we hear one rumor above the rest: the Ancestral Coalition, which, since Radama's time, has united dignitaries opposing the missionaries, has demanded punishments as examples to the converts and the rest of the kingdom's enemies.

We ask some prisoners and families who are still in the square about Vero.

"No, we don't know who you're talking about. There are so many people here, you know, we can't see all of them. There were some officers and judges who came to address everyone. A few were taken right after that, we don't know where to. Others are still inside, undergoing the trial of tangena."

Ten paces away, soldiers are throwing things onto a bonfire. I touch Voahangy's arm.

"Are they burning books?" I ask.

"It's one of the measures the Palace is taking against the Europeans' religious influence. They've seized a great number of them: the Baiboly and all the other texts that sing the praises of the vazaha god."

Voahangy lowers her voice. She tells me that everything from the missionaries' era is being combed through: all the customs, clothing, even words. The word "darkness" has been banned, because vazahas used it to slander the kingdom.

310

We're close to the buildings in the basin. My washwoman friend finally bribes a soldier to try to find out where Vero is. He looks for her among the ones still undergoing an ordeal, but doesn't find her. Now, we have to look at the bodies of the ones who already succumbed to Manamango. They've been left behind the houses for slaves or laborers sent by the authorities to drag over to the communal grave. After asking permission from the soldiers standing guard, we walk among the corpses, many of which have already been stripped by servants or robbers.

Vero isn't here either.

"Go to Andohalo," other people tell us. "That's where they're selling criminals and their families. If you have enslaved relatives that you'd like to buy back, that's where you'll have the most luck."

"Or go look in Faravohitra. I heard officers say that a few converts had been brought there."

Faravohitra is closer. We hoist ourselves up the steep slope leading to the center of town instead of the road that winds up the contour of the hill—it's faster this way. We hold onto shrubs and sometimes have to scale huge rocks.

When we get halfway up, we hear people shouting in the distance. The crowd squeezes tighter. Clouds have formed over the royal hill, as if foretelling a tragedy. It starts raining, a heavy downpour, but it's quickly swept away by a wind blowing out of the northeast. The hill becomes slippery, which slows our pace. We hear more screaming.

As the city's inhabitants converge on Faravohitra, the final village on the way to the Palace, I ask what's happening.

"The Christians!" they answer. "They burned them alive!"

We hurry toward the site of the executions, but by the time we get there the crowd is already scattering. Some flee, frightened by the enormous rainbow that's appeared over the hill, as if it's pouring out of the exact spot where the Christians were martyred. People whisper that the god of the Christians is displaying his presence and anger. Others are saying that it's the Christians' souls on their way to the market of no return called Paradisa. On the ground, there are only piles of rubble and ash left. The bodies have been taken away. No one knows the names of the Christians who were burned here.

There's nothing else we can do in this place. We have to go to Andohalo, and hope.

"I, the Queen of Madagascar, declare that no religion, whatever it may be, save that of Nampoina and Lehidama and our ancestral traditions, will ever be introduced and practiced in this country. I reject all other religions absolutely. If I had not ordered that the followers of this new religion admit their guilt themselves, they would soon have overthrown this kingdom, and all peoples would have followed them. They are considered rebels. For this reason, I have decided to punish them, according to the spirit of Nampoina and Lehidama, which has been revealed to me."

This is the Sovereign's message, transmitted by the high judges and superior officers of the People Under the Sky, in this twenty-first year of her reign.

We run to Andohalo. Crowds crush into this neighborhood on the hills; in addition to the gawkers, entire villages have traveled here in the hopes of saving relatives or friends thrown into slavery. Such public auctions attract people under normal circumstances, and the rumors have attracted a crowd three times larger than normal.

We have to elbow our way through to get to the front. After scanning the different groups of convicts, we have to face the facts: no Vero.

Just as I start to harbor a little hope, to think that perhaps Vero had been let go, a great clamor rises from the City.

"They've taken the Christians to the edge of the cliff!"

People scramble up to the edge of the Andohalo slave market, where the view is unrestricted, to both the plains and the high cliffs that tower over the southwest of the city. The other parts of the hill are already mobbed with people. Thousands of eyes are riveted onto an enormous rock hanging out into the air from the buttress: tiny figures are visible on there, some of which are in uniform.

A second clamor erupts: "They're throwing them into the ravine!"

One body breaks away from the rock, spinning like a wisp of straw, and disappears from sight.

It took forever to reach the place where the Christians were chained up, awaiting their fate. As soon as we get there, I feel my limbs drain of energy: Vero is among the convicts.

I realize that I don't know what I came to this place to do. What can I do for Vero? I can't save her. I can't even bring her a small bit of comfort. For that matter, she doesn't seem aware of what's going on around her. She's looking straight in front of her, indifferent to the muttering crowd.

"Their love of prayer is what's getting them killed," someone says. "They said they'd rather die than stop praying."

"That one there calls upon the ancestors of others," explains another, pursing his lips at Vero. "That's why they're going to make her drop."

I came only to see her one last time. Our paths will diverge here, for good, after so many years. We've arrived at a place where the river splits, and each of us has made her own choice. The branch Vero took is approaching a waterfall, and she knows it. As for the path of my own life, I leave it up to the Creator and our ancestors to decide.

The Christians are held ten paces from the edge of the cliff. A group of men, including judges and soldiers, is holding council nearby, occasionally shouting questions at the convicts.

Vero is designated the next victim.

She seems to wake up and put on a serene expression when two soldiers come to get her.

"They say that she refused to renounce the vazaha religion," someone mutters. "Why would she do that? Have the vazahas found a remedy against death?"

As the soldiers take her away, Vero turns her head back toward the crowd, and our eyes meet. I try to wave, but it means nothing. Vero smiles sadly at me, turns back around, and follows her executioners without a fight. I close my eyes. The crowd screams. She's not here anymore.

The next instant, I'm running, tearing down the slope as fast as I can, grabbing shrubs along the way.

It feels like the ravine wants to drag me down too, to devour me. I run into people, and they swear and shove me aside. Anytime I stop, I feel the ground giving way below my feet. The image of Vero's body spinning in space, about to be dashed on the rocks below, haunts my mind and soul.

"Out of the way! Let her through!"

"Did you see? Maybe she's a Christian! It looks like she's running away!"

Finally, I manage to get away from the mob. Spying a thick clump of bushes behind the road, I scamper over and crouch behind the plants, like a hunted animal. People are running all around me. I'm trembling all over. But the noise from the executions follows me: the crowd screams every time a convict is pushed over the edge. It's like thousands of voices are chanting with each Christian's fall: "There! Another! Another!"

A dozen times I try to run away, to hide somewhere. A dozen times, the screams from the crowd comes to drive me out. My mind is bruised by the waves of terror and my chest aches as if beset by poison more violent than the tangena.

"Fara! Fara! Stop, where're you going?" a voice shouts from far away.

Voahangy has taken off after me. But I'm incapable of stopping, waiting for her. I have to get out of here.

I'm lost among the people of the vast city, I'm regaining my senses again, slowly. Standing in the middle of a wide street, I'm trying to reorient myself. The surrounding hills seem identical, and all the roads look alike. I can't remember where we came from. The street is very busy. People look at me as they pass. I must be completely disheveled. I must look like a beggar.

"There!" shouts a voice. "Bring me that girl!"

People grab me and drag me toward a group of prisoners. I don't understand what's happening. But the voice of the man who barked the order seems familiar. A hoarse voice, like a disturbed breeze. Where have I heard it?

"I've found you again!"

He appears to be the leader of the troop driving a dozen captives before them. He's dressed in black and red and wears a strange headpiece set with stones. His face, neck, and hands are covered with scars. It's the seer from my ordeal in Sahasoa.

"Do you know who I am?" he says in his animal voice.

"I do recognize you, my lord. But I do not understand. I already purified my name, back in Sahasoa."

The man leans over me and whispers in my ear. "You didn't understand my question. I'll repeat it: Do you know who I am?"

"Yes, my lord. You are one of the earth husbands who took part in my judgment in Sahasoa."

"Yes, but I am also Rahantsana, the firstborn and heir of Ranakombemihisatra, the guardian of the talisman Mandatsivoho. And you killed my father."

"I haven't killed anyone, my lord."

"I am Ranaka's son. You come from a long line of evil. I was never like you. I never made my soul subservient to the vazahas."

"I don't understand."

"I should have known last time that you'd carried the slave's child. I always knew you were born for betrayal. But you took advantage of my weakness."

"What? No, this can't be . . . Creator protect me, you're Faly!"

40 *Tsito*

WHEN TOVO AND I heard the cannon fire, we jumped. At first, I thought that the cannon had been marking some important dignitary's departure.

But Tovo cried out: the slopes of the surrounding hills were packed with people. We hadn't noticed anything, fully absorbed in our conversation. My hut was in the Mahamasina valley, not far from the royal stables. The enormous Ampamarinana boulder dominated our view, like an imminent catastrophe suspended in the sky above clusters of houses.

We saw a body fall from the boulder. People screamed: "They're throwing Christians off the cliff!"

We ran after the crowd, to where the bodies had crashed to the ground. More clamors rose as we ran, and we saw two more bodies hurtle through space before disappearing from sight behind the trees. We finally reached the rocks below, out of breath, and fought our way through the amassed onlookers.

The rocks were bloody. Most of the bodies lay disjointed, grotesque. Soldiers watched the area but didn't forbid access: as at all public executions, the people had to see with their own eyes what happened to enemies of the kingdom. The fourth body especially was attracting the crowd's attention. It was a woman. We approached, trembling.

Tovo shuddered. The face was covered with dust but intact. The eyes were open, as if staring at the sky. "Vero!" It was her, straight out of my childhood. Vero, the little girl with great big eyes that shone so feverishly. A flood of memories and profound sadness washed over me.

Tovo dropped to his knees and took his sister's hand, his face flooding with tears. It was over.

I asked a soldier if we could take the body with us.

"Touching the bodies is forbidden," he answered. "Palace orders."

"But we're family," I insisted.

The soldiers refused. The orders were strict. I felt awful for my friend. That was how he lost the last of his family.

"Leave me. Please," said Tovo. "I'm going to stay with her until they take her away. To pray. I fear that our paths, too, may diverge here. I know that you want to return to Sahasoa as soon as possible and find Fara. I will endeavor to find Andriantsitoha."

I whispered a few inadequate words of comfort to my friend, clasped him by his shoulder, and left, forcing my emotions down. Another clamor went up from the crowd, signaling the last Christian's fall.

My mind was wracked with opposing thoughts. Rasoa was dead. Now Vero. What sign were our ancestors sending me? What funereal turn of fate had led me down these fatal roads? I looked at the Palace, which seemed to blaze above the city. I remembered how fascinated Fara was by this city. It was best for me to try to find Rainimahery.

The persecutions continued. I passed several trains of prisoners being taken to Analakely. One of them was led by a man dressed in ritualistic red and black garments, a seer, whose appearance sent whispers through the crowd. I felt drawn to that group. I examined the prisoners one by one, when a man attracted my attention on the other side of the street, half-hidden by the crowds.

I recognized him instantly, but I had to let the line of prisoners pass. It was Andriantsitoha. He looked so peculiar that people were stopping to stare at him. His clothes were torn across the top, leaving half of his chest visible. His mouth was twisted in mute anguish that was frightening to behold. With his wild mass of hair and his long arms dangling uselessly at his side, it was like seeing a frozen ghost, someone whose soul had left their living body.

I remembered a question he'd once asked me: "Do you think we're cursed?"

I crossed the street. "How are you feeling, my lord?"

He seemed to exert a superhuman effort to piece together what was being said to him. By approaching him, I'd dragged him back to the land of the living, against his wishes. His whole being exuded grief.

"How are you feeling, my lord?" I asked again.

He looked at me with delirious eyes. His mouth moved to form snippets of sentences. "So, the world keeps living? People keep talking, walking? Suffering is nothing. The mind is the poison. It dissolves slowly into blood. A shroud covering you while you live . . . "

"My lord, Tovo's sister is dead. Their destinies finally crossed, but in the worst of ways: she was executed."

"Destiny? The ancestors say that it's a chameleon on a tree branch. It only takes a hissing child for it to change color."

People nearby were shouting. A scuffle. Blood was boiling. We couldn't stay there. I took my former master by the arm and led him back to his house.

An hour later, I set off for Rainimahery's house.

41 *Fara*

I'M WALKING AMONG PRISONERS once again, bound by my neck and feet. Why do our ancestors attack me so? I keep looking for Voahangy in the crowd, but in vain. The washwoman is my last and only hope. I must let her know what has happened, I must send her to tell Andrianony and Rainimahery.

People watch our convoy pass. My eyes dart among them feverishly, driven by mad hope. If I can attract the attention of someone I know, maybe I'll be saved? But the absurdity of such an idea devastates me even more. Who besides Voahangy would recognize me in this big city, so far from Sahasoa?

And yet, I feel renewed hope burst within me when I think I've spotted a familiar face, there, on the side of the road. Our convoy has passed him, and I catch sight of him in between blinking; I know that I must attract this man's attention. In the same an instant, my memory reveals his identity to me: the lord of Ambohimanelo! I spin my head wildly toward him, trying to find a way to signal him without attracting the attention of Rahantsana, who could kill me on the spot.

Now I see the other man, a tall man, talking to Andriantsitoha. I stop, struck dumb. Then a wordless scream erupts from my chest and I run toward him, arms outstretched.

"Tsito! Tsito! Help me! Help me!"

"Silence, you witch!"

The first blow hits my temple and stuns me half senseless. I fall in the dust, unable to balance in my shackles. I keep screaming Tsito's name, but my cries are muffled by the noise of the crowd and the other prisoners. A heavy stick rains blows down on me, but I don't feel a thing.

Tsito. He is here, just steps away.

There is blood in my mouth. The last thing I see before losing consciousness is Voahangy's dismayed face, staring at me from the crowd.

42 *Tsito*

WHEN I REACHED Rainimahery's house, I was frustrated not to find him there, and I only stopped myself from swearing out of consideration for the family of Christians that appeared to be hiding out there. It only reinforced my premonition. I knew that I'd need my Menamaso companion soon.

The Christians gave me an odd look. I could tell they were afraid. They were wearing the heavy iron collar of convicts and had trouble moving. They asked me timidly if I was part of the brotherhood. I nodded, and they exchanged glances. A little girl and a newborn were sleeping in Rainimahery's bed.

I spoke with the father, who started telling me their story. Out of the corner of my eye, I saw his wife try to rouse the little girl. Who were these people?

"My name is Andrianony," said the father. "We live in Isotry . . . "

As he spoke, I glanced at the little girl, who by that point was sitting up at the foot of the bed. Probably the Christians' offspring. But on second glance, as Andrianony's wife brought her toward me, I thought I'd gone insane: it was Fara, as I'd known her at ten years old!

At first, the little girl didn't recognize me. I froze, my mouth hanging open. We'd met in another place, several years earlier, for a brief time. But I leapt up, trembling, wrenching myself from my stupor.

She cried out and her eyes opened wide. "Tsito!" she said, coming toward me. "You're Tsito!"

I approached her, my eyes brimming with tears, my head spinning. I took her in my arms, shaking, unable to reorder my thoughts. Hanta let go and ran to the bed. "Wake up, Manarivo! Your father's here!"

"Your . . . father?" I spluttered, watching her approach with the baby in her arms.

Andrianony explained everything that had happened over the last two hours.

Rainimahery had asked them about the two children they'd brought, jumping when they heard him mention my name.

"Tsito! It is true? And what was their village called? Sahasoa? Why didn't you tell me that when you sent the messenger? I could have brought him with me!"

"We weren't thinking about those details. We had to save them first! But if their father is here, they'll be able to see him soon, right?"

"No, he's supposed to be on his way back to Sahasoa this very moment! Where is their mother? Why did she leave them behind?"

Andrianony had explained to him that Fara had left to try to help a Christian friend and should have been meeting them afterward at their place in Isotry. Rainimahery had stood and paced nervously around the house. He'd sent one of his servants to my place, not hoping for much—he was sure that I'd left, and had resigned himself to not seeing me for a long time.

Andrianony, for his part, had sent his eldest son back to their home in Isotry, with instructions to bring Fara as soon as she arrived.

But no sooner had the boy left than he ran back. "They threw Christians off of the Ampamarinana cliff! They're saying that the other convicts were burned!"

The news had dismayed the whole household. Andrianony and his family wept bitterly. Hanta was worried, but Rainimahery tried to reassure her. "Yes, a terrible thing has happened, but your mother shouldn't be worried. She's not Christian. We'll just have to find her."

"There weren't any Christians in Sahasoa, but a lot of people died!" Hanta protested with tears in her eyes.

"Yeah, there were convoys of prisoners everywhere!" shouted Andrianony's son. "Most of them aren't Christian! They're all people suspected of conspiracy or sorcery!"

They could hear crowds bustling outside. In the end, they'd decided that, as a precaution, no one should leave the house. Except for Rainimahery, who'd gone to Isotry himself, to Andrianony's house, to find out what was going on.

Andrianony the Christian had barely finished telling me all of that when my Menamaso friend burst through the door with a woman. "Fara has been arrested! They took her to Analakely! We must save her!"

When we went outside, it felt like the City was having trouble breathing, like a great sick creature. Pieces of news flew through the streets, carried by swiftly moving groups of people.

"The talisman guardians have sworn to exterminate all sympathizers of the missionaries, down to the very last one! The high judges have been authorized to put half the city to tangena if necessary."

We heard that the Sovereign was going to give a speech and oversee the executions herself. Entire regiments of soldiers were spreading through the city, as if in confirmation.

Black clouds gathered above the royal hill. A cold breeze passed through the city.

43　*Fara*

SO, IT WAS HIM.

He survived the explosion at the magazine.

He was Ranaka's son. Now I understand all the violence and hatred that motivated him all those years. His father was beheaded and his mother died of grief. Ranjato adopted Faly, the orphan, but never revealed his parents' identities—most likely to protect him from the retribution of families harmed by the seer, to protect him from people like me and my family. Did he know that his father had tried to kill me? Did he know, when he was kissing me, clutching me?

He was different.

Yes, he knew that Ranaka had tried to kill me. He'd seen the sacrifice of Rasoaray's children himself, and was proud of it. I know now what it was that I could never stand in him: the spirit of death. The fetid breath of revenge. But the ancestors finally gave him an appearance that best matches his soul. He's a corpse. Even his voice is dead, ripped out of his throat by blazing heat.

I will not be destroyed by Rahantsana. I will not let Rahantsana destroy my family.

"Are you going to tell me where your spawn are?"

We're in one of the brick houses in Analakely. I'm alone with him, but I can hear the tangena servants busying themselves outside. I'm sitting on a mat unrolled in the middle of the bare room, my hands tied behind my back. My left eye will not open. I can feel dried blood biting at skin on that side of my face.

"I left them in Sahasoa. They stayed with their great-grandmother. It's too dangerous to bring them here."

"You're lying! You'd never leave them! Where are you hiding them? Oh, you'll talk, I promise you that!"

A man comes in. He's a kinsman of the royal family. Vague hope passes through me, but soon disappears.

"This is the girl that tried to cause problems in the crowd? I don't see why you didn't execute her on the spot. We can't waste time on cases like these."

"I did not execute her because she represents a much larger danger, my lord, and we must avert it," replied Rahantsana.

"Oh? What danger is that?"

He takes the high judge aside, into another room. I hear them talking in low voices, as outside the crowd in the basin continues to throb.

" . . . a cursed family . . . a spiderweb of apostates . . . "

I hear the high judge leave, clearing his throat. The square buzzes with movement, muffled trampling. In the distance, the hills of the great City echo back the cowherds' calls and children's cries.

I hear women come to the door. They speak with Rahantsana, whose guttural voice rises above the rest.

After a lengthy discussion, the seer comes back into the room where I sit, his face distorted into a horrible smile.

"I found them. Your time on this earth is over."

44 *Tsito*

WE HURRIED TOWARD ANALAKELY.
The sun had gone past its height and was beginning to fall. The city brimmed with confusion and fear. Any minor incident drew crowds and led to shouting and panic. Children cried as they roamed the streets, disoriented and separated from their parents. Dogs howled at nothing.

On our way, I watched soldiers dispersing the crowds. Voahangy wrung her hands in concern, praying out loud to our ancestors. She'd grown very fond of Fara, the village girl from Sahasoa; she said that she couldn't erase the memory of her bloody face from her mind. She'd tied our child onto her back with a wrapper. The thought that Manarivo could lose his mother filled her with sorrow. Her soul seemed wracked with the torment of our family tree.

A group of angry men barreled down toward us from a street corner. The crowd on the street moved as one, pushing me off to the side.

"Look out! Get off the road!" I bellowed at the others, too far away to intervene. Voahangy grabbed Hanta's arm and pulled her back just before they would have trampled her. The little girl screamed in terror. Nobody had seen her in the chaos and clouds of dust. Voahangy signaled to me that everything was good. The men were pulling a captive behind them, his face bloody, hands bound, his clothes ripped to shreds.

"We'll be there soon!" I shouted. "Keep going!"

Voahangy and Hanta were keeping up with our fast pace as best they could. Hanta now clung to Voahangy's hand so that she wouldn't get swept away. Rainimahery and I did our best to keep them safe.

Soldiers passed more and more frequently, then brought the crowd to a standstill, forming a wall of humans. Women were shoved aside, people fell to the ground.

The uniformed regiment lined up.

"Look!" someone yelled. "Dignitaries!"

But they were mounted officers, staring severely down on the common-ers. No one knew what was happening or who was crossing the City. It had to be someone very important for the soldiers to take so many precautions.

A whisper spread and grew: "The Queen!"

We heard the military fanfare coming from far away. We were powerless: the road was completely blocked off, and it would be impossible to get through. Crossing the street would mean impeding the path of a royal procession, which could warrant immediate death.

The mounted officers at the head of the procession paced nervously, ready to charge any onlookers who moved too far into the street. After them came the soldiers in blue tunics and red pants. They marched at a rhythmic quickstep, rifles shouldered, the colorful plumes in their hats rolling like waves.

Then the royal chair came into view, crowned with a red parasol and carried by eight royal slaves dressed in eight different colors of wide, sweeping lambas. A royal eagle sat on the carrier's footrest, like the prow of a ship, and two more golden eagles towered over the backrest. The litter was upholstered in crimson red, trimmed in gold, and encrusted with rubies and aquamarines. Its passage was hailed by the low rumble of a thousand mouths saying, "*Sarasara*, mistress! May you live to an old age! May illness stay away!"

Ranavalona, sitting straight in her chair, looked out at her people with a worried expression. She wore a long scarlet dress with a train that covered the entire litter and draped off of both sides. A silver diadem with pearls and red coral was set on her head. The human mass lining the streets bared their heads and bent in half as she passed.

"What are you doing?" said Rainimahery, tugging my arm down. "Have you lost your senses?"

Snapping back to reality, I knelt and stayed bent over double, eyes to the ground, while the Queen passed. It wasn't allowed, looking at sovereigns.

My mind was burning; we were so close to Fara, and yet so powerless. Every second that passed brought her closer to death. Time, cruel time, was working against us. The procession seemed infinite.

I snuck a glance up. The Sovereign's eyes stopped scanning the multitudes, focusing in surprise on something I couldn't make out. An officer followed the Queen's gaze, saw what she was looking at, and took off instantly on his horse in our direction, loosing his sword from its sheath. But the Sovereign stopped him with one sharp word. Terrified, I realized what was happening: Hanta's head had popped up from the rest, and she gazed at the Queen with her great big brown eyes, gaping in admiration and fear. Perhaps she didn't believe that anything was real, perhaps she thought that the woman reclining on that chair had descended directly from the skies, like the princesses in Bebe's tales.

Mavo met her eyes, and even turned back slightly so as not to lose sight of her as the procession moved on. Rainimahery shoved Hanta's head back down.

The Queen smiled almost imperceptibly and turned away. The royal chair passed.

But it wasn't finished. The Sovereign brought an entire entourage in her wake wherever she went. The initial flourish was followed by some members of the royal family. I peeked up at their faces, but the Crown Prince wasn't among them. The vazahas came directly afterward. They were all Europeans whom the Queen had decided to keep close to her, whom she'd named kinsmen of the sovereigns. They were lavishly dressed and looked out inscrutably over the crowd. Among them, I recognized Laborde and another man who people suspected to be a priest. The ladies in waiting followed, in silken dresses trimmed in gold, then the choirs of the Queen's musicians. Time dragged on and on. We waited until the last of the royal slaves had passed by, marking the end of the procession, and rushed toward the heart of the City.

Arriving at the wide basin, we could see bodies being dragged behind the place called Anjoma, to be discarded up toward Faravohitra. Hanta burst into tears at the sight: all the images of Bao's death were probably coming back to her. A large black bird cried and flew across the sky. We couldn't let ourselves be beaten. We pressed on.

The square was still filled with prisoners, bound and squatting in the dust. How could we find Fara in this mob? We scanned the hundreds of captives awaiting judgment. I'd noticed the brick houses set slightly back from the platform, and I sped off in their direction. But I was rebuffed by a blockade of soldiers and couldn't get by. In the meantime, Voahangy had come back from Anjoma, where she'd gone to see the bodies of the ones who'd been executed or who had perished from tangena. Fara wasn't there either.

She was in one of those houses, I was sure of it. I lifted my head to look at the City. In Faravohitra, on the hill, groups of city folk were dressed in white, sitting by the rows of long-horned huts, silently observing the processions. I shivered despite the heat, and a bittersweet wave washed over me. Must I lose her at the very instant I found her again? Memories tumbled through my head and I saw the green hills of Sahasoa, its shaded valleys where we had curled up and talked about the future, our plans, our hopes. I also remembered the suffering I felt across the oceans, far away from her, with no news of the village.

Rainimahery spied an officer he knew and approached him; they had a heated conversation. The man shook his head in suspicion and refused to let us pass. The Menamaso clenched his fists; under other circumstances, we wouldn't have even needed to ask permission to pass. As the Crown Prince's companions, we were untouchable. But the Prime Minister had handed down orders to deny any attempt to intervene in the purge. Soldiers hated the Menamasos, and they were fully capable of running us through with their bayonets. I was overcome with despair. What could we do? Rainimahery suggested he go beg the Prince to come in person, and I agreed: it was essentially our only hope.

I sent Voahangy and the children across the basin while we waited. Desperate ideas flew through my mind. I fingered the blade that I kept hidden in my clothes—I would carve a trail of blood through the troops, I would save her, or we would die together. We took shelter in the shade of a large tree, and I started pacing back and forth in front of it, like a man possessed. If only I knew which of the buildings she was in . . . My spirit was strung so tight it could snap. Suddenly, something in the crowd grabbed my attention, and I froze. A man was striding through the onlookers and prisoners' families on the far side. Something about him stopped me, and I took off after him without stopping to think.

I tried not to lose sight of the man, all the while flipping through my memories. Then the image came back to me: this man, I'd come across him this morning. His red and black clothes had attracted my attention. He'd been leading a convoy of prisoners.

Voahangy had mentioned a seer dressed in red. I had to catch up to him.

45 *Rahantsana*

IADA, MY SPIRIT CRIES, for our ancestors' word has fallen into a deep ravine where it is dying, smothered under the weight of the sacrilege perpetrated by enemies of this earth.

Yes, their opprobrious practices and incestuous ways have invaded our land. Our clans have lost their souls; nations, their sacred virtue. Even our language is being corrupted, o Iada, even words flex under their sugared speech! Our youth overstep the bounds of respect, and our cities are sinking into chaos. Our people are deserting their ancestral rice fields to be packed like swine into their cold dwelling places! The slave insults his master with impunity and places a beggar ancestor as King above the sovereigns!

Iada, your son now beseeches your favor. The son who has always been closest to your soul asks for your blessing. This was my destiny: well before I learned the first inklings of the astral sciences, I knew that I would one day follow in your footsteps. By our ancestors' will, I have inherited the most precious gift from you, which any *mpisikidy* seer must possess: intuition.

Remember, Iada: without you having taught me how, I could predict the rain and the hail, several days before the old farmers in Ambohimanelo did, simply by observing the animals' behavior. I could also unerringly say which one in a group of old men would soon pass away, simply by touching the back of his hand or the crux of his elbow.

Iada, you said this of me: "Here is a pleasant child. Only fools are like their fathers."

But it was you, my father, Ranaka, who initiated me and showed me the way. Thanks to you, the lunar calendar and arrangement of seeds had no secrets for me. You taught me plants and hidden meanings and rituals of pacification. You slashed my tongue until it bled, and the palm and four fingers of my right hand, to spread crushed fano seeds there, and I swallowed my pain so as not to disappoint you.

Remember, Iada, once my initiation was complete, you handed me an assegai and invoked the Creator's power over me: "May this boy walk the days and master the moons! May he foresee lifespans, may he be able to see the dead and know the living! Perfumed Lord, let his words never be false, let his skin be honeyed to the sovereigns of this earth, and let his word be accepted by the people!"

Iada, I beseech you. You, who could modify the course of nations and unmake kingdoms by your talent and your wisdom, like the ombiasy masters from the southern shores in the time of the vazimbas. Yes, you, whose beloved head, in my sight and my mother's, broke away from its torso and fell to the ground in a river of blood. You, whose eyes never left me that whole time, I remember it. You, who, on your way to the market of no return, told me to carry out the unfinished task. You, whose final instructions still echo in my ears today, in these trying hours:

"See. Your eyes must learn to see what they do not see, your mind must train itself to read, in lowly seeds or the movement of a leaf, what destiny awaits and how fortune is blowing. To discern signs of a curse behind pleasing traits, or the mark of death in living words. For even newborns are marked, and only ignorant men and rebels will claim those marks of evil should be ignored. Our eyes are not eyes, but friends of the earth, and our hands that hold seeds and thorns from sacred wood are naught but spades that turn the clay of intertwined fates. Our enemies are known in every era: destinies heavy as a scourge, which drag down clans and kingdoms in their wake. We must hunt them down without rest and strike them without mercy, casting them into the furthest ravine or burying them under seven layers of earth and rocks."

Iada, you did not wish for me to perish in the fire of the magazine. You helped me dress my burns. You helped me vanquish my enemies.

Grant now that the sacred virtue of the first sovereigns may envelop me. Grant that the spirit of the twelve sacred hills may show me the way and help me to fell our enemies, like the cyclone's furious whirlwinds and the tremors from the womb of the earth.

46

I SENSE DESTINY'S FLOWING CURRENTS converging on resolution. I sense all the elements that will allow me to complete my quest falling into place. I walk through the crowd. I read the signs. I know that the cursed line is not far, I sense it within my reach.

I left Fara in the high judges' hands. My informants told me that she was, today, in the company of a family of Christians who received judgment and were sent back to their homes. I obtained the names of these Christians and the location of their house. When I told Fara this, she at first tried to deny it. Then she fell to screaming and begging, groveling at my feet. Yes, it is time for justice to be done.

The only thing that remains for me to do is summon a few armed men and fall upon the evil seedlings. I will find the spawn of the cursed one and the slave—it is only a question of time. They will no longer be able to escape our ancestors' judgment. Their fate is sealed.

"They've burned the Christians' remains!"

People around me are screaming. I look up and see smoke rising from a place halfway up the royal hill. They're burning the bodies of the Christians thrown off of the cliff with the remains of those who perished at the stake. It is right that these rebels not be put in the ground, even anonymously at the side of the road, like witches. They must be burned, consumed.

Herds of people slow my progress. They're watching a man on his knees, crying, his face turned toward the sky. Sobbing, he lifts helpless hands toward the flames rising in the distance. He must be kin to one of the executed Christians. I move closer to better see his face.

Him!

The ancestors willed this meeting. For an instant, I am seized with true terror: my deepest premonitions, my soul's most secret predictions, they are all coming to pass. I am petrified, I cannot move. This man, this man before me, is the very incarnation of the sacrilegious forces that shake this earth. The very marriage of subterfuge and deceit, which could have brought the kingdom to its knees. Yet to see him weep, that is a joy. Yes, it means that opposition forces can be crushed, destroyed, even if they are powerful. Blessed be our ancestors.

Andriantsitoha.

He who had my two fathers killed, Ranaka and Ranjato. He whom I went to hunt down in his fief, just a few moons ago. So he was hiding here, in the City of Thousands!

Metal burns my skin. I place my hand at my side; it is my sword. Yes, this is it, the time has come. My hand does not tremble as I draw the sacred blade from its sheath. All destinies must reach their end.

47 *Tsito*

I LOST SIGHT OF THE SEER for a few moments in the moving crowd. I ran faster and scrambled up a small mound to better see over people's heads, but he had disappeared. I swore under my breath. Where had he gone? I couldn't let myself lose him now. Murmurs rumbled through the crowd. I saw the flames and smoke on the hill marking the Christians' end and thought of Vero. That's when I spotted the seer, just twenty paces ahead. He'd swerved off course and unsheathed a sword and was stalking resolutely toward a man who did not see him coming. His eyes glinted like death itself. People were terrified of his appearance and his weapon, and they leapt out of his way, circling back at a safe distance to watch.

I recognized who he was heading for: Andriantsitoha! I dashed forward, screaming, "Out of the way! Out of the way!" But the spectacle had attracted too many people, and I couldn't get through.

The former lord of Ambohimanelo finally saw the man coming, he looked at him with indifference. He didn't even seem to want to defend himself, not even as the other man raised his arm to slice through his flesh.

"Out of the way! Out of the way!"

But the man in red did not complete his swing. His expression turned to one of shock, and he started to vomit blood. He looked at Andriantsitoha incredulously, then his eyes went glassy, as if he were already dead, as Tovo's dagger plunged into his abdomen for the third time. Vero's brother hurriedly wiped off his blade on a corner of his clothes as the seer crumpled, then took Andriantsitoha by the arm like a child and pulled him quickly into an alley.

I ran to the seer and knelt over him, but he'd already joined his ancestors.

As I looked more closely at his deformed face, I was seized with terrible shock. Faly! Yes, Faly, returned from the kingdom of the dead. His face and body marked by the hellish magazine fire.

I heard people screaming. I got hastily to my feet and slipped into the crowd. I lost hope.

I felt that Fara's fate had slipped entirely out of my grasp.

48 *Fara*

I'M SHIVERING, but it's not from the cold water that the servants are pouring over my head and body.

It's from a fear deeper than any that the tangena could elicit: I'm seeing images of my children falling into Rahantsana's hands and dying in pain. I beg my executioners, I tell them of my children, the pieces of my soul. How could they want this? How could our ancestors let this happen? The judges and tangena servants—they too have children, family. I appeal to their mercy.

One of the servants takes a damp cloth and wipes off the coagulated blood that still covers part of my face. He bends toward me, uneasy. "There is nothing we can do for you. You must endeavor to purify your name if you want to see your children again."

The high judge enters.

He places three skins on an iron plate, then pours poison into a cup and begins the invocation of Manamango. He asks the spirit of the tangena to set malice aside so that it does not influence the course of judgment.

"Open your mouth," he says, finally, picking up one of the birdskins.

"Please, wait," I say.

"What is it?" The judge is impatient. "You must not interrupt me and disturb my prayers."

If he is an honest man, there is still hope for me. I take a deep breath before speaking.

"I am a poor woman, my lord, with no husband and no wealth. This city is not the place where my elders rest. My familial tomb is in Ambohimanelo, a week's journey from here. None of my family or friends know where I am right now. No one knows that I will be undergoing a judgment that will decide my life or death. Everyone else who's been accused has a friend, at least, or a relative. Who is going to pray for me? Who will ask that the outcome be favorable and the verdict be just?"

The tangena servants look questioningly at the judge. He looks about to say something but holds it back and stays silent.

I must keep talking; words are the source of life.

"The Lord Rahantsana arrested me in the street, far away from my kinsmen. How could I die like this, in complete isolation, while even animals have family and friends to mourn them?" Tears spring to my eyes.

He-who-calls-forth-the-tangena-spirit turns without a word and goes to get banana-leaf sap from the other room. When he comes back, he sees the two tangena servants speaking in low voices in a corner and gives them a vexed order to stop. They fall silent.

"How do you expect us to notify your family?" he asks. "We're not going to send anyone to Ambohimanelo."

Despite my weakness, my heart leaps for joy at these words, and hope springs forth in me again. I hurriedly explain to him that it won't be necessary to go all the way to Ambohimanelo, that I have a kinswoman in the City, named Voahangy, who most likely followed us and is probably looking for me at this very moment, outside, just a few steps from here.

The judge has me repeat her name, then signals to the two servants.

"I'm sure she followed me," I say. "She has to be waiting outside."

The two servants exit.

They return after a few moments and speak quietly to the judge. He looks satisfied.

"We've found your kinswoman, the one named Voahangy. She is praying for you outside of this house. It is time for us to continue our work."

"She says to tell you that your family is doing fine and that someone named Tsito is with them," whispers one of the servants.

It feels like a massive rock has been lifted from the crown of my head. Tsito is here, he will protect the children. But I still have to warn him about the danger of Rahantsana.

"May I speak with my kinswoman, my lord?" My voice trembles. "I would like to tell her to watch over my children."

They agree.

Voahangy is at the entrance. Tsito is not. We fall into each other's arms, weeping. I whisper to her about Rahantsana. Voahangy tells me that he is dead.

"Tsito is with the Menamasos," says the washwoman, crying as she dabs at my mangled face. "We will save you. Be strong!"

I thank our ancestors and heave a sigh. From this point forward, my destiny is not my own.

We must leave each other. I go back into the room and retake my place near the pit.

"Open your mouth," says the judge.

He puts the first birdskin on my tongue and tells me to swallow. The procedure is repeated twice more, then they make me drink the poison. I thank our ancestors still. I recognize the taste of tangena on my tongue—familiar, like the presence and scent of an old enemy.

I hear the invocation begin.

"Listen, Manamango, listen well. You are the judge and the primal egg, you have no ears yet you hear, you have no eyes yet you see. You have no voice but all bend to your word. Here is Rafaramanorosoa. If she is guilty of sorcery against children or against adults, if she has trampled on a tomb, if she has sung with wildcats, or if she has made use of harmful magic spells, then break her from the inside, ravage her entrails! However, if she is guilty only of bad relations with others, if she has only made poor use of others' possessions, then let her live! If her fall is merely the fall of a leaf under a caressing wind, or that of a stone betrayed by loose soil, grant her life!

"But be wary, Manamango: you are now in the deepest parts of her body, mingling with her bones and flesh. Be vigilant, for it is for you to detect bad germs, to pry out harmful seeds. You are the shield that protects us from the scourge, our fortress against destructive forces!

You are the blade that assails our enemies, the lance that pierces their lies. Your duty is to destroy everything that would harm this earth! So if her mind is prone to betrayal, if her heart contains the seeds of chaos, then strike!"

Blessed be our ancestors who have given us life.

49 *Tsito*

SEEING FALY GET RUN THROUGH with a knife, I felt my soul grow heavy under the weight of a curse. I was losing the last connection to Fara. I didn't know what else to do. I felt the vertigo of someone watching rapids sweep away their boat and their life. I saw huge rocks and jagged stones coming to rip my hopes to shreds, but I could do nothing.

Yet Voahangy had not abandoned all hope. This washwoman was like our people's very soul: tenacious, big-hearted, and merciful.

She'd hurried away, shouting back as she went. "I have to give you the children, I can't bring them with me! I asked around, I think I know where she is!"

Beaten and lifeless, I'd watched her as she set off for the houses in Analakely. Rainimahery found me there, lost in my despair and powerlessness.

Ten times, I tried to rush toward the house where Fara was dying. Ten times, my companions pulled me back and held me down. The children were crying. Rainimahery was back, but the Prince couldn't come; pressure from the Prime Minister's coalition had become too strong. Tensions at the Palace had been growing for two years. Rumor had it that an influential dignitary had secretly written to the governor of Maurice to ask for a foreign military intervention. The Commander in Chief was livid. Even the heir to the throne could no longer oppose the repressive movement. Generals wielded the real power. So, for want of the prince, Rainimahery had brought with him all the members of the brotherhood that he could find. They knew that Fara was likely lost, but they didn't want to lose me.

"Do you want to die? Do you want to lose your child, just as you've been reunited? Your death itself would be a dishonor for you and your descendants: you would be obstructing royal justice and defying the ancestors' will! Your body would be ripped apart by dogs and tossed with the garbage into the swamp!"

"Doesn't matter," I growled, my face and muscles shining with sweat. "I'm a slave, I don't have an ancestral land, I don't even have a father or mother!"

"What, did your time among white men make you lose your mind?" another man snarled as he gagged me with a wrapper and his companions held me fast. "All that reading has turned your brain inside out! No one can go to his death of his own free will! And have you thought of us for even an instant? We could all be accused of open rebellion because of you!"

50 *Fara*

I CATCH GLIMPSES of Voahangy's face through the open door. Her visible dread reflects my body breaking down.

"We ask that the outcome be favorable. We ask that the verdict be just."

I feel spent. Exhaustion, added to Rahantsana's blows, has transformed me into a field of defeat, where the tangena meets no resistance. Not even the *koba* broth that the servants have me drink can give me any strength back. Every time I vomit takes a moment of my life, like a candle flame melts off a piece of the moth's wing each time it passes by.

"And how will you love me?"

"I will love you like my eyes, the windows of my soul: without them, I am weak as a child, but with them, the world smiles at me."

"Then you do not love me, for I will be of no use to you in the darkness."

"I will love you like the door to my home, protecting me from enemies and keeping the hearth warm."

"Then you do not love me, for you push through me without shame to achieve your ends."

"I will love you like the Sovereign of this realm, mistress of our lives and our destiny."

I think about the city of wonders that the vazahas constructed at Mantasoa. There are fountains and lakes dug by man's hand, where fish of dazzling new colors swim. Buildings with tall chimneys where the purest metals burn, where fabulous works are born. Ten thousand men and ten thousand women toil there for the prosperity of the kingdom and the delight of our descendants. Weapons are forged there for the glory of the highland sovereigns, and goods are produced there to benefit the people. Like the vazahas, even more than them, Tsito will be the iron that works this rice field, the spade that turns the fertile clay. And I, Fara, I will be the wife residing in the City of Thousands, I will be the wellspring of a hundred descendants and a thousand nations.

My eyes do not leave the purple sky over the City, through the window. Someone touches my shoulder. Is it Tsito? Yes, he's come back. He is here, at my side. I know the heat of his hand. Why are my body and limbs so wracked with tremors?

51 *Tsito*

WHEN ONE OF THE MEN appeared at the door, Voahangy knew that it was finished, before he said a word. The washwoman stopped praying and bowed her head.

The man said, simply, "She is beaten."

Voahangy brought me her things: a raffia dress, a leather bracelet, a pair of sandals. She was devastated, but tried to comfort me all the same. "She died peacefully. She died smiling. She was already on her way toward the kingdom of our ancestors."

I took the children into my arms, unable to speak.

I lifted my face, blurry with tears, toward the royal hill. The sky shone with a mauve tint that bathed the Palace in soft light. All the other houses on the side of the hill took on the ocher color of the falling star.

EPILOGUE

I CAME BACK TO SAHASOA one moon later. I left the children with Voahangy at Rainimahery's house and set off alone out of caution. I was able to talk with Bebe one last time. She told me that the day of Fara's death, an egret had let out a shrill cry and landed on a tree to the east of the house. She'd seen a sign in that.

"The bird had unusual slowness in the way it folded its wings, as if using the sturdiness of the branch for just a moment to restore its equilibrium."

Seeing that, the old woman had gone back inside the hut, stricken with inexplicable sadness, and knelt in the northeast corner, her forehead against the earth. The sorrow hanging heavy on her back and spreading through her bones. She stayed prostrate until the sun had gone out and darkness had taken hold of the house.

The flowing current of destiny had followed its course since the bird came.

Bebe passed away a few days after telling me that. I held her hand until she departed for the market of no return.

During the last evening that we spent together, I felt great peace. It was like feeling our ancestors' presence. At one point while I was contemplating things, a rooster appeared at the hut's entrance, looking for leftover rice. His figure stood silhouetted in the doorframe. He glanced quickly, astonished, at the dark, unmoving forms in the house, then pecked at the ground once or twice and took off. The only sounds in the hut were the buzzing bluebottle fly and the old woman's labored breathing.

Outside, the village was slowly retiring behind its trenches. When all the cattle were back inside and the great gate stone was rolled into place, a peculiar silence fell. The night was filled with household sounds and bursts of muffled voices. The sky drew its great black veil over mankind.

Then, Bebe sat up slowly in bed and whispered a song.

> *I implore your forgiveness, O my earth*
> *I appeal to your mercy, O my earth!*
> *You who cover our dear ones*
> *You, their final shelter*
> *We trample you underfoot*
> *But you are the water's cradle*
> *And you grow the ears of rice*
> *And you absorb all sorrow*
> *O my earth*

In the City of Thousands, the bodies of those who failed the ordeal were dragged with ropes behind the place called Anjoma, to be discarded on Faravohitra, the Last Hill. They couldn't be carried above knee height, and could not be buried. We could not mourn them or weep for them.

The day the Christians were put to death, the cannons thundered twelve times, and all other rebels were arrested. Many of them were judged. Many lost their possessions and their honor. Others had their wives and children thrown into slavery. All the People Under the Sky were condemned to pay one piaster per family.

This occurred during the Alakarabo moon, in the twenty-first year of the Sovereign Queen's reign.

GLOSSARY

MALAGASY TERMINOLOGY

Ambalavelona – An illness characterized by intense mental confusion. Traditionally attributed to curses from others, it usually also caused double personalities (possession) within the victims. Collective crises of ambalavelona were experienced especially during periods of social instability.

Amboalambo – Literally "dog-pigs"; beggars, parasites, or other fringe elements more inclined to lucrative cons than honest work in the rice fields. Subjects of certain kingdoms adopted it as a nickname for the Merina invaders, to mark their distaste for the enemy's ruses of war. However, an older usage appears in historical documents, which could carry another meaning that wasn't necessarily pejorative.

Ancestral Coalition – In this story, the traditionalist party that was hostile to Christianity and the rising European influence during the times of King Radama and Queen Ranavalona.

Ancestral tomb – The *fasan-drazana*, the elevated structure where the descendants of one ancestor lay. Generally a vault accompanied by various customs or restrictions for each specific family or statutory group, in certain cases housing a considerable number of remains. The importance of ancestral tombs in the Malagasy family system is illustrated by a proverb: "*Velona iray trano, maty iray fasana*. Alive, we live in the same house; dead, in the same vault."

Andriana – Lord, sovereign; noble, related to the kings.

Atsipilavaka – A game using a disc.

Barandro – A name for rum in certain regions, particularly Betsileo. A synonym of *toaka*, the word appears mostly in stories where it plays the role of fatal or ultimate drink, bringing about the climactic ending.

Bathing Feast – The *Fandroana* (from *andro*, meaning "bath") was the royal feast that marked the first day of the Malagasy year. It was celebrated on the first day of the lunar year (on *tsinan'Alahamady*, the new moon of Aries). A time of renewal, it culminated in a ritual of sacralizing the sovereign in a bath.

Bebe – Diminutive of Nenibe.

Council of Elders – An organization of the *loholona*, or chiefs of the people, who were generally distinguished by historical merit (e.g. an individual's or group's act of bravery) or influence. They played a major advisory role at every level: village, province, and state. In many kingdoms, including Imerina, these elders' power was sometimes even greater than lords'.

Dadabe – Grandfather, a title of respect and affection.

Diamanga – An art of combat, similar to savate.

Doany – An altar used to make offerings to the ancestors, ranging from a simple rock or spring to a tomb or royal fortress.

Fahavalo – A generic word for "enemy," usually used for cattle thieves. Literally "the eighth," in reference to some arrangements of the *sikidy* system of divination.

Fampitaha – A dancing and finery competition organized by Imerina sovereigns. The most notable dancers were invited to dance at the Palace. Also denotes a game that young girls play, inspired by the competition.

Fano – *Piptadenia chrysostachys*, a type of acacia. The seeds are used in divination.

Fanorona – A game of strategy, highly important in Malagasy society and similar in difficulty to chess.

Fosa – *Cryptoptrocta ferox*, a feline-looking carnivore endemic to Madagascar, closely related to the weasel.

Great rolling gate stone – The entrance to fortified Malagasy villages was usually an enormous flat circular rock wedged between the internal wall and two solid pillars, and rolled back and forth to block or open the passage.

Hainteny – Traditional form of Merina speech, used mostly for exchanges between lovers. Later became a form of written poetry.

Haody – A salutation used by visitors upon entering a house.

Hasina – Attribute, virtue, or power attached to a being or object, rendering it sacred and worthy of respect.

Highlands – Central Madagascar, where the Imerina kingdom was. The high plateau region is uneven, sitting at an average height around 4,500 feet, rising up to some 9,000 feet. Primarily populated by the Merina and Betsileo groups.

Honors – Grades in the royal Merina army were denoted by *voninahitras* (literally "grass flower"), or honors. The ranks went all the way from one honor for a soldier to ten honors for a general. The system gave higher ranks sometimes-exorbitant privileges and extended all the way up to sixteen honors for the prime minister and commander in chief, Rainilaiarivony.

Iada – Father.

Ingahy – Sir, mister.

Kabary – Speeches in a public place, used to deliver proclamations from the sovereigns of their decisions or laws. The oratorical event held a central place in Malagasy political systems, and its spirit continues to be felt in every part of social life. Today, it is still required for marriage proposals and burials.

Karajia – An argument.

Kinsmen (to the royal family) – Including blood relatives of the sovereign and people granted the title of "family." Judicial roles were part of the distribution of the traditional privileges of lords (*andrianas*), while administering tangena was usually reserved for actual blood relatives (see: *Andriamasinavalona*).

Koba – Rice flour.

Lalao – Community games.

Lamba – A shawl traditionally worn by women.

Long-horned hut – Most traditional Merina houses were made of wood or bamboo and had an ornament extending out of the top edge of the roof at the north, made of two long rafters called the "horns" (*tandroka*) of the residence.

Mahazaka.– A thick rope, generally used with zebus.

Moraingy – Traditional wrestling.

Mpandranto – Traders on the major bartering routes.

Mpisikidy – A seer specializing in sikidy, a complex system of divination relying on a wide variety of arrangements of seeds to call upon good or bad fortune. These seers were very influential in social life.

Mpitaiza sampy – A talisman guardian. In traditional society, talisman guardians had much more prestige than seers or healers, as their talismans had both political and social functions.

Mpivavaka – Literally "people who pray." During the era of Ranavalona I, this word designated Christians specifically.

Nenibe – Grandmother.

Neny – Mother.

Ndao – Let's go!

Ntaolo – The Ancient Ones.

Ody – A remedy.

Off-season rice – The *vary aloha*, or rice planted in winter, well before the normal season, and used as backup. As the saying goes: "*Vary aloha, mahatra-po fa tsy mahavita taona.* First season rice, comes in a timely fashion but will not last the year."

Ombiasy – Wise men, skilled astrologers, and advisers to kings. According to some historians, they played a decisive role in Malagasy political structures.

Perfumed Lord – The literal translation of *Andriananahary*, a name used for God. Also Zanahary, meaning the Creator.

Piaster – Generally the Spanish piaster, introduced by Arabic traders. Divided into fractions for commercial requirements, it was also used—either whole or divided—for many rituals.

Ramose – Portmanteau of the Malagasy honorific prefix "ra-" and the French "monsieur."

Raosi-jamba – A game like blind man's bluff.

Rodobe – Literally "the act of moving together." Has also become the resulting sound.

Rongony – Cannabis leaf.

Rova – The royal palace.

Sahafa – A concave tray used to shake rice and eliminate impurities.

Sarasara – A word used to greet sovereigns.

Sefo – A malgachization of *chef*, French for "boss."

Sinibe – A large vessel for storing water provisions. Traditionally situated at the east side of the hearth in a traditional hut.

Soimanqa – A blue-feathered bird, similar to a hummingbird.

Songomby – A man-eating storybook animal.

Sorabe – Malagasy writing using Arabic characters. The practice is generally restricted to religious and sacred usages, but practically disappeared after the introduction of the Latin alphabet by English missionaries, and only exists in the form of historical manuscripts.

Sosoa – As in *vary sosoa*: rice meal, similar to porridge or risotto.

Tambolo – *Buchnera leptostachya*, a plant used to whiten teeth.

Tangena – *Tanghinia venenifera*, or sea mango. A poison used for the ordeal of the same name, the judgment of last resort in the Malagasy judicial system in different eras. Ranavalona I relied heavily on it to combat what were seen as threats to the integrity of her kingdom.

Tantara tantara – A storytelling game.

Taro – Generic name for plants cultivated for edible roots. However, in Francophone Malagasy literature, the word is especially used as the translation of *saonjo* (probably derived from Arabic or an African language), which designates the *colocacia* genus.

Tolonomby – Bare-handed combat of one or several men against a zebu.

Tompomenakely – The lord of a province. The Merina kings, specifically Andrianampoinimerina and his son, Radama I, subdivided the kingdom's territories into vassal provinces (*menakely*) and royal domains (*menabe*), giving them either indirect control or direct sovereignty. The statutes of these fiefs were also adjusted to reward loyalty to the sovereign or sanction attempts at independence.

Tonga soa – A declaration of welcome.

Tranovorona – The "bird's honeycomb." The bier in which the remains of the deceased sovereign were put.

Tromba – Possession by ancestral spirits. It holds an important place in many Malagasy traditions.

Tsikonona – Ancestral children's dinner during the Bathing Feast.

Tsindrife – Slaves also used as concubines, usually younger.

Twelve sacred hills – The Merina sovereigns held power by way of places that symbolized their legitimacy. The twelve hills, representing the dynasty's wellsprings, were the most prestigious of these places. An official list was created for King Andriamasinavalona in the seventeenth century. King Andrianampoinimerina housed twelve royal wives on these hills to secure his sovereignty after the second Imerina reunification.

Vahoaka – The people.

Valiha – A traditional stringed instrument with a stalk of bamboo as the sound box.

Vatolahy – The "male rock," a raised rock table often used in rituals or incantations.

Vazaha – A generic word for a foreigner. In common usage, frequently refers to Europeans and other whites.

Vazimba – The Merina word for the first ancestors who arrived in Madagascar in early waves of migration.

Vokaka – A beverage made from soil taken from the tomb of the kings and mixed with water. Drunk during the swearing of loyalty oaths.

Volavita – A breed of zebu with a black and white coat, often used for sacrifices.

Zafimaniry – A group from eastern central Madagascar, known for rich symbolism and sculpted woodwork.

PROPER NAMES

Ambatonakanga – Literally "the Guinea Fowl Rocks." The site of one of the first schools and churches founded by the London Missionary Society. Today, it houses a renowned Protestant parish.

Analakely – Literally "the Little Woods." A little valley from which a stream was diverted by King Radama to be used as military parade grounds. Site of the charging and judgment of Christians on March 22, 1849, under Queen Ranavalona I. It has a rich, innovative history, especially in the industrial and architectural realms. Today, the neighborhood is the heart of the lower part of the city, with a wide square to its name.

Analamanga – Literally "The Blue [or "Beautiful"] Forest." The former name of the capital (today, Antananarivo, the "City of Thousands"). It was founded by King Andrianjaka in the seventeenth century as the capital of the Merina kingdom.

Andavamamba – Literally "the Crocodile's Cave." A neighborhood in the western part of the capital city.

Andohalo – Situated in the higher part of Antananarivo, the place where sovereigns proclaimed their sovereignty or spoke to the people.

Andriamasinavalona – Descendants of King Andriamasinavalona, who reigned from 1675 to 1710. He was the first to unify Imerina, bringing about several reforms in the process. Other people were also integrated into this group if deemed worthy, and their prestige diminished little over the course of the following dynasties.

Antalaotra – People of the sea. Refers to Arabic or Arabicized peoples that settled on the west coast of the island, most likely as early as the second millennium. They had considerable influence on Malagasy society.

Bara – People from the center-south of Madagascar, traditionally semi-nomadic and pastoral.

Bezanozano – A group from the center-east of Madagascar, especially renowned for their fierce resistance to the Merina invasion in the nineteenth century. Besides older, settling populations, this diverse group also included many Merina people who had fled persecution under the sovereigns in Antananarivo.

Darafify – A mythical giant whose story is told in several Malagasy oral traditions. Historians believe that Darafify's battles and exploits are a mythologization of the conquering march of migrants in the early eras of the island.

Iarivolahimihaga – A thousand strong and powerful men.

Imamo – The region in the center-west of Madagascar whose power was equal to Imerina in the seventeenth century. In the era of King Andriamasinavalona, Imamo and Imerina intermarried and began to fuse together.

Imerina – Literally "the country that can be seen from far away." Traditionally attributed to King Ralambo (roughly 1575–1610), probably for lack of much convincing information about his predecessors.

Laborde, Jean (1805–78) – A French adventurer and industrialist who played a significant role in the political and economic history of Madagascar. Completely integrated into Malagasy society, he was accepted among the Andriamasinavalonas and had Malagasy descendants. He used his privileged relationship with Queen Ranavalona I (he was her lover) to promote industry and undertake ambitious projects. The Malagasy state's refusal to "return" Laborde's goods was one of the disagreements that served as pretext for the French invasion of 1895—after many other incidents and an underhanded agreement between the French and British governments.

Mandatsivoho – A fictitious talisman, meaning "to strike an enemy from behind as he claims victory."

Merina – People on the highlands of the Imerina kingdom.

Mojanga – Also known as Majunga or Mahajanga. A port on the northwest coast of Madagascar.

Nampoina – Andrianampoinimerina.

Radama – Lehidama.

Toamasina – Also known as Tamatave. A port on the eastern coast of Madagascar.

Zanaharitsimandry – Literally "the God who never sleeps." The talisman of the Mandiavato clan. One guardian of this talisman was Rainitsiandavana, who played a significant role in early Christianity in Imerina.

Zafimanelo – A fictitious clan of nobles.

ASTROLOGY

The Malagasy year was divided into twelve moons, or months:

- Alahamady (Aries, from the Arabic Al-hamal)
- Adaoro (Taurus, from the Arabic A-thaur)
- Adizaoza (Gemini, from the Arabic Al-jauza')
- Asorotany (Cancer, from the Arabic A-sarataan)
- Alahasaty (Leo, from the Arabic Al-asad)
- Asombola (Virgo, from the Arabic A-cunbula)
- Adimizana (Libra, from the Arabic Al-mizan)
- Alakarabo (Scorpio, from the Arabic Al-'aqrab)
- Alakaosy (Sagittarius, from the Arabic Al-qaus)
- Adijady (Capricorn, from the Arabic Al-jadi)
- Adalo (Aquarius, from the Arabic A-dalu)
- Alohotsy (Pisces, from the Arabic Al-hout)

Each day of each moon was associated with a specific destiny, called *vintana*. Beyond the complex interactions of *vintanas*, the calendar was a way of finding spatial characteristics that applied at every level, from each individual hut to the known world.

CHRONOLOGY

A brief timeline of the Imerina Monarchs: late eighteenth to early nineteenth centuries

1785 Beginning of the reign of Andrianampoinimerina (known in this story as Nampoina), called *Ny Ombalahibemaso*, or the Bull with Large Eyes. This great reforming king's unifying vision (summed up by his famous campaign known as *ny riaka no valam-parihiko*, or "the seas are the limits of my rice fields") has become dogma in Merina cultural history. Andiranampoinimerina has very few relationships with Europeans. Illiterate, but cognizant of the value of writing, he gathers ombiasy seers from the coastal regions to tutor his son, Lehidama, the future king Radama I.

1810 After Andrianampoinimerina's death, his son Radama is proclaimed king. He continues his father's project of expansion, creating an army organized and outfitted in the European style, and opens the country to foreign influence. Most notably, he will welcome the first missionaries from the London Missionary Society (LMS).

1816 The LMS sends its first mission to Toamasina on the east coast, consisting of the Reverends Jones and Bevan and their families. Everyone will perish except for Rev. Jones, who will withdraw to Maurice for some time, before returning to Antananarivo in 1820, where he will be received by Radama I. At that time, Jones will establish the first missionary school in Madagascar.

1828 Radama I dies at the age of 35. His first wife, Mavo, is proclaimed queen, under the name Ranavalona I. Mavo's reign has generally not been explored in literature outside of the persecution of Christians. Many historians have tried to explain that characterizing Ranavalona as a brutal, bloody queen is reductive, and that in reality her reign actually did quite a lot to further her two predecessors' visions.

1849 The persecution of Christians reaches its peak on March 28 (Alakarabo 6) in Antananarivo. Four converts are burned at the stake in Faravohitra, and fourteen others are thrown off of the Ampamarinana hill.

ACKNOWLEDGMENTS

This grand adventure would never have seen the light of day without advice and warm encouragement from Sherry Simon, Dominique Ranaivoson, Leonard Fox, Patricia Bardou and Gaël Leclech, Ephrem Razafimanantsoa, and Karen Rakotonirina-Razafimanantsoa. Many thanks especially to my devoted reader, Sylvana Ranaivoson.

My thoughts are also with Daniel Simeoni, who left us too soon. Although he never read a line of this work in his lifetime, his passionate desire to walk this path with me into the universe of Malagasy culture and his unique perceptions both left their clear marks on this book.

NAIVO

My thanks to everyone who got Naivo's book into my hands: Michèle Rakotoson, Bao Ralambo, the Tana Water Front bookstore, and many others. Lova Rasoazanatsalama and Loic Razakarijaona deserve a medal for guiding me all around Antananarivo the first time I traveled there.

This grand adventure into English was supported by many people, to whom I am eternally grateful: Michael Moore and the 2015 PEN/Heim grant committee; Susan Harris, Eric M. B. Becker, Karen Phillips, and the rest of the team at Words Without Borders; D.W. Gibson and the Art OMI staff; Albertine Books; Razia Said; Emily Wolahan and the crew of Two Lines. Special undying thanks to Jack, Nathan, Joshua, and Brinda at Restless Books for believing in this endeavor.

I owe a large debt of gratitude to everyone who supported my family as it grew by one during this process. And as always: Jeremy, your love and encouragement makes all this possible.

Finally, to Naivo: Thank you for your writing.

AMC

ABOUT THE AUTHOR AND TRANSLATOR

Naivoharisoa Patrick Ramamonjisoa, who goes by the pen name **NAIVO**, has worked as a journalist in his home country of Madagascar and as a teacher in Paris. His first novel, *Beyond the Rice Fields*, was published in its French original version in March 2012 by Éditions Sépia in Paris. This work, which describes the violent cultural clash and mass killings that arose in the early-nineteenth-century Madagascar in reaction to the arrival of British missionaries and the rise of Christianity, is the first Malagasy novel ever translated into English. Naivo is also the author of several short stories, including "Dahalo," which received the RFI/ACCT prize in 1996, and "Iarivomandroso," which was adapted for a theatrical production in Antananarivo, Madagascar. He recently released a short story collection entitled *Madagascar entre poivre et vanille*, which explores various topics pertaining to contemporary Madagascar including the socialist era, the recurrent political coups, the corruption of the judiciary system, and the monarchic and colonial resurgences.

ALLISON M. CHARETTE translates literature from French into English. She received a 2015 PEN/Heim Translation Fund Grant for *Beyond the Rice Fields*, the first novel from Madagascar to be translated into English. She founded the Emerging Literary Translators' Network in America (ELTNA. org), a networking and support group for early-career translators. Allison has published two other book-length translations, in addition to short translated fiction that has appeared in Words Without Borders, The Other Stories, Tupelo Quarterly, InTranslation, the SAND Journal, and others. Find her online at charettetranslations.com.

RESTLESS BOOKS is an independent, nonprofit publisher devoted to championing essential voices from unexpected places and vantages, whose stories speak to us across linguistic and cultural borders. We seek extraordinary international literature that feeds our restlessness: our curiosity about the world, passion for other cultures and languages, and eagerness to explore beyond the confines of the familiar. Our books—fiction, narrative nonfiction, journalism, memoirs, travel writing, and young people's literature—offer readers an expanded understanding of a changing world.

Visit us at www.restlessbooks.com.